PRAISE FOR THE NOVELS OF BARBARA DAVIS

"This intriguing novel is magically woven together with sorrow, surprises, and happiness, just like the wedding gowns of 'The Dress Witch.'"

—Historical Novel Society

"Historically sound with a thread of supernatural intrigue, this exploration of shared experiences, learned adaptations, and the power of trust is a book that fans of Catherine Ryan Hyde, Erica Bauermeister, and Lucinda Riley will fall in love with."

—*Booklist*

"Fans of Tana French, Alena Dillon, and Hannah Mary McKinnon will adore Davis's multilayered tale of intrigue, romance, and long-held biases set straight."

—*Booklist*

"*The Last of the Moon Girls* is reminiscent of two of my all-time favorites, Sarah Addison Allen's *Garden Spells* [and] Alice Hoffman's *Practical Magic*, because it's witchy, full of plant magic, and painfully human."

—Kristin Fields, bestselling author of *A Lily in the Light*

"A story of love, hope, redemption, and rediscovering who you were meant to be . . . will resonate with readers who love a tale full of heart and soul."

—Camille Di Maio, bestselling author of *The Memory of Us* and *The Beautiful Strangers*

T0037290

"Infused with honesty, friendship, and a touch of romance. Davis creates nuanced and well-developed characters . . . A carefully woven tale that the reader won't soon forget."
—Emily Cavanagh, author of *The Bloom Girls* and *This Bright Beauty*

"Brimming with compassion and a refreshingly grown-up romance . . . An uplifting tale about starting over and how letting go of our nevers just might be the only thing that lets us move forward."
—Emily Carpenter, author of *Until the Day I Die*

"Heartfelt and beautifully written."
—Diane Chamberlain, *USA Today* bestselling author of *Pretending to Dance*

"A beautifully crafted page-turner . . . Part contemporary women's fiction, part historical novel, the plot moves seamlessly back and forth in time to unlock family secrets that bind four generations of women . . . This novel has it all."
—Barbara Claypole White, bestselling author of *Echoes of Family*

"Everything I love in a novel . . . Elegant and haunting."
—Erika Marks, author of *The Last Treasure*

"A book about love and loss and finding your way forward. I could not read it fast enough!"
—Anita Hughes, author of *Christmas in Paris*

"One of the best books out there, and Davis is genuinely proving herself to be one of the strongest new voices of epic romance."
—RT Book Reviews (4½ stars)

the
ECHO
of
OLD
BOOKS

OTHER BOOKS BY BARBARA DAVIS

the

ECHO

of

OLD

BOOKS

A NOVEL

BARBARA DAVIS

LAKE UNION
PUBLISHING

Published by Lake Union Publishing, Seattle

www.apub.com

Amazon, the Amazon logo, and Lake Union Publishing are trademarks of Amazon.com, Inc., or its affiliates.

ISBN-13: 9781662511608 (hardcover)
ISBN-13: 9781542038164 (paperback)
ISBN-13: 9781542038157 (digital)

Cover design by Faceout Studio, Spencer Fuller
Cover image: ©Vasya Kobelev / Shutterstock; ©VolodymyrSanych / Shutterstock; ©PhetcharatBiRTH / Shutterstock; ©tomertu / Shutterstock; ©SUFAIR / Shutterstock; ©Franck Boston / Shutterstock; ©BONNINSTUDIO / Stocksy United; ©Todd Korol / Stocksy United

Printed in the United States of America
First edition

*This book is dedicated to the librarians
and the booksellers . . .
Custodians of imagination, feeders of hungry hearts,
matchmakers of the written word.
Where would we be without your labors of love?*

Seated in my library at night, and looking on the silent faces of my books, I am occasionally visited by a strange sense of the supernatural.

—Alexander Smith

PROLOGUE

July 21, 1954
Marblehead, Massachusetts

It arrives on a bright summer day.

A large manila envelope with the word PRIORITY stamped in two places across the front in red ink. I stare at it, lying atop the scarred leather blotter along with the rest of the day's mail. The writing on the front is familiar, as is the name of the sender.

I drop into my chair, breathe in, let it out. Even now, with so many years gone, the memories are tricky. Like the ache of a phantom limb, the source of the pain may be gone, but the reminder of what's been lost, so sudden and so keen, takes me unaware. I sit with that pain a moment, waiting for it to fade.

Afternoon sun spills through the blinds of my study, painting slats of buttery light on the carpet and walls, shelves lined with books and awards, bits of this and that collected over the years. My sanctuary. But today, it seems my past has found me.

I open the envelope and spill the contents onto the desktop. A rectangular parcel in plain brown paper and a small envelope with a note paper-clipped to the outside.

Forwarding to you, per the enclosed letter.

There's no mistaking Dickey's careful hand.

My nephew.

We rarely speak these days—the years have made conversation awkward—though we still send cards at the holidays and on birthdays. What would he be sending me?

I tease the single sheet of stationery from its envelope, laying it open on the blotter. Not Dickey's handwriting here but another's. Also familiar. Sharp, angular letters, heavily slanted. Letters penned by a ghost.

> Dickey,
> After all that has passed between myself and your family, you will no doubt think me bold in contacting you. I am keenly aware of the fallout resulting from my connection with your family and am reluctant to put you in the middle once again, only I find there are matters that, after so many years, require clarification. And so I must beg one last favor. I ask that you forward the enclosed package to your aunt, whose whereabouts I have lost track of over the years. I assume the two of you are still in contact, as you were always her favorite, and I recall her entrusting you, on one particular occasion, with a communication of some delicacy. It is this memory that emboldens me to enlist your help now. It is my wish that the package be sent on undisturbed, as the contents are of a private nature, meant for your aunt's eyes only.
> With deepest regards and gratitude,
> —H

The room feels small suddenly, airless and close, as I eye the neatly wrapped package. Thirteen years without a word and now, out of nowhere, a clandestine parcel sent via our old go-between. Why now? Why at *all*?

My hands are clammy as I tear the coarse brown paper. An embossed leather spine appears. A marbled blue cover. A book. The title, lettered in gold, hits me like a fist.

Regretting Belle.

I swallow the ache in my throat, the jagged sensation so fresh it steals my breath. I've been numb for so long, so careful not to remember, that I've forgotten what it feels like to be sliced open, to bleed. I brace myself as I flip back the cover, then press a hand to my mouth, gulping down a sob. Of course there's an inscription. You never could pass up the chance to have the last word. What I haven't prepared for is your voice filling my head as I read the words you've scribbled on the title page—a dart aimed squarely at my conscience.

How, Belle? After everything . . . how could you do it?

ONE

ASHLYN

There is nothing quite so alive as a book that has been well loved.

—*Ashlyn Greer,* The Care & Feeding of Old Books

September 23, 1984
Portsmouth, New Hampshire

As was often the case on Sunday afternoons, Ashlyn Greer was on the hunt. This time in the messy back room of a vintage boutique situated two blocks from An Unlikely Story, the rare bookstore she'd owned and operated for nearly four years.

She'd received a call yesterday from Kevin Petri, the boutique's owner, alerting her that a guy from Rye had brought in several cartons of books and he didn't have room to stock them. Did she want to come take a look?

It wasn't the first time she'd spent her lone day off digging through boxes for lost treasure. More often than not, she came away empty-handed—but not always. Once she'd scored a first printing of *All Creatures Great and Small*, unread as far as she could tell. Another time she had rescued a first-edition *Lost Horizon* from a carton of old cookbooks. It had been badly neglected, but after an extensive rehab, she netted a tidy profit. Such finds didn't happen often—in fact, they almost never did—but on the rare occasions when they did, the thrill made all the digging worth it.

Unfortunately, today's boxes weren't looking particularly promising. Most of the books were hardbacks, recent bestsellers by Danielle Steel, Diane Chamberlain, and the much-lauded king of "ugly cry" novels, Hugh Garret. Esteemed authors, to be sure, but hardly rare. The second carton offered a more eclectic mix, including several health and nutrition books, one guaranteeing a flat tummy in thirty days, another touting the benefits of a macrobiotic diet.

She worked quickly, careful not to hold on to any of the books for too long, but it was hard not to pick up subtle vibrations as she returned them to the carton. They had belonged to someone who was sick and afraid, someone worried about running out of time. A woman, she was almost certain.

It was a *thing* she had, a gift, like perfect pitch or a perfumer's nose. The ability to *read* the echoes that attached themselves to certain inanimate objects—books, to be precise. She had no idea how it worked. She only knew it had started when she was twelve.

Her parents had been having one of their knock-down-drag-outs and she'd slipped out the back door and hopped on her bike, pedaling furiously until she reached the cramped little bookshop on Market Street. Her safe place, as she'd come to think of it—and still thought of it.

Frank Atwater, the store's owner, had greeted her with one of his taciturn nods. He knew what it was like for her at home—everyone in town knew—but he never once broached the subject, opting instead to offer a refuge when things between her parents became unbearable. It was a kindness she'd never forgotten.

On that fateful day, she had made a beeline for her favorite corner, where the children's books were stocked. She knew every title and author by heart, as well as the precise order in which they were shelved.

She'd read them all at least once. But that day, three new books had appeared. She ran her fingers along the unfamiliar spines. *The Story of Doctor Dolittle*, *The Mystery of the Ivory Charm*, and *The Water-Babies*. She pulled *The Water-Babies* from the shelf.

That's when it happened. A zingy little shock running along her arms and into her chest. And so much sadness, she suddenly couldn't breathe. She dropped the book. It landed at her feet, splayed open on the carpet like a felled bird.

Had she imagined it?

No. She'd *felt* it. Physically. A pain so real, so raw, that for an instant, tears had sprung to her eyes. But how?

Wary, she retrieved the book from the floor. This time, she let the feelings come. A throat scorched with tears. Shoulders racked with loss. The kind that showed no mercy and had no bottom. Back then, she'd had no frame of reference for that kind of anguish, the kind that imprinted itself on the body, etched itself into the soul. She simply sat there, trying to make sense of it—whatever *it* was.

Eventually, the anguish ebbed, losing some of its sharpness. Either she'd grown used to the sensation or the emotions had simply bled themselves out. She wasn't sure which. All these years later, she still wasn't sure. Could a book change its echoes, or were the emotions she registered of a more indelible nature, forever fixed in time?

The next day, she asked Frank where the new books had come from. He told her they'd been brought in by the sister of a woman whose son had been killed in a car crash. Finally, she understood. The suffocating sadness, the crushing sensation beneath her ribs, was grief. A mother's grief. But the *how* still eluded her. Was it really possible to register the emotions of another person simply by touching an object that had belonged to them?

Over the next few weeks, she attempted to re-create the sensation, plucking titles from the shelves at random, waiting expectantly for another peculiar jolt of emotion. Day after day, nothing came. Then one afternoon, she picked up a battered copy of Charlotte Brontë's *Villette* and a fierce surge of joy rippled through her fingers, like the rush of cool water, light and bubbly but startling in its intensity.

Then came a third book. A volume of poems by Ella Wheeler Wilcox called *The Kingdom of Love*. But the book's stale masculine energy felt strangely at odds with its romantic title, proof that a book's echoes had little to do with genre or subject matter. Rather, a book's energy seemed to be a reflection of its owner.

Eventually, she got up the nerve to tell Frank about the echoes. She was afraid he'd tell her she'd been reading too many fairy tales. Instead, he listened intently as she poured it all out, and then he surprised her with his response.

"Books are like people, Ashlyn. They absorb what's in the air around them. Smoke. Grease. Mold spores. Why *not* feelings? They're as real as all those other things. There's nothing more personal than a book, especially one that's become an important part of someone's life."

Her eyes had gone wide. "Books have feelings?"

"Books *are* feelings," he replied simply. "They *exist* to make us feel. To connect us to what's inside, sometimes to things we don't even know are there. It only makes sense that some of what we feel when we're reading would . . . rub off."

"Can you do it? Feel what's rubbed off, I mean?"

"No. But that doesn't mean others can't. I doubt very much that you're the first. Or that you'll be the last."

"So I shouldn't be scared when it happens?"

"I don't think so, no." He scrubbed at his chin a moment. "What you're describing is a kind of gift. And gifts are meant to be used. Otherwise, why have 'em? If I were you, I'd figure out how to get better at it, practice at it, so you know how it works. That way, you won't be scared when it happens."

And so she had practiced. She'd also done a bit of sleuthing. With Frank's help, she had discovered that there was an actual name for what she'd experienced. *Psychometry.* The term had been coined in 1842 by physician Joseph Rodes Buchanan, and in 1863 a geologist named Denton had published a book entitled *The Soul of Things*. In short, she was a kind of empath, but for books.

Frank had been right. Books *were* like people. Each carried its own unique energy, like a signature or fingerprint, and sometimes that energy rubbed off. Ashlyn scrubbed her palms along the thighs of her jeans now, trying to erase the sadness that had leached into her fingers from the box of discarded cookbooks. It was the downside of her so-called gift. Not all echoes were happy. Like humans, books experienced their share of heartache—and like humans, they remembered.

Over the years, she had learned to limit her exposure to books imbued with negative echoes and to shun certain books entirely. But on days like today, avoidance wasn't possible. All she could do was work quickly.

The final box contained more novels, all in great shape, but nothing she could use at the shop. Then, as she neared the bottom of the carton, she came across a paperback edition of Kazuo Ishiguro's *The Remains of the Day*.

It was nothing special. In fact, it was rather shabby, its pages yellowed almost to brown, its spine deeply creased. But its echo was impossible to ignore. Intrigued, she laid the book in her lap, pressing her palm against the cover. It was a game she played sometimes, trying to guess whether a book contained an inscription and, if so, what it might say.

She loved imagining how a particular volume had found its way into a reader's hands—and why. Why that book especially, and for what occasion? A birthday or graduation? A promotion?

She'd read a lot of inscriptions over the years, some sweet, some funny, some so poignant they'd brought tears to her eyes. There was something deliciously intimate about opening a book and finding those few scribbled lines on the flyleaf, like being given a glimpse into its emotional life, which had nothing to do with its author and everything to do with its reader.

Without a reader, a book was a blank slate, an object with no breath or pulse of its own. But once a book became part of someone's world, it came to life, with a past and a present—and, if properly cared for, a future. That life force remained with a book always, an energetic signature that matched its owner's.

Some books carried mingled signatures and were harder to read, usually in the case of multiple owners. That was the vibe she was getting from the copy of *The Remains of the Day*. Lots of layers. Very intense. The kind of book that almost always had an inscription. And as she flipped back the cover, she saw that this one did.

> *Dearest,*
> *Honor isn't about blood or a name.*
> *It's about being brave and standing up for what's*
> *right. You, my love, have always chosen honorably.*
> *Of that, you may always be proud,*
> *just as I am proud of the man I married.*
> *—Catherine*

It felt like a reassurance of some kind, words of comfort offered to a troubled heart, but the energy the book gave off, a dank, weighty sensation that felt like doubt, along with threads of guilt and regret, hinted that *Dearest*—whoever he was—had been less than convinced.

Ashlyn closed the book, placing it firmly on the *no* pile, then reached for the final book in the carton. Her belly did a little flip as she lifted it out, the kind that meant she may finally have discovered something worthwhile. It was a small volume but quite beautiful. Three-quarter Moroccan leather, ribbed spine, marbled blue boards—and, unless she missed her guess, hand-bound.

She held her breath as she examined it. Little to no shelf wear. Binding tight and square. Text block yellowed but otherwise solid. She peered at the embossed gold lettering on the spine. *Regretting Belle*. Not a title she was familiar with. She frowned as she continued to study the book. There was no sign of an author's name. No publisher's name either. Odd, but not unheard of. But something was *off*.

The book was strangely quiet. Silent, in fact. The way a new book felt before an owner's echo rubbed off. An unwanted gift, perhaps, that had gone unread? The thought made her sad. Books given as gifts should *always* be read. She turned back the cover, hunting for the copyright page. There wasn't one. There was, however, an inscription.

How, Belle? After everything . . . how could you do it?

Ashlyn stared at the single line. The script was jagged, the shard-like words intended to cut, to wound. But there was sadness, too, in the spaces between, woven through the ellipses, the desolation of a question unanswered. The inscription was neither signed nor dated, implying that the recipient would have required neither. An intimate acquaintance, then. A lover perhaps, or spouse. *Belle*. The name leapt off the page. Might the book's recipient have also been its namesake? The giver its author?

Intrigued, she began flipping pages, on the lookout for an author's name, a publisher's imprint. But there was nothing. No trace of how this strange and beautiful book had come into the world.

The absence of a copyright page suggested the book might be in the public domain, meaning it would have to have been written before 1923. If so, it was in amazing condition. But there was another possibility, one that seemed more likely. The book may have been rebound at some point and the binder had been unable to include the original copyright page.

Some of the pages may have been damaged or lost. It certainly happened. She'd been tasked with rebinding books that came into the shop in grocery bags, loose pages held together with twine or rubber bands, warped boards left to mold in damp basements, attic finds whose pages were so dry they crumbled when touched. But never had she come across a book missing *all* traces of its origins.

People rehabbed old books for all sorts of reasons, but those reasons almost always fell into one of two categories: sentiment or collector value. In either case, preserving the author's name would be critical. Why would someone go to the trouble and expense of having the book rebound and then omit such important details? Unless the omission had been intentional. But why?

Lured by the promise of a literary mystery, Ashlyn laid the book open. She had just turned to the first chapter when a jolt of what felt like current surged through her fingers. Startled, she jerked her hand back. What had just happened? A moment ago, the book had been silent—pulseless—until she opened it and roused whatever lay within, like the flashover that occurs when a door is suddenly thrown open and a small fire erupts into a fully involved blaze. This was a new experience, and one she definitely intended to explore.

Breath held, she placed the flats of both hands against the open pages, bracing for what she now knew was coming. Every book presented differently. Most registered as a subtle physical sensation. A humming in her jaw, a sudden flutter in her belly. Other times, the echoes were more intense. A ringing in her ears or a stinging sensation in her cheeks, as if she'd just been slapped. Occasionally, they registered as tastes or smells. Vanilla. Ripe cherries. Vinegar. Smoke. But this felt different, deeper somehow and more visceral. The taste of ash sharp on her tongue. The ache of tears scorching her throat. A searing pain at the center of her chest.

A heart in ruins.

And yet she'd felt nothing until she opened the book, as if the echoes had been holding their breath, biding their time. But for how long? And *whose* echoes? The inscription—*How, Belle?*—was clearly intended for a woman, yet the book gave off a decidedly masculine energy.

She examined the spine again, scoured the flyleaf, the verso, the endpapers, hoping to find some clue as to the book's origins. Again, she came up empty. It was as if the book had simply manifested out of thin air, a phantom volume existing out of literary time and space. Except she was holding it in her hands. And its echoes were very real.

She lifted her palms from the pages, shaking out the fingers of her right hand in an attempt to dispel the dull ache in her palm. The scar was playing up again. She peered at the crescent-shaped lesion running from her little finger to the base of her thumb. A shard of glass inadvertently grabbed in a moment of panic.

The wound had healed without incident, leaving a curved line of puckered white flesh cutting across her life line. Ashlyn pressed a thumb deep into her palm and flexed her fingers repeatedly, an exercise they had given her after the accident to prevent contracture. Maybe it was time to slow it down a little in the bindery and give her hand a rest. And speaking of the bindery, it was time to get back to the shop.

After returning the *no* books to their respective boxes, she carried the mystery volume to the front, where she found Kevin lovingly polishing a pink Bakelite radio.

"Looks like you got lucky this time." He picked up the book, opened it briefly, then closed it again with a shrug. "Never heard of it. Who's it by?"

Ashlyn looked at him, astonished that he could be oblivious to the emotions boiling up from the book. "I have no idea. There's no author name, no copyright page, not even anything about who the publisher was. I'm thinking it may have been rebound at some point. Or it could be a vanity press kind of thing—a few copies of Uncle John's novel printed for family and friends."

"And someone will actually want a book like that?"

Ashlyn shot him a conspiratorial wink. "Probably not. But I'm a sucker for a mystery."

TWO

ASHLYN

Where is human nature so weak as in a bookstore?

—*Henry Ward Beecher*

Ashlyn locked the door behind her, savoring the reassuring calm that descended each time she stepped through the door of An Unlikely Story, the sense that she was wholly and completely where she belonged.

The shop had been hers for almost four years now, though in a way it had *always* belonged to her. Just as she had always belonged to *it*. As far back as she could remember, the shop had felt like home, the books lining its jumbled shelves like trusted friends. Books were safe. They had plots that followed predictable patterns, beginnings, middles, and endings. Usually happy, though not always. But if something tragic happened in a book, you could just close it and choose a new one, unlike real life, where events often played out without the protagonist's consent.

Like a father who couldn't hold a job. Not because he wasn't smart enough or skilled enough but because he was simply too angry. The entire neighborhood had known about Gerald Greer's temper. They'd either experienced it firsthand or heard it spilling out of the windows on a near-daily basis. Berating her mother for overcooking the pork chops, buying the wrong brand of chips, or using too much starch on his shirts. Nothing was ever right or good enough.

People used to whisper that he had a drinking problem, but she never knew her father to keep liquor in the house. Good thing, too, according to Grandma Trina, who had once grumbled that her son-in-law was never more than one ruined dinner away from burning down the house. The last thing he needed was an accelerant.

And then there was her mother, the shadow figure who could generally be found in her room, watching game shows or sleeping away her afternoons, aided by the seemingly bottomless vial of yellow pills in her nightstand. Her *coping pills*, she'd called them.

The summer Ashlyn turned fifteen, Willa Greer had been diagnosed with uterine cancer. There'd been talk of an operation, followed by chemo and radiation, but her mother had refused treatment, concluding that there was nothing in her life worth hanging around for. She was dead within a year, buried four weeks to the day before Ashlyn's sixteenth birthday. She had chosen death over her family—over her daughter.

Ashlyn's father had been strangely unmoored by the loss of his wife, shutting himself up in his room or staying away from home entirely. He ate little and rarely spoke, and his eyes took on an unsettling emptiness. And then, on the afternoon of her sixteenth birthday, during the party her grandmother insisted on giving her—a party she hadn't wanted—her father had climbed up to the attic, braced a loaded Winchester side-by-side beneath his chin, and pulled the trigger.

He had *chosen* too.

She'd gone to live with her grandmother after that and had spent her Thursday afternoons with a therapist who specialized in children and grief. Not that it had done much good. Two parents gone in the space of a month, and both had *chosen* to leave her. Surely the fault lay with her. Something she'd done or *not* done, some awful, unforgivable flaw. Like a disfiguring birthmark or faulty gene, the question had become a permanent part of her. Like the scar on her palm.

After her parents' deaths, the store had become her sanctuary, a place to retreat from the stares and whispers, where no one gave her sideways looks and snickered about the girl whose father had blown his brains out while she was blowing out her birthday candles. But it wasn't only her father's suicide that had marred her early years. She'd always been different, skittish and withdrawn.

A freak.

It was a label she'd earned on the first day of seventh grade, when she'd burst into tears after being issued a battered social studies textbook dripping with self-loathing. The echoes had been so bleak and so bottomless—so uncomfortably familiar—that she'd found it almost unbearable to touch the book. She'd begged the girl beside her to trade but had refused to say why. In the end, her teacher had issued her a different book, but not before the entire class had a good laugh at her expense.

Years later, the memory still stung, but she'd eventually come to accept her strange gift. Like the ability to paint or play the violin, it had become a part of her and was even a comfort at times, the echoes a stand-in for actual friends, who might judge or abandon her.

Ashlyn shook off the thought as she deposited her tote on the counter and ran her eyes around the shop. She adored every inch of its cozy clutter, the threadbare carpets and warped oak floors, the scent of beeswax mixed with lingering traces of Frank Atwater's pipe tobacco, but as she eyed the stack of books waiting for her on the front counter, the shelves that needed dusting, the windows that were long overdue for a wash, she regretted not following through on her plan to finally hire someone to help with day-to-day tasks.

She'd nearly placed an ad last month, had gone so far as to write the copy, but ultimately she had changed her mind. It wasn't the money. With the bindery business taking off, the shop pulled in more than enough to support a staff. Her reluctance had to do with preserving the sanctuary she'd built for herself, an insular world of ink and paper and familiar echoes. She wasn't ready to let someone else in, even if it meant more free time. Perhaps *especially* if it meant more free time.

Ashlyn glanced at the old depot clock as she peeled out of her jacket and tossed it on the counter. It was nearly four and she had an hour's worth of reshelving to tackle before she could change hats and head to the bindery. Today's stack was especially diverse and included titles such as *The Art of Cooking with Herbs & Spices*, *A Guide to Bird Behavior: Volumes I & II*, *The Poetical Works of Sir Walter Scott*, and *The Four Dimensions of Philosophy*.

The varied interests of her customers never ceased to amaze her. If someone, somewhere, was interested in a subject, no matter how obscure, there was a book about it. And if there was a book about it, someone, somewhere, wanted to read it. Her job was to connect the two, and it was one she took very seriously. She'd grown up believing a person could learn absolutely anything from books, and she still believed it. How could she not when she spent her days in such rarefied air?

When the shelving was finished, she polished the counter and restocked the handouts in the rack at the front of the store, including the latest issue of the store's monthly newsletter. The windows would have to wait for another day. After sixty years in business, the place was long past gleaming, but there was a warm patina to the scarred floors and overcrowded shelves that her customers seemed to appreciate, and perhaps even expect.

In the bindery, situated at the back of the shop, Ashlyn flicked on the overhead fluorescents, almost uncomfortably bright after the shop's softer reading lamps. The room was small and cluttered, but there was an organized chaos to the clutter. On the right, just inside the door, sat the sewing frame, used to stitch pages together, and a rack of endpapers in various colors and patterns. The left side of the room was dominated by an ancient cast iron standing press, which had once conjured images of the Spanish Inquisition until Frank had shown her how it was used to press books.

A workbench occupied most of the back wall. Above the bench, shelves held the various tools of the trade: book weights, awls, sanding blocks, bone folders, an assortment of mallets and spatulas. There was also an array of less specialized supplies, household items like waxed paper, binder clips, and the old blow-dryer she used to remove sticky labels from garage sale finds. At the end of the bench, a glass-front case housed an assortment of solvents and adhesives, pots of dye and tubes of paint, mull and tape to strengthen spines, Japanese tissue to repair torn pages.

The sight of it all had intimidated her once. Now each tool felt like an extension of her love of books, an extension of herself. After her father's *accident*, as Grandma Trina insisted on calling it, Frank had offered her a proper job. It was just dusting and emptying wastebaskets at first, but when he caught her hovering in the doorway of the bindery one day, watching with breath held as he painstakingly dissected a first-edition Steinbeck, he had waved her over and given her her first lesson in book restoration.

She had proved a quick study, and after a few weeks was allowed to help regularly in the bindery, handling less valuable books at first, then moving on to rarer and more costly volumes. Years later, book restoration had become an almost sacred vocation. There was something enormously rewarding about taking something that had been neglected, even mistreated, and making it new again, deconstructing it with the greatest of care, then putting it back together again, its spine straightened, its scars removed, its tired beauty restored. Each restoration was a labor of love, like a kind of resurrection, a broken and discarded thing given new life.

Today, her first order of business was to check on several pages from a volume of Tom Swift she'd left soaking in a large enamel tub, in hopes of removing the copious amounts of glue applied during an ill-advised do-it-yourself rebinding attempt. Glue could be a bit of a high-wire act, even for a skilled binder. In the hands of an enthusiastic amateur, it generally spelled disaster.

Using a small spatula, she reached into the water, gently teasing the mixture of glue and old tape from the edge of the top page. Not ready yet, but another few hours should do it. Once she got them dry, she would reassemble the text block, add new boards and endpapers, then re-emboss the repaired spine. It wouldn't be cheap, but the book would leave the shop with a new lease on life, and with any luck, Mr. Lanier would know better than to attempt any future home repair.

When she was satisfied that she'd done what she could, she dried her hands and flipped off the overheads, her mind already wandering upstairs to her apartment, to her reading chair and the words that had already etched themselves in her mind.

How, Belle? After everything . . . how could you do it?

The words were still with her as she stepped through the door of her apartment and kicked off her shoes. Like the shop, Frank Atwater's apartment had become a second home growing up. Now, it, too, was hers.

When things were rough at home, Frank and his wife, Tiny, had provided a place to come after school, to have a snack and do her homework or just curl up on the sofa and watch *Dark Shadows*. When Tiny suffered an aneurism and died suddenly, Ashlyn had done everything in her power to fill the hole left by her absence. In return, Frank left her everything when he died six years later. *The daughter I was never blessed with*, the will had said. *A joy and a comfort in my time of sorrow.*

She missed him terribly. His unfailing kindness, his quiet wisdom, his love of all things written. But he was still here, in the old ormolu clock that remained on the mantel, the weary leather wingback near the window, his cherished collection of Victorian classics, each brimming with echoes of a life well lived. She'd done some updating before moving in, resulting in an eclectic mix of Victorian, contemporary, and arts and crafts that worked surprisingly well with the apartment's high windows and exposed brick walls.

In the kitchen, she popped last night's leftover kung pao in the microwave and ate it straight from the carton, standing over the sink. She was itching to dive into *Regretting Belle*, but she had strict rules about food and books—one or the other, never both together.

Finally, after swapping her jeans for sweats, she retrieved the book from her tote, flicked on the funky arts and crafts reading lamp she'd discovered at a yard sale last summer, and settled into the old wingback near the window. She sat a moment with the book balanced on her knees, steeling herself for the emotional storm she knew was coming. Then she pulled in a breath and opened to the first page.

Regretting Belle

(pgs. 1–13)

27 March 1953
New York, New York

You will perhaps wonder why I've gone to this trouble. Why, after so many years, I should endeavor to undertake such a project. A book. But in the beginning, it wasn't meant to be a book. It began as a letter. One of those cathartic outpourings one never really intends to send. But as my pen began to move, I found I had too much to say. Too much regret to fit on a single page—or even several pages. And so I have moved to my desk, to my typewriter—my father's old Underwood No. 5—where I now sit, pounding out the words I have swallowed for a dozen years, the question that continues to haunt me.

How? How, Belle?

Because even now, after all the mistakes I've made with my life—and I've made many—you are the one I regret most. You have been the capital error of my life, the one regret for which there can be no absolution, no peace. For you or for me.

In this life, there are losses that can never be anticipated. Grief that comes at you out of the darkness. Blows that land so swiftly and deftly that there's simply no way to prepare for them. But sometimes you do see the blow coming. You see it and you stand there and let it knock you down. And later—years later—you're still asking yourself how you could have been such a fool. You were that kind of blow. Because I saw you coming that very first night. And I let you knock me down anyway.

The memory of that meeting is still caught in my craw, a cancer no amount of living has managed to cut out, and while reliving it now gives me no pleasure, doing so may yet bring me some peace. And so I must begin it and step back in time. Back to the night it all began.

~

27 August 1941
New York, New York

I run my eyes around the ballroom of the St. Regis Hotel, trying not to fidget in my hired suit. Nothing marks one out as an impostor quite like fidgeting, and an impostor I most certainly am.

While studying the assembled company—men of industry and their pampered society wives, washing down crab puffs with chilled Veuve Clicquot—it's almost possible to forget there was ever such a thing as the Great Depression. Perhaps because it touched this shiny, silky set more lightly than the rest, reserving its worst for those of more modest means.

It's hardly surprising. Deserved or not, the affluent will always enjoy a soft landing. But to add insult to injury, many of those whose fortunes remained intact now seem determined to flaunt their survival with blatant exhibitions of wealth—like the one I'm witnessing tonight.

The party is in full swing, awash in excess and good taste, the champagne flowing, the dance floor a sea of white-tie and designer gowns that will never be worn again. There's a full orchestra, tables groaning with prawns and cut-crystal bowls of caviar, ice sculptures of plump-cheeked cherubs, and champagne cocktails endlessly circulating on gleaming silver trays. The opulence is breathtaking. And utterly unapologetic. But then nothing less is to be expected on such a night. One of its princesses has gotten herself engaged to one of its princes, and I'm here to witness the well-wishing—and to get a look at the princess in her natural habitat.

I'm here not as an invitee but as the guest of a friend, on a mission to rub elbows, if I can manage it, with the tastemakers of America's great city. Those esteemed descendants of New York's renowned "Four Hundred," whose name arose from the number of guests Caroline Astor's ballroom was said to have held. And like Mrs. Astor's ballroom, only the crème de la crème of New York society has made the cut tonight. I, of course, would never have made such a list. I've not the pedigree for it. Or any pedigree. Rather, I am a clever and well-placed hanger-on, a social climber on a mission.

I've spotted two of the Cushing sisters among the crowd, Minnie and the newly married Babe, along with their marriage-broker mother, Kate, known to her friends as "Gogsie" of all things. Also represented are the Whitneys, the Mortimers, the Winthrops, the Ripleys, the Jaffrays, and the Schermerhorns. Conspicuously absent from this evening's festivities—though not unexpectedly—is any member of the Roosevelt clan, who are reportedly out of favor with our host. No one seems to mind. There's plenty of quality on hand to make it up. Pretty people doing pretty things in pretty clothes. And there, a few feet away, looking like an impeccable bulldog in his evening clothes, is the man who's paying for it all—the Great Man himself—surrounded by his powerful new friends.

And not far off—never far off—the Great Man's daughter. I speak not of Cee-Cee, who was auctioned off some years back to the son and heir of the Aluminum King. I refer to the younger daughter, the one whose engagement party I've been roped into attending tonight. To you, dear Belle, whose photograph recently appeared in the Sunday News, along with that of your polo-playing fiancé—Theodore. The third descendant of his original namesake.

I spent an uncomfortable few moments watching the two of you dance when I first arrived, totting up his qualities and comparing them with mine—as one tends to do. The flawless cut of his jacket, the breadth of his shoulders, the shining gold waves combed back from his brow. And his face, chiseled like a good piece of marble, tan and square, and faintly bored as he steered you about the parquet, as if he'd much rather be in one of the rooms upstairs, smoking cigars and betting away chunks of his father's fortune on a bad hand of cards. (Assuming the gossip is to be believed, of course.)

I thought the two of you suited then, your arms loosely linked as you moved around the floor with mechanical precision. I came to the same conclusion when I saw your engagement photo in the paper: a pair of beautiful, empty specimens. Equally privileged. Equally bored. But now, as I study you from across the room, separated from him at last, you look nothing like the woman in the paper, and for a moment, as I stand taking you in, I lose my train of thought entirely.

You're perfectly stunning, draped in a sheath of teal-colored silk that clings to your body like a second skin and seems to change color as you move. Blue, then green, then faintly silver, like the scales of some great fish. Or a mermaid in a fairy tale.

You're wearing long teal gloves to match and a simple strand of silvery-grey pearls at your throat. Your hair, shiny dark, is swept back, piled up in waves at your crown, exposing the perfect pale heart of your face, the small Cupid's mouth, the pointed chin with its faint cleft. An arresting face. The kind that imprints itself on the soul like a photographic negative. Or a bruise.

You sip absently from a glass of champagne, and as your eyes roam about the room, they catch mine. It's a strange moment, as if some unseen current has passed between us, like the pull of a magnet. A force of nature.

I incline my head slightly, the barest and coolest of nods. I suppose I think myself charming. I must to make such an ass of myself. You turn away, as if you haven't seen, and begin to chat with a woman sporting a rather unfortunate hairpiece, and I notice that the pearls you're wearing hang past your shoulder blades, swinging like a pendulum halfway down your bare back. The effect is mesmerizing.

I'm still staring when you dismiss your companion and turn to look at me, as if you've been aware of my eyes the whole time. You hold my gaze. A reproach? An invitation? I have no idea. Your face is blank, giving nothing away. I should know it then and there, in that instant of icy incandescence, that you will always hold some part of yourself from me. But I don't see it. Because I don't want to.

I half expect you to step away as I approach, to vanish into the crowd, but you stand your ground, eyes still on mine over the rim of your coupe. You look young suddenly, vulnerable in a way I haven't noticed until now, and I have to remind myself that you've just celebrated your twenty-first birthday. "Careful," I say, smiling smoothly as I slip up beside you. "It'll sneak up on you. Especially if you're not used to it."

You toss me a cool look. "Do I look like I'm not used to it?"

My gaze slides over you, lingering on your throat, the slender arch of your collarbone, the rise and fall of your breath, a little faster than it was a moment ago. "No," I say finally. "Not now that I look more closely."

I extend a hand and give you my name. You give me yours in return, as if it's possible to be in the room without knowing it already.

My eyes linger briefly on the diamond glinting from your ring finger. Pear-shaped and at least three carats, though I'm hardly an expert in such things. "Best wishes for your engagement."

"Thank you," you say, letting your eyes drift away. "It was kind of you to come."

Your voice, startlingly low for someone so young, gives me pause, but I'm amused, too, by your smooth delivery. You clearly have no idea who I am. If you did, you'd hardly be so polite.

You look me up and down again, lingering on my empty hands. "You're not drinking." You crane your neck, casting about for a waiter. "Let me get you a glass of champagne."

"No, thanks. I'm more of a gin-and-tonic man."

"You're British," you say, as if you've only just worked out that I'm not one of your set.

"*I am, yes.*"

"*Well, you're certainly a long way from home. Might I ask what has brought you to our shores? Because I'm certain you didn't fly all the way across the big blue ocean just to attend my engagement party.*"

"*Adventure,*" *I say simply, evasively, because it won't do to admit what has really brought me to the St. Regis tonight. Or to the States, for that matter.* "*I'm here for adventure.*"

"*Adventure can be dangerous.*"

"*Hence its attraction.*"

You run those wide-set amber eyes over me again, long and slow, and I find myself wondering what it is you see—and how much you see. "*And what sort of adventure suits you?*" *you ask, with that air of boredom you sometimes assume as a defense.* "*What is it you . . . do?*"

"*I'm a writer.*" *Another evasion, but a smaller one.*

"*Really. What do you write?*"

"*Stories.*"

We're getting warmer now, closer to the truth, but not quite. I can see that your interest has been kindled. The word writer *has that effect on people.*

"*Like Hemingway?*"

"*One day, perhaps,*" *I answer, because that part at least is true. One day I might write like Hemingway. Or Fitzgerald. Or Wolfe. At least, that's the plan.*

You wrinkle your nose but make no comment.

"*You're not a fan of Mr. Hemingway?*"

"*Not especially. All that bristling machismo.*" *Your eyes wander out to the dance floor, and for a moment I think you've grown tired of our conversation.* "*I'm more of a Brontë girl,*" *you say at last over the muted brass of* "*Never in a Million Years*" *drifting from the bandstand.*

I shrug vaguely. "*Brooding heroes and windswept moors. Very . . . atmospheric. But a little gothic for my taste.*"

You tip back your glass, draining it, then give me a sideways look. "I thought the English were terrible snobs about books. Nothing but the classics."

"Not all of us. Some of us are actually quite modern, though I'll admit to being a Dickens fan. He wasn't terribly romantic, but the man knew how to tell a story."

You lift one silky, dark brow. "You've forgotten about the dubious Miss Havisham and her awful cake. That isn't gothic?"

"All right, I'll give you that one. He did stray to doomed young lovers now and then and reclusive women in ruined wedding gowns, but as a rule, he wrote about social issues. The haves and have-nots. The disparity between classes."

I wait, keeping my face blank, wondering if you'll take the bait. I'm trying to draw you out. Because I've already formed an opinion of you and suddenly, inexplicably, I want very badly to be wrong.

"And which are you?" you shoot back, neatly turning the tables. "A have or a have-not?"

"Oh, definitely the latter, though I aspire to more. One day."

You cock your head, eyes slightly narrowed, and I see a new question gathering there. A self-admitted adventurer with neither money nor prospects, and here I am rubbing elbows at your pretty little party. Drinking your father's champagne and being impertinent. You want to know who I am and how someone like me got my foot in the door. But before you can ask, a stout woman in rusty black taffeta seizes you by the arm, all smiles beneath her chalky layers of powder.

She runs an eye over me, dismissing me as no one of import, and presses a kiss to your cheek. "Bonne chance, my dear. To both you and Teddy. No doubt your father is pleased. You've done well for yourself. And him."

You respond with a smile. Not your real smile—the one you reserve for functions like this. Practiced and mechanical. And as I watch you simper, I can't escape the feeling that the woman standing beside me, this glittering belle with her silk and her pearls, is a sham, a player in a lavish costume drama, a well-oiled being comprised of wheels and gears.

The smile slips the instant the woman departs, gone as suddenly as it appeared. You look deflated without it, less shiny somehow, so that I almost feel sorry for you. It's the last thing I expected to feel this evening and I find myself annoyed. Sympathy is an indulgence men in my line of work can ill afford.

I incline my head, the barest of nods. "If I didn't know better—and I suppose I don't—I might almost think the lady unhappy. Which is surprising, considering she's managed to land one of the most eligible bachelors in all of New York. Oil. Property. Horses. Quite the specimen too. A golden boy, one might say."

You stiffen, piqued by my tone. And by the fact that I've seen through your shiny veneer. "You seem to know quite a lot about my fiancé. Are you a friend of Teddy's?"

"Not a friend, no. But I know a little about your young man and his family. Interesting collection of friends they've managed to surround themselves with. Not all top-shelf but definitely . . . useful."

A hard little crease appears between your brows. "Useful?"

I respond with a chilly smile. "Everyone needs friends in low places, don't you think?"

You're off-balance now. You don't know what to make of my words. Are they a threat? A request for an introduction? A sexual reference? You raise your glass to your lips, forgetting you've already drained it, then lower it again with a huff. "Are you here by invitation?"

"I am, yes. Though I fear my date's gone missing. She stepped away some time ago to powder her nose and hasn't returned."

"And who might your date be? I hate to ask, only it is my party."

"I'm here with Goldie," I say simply, because no last name is necessary when talking about Goldie.

Your nostrils flare at the mention of her name. "I would have thought someone who seems so concerned with the quality of my fiancé's friends would be more careful about his own choice of companions."

"I take it you don't approve?"

"It's not for me to approve or disapprove. I just wasn't aware that she'd been invited. I'm not accustomed to rubbing elbows with the sort of woman who'd own a string of gossip rags."

"Only one is a 'gossip rag,' as you call it. The rest are legitimate newspapers."

You toss your head and look away.

"You don't think a woman belongs in the newspaper business?"

Your eyes snap back to mine, sharp and overbright. "I think a woman belongs in whatever business she chooses, so long as it's respectable. But that woman . . ." You go quiet as a waiter approaches, exchanging your empty champagne glass for a full one. You take a small sip, waiting until he's moved away, then lean close. "You should know that there's nothing remotely respectable about that woman."

"I take it this is about her stable of young men?"

You blink at me, startled by my bluntness. Or at least pretending to be. You're the kind who judges on superficialities rather than bothering to learn what might lie beneath. Disappointing, but probably better for me in the long run.

"You knew? And you still came with her? To an event like this?"

"She had an invitation and I wanted to come."

"Why?"

"To see your sort in their natural habitat. Besides, she makes no secret of it. To me or anyone else."

"And you're comfortable being part of a . . . stable?"

I shrug, relishing your outrage. "It's a matter of symbiosis, an arrangement that works for both of us."

"I see."

Your cheeks have gone a deep shade of pink and I'm reminded once again how young you are. Five years my junior, but for a man, those years amount to an eternity. Perhaps you've been sheltered from the real world of men and women, from how it all . . . works. Suddenly I find myself wondering exactly what you do know—and how you know it. I fight the urge to step back, to put distance between us. You feel dangerous all of a sudden, the pristine coolness of you at odds with the low flame that's begun to flicker in my belly. I clear my throat, force my brain to pick up the thread of our conversation.

"It's sweet of you to worry about my reputation, but I'm a big boy. I will give you a word of advice, though. Sometimes a silk purse is really a sow's ear—and vice versa."

You look at me, baffled. "What is that supposed to mean?"

"It means that in my experience, a rough exterior often masks something quite fine, while a sheen of respectability frequently disguises the opposite."

Your nostrils flare again, as if scenting the enemy. I am the enemy—or will be when you know me better. For now, though, you're intrigued by our wordplay. A smile tugs at the corners of your mouth. Closer to your real smile, I think, though held carefully in check.

"Is this your idea of clever party banter? Tortured metaphors?"

"Just a reminder that people aren't always who they pretend to be."

You sweep your eyes over me, slow, assessing. "Does that go for you as well?"

It's my turn to restrain a smile. "Oh, me most of all."

I nod politely then and step away. I've just spotted Goldie, who has reappeared with a fresh coat of shellac in place and a keen light in her eye. I join her at one of the bars, glad for the gin and tonic she presses into my hand. I take a long pull, fighting the urge to glance back at you. You're a thread I don't dare pull. Not because I'm afraid you won't survive the unraveling but because I'm certain—even in this early moment—that I won't.

Eventually, I do turn, though, and find your eyes still on me, and I realize that even at this distance, I'm not safe. You're simply dazzling, an icy-cool Eve in your slithery teal silk—the belle of the ball.

Belle.

It's how I thought of you that night, how I'll always think of you. Not by the name your family gave you but as my Belle. Because I sense it again as I pretend not to feel your eyes on me, the certainty that there's another woman hiding behind that chilly facade—one who has nothing to do with the glittering charade playing out around her.

Or perhaps it's only what I need to believe now—these many years later as I sit at my typewriter, spilling it all out—a delusion I cling to because it's easier than admitting I could ever have let myself be so thoroughly deceived.

THREE

ASHLYN

Beneath each faded jacket and scarred board is a life, a noble deed, a bruised heart, a lost love, a journey taken.

—*Ashlyn Greer,* The Care & Feeding of Old Books

September 26, 1984
Portsmouth, New Hampshire

Ashlyn sipped her coffee with closed eyes, fighting a dull headache and a vaguely queasy sensation in the pit of her stomach. It happened sometimes after handling a book with intense echoes. Like a hangover or early symptoms of the flu. She knew better than to spend long stretches of time with a book like *Regretting Belle.* Dark books, she called them, books with echoes too intense to be shelved with regular stock.

The fact that customers didn't know about the existence of echoes didn't mean they couldn't feel them. She'd seen firsthand the effects a dark book could have on the unsuspecting. Dizziness. Headache. An unexpected rush of tears. Once, a customer had pulled a copy of *Vanity Fair* from the shelf and been so overcome she had to ask for a glass of water. Poor woman. That was the day Ashlyn decided to purge the shelves.

She'd hung a CLOSED FOR INVENTORY sign on the door and over the course of the next three days had gone shelf by shelf, touching every book in the store, culling those with echoes she deemed too dark to be handled by the unsuspecting. There had been twenty-eight in all, some quite valuable. They were all safely out of reach now, quarantined in a glass-front cabinet in the shop's storeroom. *Regretting Belle* would almost certainly end up there when she finished it.

She eyed the book, lying beside her tote now on the kitchen counter. After three readings, the opening chapter had imprinted itself on her brain. An incendiary first meeting between lovers—at an engagement party, no less. Hardly an auspicious beginning. But then, the title made it clear that there would be no happy ending for the lovers.

Which probably explained why she hadn't been able to bring herself to move on to chapter two. The truth was she still hadn't decided what it was she'd been reading. Was it a memoir? The first chapter of a novel? A beautifully bound Dear Jane letter? She had no idea. What she did know was that allowing herself to become immersed in a doomed romance—even one in a book—wasn't a particularly good idea. Not when she'd fought so hard to pull herself back from the brink after her own marriage had imploded in such spectacular fashion.

A series of affairs, a divorce not quite finalized, and a death she hadn't seen coming. And yet it hadn't seemed right to call herself a widow after Daniel died—nor could she accurately call herself divorced, though their marriage had effectively ended months before. And so she'd found herself in a kind of limbo, with a brand-new therapist and no idea what came next. Once again, she had retreated to her safe place. But safety had come at a price.

She was painfully aware of the contraction her life had undergone over the last four years. Her lack of a social life or any serious professional circle. Her strict avoidance of anything that might lead to romantic involvement. It made for a narrow existence, a blur of sameness with little to distinguish one day from the next. On the other hand, there were no disasters, which made the sameness worth it. Most of the time.

Perhaps that explained why she found *Regretting Belle* so compelling. Because it offered an escape from the sameness, a journey that didn't require leaving the relative safety of shore.

But it was more than that and she had known it the moment she opened the book in Kevin's back room. There was a connection she couldn't quite identify, something prickly and familiar lurking beneath all the bitterness and betrayal—a sense of things left unfinished. It was how her own life felt, as if she'd been placed in a state of suspension, waiting, breath held, for some unseen shoe to drop. Like an interrupted story or an unresolved chord.

The realization was an uncomfortable one. And not easily set aside now that she was aware of it. All because a guy from Rye had dropped off a couple of cartons of books at Kevin's shop.

Not that it was the first time she'd been caught off guard by a book's echoes. It happened quite often, actually. Secrets so scandalous, they singed the tips of her fingers. Sadness that felt like a stone lodged in her throat. Joy so fierce, it made her scalp prickle. There wasn't much she hadn't come across. But she'd never experienced anything close to what she felt while holding *Regretting Belle*.

Her eyes slid to the book. Even closed, she could feel the pull of it, the allure of its anonymity, its careful, inscrutable prose, beckoning to be read after who knew how long.

And the echoes.

Over the years, she'd come to think of them the way a perfumer described the notes of a scent. Some were simple, others more complex—subtle layers of emotion combined to create the whole. Top, heart, and base.

With *Regretting Belle*, the echoes were complex, heavy, and slow to lift. Against her better judgment, she placed a hand on its cover. It was bitterness that came through first, hot and sharp against the pads of her fingers. That was the top note, the initial impression. Next came the deeper and rounder heart note, betrayal, which carved a hollow place beneath her ribs. And finally, there was the base note, the most resonant of all the layers—grief. But *whose* grief?

How, Belle?

The more she thought about it, the more convinced she was that the beautiful and mysterious Belle had been more than a product of the author's imagination. He'd made it clear that Belle was a nickname he'd given her. Her *real* name had been carefully omitted, as had his own. In fact, none of the characters had been given actual names. Was it because their real names would have been easily recognized?

Frowning, she fanned through the pages, as if the answers might be pressed in between, like an old love letter or prom corsage. They weren't, of course. If she wanted answers, she was going to have to work for them. Surely there was someone in her Rolodex, a professor or librarian, who might be able to shed some light on the mystery. Or maybe there was an easier way. If Kevin knew the name of the man who'd brought in the boxes, she might be able to contact him.

Downstairs, in the shop, she flipped to the Gs in her Rolodex, locating Kevin's number. After two rings, a woman answered. Ashlyn recognized the voice. It was Cassie, the gum-cracking Madonna wannabe who worked at the boutique when her band was between gigs.

"Hey, Cassie, it's Ashlyn from An Unlikely Story. Is Kevin around?"

"Oh, hey. Nope. He and Greg left this morning for a week in the Bahamas. I'm wicked jealous."

"So who's running the show?"

"Me, I guess. Something I can help you with?"

"I was hoping to talk to him about some books that came in last week. I bought one of them and I have some questions about it. I was hoping he might have a contact number for the guy who brought them in."

"Ooh-kay . . . definitely don't know anything about that."

Ashlyn pictured her smacking her gum into the phone and tried not to be annoyed. "Do you know if Kevin keeps information on the people who come in to sell things?"

"Sorry. That's all him. He'll be back in the store next Wednesday, though."

"Thanks. I'll give him a call then."

Ashlyn hung up and returned to her Rolodex. A week was too long to wait.

By the time Ashlyn turned the CLOSED sign around that evening, she'd spent a collective hour and a half on hold and had left seven messages, including one for Clifford Westin, an old friend of Daniel's and the current head of UNH's English department; another for George Bartholomew, a professor at UMASS who happened to be a customer; a pair for two rival rare-book dealers; and three for librarians.

Unfortunately, she'd come up empty. No one had ever heard of *Regretting Belle*. She was going to have to expand her search. The local chapter of the Antiquarian Booksellers' Association might be able to help. Or the International League of Antiquarian Booksellers. There was always the copyright office at the Library of Congress, but the prospect of navigating all that red tape was daunting. Still, it might be where she ended up.

Now, as she tallied the day's receipts, her eyes slid to the book again, more determined than ever to ferret out its secrets. The possibility of making some earth-shattering academic discovery, of stumbling upon a previously unknown work and seeing that discovery written up in a refereed journal like *The Review of English Studies* or *New Literary History*, was the unspoken dream of every rare-book dealer. But her interest wasn't academic. It was visceral, personal in a way she couldn't explain.

And so she would read on.

Regretting Belle

(pgs. 14–29)

4 September 1941
New York, New York

A week after our first meeting, I find myself at a dinner given by Violet Whittier and her husband, an intimate affair held in honor of your betrothal to the illustrious Teddy. The evening was Goldie's idea, though I'm not sure how she arranged it. Perhaps it had to do with some former indebtedness, a willingness from time to time to kill a less-than-flattering story, though I have no proof of that.

You tense for an instant when you spot me among the other guests, not so much that others would notice, but I notice and find myself smiling as you resume your tour of the room, a cool flame in pewter-grey silk, flitting amongst all the pretty people, pausing now and then, leaving a trail of coolness in your wake as you move on.

People use the word breathtaking—*no doubt I've used it myself—but it dawns on me as I watch you from behind my watered-down gin and tonic that I've never truly grasped the meaning of the word. Until now, that is, when I suddenly find all the air has gone out of the room.*

There's a subtle shimmer about you, a play of light that seems to cling to your skin, and for a moment I fancy I can see the cold rising from you in silvery little waves, the way the heat rises from the pavement in summer. I feel an utter fool, a boy smitten. Preposterous, since I'm not a boy. Still, I can't look away. You're ice and steel, insulated by your coolness, but your frosty exterior has the opposite effect on me, the pull of it—of you—so strong, it feels like a threat.

Being near you is necessary, I remind myself. A means to an end. But it shouldn't bring me such pleasure. Or such discomposure. My work demands a certain level of aloofness, the ability to hold myself apart, to observe from a distance. Clear-eyed, steady, always, always maintaining the illusion. It's a calling for which I'm particularly well suited. And yet, as I stand in your wake, staring after you, I'm anything but clear-eyed.

You muddle me, madam, turning all my intentions to dust until I almost forget I've been invited for a reason and that were this not the case, our paths would never have crossed. The thought hits hard, an awareness that I might have been spared from what I'm suddenly certain is to come. I'm a moth in thrall to a chilly flame, lost before the game has even begun.

I must be more guarded, I remind myself, but I'm too intrigued to be guarded, too . . . yes, I'll say it . . . too smitten with you. Our hostess, in the manner of all good hostesses—or perhaps as part of some earlier plan—takes me by one arm and Goldie by the other, steering us about the room like a pair of human bookends, dropping our names over and over until we're at last face-to-face with the guests of honor.

Your Teddy is all politeness, smiling and nodding like the great handsome clod he is. You wind your arm through his, but there's a kind of show to the gesture, a display of solidarity rather than affection. Or is it an instinctive need to protect yourself, an uncomfortable awareness of the invisible current arcing between us? Perhaps it's only what I want to see. Perhaps you two are actually mad for each other and you're not nearly as bored with him as I imagined that first night.

You manage a smile when we're introduced—that counterfeit smile again—but even that falters when our hostess introduces Goldie, then immediately slips away, leaving the four of us uncomfortably on our own. Your eyes linger on the heavily jeweled hand resting on my sleeve, then slide to the rather ample bosom pressed against my arm. It's all you can do not to curl your lip in disgust.

You catch my eye, one dark brow slightly raised. I assume the look is meant to shame me. It doesn't. I nod stiffly before excusing myself. Your eyes drill my back as Goldie and I drift away, and I feel a small lick of annoyance aimed between my shoulder blades. You're relieved to be free of me but miffed, too, at having been dismissed so publicly. A novelty, I'm quite sure.

Later, I manage to get some time alone with the golden-haired Teddy. I've done my homework and know his particulars. Theodore. Teddy for short. Middle name Lawrence, like his father and grandfather before him. Born April 14, 1917. Attended The Browning School through the first half of eleventh grade, where he managed to letter in three sports before his abrupt and carefully hushed-up departure. Last year and a half of grade school served with the priests at Iona Prep before eventually moving on to Princeton, where he distinguished himself as captain of the polo team, solidified his reputation as a prolific lout and lush, and was voted least likely to be sober for graduation. Horses weren't the only things Teddy liked to ride in those days, and I can't help wondering how much you know—and if he's mended his ways.

He's cupping a drink as I approach. Whiskey, I'm guessing. And judging by the glassy sheen of his silver-green eyes, not his first. He flashes his teeth as I hold out a hand, pretending to remember me. I congratulate him on his good fortune and his soon-to-be bride, just to break the ice, then steer the conversation to the news of the day. What he thinks about the US joining the war effort in Europe. How he feels about Roosevelt dragging his feet, despite Churchill's repeated pleas for help. How he feels about the Vichy handing over Paris to the Germans.

He frowns into his nearly empty glass a moment before looking up again. He blinks those too-wet, too-wide eyes at me and wags his great brick of a jaw, as if searching for the appropriate response. The silence is beginning to grow awkward when he finally finds his tongue. "I'd say the Frenchies should fight their own battles this time around and leave us the hell out of their wars. If you ask me, Americans should be more concerned with what's going on right here under their noses than with what's happening across the Atlantic."

And here it is—the stuff I came for. I keep my face bland. "Such as?"

"The money, of course. And who's got control of it. If we're not careful, we'll soon find ourselves at the complete mercy of the bastards—if we're not there already."

"And which bastards would they be?"

"The Steins. The Bergs. The Rosens. Take your pick."

He means the Jews, of course. "All of them?"

He blinks, slow and heavy, impervious to my sarcasm. "Well, the rich ones, anyway. Which is most of them. Making money off everyone else instead of doing an honest day's work. Buying up every goddamn thing they can get their hands on."

The irony of the moment is almost more than I can stomach. I have to grit my teeth to keep from pointing out that he's never done a day's work in his life and his family owns stock in half the railroads, oil companies, and shipyards in the United States, not to mention miles of real estate on both the East and West Coasts.

He's gotten up a head of steam now, his face flushed with the effort of stringing so many sentences together. But he's proud, too, to have been able to pull out his little speech at the proper moment, as if he's been waiting for an opportunity to express his opinion—even if it isn't wholly his own.

I nod somberly behind my gin and tonic. "Sounds like you've given this a good deal of thought—about who's to blame for your country's current plight, I mean. The Rosens and their lot."

He frowns as if I've said something ridiculous. "It doesn't really take much thought, does it? Who do you think caused the damn crash to begin with? Now they're trying to bankrupt us with somebody else's war. They will, too, if we don't cut them off at the knees. Them and the communists with their Union thugs. They've already got Roosevelt's stones in a jar. Congress will be next, mark my words."

His words have the savor of regurgitation, like a schoolboy doing an impersonation of the headmaster, and I suspect he's merely parroting someone else's opinion. Probably because he's never bothered to form one of his own. I keep that suspicion to myself, of course, along with the rest of my suspicions. Goldie didn't orchestrate our invitation to this posh little hooey just to watch me get tossed out on my ear.

Teddy, having spat out the last of his political talking points, abruptly shifts to more general topics, eventually working the conversation around to horses and polo. Not that I'm surprised. I'll wager they're the only subjects upon which he actually possesses an opinion of his own. But then I suppose when you're as rich and handsome as young Teddy, you needn't be clever. The world will always be forgiving for an Adonis with a trust fund—however thickheaded.

I endure long enough to wrangle introductions to a few of his friends— or to be more precise, his father's friends, with whom it might be advantageous to have a connection—so our conversation isn't a complete waste. Connections are the point, after all. But when the dialogue begins to peter out, I point to my empty glass and excuse myself, not sure who I despise more—him, for being an utter fool, or you, for even considering marriage to a man so clearly your inferior.

I've barely gotten my drink refilled when our hostess calls us in for dinner. I feign surprise at learning that you and I are seated next to one another. In truth, it's no accident, nor is the fact that Teddy is stationed at the opposite end of the table, as far from us as possible. Goldie is seated at his elbow, flirting openly in order to keep him occupied. I watch, amused as she lays one of those heavily jeweled hands on his arm and dips her head toward his, whispering into his ear. You are not amused.

Your eyes wandering repeatedly to their end of the table is the tell. Again, not so much that others would notice, but enough that I do. But eventually, halfway through the soup course, I manage to gain your attention long enough to begin a conversation.

"I'm both pleased and surprised," I say, with my most charming smile, "to find myself seated beside the guest of honor."

"One of them," you respond snippily. "There are two of us."

"Yes, of course. But I'm lucky enough to be sitting beside the better half."

You sniff, brushing aside the compliment. "Wouldn't you prefer to be sitting beside your . . . date? I'm sure she's missing you terribly."

"Oh, I don't know." I smile blandly, glancing pointedly to the end of the table, where Goldie and Teddy seem to be getting on famously. "She looks to me as if she's having rather a good time. Your fiancé seems quite engaged."

"I'm sure she's a brilliant conversationalist."

Your remark drips with venom, and it's all I can do not to bark out a laugh. "Surely you're not worried about Teddy falling victim to Goldie's charms."

You set down your soupspoon and eye me coldly. "Don't be ridiculous. She's hardly Teddy's type."

I want to point out that Goldie is exactly Teddy's type—loud and blonde and brassy—and that he isn't half-good enough for her—or you. I want to, but I don't. One of two things is true. Either you wouldn't believe me or you already know I'm right. "Who is his type?" I say instead. "You?"

Your gaze drifts back down the table, lingering icily. "Certainly not someone who calls herself Goldie. It's a name for a spaniel. Or a vaudeville performer."

I smile, amused by your cattiness. "It's to do with the hair, I think. Her father used to call her Goldilocks when she was little. It stuck."

"What a charming story. She told you that herself, I suppose?"

"She did. Apparently, they were quite close. What about you? Did your father have a pet name for you?"

"I was never my father's pet. That would be my sister."

Your cool indifference has fallen away, exposing nerves left raw by some childhood wound. It's not a door I expected to be invited through—at least not this soon—but I have no intention of ignoring it. "What name did he give your sister?"

"Treasure. He called her My Treasure.*"*

There's a broken-glass quality to your voice I'm not meant to notice. I do, though. How could I not, when all at once, despite the collective hum of conversation, we seem to be the only two people in the room? The wine has loosened your tongue, and the unguarded moment feels both awkward and illuminating. Here, at last, is the real Belle, the woman I suspected from the beginning was lurking beneath that counterfeit smile. The one ungoverned by gears and levers. It's in this moment, this fleeting, evanescent instant when the veil slips and you're briefly exposed, that I realize I'm truly lost.

Damn you.

I change the subject as we move on to the fish course, remarking on how much better everything seems to taste when one is away from home. "Or maybe it's to do with the war and how scarce things have gotten back home. Sugar, butter, bacon are all on rations now, and there's talk of more if the thing drags on. I hope the US will be better prepared than we were."

"My father says we're not getting dragged into it this time. The last war taught us that we need to stay home. Teddy thinks so too."

"And what do you think?"

Your shoulders twitch, not quite a shrug. "I don't think about it. Not really."

Your response annoys me. The vagueness of it, as if I've just asked your opinion on some obscure mathematical problem. "Too busy?"

"Women aren't usually consulted on wars. We send our husbands and brothers and sweethearts to do the dying, hold the pieces together while

they're gone, then pick up what's left when they come home—if they come home—but we're seldom asked what we think."

My annoyance falls away as I digest your response. I'm both surprised and relieved to find you're not quite as cool—or as empty—as I originally feared. The revelation makes me strangely glad. "That's quite an answer for someone who hasn't given the subject much thought."

"And what are your thoughts? You have some, presumably. Tell me, are you as mad at us Yanks as everyone else back home?"

"It's not a question of being mad. We're afraid of what might happen if the United States stays out. Hitler certainly hopes you do. And so far, he seems to be getting his way."

"I assume you're an interventionist."

"I'm an observer, watching from a distant shore."

"Speaking of distant shores, you never did say what brought you to ours."

I remain focused on my plate, extricating a bit of bone from my salmon. "Didn't I?"

"No. You only said you were looking for an adventure."

I look up then with an innocent smile. "Isn't everyone? Aren't you?"

You nod, acknowledging the evasion. "And have you found it? This adventure you're after?"

"Not yet, but I've only been here a few weeks."

"And how long will you be staying?"

"It's open-ended at this point. Until I get what I'm after, I suppose."

"Which is?"

"Oh no, let's not do that one again. Ask me something else."

"All right." You dab prettily at your mouth, leaving a smear of garnet on your napkin. "How long have you been writing?"

My eyes are still riveted to your napkin, to the imprint of your mouth, and for a moment I find myself annoyingly flustered. It's a simple question, perfectly safe. The kind of thing one might ask on a first date. I tell myself to breathe, to straighten up.

"I can't remember a time when I didn't," I finally manage. "My father was a newspaperman and I wanted to be just like him when I grew up. When I was ten, he set up a small desk for me in his office and gave me one of his old typewriters, a great, shiny black thing I still use today. It was the same machine Hemingway wrote on. My father was an enormous fan. I would sit there for hours, banging away at nonsense. When I finished, he would read what I'd written, marking it up with his pencil, making notes in the margins: Stronger verbs. Less shilly-shallying with descriptors. Tell them what's important and leave out the rest. *He was my first editor and a lover of the* dear old colonies, *as he called them. Which is probably the real reason I'm here. He loved New York and always made it sound so wonderful."*

"I suppose he's terribly proud of you."

"He's dead, I'm afraid. Almost ten years now. But I'd like to think he was."

Your eyes go soft. "I'm sorry."

It's the pat answer when someone mentions a death, the polite answer, but the catch in your voice tells me you mean it. And then I remember Goldie telling me that you lost your mother at a young age. A prolonged illness, I can't remember what. I only recall that she died in some private hospital upstate. It was one of those bits you simply file away, in case you need it at some point for background, but I never connected the death to a flesh-and-blood person, because you weren't flesh and blood then. Now, with you sitting so close our elbows occasionally brush, the story registers quite differently.

"Thank you. That's very kind of you."

"And your mother? Is she . . ."

"Still alive but back in Berkshire, I'm afraid. I'd hoped she'd come over with me, but my father's buried in the churchyard in Cookham and she refused to leave him. Stubborn as a goat—which is exactly what she used to say about my father. They were cut from the same cloth, those two. A match made in heaven, if you believe in that sort of thing."

"And do *you?"*

Your face gives nothing away, but there's a hint of sadness in the question, a whiff of resignation you can't quite hide. I manage a smile, though it feels like an apology. "I've seen it firsthand, so I suppose I must. But I'm not the one who's just gotten myself engaged. The more pertinent question is, Do you?"

You're spared having to answer when a server appears to clear our plates and deliver the next course. I sip my wine as dishes are whisked away and replaced with new ones. I've been rather free with my talk, I realize, allowing personal details to creep in where they have no business. I'm seldom careless, especially with a thing as perilous as the truth, but you have a strange effect on me. You make me forget what I'm about—and why I'm about it.

Through most of the next course, you chat with your other neighbor—a railroad man named Brady with whom I spoke briefly during cocktails. I pretend to focus on the bloody cut of beef on my plate as I eavesdrop on the discussion unfolding across the table, a hearty endorsement for Charles Lindbergh—or Lucky Lindy, as he's now called—and his strident assertion that Hitler's brutality in Europe has nothing to do with the United States. A theme seems to be emerging.

You eventually push your untouched plate away and turn to me, picking up the conversation where we left it. "I've never met a writer before. Tell me more about your work."

"What would you like to know?"

"Are you working on a story now? One about an adventurous Brit, perhaps, who travels across the big blue ocean to learn all about the glamorous Americans?"

"Yes," I tell you, because it's exactly what I've come to write. But it isn't the whole truth. The whole truth you will find out later, but by then, the damage will be done. Time to pivot before you become too curious. "And now it's my turn to ask a question. A little birdie told me you recently acquired several horses from Ireland. Is this an interest of your own, or is it to do with your intended's love of all things equine?"

"This birdie—is she here with you this evening?"

"I never said the birdie was a she, but yes."

Your eyes flick to the opposite end of the table, where Goldie is snickering at whatever your fiancé has just said. You let your gaze linger, thoughtful, discreet. When you finally look at me again, the corners of your mouth are tilted up, lending you a faintly feline appearance. "She doesn't mind my name coming up during your . . . pillow talk?"

I shrug for effect. "She's not especially territorial, at least not where I'm concerned. She doesn't mind that I'm curious about you."

"Am I going to be part of your story, then? Is that why you've turned up twice now? To study the modern American female and then write about your observations?"

I regard you from behind my wineglass, head tipped to one side. "Would you fancy being written about in that way? A two-page spread complete with photos—A Day in the Life of an American Heiress?"

Your eyes flash a warning, on the off chance that my question isn't hypothetical. "I don't fancy being written about in any way."

I offer another one of my disarming smiles. "You need have no fear. I prefer to leave that sort of thing to your Mr. Winchell. He's better at it than I could ever be. I'm genuinely curious about the horses, though. You don't seem like the stable type to me."

You arch a brow. "Don't I?"

"No."

"What type do I seem?"

You're flirting with me, deploying that voice and those smoky amber eyes in a way your fiancé is meant to notice. Giving him a little of his own back. I'm happy to play along. Only I wonder if you're up for such a grown-up game.

"I don't know yet," *I answer truthfully.* "I can't quite get round you. But I will—eventually."

You blink at me, surprised by my bluntness. "Are you always so sure of yourself?"

"Not always. But sometimes I look at a puzzle and already know where all the pieces go."

"I see. I'm a puzzle now."

I sip my wine, in no hurry to answer. "Every woman is a puzzle," I say finally. "Some harder to solve than others. But then, I've found it's the difficult ones who are most worth the effort."

It's rubbish, really, man-about-town nonsense made up on the spur of the moment, but it sounds right coming out of my mouth. Mysterious and just the tiniest bit lurid, a velvet gauntlet thrown down in the middle of dinner. I'm rather pleased with myself when I see a faint bloom of pink creep into those pale cheeks. A blush suits you.

"You're wrong," you assert in a tone too warm to be convincing. "I am the stable type. Or at least I'm trying to be."

"Because good wives are interested in the things their husbands are interested in?"

"It has nothing to do with Teddy. Or almost nothing. Last spring he took me to Saratoga to see some of his Thoroughbreds. They were getting ready for their first baby race. We got up early to watch the exercise riders take them through their paces. They were so beautiful, sleek and strong and fast as the wind. I knew then and there that I wanted my own. We keep a few horses at our place in the Hamptons, but those are just for riding. Thoroughbreds are athletes. It took some doing, but I eventually talked my father into buying me a pair for my birthday."

I stare at you, digesting what you've just said and the way you said it. As if it were nothing at all. "Your father bought you a pair of racehorses . . . for your birthday?"

"A sweet bay filly and a chestnut colt. And a made-over stable to keep them in. I know, it sounds frightfully stuck up, but it was mostly just to shut me up. He's convinced I'm going to lose interest now that he's given in. He says I have a short attention span."

"Do you?"

"It depends."

"On?"

"On how interesting I find something."

"And you find horses interesting?"

"I do. There's so much to know. There's an entire language to it. That's the first thing you learn if you want to be taken seriously, and I do. I've also had to bring myself up to speed on the whole breeding business. I had no idea there were so many factors to weigh when it comes to males and females. You really have to know what you're doing for everything to work right."

You're so charmingly chatty, so absorbed in discussing your new hobby as the dessert is served, that you don't realize that a casual eavesdropper, such as the young man currently placing a slice of pear tart in front of you, might mistake our conversation for something else entirely. It's all I can do to keep a straight face.

"Is that so?"

"Oh yes. It's an actual science. There's loads of literature on the subject, but a book will only take you so far. My friends think me terribly unladylike for being interested in that end of things, but I've found if you want to get good at something, you need actual experience." There's a kind of purr to your voice now, throaty and feline. You pause, flashing me a cunning little smile. "You can't be timid about things. You have to jump right in and get dirty. Wouldn't you agree?"

I nearly spit out my wine. I mistook you for an innocent, inexperienced and naive. Now I see that I was wrong. You're perfectly aware of what you're saying—and of how it might be misconstrued. In fact, you're enjoying yourself enormously. "Yes, I suppose I do," I say, fighting to keep a straight face. "And what has jumping in taught you?"

"Oh, lots. For instance, one must be very selective when choosing a male. There's temperament to consider. And past performance. Size and stamina. All very important to a satisfactory outcome."

I put down my glass and take a moment to dab at my mouth. If you're inclined to play games, who am I to spoil your fun? I'm fond of games myself. But I play to win. "And have you chosen wisely, do you think?"

Your smile widens. You're pleased that I've decided to play along. "I'm afraid it's too early to know at this point. Time will tell, I suppose."

I nod my thanks to the young man who has just filled my coffee cup, then lift the cup to hide my own smile. "I should like to see these horses of yours."

"And I'd like to show them to you," you answer sweetly as you slice into your pear tart. "Perhaps we can manage it sometime."

"I'm free tomorrow afternoon, as it happens, and I rather fancy a trip to the Hamptons. I hear it's pretty country."

Your eyes skitter to mine, a rabbit in a snare. You haven't prepared for this—for what happens when the hunter you've led on such a merry chase finally catches you—but having sprung the trap, you bear up nobly. "Do you ride?"

"Passably," I reply coolly, delighted to watch you squirm. "It's been a while, but it's not the kind of thing you forget, is it?"

"I don't suppose it is, no."

"Are we on for tomorrow, then?"

To my surprise, after the barest of glances toward Teddy, you agree to meet me at your father's stables at two the following afternoon. I catch Goldie's discreet congratulatory nod. She can't know about the date I've just made, but she senses that I'm pleased with myself.

Perhaps too pleased.

The meal is quickly winding down, and I'm aware that the moment we leave the dining room, we'll part company for the night, and that for now I must watch you hover at Teddy's side and content myself with thoughts of tomorrow.

FOUR

ASHLYN

We read not to escape life but to learn how to live it more deeply and richly, to experience the world through the eyes of the other.

—*Ashlyn Greer,* The Care & Feeding of Old Books

September 27, 1984
Portsmouth, New Hampshire

Ashlyn flinched as she flipped on the bindery overheads, wishing she'd had that second cup of coffee. She'd come down early to begin work on Gertrude Maxwell's latest garage-sale rescue—a set of cloth-bound Nancy Drew mysteries intended as a Christmas gift for her granddaughter—but she wasn't feeling particularly motivated.

Her eyes felt gritty and she could still feel the remnants of a headache at the back of her skull. She'd stayed up too late again, revisiting passages from *Regretting Belle* she found particularly intriguing. And it was *all* intriguing. Hints that the author's motives might be less than honorable. Cryptic references to the illustrious Goldie. The delicious wordplay exchanged during dinner.

It had taken a supreme act of will to finally set the book aside and turn out the light. She longed to know what had transpired the next day at the stables, but first and foremost, she wanted to solve the mystery of the book's origins.

Perhaps it was a lost manuscript, abandoned by its author, then unearthed and bound sometime later. Or more likely, the work of an aspiring writer who'd been unable to find a publisher. But neither scenario explained the lack of an author name.

Which left . . . what?

She'd all but ruled out an oversight on the binder's part. It was possible, of course. But she found it unlikely that anyone capable of turning out such a beautiful book would have been sloppy enough to omit the author's name, the publisher's name, *and* the copyright page. And there was the prose itself, dripping with disdain. For Belle's father. For Teddy. At times, for Belle herself. But nothing that might give away the names of the actual players. It all felt too careful.

She had jotted down two names last night. Kenneth Graham, who'd helped her find a buyer for a rather fine copy of *The Vicar of Wakefield* she had acquired at an estate sale last year, and Mason Devaney, a Boston shop owner, who periodically penned articles on literary sleuthing.

Ashlyn checked the clock over the workbench. It was still a bit early for phone calls. Maybe she'd get some work in before the shop opened and put the calls off until lunchtime, when she was more likely to reach someone.

She had just donned a pair of white cotton gloves, preparing for a more thorough examination of *The Hidden Staircase*, when she heard the shop phone ring. Groaning, she peeled off the gloves and sprinted up front. Frank had been adamant about not being disturbed while working on bindery projects, but he'd had staffers to tend the shop while he worked in the back. For now, at least, she was on her own.

"Good morning. An Unlikely Story," she answered, summoning a modicum of morning cheer.

"I was told you rang."

"Kevin?"

"At your service."

"I thought you and Greg were in the Bahamas."

"We were. But so was Tropical Storm Isidore, so we scrammed while we could still get a flight out. Just as well. It was wicked hot, and we were both red as lobsters. Anyhow, I'm back, and I'm calling, though not because you asked me to. I was in the back room just now, going through some boxes that came in the day before we left, and I found something you might be interested in."

"What?" She didn't ask if it was a book. Of course it was a book. "What did you find? And how much is it going to cost me?"

"That's for me to know and you to find out. All I'll say is you're definitely going to want to come by."

"Just tell me, Kevin."

"Now, where's the fun in that?"

"Can you at least tell me what we're talking about? Do I bring a checkbook or the title to my car?"

Kevin barked out a laugh. "We're not talking Gutenberg Bible. I just said you'd be interested. And you will be. I'd bring it myself but I'm alone, which means you'll have to come fetch it."

"Fine. But you're being awfully mean. You know I can't get there until I close."

"See you at six, then."

There was an abrupt click and the line went dead. Ashlyn stared at the heavy black receiver, realizing that in her excitement, she'd forgotten to ask him about the guy from Rye.

~

At six on the dot, Ashlyn locked up the shop and walked the two blocks to Going Twice. Kevin was behind the counter, working on a sheet of price tags.

He glanced up at her with a bland smile. "Hello. What brings you by?"

"Very funny."

"Hey, my vacation got canceled. You have to let me have *some* fun."

"Are you about done?"

"Okay," he said, feigning a pout. "But you're going to wish you were nicer to me." He grinned conspiratorially as he reached beneath the counter, eventually producing a small book with marbled blue boards. "Ta-da!"

Ashlyn felt the hair on the back of her neck prickle as she took the book from his hand. It was an exact copy—or very nearly exact—of the one she now carried in her tote. The same size, the same Moroccan leather, the same hubbed spine. Though not quite the same boards, she saw on closer inspection. The blue was a shade off, a little greener. She peered at the spine, at the title embossed in gold.

Forever, and Other Lies.

Once again, the author's name and publisher were absent—as were any traces of a discernible echo. She was tempted to flip back the cover then and there, to verify what she suspected lay within, but she didn't *need* to. She already knew what she was holding, and she wanted to be alone when she finally opened it.

"I can't believe it. It's nearly identical. Where did you find it?"

"The guy—the one from Rye—brought in four more boxes the day I left for vacation. I didn't have a chance to go through them until today. I knew you'd want it the minute I saw it. What did you ever make of the first one?"

"Nothing yet. No one's ever heard of it. It's like the book never existed."

"That's weird, right?"

"Pretty weird, yeah." And now there were two, which probably meant it was about to get even weirder. "I made a few calls to people I thought would be able to help, but so far, no luck. Maybe I'll do better with this one. What do you want for it?"

"Don't you want to at least have a flick through? To make sure it's what you think it is?"

Ashlyn shook her head. "I'm already sure. How much?"

Kevin scrubbed at his chin, eyes narrowed thoughtfully. "I've never once held you up for a book. In fact, I gave you the last one. But this is different. You *want* this one. You *need* this one."

Ashlyn regarded him with surprise. She'd never known him to have a mercenary streak, but he wasn't wrong. She *did* need this one. "All right. Name your price."

"It's yours . . . ," he said, pausing for effect, "for a box of cocoa bombs from Seacoast Sweets. And don't try to haggle. That price is firm."

Ashlyn broke into a grin. "You've got yourself a deal. I think they're already closed, though. Can I send them tomorrow? I promise I'm good for it."

"Fine. But remember, I know where you live."

"Also . . . I need one more favor."

Kevin responded with an exaggerated eye roll. "You're becoming a problem child."

"I know. But this is easy. The guy. The one who brought in the boxes. I was hoping you might have a number for him. I'm not going to harass him or anything. I just want to ask him a few questions."

Kevin's face went blank. "Afraid I can't help you there. All I know is his father died a few months back and he's been cleaning out the old man's house. Brought in some pretty choice stuff, too, including some great old vinyl I'll probably end up keeping for myself."

"Didn't you have to write him a check for all that choice stuff?"

"Normally I would, but the guy wouldn't take a nickel. Said he didn't want to think of it all sitting in a heap at the dump. Wasn't here fifteen minutes, and that's both trips combined."

"Don't you have to keep records, like a pawnshop?"

"Nah. That's in case someone's trying to fence stolen property—jewelry, stereos, that sort of thing. No one's going to jail for an old Partridge Family album. For a while, I scribbled names and addresses in one of those old composition books, but eventually, I got lazy and quit. Weird stuff does happen, though. Relatives show up demanding Grandma's stuff back after you've shelled out money for it. It can get messy. Come to think of it, maybe I should buy a new composition book. That doesn't help you now, though. Sorry."

Ashlyn waved off the apology. "Never mind. It was a long shot. I'll just keep sleuthing."

"You think they might actually be worth something?"

"No, it's nothing like that. I've just never run across anything like . . . whatever this is. I'm not very far into the first book, but what I've read so far feels so personal. Like it was written for an audience of one."

"Like a letter?"

"A really *long* letter. Or a journal, maybe. But why go to the trouble of having something like that professionally bound?"

Kevin shrugged and gave his head a scratch. "If there's one thing running this store has taught me, it's that there's no end to the emotional weight people attach to their stuff. Who knows? Maybe the answer is in the second book."

"Maybe." Ashlyn slid her tote up onto her shoulder. "Guess I better get reading."

Ashlyn could feel the new book burning a hole in her tote as she made the brisk two-block walk back to the shop. A sequel or a prequel? An unconnected stand-alone? She had no idea which yet, but she intended to find out. Key in hand, she tore up the stairs to her apartment, not even bothering to kick off her shoes before dropping into her reading chair and flipping on the lamp.

There could be no doubt that the books were meant to resemble one another, but side by side, the differences between them were more evident. A slightly waxier leather had been used to bind *Forever, and Other Lies*, and the bands on the spine were cleaner and sharper.

She picked up *Forever, and Other Lies*, holding it flat against her palm. Like its mate, it showed little sign of wear. And like its mate, it was strangely quiet. No echoes of any kind—at least while closed.

Breath held, she turned back the cover, braced for the waves of searing anguish she'd come to expect from *Regretting Belle*. At first, there was nothing, but after a moment, she became aware of a faint humming in the tips of her fingers. It was a cool, shivery sensation, quite different from what she'd been bracing for. She forced herself to remain still, letting the sensation build, a curious blend of numbness and pins and needles prickling up her arm like a slow-spreading frost, curling around her ribs and along her throat. Top note . . . heart note . . . base note.

Accusation. Betrayal. Heartbreak.

Ashlyn exhaled sharply as the intensity increased. This was nothing like *Regretting Belle*, which had nearly burned her fingers with its festering hostility and pent-up pain. In fact, this was the exact opposite. It was cold and cutting, like a January wind, and strangely . . . *bloodless*.

It was an odd way to describe anger, which usually registered as hot and sharp, like a slap. But there was no heat here, only a blue-white conflagration that felt like fire but wasn't. No, that wasn't right. It wasn't anger she was picking up. It was despair. A void so deep, so achingly familiar, it made her throat clench.

The echoes were feminine.

Ashlyn stared at the open book, trying to wrap her head around what she appeared to be holding—and who had almost certainly written it. She held her breath as she turned to the title page. And there it was. A single line of slanted script.

How??? After everything—you can ask that of me?

The word *me* was underlined, not once but twice, and there was an angry blot of ink marring the question mark. Instinctively, she opened *Regretting Belle* and read the inscriptions together. A question and a response.

How, Belle? After everything . . . how could you do it?

How??? After everything—you can ask that of me?

Forever, and Other Lies

(pgs. 1–6)

August 27, 1941
New York, New York

A girl isn't supposed to fall in love at her own engagement party.

She isn't supposed to, but I did. But then, for a skilled pretender, I was easy prey. And you were quite skilled, as I soon learned.

But I won't rush ahead. I must set the stage first, if I'm to tell it properly. And that's what this is about. Telling it properly—as it really *happened, rather than how you have reinvented it in your pretty little book. And so I'll begin at the beginning, on the night the whole thing started, in the ballroom of the St. Regis Hotel.*

I had accepted a proposal of marriage from a young man I more or less grew up with. Teddy, whose father was one of the wealthiest and most prominent men in New York and a business associate of my father. It was all rather tidy. Or so my father thought when he arranged it. A merger of our families' fortunes.

Oh, I fought it. I had no wish to marry anyone in those days. I was barely twenty-one—still a child in many ways—and had seen my sister obediently married off, had watched her wither under her husband's heavy hand and the incessant needs of the children she produced at alarmingly regular intervals.

Cee-Cee was a prominent figure in my childhood, particularly after my mother's death. Nine years my senior, she wielded a firm hand in raising me, but then in those days, she wielded a firm hand in just about everything. She ran my father's house with astonishing efficiency, managing the help, planning meals, and at the age of seventeen, assuming the role of hostess when he entertained. She became, in my eyes—and in my father's, too, for a time—the lady of the house. But I saw how marriage diminished her, leaving her smaller somehow, less visible and less valuable.

As far as I could see, my sister's chief contribution as a wife was that of a broodmare, and I found the prospect appalling. I wanted a life of my own: school, travel, art, adventure. And I meant to have it too. So you can imagine my surprise at finding myself in the ballroom of the St. Regis, standing at Teddy's side in a new gown by Worth, being toasted by a veritable Who's Who of New York society. But then, my father can be very persuasive when he's made up his mind about a thing. And he'd made up his mind about Teddy.

"To the happy couple!"

The collective cry rings in my ears after yet another toast. I lift my glass when I'm supposed to, smile when I'm supposed to. I'm my father's daughter, after all, and have been well trained. But inside, I'm numb. It's as if I'm peering through a window, watching it all happen to someone else. But it isn't. It's happening to me, and I can't imagine how I've let it.

I slip away as soon as I can manage it, leaving Teddy to talk polo ponies with his club cronies, and search out a quiet corner. The heat of too many bodies combined with the whir of conversation and music is giving me a headache. But really, I'm nauseated by the thought that I'll soon end up like my sister. Bored. Bitter. Invisible.

Teddy isn't George, I remind myself as I grab a glass of champagne from a passing waiter and toss it back. Teddy is athletic and dashing, highly accomplished by masculine standards—which I've learned are the only standards that matter—and is considered a worthy catch by just about every woman in New York. The problem, I realize as I glance about for another tray of champagne, is that I don't want to catch anyone. Parties and dinners and bland conversation. Holidays at all the fashionable places and endless changes of clothing. God help me.

Malleable, my father once called Cee-Cee. Because she understood things like loyalty and duty. It was the day he informed me that I was to marry Teddy. When I said I wasn't interested in marriage, he explained with strained patience that sometimes we must do what's required for the greater good. He was talking about his greater good, of course, protecting the less-than-tidy empire he'd managed to build when the Volstead Act was passed.

Teddy and his pedigree were meant to help with that, our marriage a strategic alliance intended to advance the collective family cause and remove the stench of new money and a decade of illegal Canadian whisky. But marriage should be more than an alliance. Or so I naively assumed. I'm fond of Teddy, the way one is fond of an unruly puppy or clumsy cousin, but I feel nothing when he kisses me, nothing warm or stirring.

My experience with men at this point in my life has been limited—which is as it should be for a young lady only three years out of an all-girls school. But somewhere along the way, I picked up the idea that there should be more to the business of men and women than submission and duty, something visceral connecting us, something chemical and elemental.

These are the thoughts running through my head as I glance around and see you for the first time. I look away, startled by my own thoughts and the creeping heat I feel moving up my throat and into my cheeks. But after a few more sips of champagne, I look for you again. And there you are, tall and dark-haired with a longish face and piercing blue eyes, still watching me. The hint of a smile tugs at the corners of your mouth, as if you're amused but would rather not show it.

There's a mocking quality to your expression that makes me self-conscious, and makes me a little angry, too, an audaciousness that causes my *skin to tingle. I meet your gaze, willing myself not to look away, even as you begin to walk toward me. I swallow what's left in my glass as you come to stand at my side.*

"Careful," you say, your voice low and sinuous. "It'll sneak up on you. Especially if you're not used to it."

I sweep you with my eyes, doing my best to appear dismissive. "Do I look like I'm not used to it?"

"No," you reply, raking a shock of dark hair off your forehead as you run your eyes over me. "Not now that I look more closely."

Something about the look unsettles me, like a cloud of butterflies has suddenly been let loose in my belly. Or perhaps it's just that you're standing so close. There's a hint of a five-o'clock shadow along your jawline, suggesting you didn't have time to shave before the party. Your evening clothes, though proper white-tie, seem not to fit as well as they could, your jacket the tiniest bit shy at the cuff, the seams at your shoulders slightly puckered. A rented suit most likely, rather than one owned for occasions like this.

I notice you're not drinking and suggest a glass of champagne, but you decline in your cool, clipped British tone. Educated but not quite posh. It suddenly occurs to me that I don't know you, despite the fact that you've obviously been invited to my engagement party.

I study your face as we talk about books, trying to discern what it is that makes you handsome, since, taken one at a time, your features fall a bit short of the classic definition. Your nose is narrow and a little long, giving you the look of a raven, your mouth both too wide and too full above a sharply clefted chin. No, I decide. Not nearly as perfect as I'd thought at first glance. But your eyes, an arresting pale blue with a dark ring at the perimeter, hold mine longer than is comfortable, and suddenly I can't think of anything to say.

I'm relieved when Elaine Forester appears. She's the mother of one of Cee-Cee's friends, and her husband, whose family tea fortune evaporated after The Crash, is a longtime associate of my father's. I'm hoping you'll take the hint and wander off, but after a few simpered platitudes about Teddy and my good fortune, Elaine moves away and we're alone again.

You lean in and offer your congratulations, softly, like you're telling me a secret. I can't help feeling I'm being mocked. I shrug off the words, barely remembering to say thank you. But you're not through being insolent. Not by a long shot. You launch into a dossier on my fiancé, a catalog of all his traits and accomplishments. But your words are meant as an insult rather than praise. You even suggest I'm unhappy with my engagement. As if we haven't just met and you somehow have the right to an opinion.

I ignore the impertinence and ask how you happen to be at my party, since I don't know you. Your name, when you give it, is unfamiliar. Your date's name, however, which you drop without batting an eye, is familiar, though not in a way that reflects well on you. Everyone in New York knows the infamous Goldie.

Still, I find myself at a loss for words, astonished that she's somewhere in the crowd, drinking my father's champagne and getting up to god knows what. How on earth did one of the city's most notorious women—a self-styled newspaperwoman, of all things—manage to wrangle an invitation to my engagement party? Undoubtedly the work of my betrothed, who never misses a chance to get his name and face in the paper.

I should have known then and there what kind of man you are, running around with a woman at least ten years your senior. A woman, I might add, known for keeping a stable of young men at her beck and call. All I can think is, What kind of man gets mixed up with a woman like that? I believe I even say something to that effect. You stiffen a little, informing me in that snooty accent of yours that people aren't always who they pretend to be—you least of all.

What a fool I was to not take you at your word.

Forever, and Other Lies

(pgs. 7–10)

September 4, 1941
New York, New York

*Imagine my surprise at seeing you a week later at the Whittiers' dinner party.
You're with her again. She of the too-yellow hair and the too-tight dress and
the snorty bray of a laugh. She of the checkered past and silly name.*

Goldie.

*You move about the room in tandem, arms linked, smiling coolly as
you're introduced to my friends. You in your superbly cut dinner jacket—a
gift, I assume, and very generous. Her in plum-colored moiré that clings
like a second skin. She's handsome, I'll grant. Well put together and perfectly
made up. But with a few more miles on her than most men your age would
find appealing. But perhaps you like that sort of woman.*

*I watch the way your eyes take in the room, as if you're taking notes,
gathering names and faces, pairing them with fortunes perhaps. I pretend
not to care where you are as cocktails drag on, to not notice you chatting
with Teddy, but it's impossible. Your presence—the fact of you—sets my
nerves jangling. It isn't the way your eyes snag mine from time to time. Or
the tiny smile that lifts the corners of your mouth when they do. It's that I*

can't think why you've turned up again like the proverbial bad penny. What do you want with us? With me?

I'm relieved when we're finally called to dinner. The seating arrangements have been decided in advance, staked out with place cards of creamy ivory vellum, which will allow me to keep an eye on you from a safe distance.

Strange that the word safe should pop into my head at such a moment, as if your mere presence poses some kind of danger. It's ridiculous, really. How could I be unsafe in such a lovely room, surrounded by people with such impeccable pedigrees?

I smile serenely as I look about for Teddy, expecting him to join me. And then I see that your place card and not his rests beside mine. A fact that doesn't appear to surprise you at all.

My fiancé has been seated at the opposite end of the table—beside your date, conveniently enough. Her eyes lift to mine as I take my seat, as if she knows I'm watching. I expect to see jealousy, the petulant glare of a woman whose escort has been lured away by another. I've grown used to that kind of look from women. Especially those who had hopes of landing Teddy for themselves. But there's only a cool appraisal in the look she gives me. Watchful. Curious. As if she's trying to decide what to make of me.

I'm the first to look away, unsettled by her open regard, but I see your eyes snag hers for the merest instant. I don't know how you arranged it—you never did say—but something about the look leaves me certain that this second meeting is no accident. Out of politeness—or perhaps because I've already drunk too many cocktails—I allow you to draw me into conversation. We speak of horses, or at least we begin that way. My newfound interest in Thoroughbred racing, my recent trip to Saratoga for the Spinaway Stakes, my birthday present from my father.

Eventually, or perhaps inevitably, we land on the subject of breeding. Whether it was my mention or yours, I do not recall. You ask how I happened to become interested in such a subject. You're so condescending and snide, so sure of yourself and your smooth British charm, that I find myself *gritting my teeth. You're goading me with that bland smile of yours, writing me off as some rich little miss who asked for a pony for her birthday and got two, but I refuse to be underestimated. Suddenly, I want very badly to put you in your place.*

And just like that we're no longer talking about horses. You know it and I know it, but we both keep sparring, raising the stakes with each clever innuendo and double entendre, skating perilously close to the edge of indecency.

It's a place I've never been, this sensual war of words. And yet it feels startlingly familiar. A déjà vu of the body. A knowing—of where it might lead and how it might end. All at once, I understand the danger I sensed earlier. It's this. This moment of needing to prove something to you. And perhaps to myself. Something even I don't understand.

You're smirking, clearly pleased with yourself, and I'm furious for becoming tangled in my own web. I don't know how to get out of it without exposing myself as the novice I am, and I'd sooner bite off my own tongue than give you that satisfaction. And so I play on, brash, reckless, and completely out of my depth, as I suspect you well know. I mean to shock you, but you're not shocked at all. Far from it.

In the end, you call my bluff.

Your eyes hold fast to mine—a deeper blue than I had previously noted, with small gold flecks around the pupils—and suddenly I'm terribly warm, which I suppose is what usually happens when one plays with fire.

"I should like very much to see these fine animals of yours," you say with that lazy smile you've perfected to keep little fools like me off-balance.

"And I should very much like to show them to you," I answer, because what else can I say? You've laid your cards on the table, and I must do the same. "Perhaps we can manage it sometime."

"I'm free tomorrow afternoon," you suggest smoothly. "And I rather fancy a trip out to the Hamptons. I hear it's pretty country."

And just like that, I'm caught.

FIVE

ASHLYN

Restoration is a long and involved business, particularly when the damage is extensive. Progress will be slow. Expect setbacks. Exercise patience. Persist.

—*Ashlyn Greer,* The Care & Feeding of Old Books

September 28, 1984
Portsmouth, New Hampshire

Ashlyn reminded herself to focus on the job at hand as she worked to remove a strip of old linen tape from the second of Gertrude's Nancy Drew books, but it was difficult when all she could think about was the mystery surrounding her latest literary find.

After several chapters of *Regretting Belle* with its decidedly masculine slant, it had been fascinating to immerse herself in *Forever, and Other Lies* and see the lovers' first meeting through Belle's eyes. The details of that night in the ballroom of the St. Regis. The nearly identical lines of dialogue. The mutual, slow-smoldering attraction. It all synced up neatly.

Perhaps . . . too neatly?

She was convinced the books weren't actually works of fiction, that the characters were real, that the love story—if it could be called a love story—was real. But what if she had it wrong? What if they were something else entirely? What if they'd been conceived as a kind of *metafiction*, a literary gimmick designed to hook readers with the *illusion* of two distinctly different voices? A pair of lovers with old axes to grind. A kind of romantic whodunit.

It was an intriguing concept and might explain the lack of a publisher's imprint on both books. Experimental fiction of the quirky, rule-breaking variety was still a heated topic among the literati. Thirty years ago, such books would likely have been passed over in favor of safer projects. Perhaps the author had resorted to a print-on-demand publisher, as Ernest Vincent Wright had done in 1939 when he couldn't find a publisher for his novel *Gadsby*. (Not to be confused with Fitzgerald's *The Great Gatsby*.)

By design, Wright's book hadn't included a single word containing the letter *E*—the most common letter in the English language. Legend had it, the author had tied down the *E* key on his typewriter, assuring that no stray instances of the vowel would appear in the manuscript. The book had barely raised an eyebrow in its day but had eventually earned its own curious brand of notoriety. Today, a collector lucky enough to locate a copy would be looking at a $5,000 price tag.

Was it possible she'd stumbled onto something of that sort? Possibly. But it didn't explain the echoes. No amount of clever writing could account for what she felt when she touched them. The echoes weren't a gimmick. They were real, dark and visceral aftershocks from the past. But *whose* past?

Her hands went quiet as she imagined *Regretting Belle* and *Forever, and Other Lies* being pulled from their shelves and packed into boxes, bound for Kevin's store, with its lava lamps and Bakelite radios. And now they'd found their way to her. Was it possible there was a reason she'd been the one to rescue them from Kevin's back room? That she was *meant* to solve the mystery?

The thought continued to nag as she picked up a bookbinding knife and made her first cut, then carefully detached the front and back boards from the text block. It was an intriguing idea, but she had next to nothing to go on. None of the characters had proper names, and there wasn't much she could do with names like Belle and Cee-Cee. There was Goldie, of course, but that, too, appeared to be a nickname. But hadn't Belle mentioned that everyone in New York knew Goldie's name? Surely that was worth looking into. How many women had owned newspapers in 1941?

She felt a fizz of excitement as she made a beeline for the shop's journalism section. It was probably a long shot, but it was a place to start. Sadly, the journalism shelf contained exactly eight books, all of them to do with foreign correspondents during the first and second World Wars, including a tired copy of *A Moveable Feast*, a rather nice edition of *Hemingway on War*, and a copy of *The Face of War* by Martha Gellhorn, Hemingway's third wife. Not surprising. Frank had been fascinated by all things Hemingway.

She checked American history next, but most of the titles dealt with either war or politics. Moving on to commerce and industry, she found plenty of books on mining, railroads, and the auto industry, but nothing to do with the newspaper business.

This was clearly a job for Ruth Truman. In fact, Ruth should have been her first call. Though now part-time, she'd chalked up nearly thirty years as a librarian and was an absolute godsend when it came to research.

Ashlyn flipped through her Rolodex, located the number for the Portsmouth Public Library, and picked up the old black receiver.

"Good morning. Ms. Truman speaking. How may I help you?"

Ashlyn found herself smiling. Ruth Truman sounded exactly the way a librarian was supposed to sound: capable, courteous, and crisply efficient. "Hey, Ruth. It's Ashlyn from An Unlikely Story."

"Ashlyn. It's nice to hear from you, dear. It's been a while."

"Since I pestered you, you mean?"

"Don't be silly. I'm always happy to help if I can. What is it you need?"

"I've run across a book that I'm trying to trace. The title is *Regretting Belle*, but I don't know who wrote it. And I don't mean I'm trying to find the book. I actually *have* the book. But there's no author name anywhere. No copyright page. Nothing. It's completely anonymous."

"And you hope I can tell you who wrote it?"

"Actually, I'm hoping you can help me identify one of the characters. A woman who went by the nickname Goldie."

"Hmm. *Regretting Belle* and Goldie. That isn't much to go on. What else have you got?"

"She lived in New York and owned a string of newspapers in 1941. That's all I know, really. Oh, and she was kind of . . ." She paused, searching for an age-appropriate word. "Loose," she finally supplied. "She liked young men—a lot."

"Well, bully for her," Ruth shot back with a chuckle. "Nice to know someone was having fun back then."

"So what do you think? Is it possible to track down this mystery woman with so little to go on?"

"Well, I can't guarantee anything, but I'll do my damnedest. Just let me make sure I have it all: 1941. Goldie somebody or other from New York. Owned a string of papers and liked 'em young. Sound about right?"

"Sounds exactly right."

"Okay. Let me start digging. I'm by myself at the desk this week, so it might not be right away, but if her name's in print, I'll find it."

"You're a peach, Ruth. I owe you huge."

Ashlyn had no more than hung up when she heard the bells on the shop door jangle. She looked up, surprised to see Kevin. "What are you doing here in the middle of the day? Playing hooky?"

"I was out to grab lunch, so I thought I'd bring you this." He reached into his back pocket, extricating a bit of paper.

Ashlyn frowned at the folded envelope he handed her. "What is it?"

"Look at it. Not in it—*at* it."

She unfolded it, scanning the neatly typed address: *Richard Hillard. 58 Harbor Road. Rye, NH.* She looked up, perplexed. "What is it?"

"I ran across it at the bottom of one of the boxes the mystery guy brought in. Wasn't sure if you still needed to get a hold of him, but I thought I'd bring it by."

Ashlyn nearly threw her arms around him. "Thank you! And yes, I still want to get in touch with him. This is fabulous!"

"So what's the deal? Are they long-lost works of Fitzgerald or somebody? Please tell me I didn't let a fortune slip through my fingers."

Ashlyn shot him a grin. "I seriously doubt it. Finds like that are fairly rare, though the books *are* pretty unusual, so I suppose they might be of academic interest to someone. I'm just hoping to find out who wrote them. It's only a hunch at this point, but my gut tells me they're not fiction. I'm hoping Mr. Hillard will be able to at least verify that."

"Just leave my name out of it if you plan on getting all stalky, okay?"

"I'm not going to get stalky. I promise. I just want to ask a few questions." She held up the envelope, looking more closely, and felt her hopes fall. "This is postmarked April 4, 1976. Eight years ago. And it's from AARP. How old was the guy who brought the boxes in?"

"He looked to be about my age, but he said the books belonged to his dad. I'm guessing Richard Hillard was the dad. Worth checking out anyway. Dial 411 and ask for a number for a Richard Hillard in Rye. If you get a number, call it and see who answers. But don't get your hopes up. The son didn't seem like much of a talker. I got the impression he just wanted to be done with the whole clearing-out business."

Kevin's warning continued to echo as Ashlyn dialed Richard Hillard's number. As it turned out, getting the number had taken one phone call and exactly two minutes. The tricky part would be broaching the subject with a total stranger without sounding creepy or deranged—or as Kevin put it, all stalky. She was still pondering what to say when she began to dial. After four rings, there was an abrupt click.

"I'm not here. Leave a message."

No name. No greeting to speak of. And no indication that whatever message she left would ever reach anyone named Hillard. For a moment, she considered hanging up. She hated answering machines. She was never quite prepared, never sure she'd have enough time to say what she needed to. But at the moment, it was the only lead she had.

"Hi," she blurted too cheerfully, too breathlessly. "My name is Ashlyn Greer. I'm the owner of a rare bookstore in downtown Portsmouth. I'm trying to reach a Mr. Hillard regarding a book of his, which I recently acquired. Well, two books actually. I just have a few questions. I won't take up a lot of your time. If you could call me back, I'd appreciate it."

She was so flustered she nearly hung up without leaving her number, and ended up blurting it out clumsily, twice, then followed it up with another rather pitiful plea for a return call. So much for not sounding creepy.

Ashlyn had just flipped the OPEN sign to CLOSED when the shop phone began to jangle. She rushed back to the counter and made a grab for the receiver. "An Unlikely Story."

"Yes, I'm returning a call from a Ms. Greer."

Ashlyn's pulse ticked up a notch. "Who's calling?"

"Ethan Hillard. Someone left a message on my father's machine this afternoon."

"Yes!" she blurted. "This is Miss Greer. Thank you so much for returning my call. I wasn't sure I'd actually hear back."

"Your message said you're in Portsmouth."

"Yes. On Market Street. I hated to call out of the blue, but I had a few questions about some books I recently acquired. I was hoping you could answer them."

"Sure. I guess. What can I help you with?"

Ashlyn's mind raced. Why hadn't she made a list of questions? Now that she had him on the phone, she didn't know where to start. "I guess my first question is about how old they are. Do you know when they were published?"

"Do I know . . ." There was a lengthy pause. "Which books are we talking about?"

"Oh, sorry. Of course. You have no idea which books I mean. I was asking about *Regretting Belle* and *Forever, and Other Lies*."

"I'm afraid you've got the wrong guy. Come to think of it, how *did* you get my number?"

"The owner of Going Twice—the boutique where you left the books— found an envelope in one of the boxes with your father's address on it. I called directory assistance and got the number. Normally I wouldn't bother you, but under the circumstances . . . Well, these are very special books."

There was another long breath. Annoyance or impatience. "They may well be, Ms. Greer. But I'm afraid I didn't write either one of them."

"No, I didn't think you had. I was just hoping you might be able to tell me who did—or anything about them, really."

"I'm sorry. Did you say you own a bookstore?"

"Yes. In Portsmouth."

"I guess I'm confused. You're calling about a pair of books I've never heard of and you want me to tell you who wrote them?"

"I'm so sorry." She needed to slow down and start at the beginning. "I should have been more clear. I own a rare bookshop called An

Unlikely Story. A few weeks ago, you brought several boxes of books to a vintage boutique. The owner is a friend of mine. He calls me when he gets books in that he thinks might be of interest to my shop."

"Excuse me. I was under the impression that you were calling about *my* books. Books I'd written."

Books *he'd* written? Finally, Ashlyn understood. "Right. I can see now why you were confused. I didn't realize you were a writer. What kinds of books do you write?"

"Sleep aids, mostly. Nonfiction. Political history. Very . . . academic."

"That sounds interesting."

"I assure you, it's not. But I think I understand. You're talking about the boxes I donated a few weeks ago. Those books belonged to my father."

Finally, they were getting somewhere. "Yes. Your father's books. I'm sorry, by the way. About your father's passing, I mean."

"Thank you. He was a bit of a pack rat where books were concerned, where everything was concerned, actually. I needed to clear shelf space for my own books. A neighbor gave me the name of the shop in Portsmouth."

"Do you happen to remember a pair of books with blue marbled boards? Three-quarter bound in Moroccan leather? Gold embossing?"

"I can't say I recall any of them specifically. There were so many. I assume you think they might be worth something?"

"No," Ashlyn replied carefully. "Not *worth* something. Not exactly. But they're . . . intriguing."

"Intriguing how?"

"There's no author name on either one of them. No copyright pages either. But the stories are unusual too. Out of the mainstream, you might say."

"So we're talking about fiction?"

"I don't think so."

"Memoir, then? Or autobiography?"

"That's the thing. I can't tell. They may be both. Or neither. I've made a few calls, but so far I haven't found anyone who's heard of either title, though it's hard to research a book when you don't know the author's name. That's why I called you. I was hoping you might shed some light on the mystery."

"Sorry. As I said, the books belonged to my father. A few may have been my mother's. All I did was take them off the shelves and pack them into boxes. Beyond that, I really can't help you. You do seem awfully interested, though, for books that aren't worth anything."

Ashlyn hesitated. He suspected her of withholding something. And wasn't she? But how could she explain what she had experienced the first time she opened *Regretting Belle*, that her touch had unleashed someone else's emotional storm? Ethan Hillard was the only lead she had. She couldn't afford to scare him off with a lot of woo-woo talk. And she would if she opened that particular door.

"I am interested," she answered at last. "But not because they might be valuable. I've never run across anything like them. Their stories are sort of woven together, like an argument taking place across the pages. But they're so completely anonymous. Purposely anonymous, it seems. I can't imagine why anyone would go to the trouble of writing a book, then leave their name off it."

"Writers have been doing it for hundreds of years."

"Yes, but they generally use a pseudonym, like Ben Franklin and Silence Dogood. But these books have *no* author. Literally no name of any kind, anywhere. I get not wanting the details of your love life splashed all over the place, but then why write them down at all?"

"So you're saying the characters are real? That what's written in them actually happened?"

He hadn't bothered to hide his skepticism and it annoyed her. "I think they might be, yes. The books dovetail perfectly as far as narrative goes, but the voices are completely different. One is written by a man, the other by a woman, but they tell the same story. A love affair that clearly ended badly. The writing is so tortured and raw. Beautiful, actually, but ultimately sad. Both of them determined to acquit themselves of blame for whatever happened between them. They're quite extraordinary."

"A love that ended badly? Sounds anything *but* extraordinary, if you ask me. Interesting premise, though, telling it in two books. A clever way to double your sales."

"I thought that, too, at first, but my gut tells me that isn't what this is. I think it really happened. All of it, just like it's written. I just don't know who it happened *to*."

"And you thought I might?"

"It was worth a shot. I thought maybe you'd seen the books growing up or might even have read them."

"I don't read much fiction, actually. No, that's not true—I don't read *any* fiction."

"I understand. I just thought your father might have mentioned them at some point, or that you might have some idea how they'd found their way onto his shelves."

"I'm sorry. I can't help you there. I won't pretend to understand why you care about something that may or may not have happened between people who may or may not have existed, but I wish you luck with your sleuthing."

"Right, then," Ashlyn said, acknowledging his wish to end the conversation. "Thanks so much for returning my call. I'm sorry to have bothered you."

She hadn't actually expected Ethan to solve the mystery with a single phone call, but she couldn't help feeling deflated as she hung up. Unless Ruth came through with something on the illustrious Goldie, her chances of finding out what really happened between the lovers were practically nil.

Maybe Ethan was right. Maybe the whole thing was ridiculous and she should let it go before she became any more distracted. The books were already taking up hours that would be better spent in the bindery. But even as she acknowledged the wisdom of abandoning this strange new obsession, she felt the pull of it. Of *them*—whoever they were—and their unfinished story, beckoning her to read on.

Forever, and Other Lies

(pgs. 11–28)

September 5, 1941
Water Mill, New York

I arrive at the farm two hours early and pull up to the courtyard behind the stables. I'm early on purpose, to get myself planted and remind myself that today we'll be on my turf—and that I'll not let you have the upper hand. I was caught off guard last night, surprised to find you milling about the Whittiers' drawing room with your aging amour glued to your side. But I'm prepared now for whatever game you might be playing. Forewarned, as they say, is forearmed.

I check my watch for what must be the hundredth time, regretting last night's rashness with every fiber of my being and wishing I'd had the sense to make some excuse when you invited yourself. At least I summoned the wits to refuse your offer that we drive out together, opting instead to borrow one of my father's cars. No one asked where I was going when I left the house, and I didn't volunteer. I'm lucky in that way. When no one cares about you, they don't wonder where you are or when you'll be back.

Another look at my watch. I'm edgy after the long drive from the city, still questioning my decision to come at all. I could have phoned you this morning and begged off, blamed it on the weather or a forgotten appoint-ment. Goldie's number would have been easy enough to track down, and she would almost certainly know how to reach you. But it would have felt like surrendering, and I find I've surrendered quite enough of myself lately. To my father, my sister, Teddy. I refuse to add you to the list. And so I'm here, waiting under the eaves, watching the rain fall, and waiting for the crunch of tires on the gravel drive.

I've always loved Rose Hollow, even on rainy days. I love the wide-open feel of it and the clean blue sky, the sprawling house of weathered gray stone with its chimneys and dormers and climbing roses. And farther out, past the stable and the apple trees, the rolling green ground where it rises up and then falls away, creating the shallow bowl where my mother used to take me sledding when I was little.

She used to love it here, too, away from the noise and the grit of the city. I'm like her in that way. In many ways, really. More than I knew back then and more than makes my father and sister comfortable. But it does me good to come, especially now that no one else does. It belongs to me now, by default if not by deed, though being here sometimes makes me sad. Perhaps that's why my father stopped coming. Memories he can't bear to own—of the days before he sent my mother away. I remember, though. Even if he wishes I didn't.

I remember Helene—Maman, as I called her when we were alone. How she smelled of lilies and rainwater and spoke like a duchess with her soft French lilt. How her eyes—amber-brown like my own and always so sad—would close when she prayed. Strange prayers she taught me to say, too, with strange words that felt too big for my mouth. How she would thumb through the album of old photos she kept hidden under her mattress, the stories she would tell, stories meant only for us. And I remember how she was punished for all of it when my father found out—and how it eventually broke her.

Even now, my throat aches with her memory. She was too tender for a man like my father, too fragile for the kind of life he expected her to live. Shut off from her family in France and isolated from her friends in the States, she'd been left to flounder alone after the births of each of her children, mired in loneliness and depression. And the guilty abyss after the brother I never knew wandered away during luncheon at a friend's home and stumbled into a pond. Ernest, dead at age four.

All of it had left her brittle, prone to weepy, sometimes debilitating bouts of melancholia, a character flaw my father had been unable to forgive. Tears are a waste of time, *he used to say.* A sign of weakness, of failure. He *meant it, too, as I learned firsthand when I turned on the tears in response to his edict that I get myself engaged by year's end.*

He's happy enough now, I suppose. Now that I've finally agreed to marry Teddy. I fought it as long as I could, but my father eventually won the day, as he always knew he would. I, however, am not happy—as you have somehow guessed.

I have no wish to become a shadow, which is what women in families like mine become: obedient, hollowed-out things who fade into the background the moment their usefulness as a bargaining chip is at an end. We see to the menus, raise the children, keep up with the latest fashions, grace our husband's table when he entertains, and look the other way when a pretty young face turns his head. But I've always wanted more for myself. I imagined a life that actually counted for something, left something worthy in its wake. I have no idea what form that life might have taken. Something to do with the arts, perhaps, or maybe a teacher, but now, as Teddy's wife, I'll never know.

For an instant, I'm astonished to find my thoughts wandering almost wistfully to your Goldie with her newspaper empire and her unapologetic life. What might that be like? To captain your own ship and command your own fortune, to live unfettered by the opinions of others.

I'll never know that either.

The realization lands me back to earth with a bump as I stare at the diamond on my left hand—an uncomfortable reminder. I'll be married soon, which is all I'm expected to want. I'll have a grand New York estate, a respected last name, and bear a brace of sons to carry it all on. My daughters will marry well, dutifully, as Cee-Cee did several years ago. As I will as well, as soon as I can bring myself to set an actual date.

Fin, as Maman *used to say—the end.*

But there's no time to dwell on the finality of such thoughts. I've just caught the sound of your tires and my stomach does a little somersault. I look out over the lawn to see a car coming up the drive, and I realize that while part of me was hoping you wouldn't show, another part hoped very much that you would.

I watch as you climb out of the car, a sleek and splashy silver thing with lots of chrome, and I know without asking that you've borrowed it from her. *It isn't your style, which feels like an odd thing to know about you, since I don't know you at all.*

You look relaxed in your Harris tweed jacket and loose wool slacks, a worn pair of brogues on your feet, and a hat perched at a jaunty angle on your head. These are your real clothes, I say to myself as you approach. This is who you really are. Not a member of the smart cocktail set but a country type, unfazed by the rain, at home in both your clothes and your skin.

I'm in traditional riding clothes, a jacket of gray flannel, bone-colored jodhpurs, and chestnut riding boots whose fresh-from-the-box sheen marks me out as a newcomer to the equestrian life. A gift from Teddy, who is very particular about things like riding attire. I don't know why I bothered, really. The weather made it clear that there would be no riding today, but I felt obliged to put on a proper show. Members of our circle have a uniform for every occasion, preferably with the right label sewn in. We wear them not because they're comfortable or even appropriate for the activity of the moment but because it's what's expected, and we must never veer from what's expected.

You pull off your hat as you duck under the eaves, giving it a shake to dislodge the raindrops clinging to the brim. "Filthy day for a ride," you say, grinning. "What shall we do instead?"

You look younger out of doors, more rugged shed of your expensive evening clothes, though I can't deny that you manage to pull it off rather well. You're something of a chameleon, I suspect, the kind of man capable of melting into his surroundings when he needs to. I find myself wondering why someone might need such a skill, then recall your eyes last night, moving methodically about the room, as if snapping photographs without a camera. Of what or whom?

It occurs to me suddenly that this is the first time we've been alone. The boys who look after the stables have gone to lunch and the trainer called out due to the weather. There are no eyes on us now, no niceties to observe. Why that should rattle me, I don't know, but it does. It's not that I'm afraid of you. I'm not. Mostly. But I don't feel quite myself when you're near.

You're staring at me, I realize, waiting for a response. "I suppose I could give you a tour of the stables," I say. "And introduce you to the horses."

"Your birthday presents, you mean?"

You're mocking me again, with that upturned mouth and those cool blue eyes, but instead of being annoyed, I find myself smiling. "Yes. My birthday presents."

Your jacket and tie are flecked with rain, your shirt dappled with translucent spots. You smell of starch and warm, wet wool, with a hint of shaving soap underneath. I step back from the assault of it, masculine and vaguely unnerving. "I'll see if I can scare you up a towel so you can dry yourself off."

"I'm fine. But I'd love the tour." Your eyes slide down my body, lingering briefly on my boots before sliding back up again. "Nice togs, by the way. Very . . . horsey. Shame to waste them. But perhaps we'll ride another day and you can get some proper use out of them."

I turn away, less charmed now by your teasing. You follow me down the breezeway to the double sliding doors that lead into the stable. The patter of rain recedes as we enter, replaced by a thick, insular quiet.

It's cool and dim inside, drowsy feeling with the mingled smells of damp hay and horse dung hanging in the air, and I'm reminded of the day I was caught napping in the horse bedding, back when my parents kept a pony for my sister and me. It was raining that day, too, and I hated that Mr. Oliver wasn't allowed to come into the house where it was warm, so I curled up in his stall to keep him company. My parents turned the house inside out looking for me, my mother frantic that, like poor Ernest, I'd met some terrible fate. When the stable boy finally found me and brought me up to the house, my father shook me so hard I chipped one of my baby teeth.

A soft whistle pulls me back to the present. You're standing beside me with your neck craned, taking it all in. The high-timbered ceiling and newly added windows, the freshly bricked center aisle, the gleaming doors and ornate stall partitions.

"This is some place," you say finally. "Quite posh for a barn. Not new, though, I'm guessing from the look of the stone."

"No. The house was built in 1807. The stable came a little later, though back then, I suspect it housed pigs or sheep. It was fine for a pony when I was little, but we had to raise the roof before we could bring the new horses."

"I'll wager that set old Pater back a few quid."

I shrug, realizing I have no idea what any of it cost. "He considered it a business expense."

You look surprised. "He thinks you've got a shot at making money with this new hobby of yours?"

"Not that kind of business."

"Dare I ask?"

I nearly laugh. I hardly know you—don't know you at all, really—but my early impression is that you're a man who would dare almost anything. "It was to do with Teddy," I say quietly. "With me agreeing to marry him."

"I see. Your father thought if he gave in about the horses, you'd see the merits of the life you'd have as Teddy's wife and be more likely to accept his proposal."

"Something like that."

"So . . . a bribe."

"It's the way he works. He buys what he wants." And crushes what he doesn't, *I think but don't say. I've already said more than I should.* "Let's meet the horses."

I'm grateful when you fall in beside me, leaving whatever it is you're thinking unsaid. With any luck, you'll be too distracted by the horses to return to the subject. Talking about my father to you feels wrong. Not because anything I might say would be untrue but because I've been raised to keep family matters within the family. It's a code my father has drilled into all of us, to my mother and my sister and me. Loyalty to the family and obedience to its head—to him. I've seen what happens when someone betrays the code.

"How many horses do you keep here?" you ask, forcing me back to the moment.

"There are six stalls but only four horses at the moment." I point to the *first two stalls on the left.* "These two are companion horses. Strictly for riding."

Two sets of curious eyes peer back at us, the first belonging to a smooth-riding roan named Bonnie Girl, the second to a stout black gelding my sister named Nipper because of his tendency to bite when he was young. He never bit me. But then, Cee-Cee has never been an animal person—or a people person, for that matter.

Bonnie Girl whickers as we approach, nostrils flared, ears flicked to attention. She smells freedom, can taste it, and I'm sad that I can't oblige her. She whickers again and nuzzles my palm. I turn my face to hers, dropping a kiss on the velvety red muzzle, wishing I'd thought to at least bring them a treat.

"Sorry, girl." She nudges my cheek as if to absolve me of my neglect. I pat her affectionately and bestow another kiss.

"She's fond of you."

"We've been together a long time. My parents bought them when I outgrew my pony. One for me and one for my sister."

"Which was which?"

I open my mouth to say something I shouldn't, then catch myself and shrug instead. "Cee-Cee wasn't really a horse person, so I ended up with them both. They're getting up in age now, but they still ride well."

"Are these the horses we were supposed to ride today?"

I nod, reaching over to stroke Nipper's forelock. "I hate that we can't take them out. I don't come as much as I used to. I think they would have enjoyed a day out."

You smile and give Nipper's neck a pat. "I think I would have enjoyed it too."

Nipper whinnies and shakes off the touch but immediately leans in for another. Wary but hungry for connection, needing to be touched, to be seen. I look at him in his box, obedient, expectant, hoping I'll reach for the stall latch and lead him out, and I suddenly feel a wave of sadness.

"Poor thing," I say softly. "It's no fun being penned in all the time, is it? Waiting for someone to turn you loose?"

You drop your hand and turn, saying nothing for a moment. I pretend not to notice you studying me, but the weight of your gaze makes the back of my neck tingle. What? I long to shout. What is it you see? But part of me is afraid to know. Most of me, really. I've always been so careful about how much I let the world see. But it doesn't seem to matter. You see it all, especially the parts I don't like. And you want me to know that you see them.

"Are we still talking about the horses?" you say when the silence grows awkward. "Waiting to be turned loose, I mean."

Your voice is thick in the quiet and vaguely unsettling. I feign amusement, knowing full well I haven't pulled it off. Still, I must keep up the pretense. "Of course I'm talking about the horses. What else would I be talking about?" I step away then, a little too abruptly, and wander toward the stalls on the opposite side of the aisle. "Come see my presents."

You move to my side, your eyes still on my face. You want to press me for more, but you don't, as if you're afraid I might startle and skitter away. You're right about that. I might.

"This is Cracker Jack Prize," I say, pointing to a sleek, dark bay with bright eyes and a thin white blaze streaking his muzzle. "He was foaled in '39, which means he's still a baby in horse years."

"Quite a looker."

"Isn't he? The trainers say he's going to be a champ. A good brain and a brilliant pedigree. His sire was Dark Upstart out of Lexington, a high earner until he had to be retired because of a slab fracture."

You look surprised and a little impressed. "And here I was thinking you're a novice. You sound like a pro with all that horse jargon."

I smile and relax a little, pleased by your praise. "I told you. Lots of reading."

"He seems a bit standoffish compared to the others."

"Horses aren't like people. It's not love at first sight. It takes time to develop a bond. I practically grew up with Nipper and Bonnie Girl. They were like pets. But it's different with racing horses. They're athletes rather than companions. And neither will be here long. This is just a 'getting to know you' visit until they're green broke."

"Which means?"

"Responsive to cues. Comfortable with a saddle. But that's just the start. When they're old enough to course train, they'll be moved to Saratoga."

"With Teddy's horses?"

I stiffen, perturbed that his name has come up again. "Yes, I suppose. Cracker Jack will be prepped over the winter and spring and hopefully start racing as a two-year-old next summer."

You step past me to peer into the last stall. "And who is this beauty?"

I eye the chestnut filly with her strongly chiseled face and perfectly matched half socks, a beauty despite her less-than-glamorous pedigree, and I feel a fresh pang of guilt. "I don't know, actually. I haven't named her yet. The trainers aren't quite as keen on her, but I think she has a lot of promise. At least I hope she does. For now, I've been calling her Little Girl. Not *terribly original, but it'll do until she gets her official name. I need to hurry up and decide, though, before I run out of time."*

"Out of time?"

"Naming a Thoroughbred is a big deal. There are all kinds of rules you have to follow, like names not being more than eighteen characters. And there's a whole process. You submit six names in order of preference to the Jockey Club, and they have the final say."

"How is that fair?"

I shrug. "Those are the rules. I'm leaning toward Sweet Runaway as my top choice. No guarantee they'll let us have it, but at the moment, it's my top pick."

You have the strangest look on your face as you listen to me speak, an intensity that makes me want to look away. "Name her Belle's Promise," you say abruptly.

"Belle's Promise?"

"You said you think she has promise."

"I did, but who's Belle?"

"You are." You look away briefly, almost boyish. "It's the name I gave you the night we met. You were the belle of the ball that night. As I suspect you are on any night, in whatever room you happen to find yourself. At any rate, it's how I've been thinking of you ever since."

Your words make my cheeks go hot. "You've been thinking about me?"

"Don't be coy. It doesn't suit you."

"We're strangers," I remind you, my voice alarmingly breathless. "You have no idea what suits me."

"I'd like to fix that."

I toss my head with a nervous laugh. "Well then, if I'm to be Belle, what shall I call you? Hemingway, perhaps? Or Hemi?"

"I don't care. As long as you call me."

I look away. You're flirting with me and I don't like it. Or perhaps I like it too much. I try to step away but your hand grazes my arm, the barest of touches.

"Don't go. Please."

"Why are you here?" I ask bluntly. "What is it you want?"

"I told you—to talk. Presumably, we would have talked while riding. We'll just do it without the horses."

You wander back toward the open stable doors and locate a pair of battered stools, then drag them to the doorway. I watch, exasperated, as you hang your hat on a nearby nail, plant yourself on one of the stools, and wait—another man used to getting his way. Against my better judgment, I join you.

The rain is falling harder now, and it's as if a thick gray curtain has been drawn around us. It's just us and the thrum of rain on the roof. My senses are suddenly heightened, every nerve at attention.

You smile, attempting to disarm me. "What should we talk about?"

I pluck an imaginary bit of lint from my sleeve and flick it away. "You called the meeting. You get the first question."

"Very well. Tell me about growing up."

I blink at you, puzzled. "Growing up?"

"I want to know it all. Did you wear your hair in braids? Who was your first boyfriend? Did you like school?"

"No to the braids," I reply, though I have no idea why you'd care about such a thing. "I don't remember my first boyfriend's name. And I hated school. No, that's not true. I didn't hate all of it. I hated the girls I went to school with. And the headmistress, Mrs. Cavanaugh, who didn't like me because I asked too many questions and doodled during class."

"Doodled?"

"In my composition book."

"Your boyfriend's name?"

"Poems," I say simply.

"You write poetry?"

I see I've surprised you. I've surprised myself too. I haven't thought of those silly poems in years, and I wonder why they've suddenly sprung to mind. "I was a girl. It's what girls do. Write silly poems about our angst."

"Love poems?"

I toss my head with a little laugh, dimly aware that the gesture might be mistaken for a flirtation. "What did I know about love? I was a child. No. I wrote nonsense. Rubbish about a caged bird who dreamed of leaving her bars behind, of soaring high above the city and flying far, far away. And there was one about being lost in one of those hedge mazes. The hedges kept growing taller and taller and I couldn't find my way out."

"Sounds deep."

"It was tosh, as they say on your side of the pond. But I was a fanatic about poetry back then. I read everything I could get my hands on, some of it unacceptable for a girl my age. I was convinced I was going to be Elizabeth Barrett Browning when I grew up."

You study me strangely, as if searching for something. "When were you going to tell me this?"

The question feels odd, the kind of thing you ask someone you've known for years. "Tell you how? When? We've only just met."

Your mouth curls in a way that's vaguely sensual. "I keep forgetting."

I don't know how you've managed it, but you seem to be sitting closer now, as if the world has suddenly shrunk to just this doorway, to just you and me and our words, mingling with the falling rain. And yet, when I blink, I see that your stool is exactly where you first placed it. I drop my eyes, stare at my boots.

"The night we met," you say, then add, "at the St. Regis"—as if I need reminding—"we talked about books, about Hemingway and Dickens and the Brontës, and you never once let on that you wrote."

"Because I don't." My tone is too emphatic, too defensive. I soften it. "It was just one of those childish fantasies you grow out of. You know how it is. You're suddenly passionate about something, so passionate that for a while it consumes you; then something happens and it's over."

"What happened?"

I squirm a little, uncomfortable with the memory. But you're watching me so carefully, so completely. "Mrs. Cavanaugh," *I answer finally.* "She confiscated one of my notebooks and showed it to my father. It was . . . I was in my Sappho phase at the time. The* blushing apple, ungotten, ungathered. *I had no idea what any of it meant, and I didn't care. It was about the words, the rhythm of them, the ache they conveyed. I longed to re-create them somehow, in my own words, so I began experimenting, trying to emulate that beautiful lyricism. My father was appalled by what I'd* written. Smut, he called it. *He made me hand over all my notebooks, then made me watch as he ripped out the pages and tore them to shreds. I was forbidden to even read poetry. For a while, I kept a journal under my bed and continued to scribble, but my sister found it and squealed. That was the end of my poetry career."*

"How old were you?"

"Fourteen. Fifteen, maybe."

"And you haven't written since?"

"No."

"But you could. Now, I mean."

I shrug, shift my eyes from yours. "There's no point."

"Beyond having something to say, you mean?"

"But I don't."

"I don't believe that."

"I'm not like you," *I say flatly, because you might as well know it now, before this strange unraveling of my inner self goes too far.* "I have no depth. No . . . substance, I guess you'd call it. Unless you count a trust fund as substance. I'm not the sort to sail around the world and chase dreams or thumb my nose at convention like your friend Goldie. I thought I was once, but I was quickly disabused of the notion. I'm exactly what you thought me when you asked me about the horses—the spoiled daughter of a very rich man who's used to getting everything she wants."

"And the price of everything *is obedience?"*

I hold your gaze, braving those eyes that seem to see through me. "Don't feel sorry for me."

"I don't. We all make our choices. Business. Politics. Marriage to someone we'll never be happy with. It's called compromise."

"Is that what you're doing with Goldie?" I say, wanting desperately to turn the tables. "Compromising?"

You sigh. "Goldie again. All right. What do you want to know?"

"Are the two of you . . ."

"Lovers?" you supply. "No need to be shy. I'm happy to share all the juicy details, only brace yourself. It's rather lurid."

I sit very still, determined not to let you shock me.

"The truth is, my relationship with Goldie is . . ." You pause, scrubbing a hand across your chin. "How do I put this delicately? Financial in nature."

My eyes widen despite myself. "You're taking money from her? For . . . No." I hold up a hand. "Never mind. I don't want to know."

"My, my, my. You do have a naughty mind, don't you?"

"Me? You're the one—"

You grin, as if I've said something terribly funny. "She's adding a magazine to her list of publications and she's offered me a spot as a writer. Slice-of-life stuff. The odd social piece. Not exactly Hemingway but it'll pay the bills until something better comes along. And I'll get to rub elbows with American toffs like you. Who knows, I might even get a paid trip or two out of it."

"And what about the novel you talked about publishing one day? When does that happen?"

It's your turn to look away. "That dream's a ways off, I'm afraid."

"No time?"

"No pulse."

I frown. "What does that mean?"

"It means there's no blood going to it. So until I figure out how to resuscitate it . . ."

"*You'll write slice-of-life pieces and escort your boss to social functions?*"

"*In the interest of full disclosure, I'm staying at Goldie's until I find my own flat. Separate rooms.*"

I eye you skeptically.

"*I haven't slept with her,*" *you say firmly.* "*Nor do I plan to sleep with her.*"

I roll my eyes. "*I'm not sure anyone ever plans to sleep with her. She's like a big blonde spider.*"

"*Do I detect a note of jealousy?*"

"*Jealousy?*" *I hurl you a chilly look.* "*I'm engaged to one of the most eligible men in New York.*"

You slide off your stool and wander toward the open doors with your hands in your pockets, looking out over the rain-soaked stable yard. "*Before, when I talked about marrying someone you'd never be happy with, I was talking about Teddy. Shall I tell you why?*"

"*I'm not interested in what you think of my fiancé.*"

"*Are you afraid of what I'll say? Afraid I might be right?*"

"*I'm not afraid of anything you could say to me.*"

"*Aren't you?*"

Before I know it, you're standing in front of me again. I stiffen, unnerved by your sudden closeness. I need to put space between us, but short of ducking under your arm and out into the rain, there's nowhere to go. Instead, I tip back my head and meet those cool, clear eyes. "*No.*"

"*Not even if I said I want to kiss you?*"

You don't wait for permission, but I give it as your lips close over mine, and it strikes me, as my body sways against yours, that this has always been where you and I were going. That the quiet fire that reared its head the first time I saw you would rush up one day and catch me unaware. That given the chance, it would consume me. And that I would let it.

This is what it's supposed to be like, *I think as our breaths mingle and my bones begin to melt.*

This. This. This.

Regretting Belle

(pgs. 30–39)

5 September 1941
Water Mill, New York

There are a hundred reasons not to kiss you, a thousand, a million, but I can't think of any of them as your eyes touch mine. Your mouth is there for the taking, your breath coming shallow, a tiny pulse ticking at the base of your throat, frenetic, like a bird's.

I expect you to pull away and half hope that you will, to spare us both the mess we're about to make. Instead, you yield with a completeness so breathtaking, I'm not sure which of us is the giver and which the taker. I'm lost in the feel and taste of you, the need for you that I've been trying to talk myself out of from the first moment I saw you. The fact of it—of this thing that's been done and can now never be undone—guts me as our mouths continue to explore. Finding. Taking. Yielding.

Still, it was never part of the plan, and I can't quite believe I'm allowing myself to be so reckless. Part of me—the part still capable of rational thought—is somehow certain that this is new for you, that you've never yielded to anyone in this way. The thought is a heady one, the way I suspect morphine injected into a vein might feel. A euphoric kind of unspooling you never want to end. But it must end—and does.

Even now, so many years later, I can't say which one of us finally came to our senses and pulled away. I'd like to think it was me, but it's hard to imagine.

That kiss was the start of so much. More than I ever knew I wanted. More than I ever thought I could bear to lose. But it wasn't only the kiss. From the first moment, the first words you spoke, I was caught in your undertow, drawn so far out to sea that the water was over my head almost before I knew it. And you let me believe you felt it too.

To this day, I don't understand how you could have kissed me like that—as if there were nothing you wouldn't give me—and not have meant it. Or perhaps you did mean it in that first breathless moment of weakness and all the breathless moments that came after. Perhaps it was only later, when the newness began to wear off and the reality of what you would have with me—and what you wouldn't—became clear, that you changed your mind.

We saw each other the next day and the day after that. Do you remember? We'd meet at the stables in the afternoons and ride together or walk in the woods where we knew we wouldn't be seen, holding hands, stopping now and then for long, slow kisses. I was ridiculously happy, content to simply be with you, pretending it wasn't odd that we never spoke of your engagement.

Like a land mine carefully stepped around, we pretended Teddy didn't exist. Because saying his name, acknowledging the reality of him, might break the spell that had wound itself around us.

We seemed to exist out of time in those stolen moments at Rose Hollow, in a world of our own making, a world of only us. And in those early days of . . . what should I call it? Madness? Yes, that's what it was. In those early days of madness, I nearly forgot what I'd come to the States to do. I was bewitched, gullibly, hopelessly mad for you. And I let myself believe you were mad for me too. The memories are still raw. Like breathing things, they wait for me when the lights go out, and suddenly, against my will—or perhaps not—it's yesterday.

~

It's the first day of autumn and you've packed a basket. We drive out to the lake and spread a blanket on the grass. We eat cucumber salad and cold roast chicken, sitting cross-legged on a blanket found in the trunk of Goldie's borrowed Zephyr.

It's your turn to ask about my childhood. I tell you about my parents and the kind of marriage they had, that my father was my hero. There are stories about shoestring holidays at the shore in Bournemouth, my brief stint with the cricket team, my misspent days at university. Finally, I tell you about my father dying a few years ago—a blood clot no one saw coming—and how his old boss at the London Observer *hired me out of loyalty, even though I'll never be the writer my father was.*

You listen to it all with your eyes closed and your face tipped to the sun, a hint of a smile playing at the corners of your mouth, as if you're seeing and smelling and tasting every word. But your eyes open when I say that last part, and search my face.

"Do you believe that? That you'll never be as good as your father?"

"Everyone believes it. Except my mum, of course." I manage a half-hearted grin. "She thinks I hung the moon. But it's her job to believe in me."

"I believe in you," you say softly.

I look away, swallowing the words that are on the tip of my tongue. That you shouldn't—and won't when you know what I'm really after. "How is that possible?" I say instead. "When you've never read a word I've written."

"That's not true. I've read all your stories. For weeks now."

I wave the words away. "Those aren't me. That's just the stuff I write to get paid."

"So let me read the novel."

"No."

"Because it has no pulse?"

"Yes."

"I still don't understand what that means."

"It was something my father said to me once after he read a piece I'd written. I've never forgotten it. He said all truly good writing—fiction or nonfiction—has a heartbeat, a life force that comes from the writer, like an invisible cord connecting them to the reader. Without it, the work is dead on arrival."

"Did your father's writing have a heartbeat?"

I smile. I can't help myself. "Like thunder. Unfortunately, it isn't genetic. You don't inherit it, and you can't imitate it. It's something that's unique to every writer. But you have to find it."

"And how does one find the heartbeat?"

"I asked my father the same thing."

"And his answer was?"

"By writing. And then writing some more. He rode me hard."

"Because he believed in you," you say quietly. "You were lucky to have someone like that in your life, someone who wanted you to be and have what you wanted."

I study your face as I sink my teeth into one of the apples from the basket, wondering about the sadness that's suddenly crept into your tone. I want to know who put it there and why, and how I can make it go away. It's not the first time I've sensed it, the melancholy air that settles around you when you think no one's looking. The way your gaze drifts from mine when I ask certain questions.

"I can't imagine you ever went without much as a tyke," I say between bites, aware that I'm risking that frosty veneer you often don when I probe too deeply.

You pluck several blades of grass and begin braiding them in your lap. You're silent for a time, your eyes carefully averted, and I assume you've decided to let the remark pass. Finally, you look up. "I would have liked a family vacation at the beach," you say quietly. "I would have given anything for a summer like that."

I crane my neck, taking in the bucolic setting, the soft roll of deep-green hills, the shimmery surface of the lake beyond the brightly leafed trees, and I can't quite find it in me to feel sorry for you. "How tragic," I reply drolly. "Having to suffer all those summers in a place like this. And then having to wait so long to get your birthday ponies. However did you survive it?"

"Yes, that's me," you fire back, flicking the braided blades of grass away. "A spoiled brat who's never known a day's disappointment."

You've gone sulky now, hoping to mask the fragility you're always trying so valiantly to hide, but I see it. I've always seen it. Your inexplicable and incandescent sadness.

No, I realize suddenly, startlingly. Not sadness. Resignation. For things left unfinished, unattempted, unrequited. For what could have been but won't ever be, because you've chosen something else. Something less. Something safe.

"Go on," you say peevishly. "Tell me what else you think of me."

I hurl my half-eaten apple into the trees and wipe my hands on my trousers. I want to reach for your hand, to wind my fingers through yours and never let go, but it isn't a good idea. Not when you're looking at me with daggers in your eyes.

"I think," I say gently, "that when one grows up with the kinds of privileges you have, it's easy to forget that not everyone had such a cushy childhood. It doesn't make you a brat—necessarily—but it does mean you're less likely to understand how the real world works. Money has a way of sparing the haves the kinds of trials the have-nots grapple with on a daily basis. There's nothing you can't buy or arrange. Nothing out of reach."

"So after a handful of afternoons together, you know all about my dreams and disappointments, do you?" Your chin lifts a notch. "It might interest you to know that I'd trade every one of my Hampton summers for one shoestring vacation in Bournemouth."

The heat in your voice, such a departure from the chill you normally exude when piqued, surprises me. I've touched a nerve. Not pride. Something else. "I didn't mean to presume—"

"Never mind. I don't want to talk about summers anymore."

"Tell me about your mother, then."

You go strangely still. "Why?"

My conscience prickles. I'm aware that I've wandered into uncomfortable territory. Still, I press on, determined to draw you out. "Because no one ever mentions her. Your father comes up over and over, but you never talk about your mother. What was she like?"

Your eyes cloud and drift from mine. You're silent for a long time. So long, I think you've decided not to respond. Finally, you answer without looking at me. "She was French."

"Surely there was more to her than that."

I watch as you deliberate. Am I worthy of your memories, of exposing your vulnerable places? Finally, your face softens, and I see just how badly you want to talk about her——as if you've been waiting for the chance to share her with someone. "There was. So much more. She was wonderful and so lovely. Always the most stunning woman in the room."

"The belle of the ball," I say softly. "Like her daughter."

"No. Not like me. Not like anyone I've ever known." Your eyes cloud again, and your expression grows wistful. "She was . . . exceptional. She had this dreamy, faraway quality about her. As if she came from an entirely different world than the rest of us. It's what I loved most about her. But my father never quite forgave her for it."

"Because she was French?"

"No. It wasn't that. Or it wasn't only that." You smile then, and for a moment, your eyes kindle with girlish memories. "We had secrets, she and I, from my father and my sister. Stories she only told me and then made me swear not to tell. She used to call me ma toute-petite—my little one."

"She sounds wonderful."

"Her name was Helene." Your face softens when you say the name so that it comes out like a sigh. *"It fit her perfectly. She was like a fine piece of porcelain—beautiful but not meant to be handled every day."* The light in your eyes fades and your voice goes flat. *"She got sick when I was little."*

"I'm sorry," I say. And I am. Because I already know what's coming. I've heard things. And not only from Goldie. Still, I have to ask, because you can't know I know. *"What happened?"*

"She had a sort of episode one night at a dinner party my father was giving for some important investors. There was an awful scene. The doctor came and gave her something to calm her, but the next day she went away . . . to a hospital. A sanitarium. She never came home. A year later, we got a call that she died."

Your voice falters and you stop talking. I know there's more, but I don't push. Instead, I wait. When you continue, your eyes are bright with unshed tears. *"I never got to say goodbye."*

I reach for your hand, watching you closely as I fold your fingers into mine. *"It must have been terrible for you to lose your mother so young. And your father—he must have been shattered when the call came."*

"Shattered," you repeat woodenly, staring at our joined hands. *"Yes, I'm sure he was. The talk after she went away was bad enough. A wife losing her oars in the middle of a dinner party is appalling, but dying in a madhouse and having it printed in all the papers was nothing short of a disaster for a man who'd spent most of his life managing appearances. Still, he knew how to play it. Long-suffering husband turned tragic widower. The tabloids ate it up. Most of them, at any rate."*

It's the first time I've heard you utter a word against your father, and the harshness of your tone makes it doubly surprising. *"You don't like him very much, do you?"*

You flinch at the question, as if realizing you've said too much. *"Please forget I said any of that. I was a child and I was hurting. I needed someone to blame."*

"And your sister?"

"What about her?"

"How did she take the news?"

You offer another of your evasive shrugs. "People deal with loss in different ways."

"Were the two of you close?"

"She raised me," you say, not quite an answer. "After my mother went away. She had just turned seventeen, but she stepped into my mother's shoes as if she'd been training for it all her life. She dedicated every waking moment to taking care of my father, running his house, writing his letters, hosting his dinner parties. She became indispensable to him."

There was something vaguely discomfiting about the description, not blatantly unsavory but not quite natural either. "A little odd, isn't it? A seventeen-year-old playing lady of the manor? At that age, most girls are worried about clothes and boys, not approving the weekly menu and playing hostess."

You smile, a brittle smile that leaches the warmth from your eyes. "Cee-Cee was never most girls. She was so driven, even then, willing to throw herself on a live grenade if my father required it of her—which he did from time to time. We were never close—not before my mother died or after—but she took care of me. She took care of everything. It's hard to fault that kind of loyalty."

"And yet, something tells me you do."

"Of course I don't."

"It's just us," I say gently. "You don't have to defend her. Or your father. Not to me."

"I don't know what you mean."

"I just mean you seem a little protective. You button up the minute I ask about either one of them. And if you do happen to slip and say what you think, you immediately backpedal."

"Privacy means a great deal to my father. And loyalty. In fact, they're everything. Family first. Family last. But he has good reason."

"Does he?"

"My father's a very wealthy man, and there are people who don't think that's okay. They'd love nothing more than to see him taken down a few pegs."

"Who are . . . they?"

"Business rivals, mostly. And the papers."

"Like the one I work for," I remind you. We're getting into tricky territory now. "Why should the newspapers want to take down a private citizen? Has your father done something to warrant being taken down?"

"Over the years, there have been . . . stories. Rumors." You drop your eyes then and look away. "Not nice ones."

"What kinds of rumors?"

You pull your hand free and look at me with your mouth clamped tight. "You sound like a newspaperman."

"Or a man who wants to know all about you."

"And which are you?"

Your frosty mantle is back in place as you study me. Still, I'm dazzled as I look at you, the way the sun creates shadows beneath your cheekbones, the play of the breeze as it lifts your hair off your face. "The latter," I say quietly. "Very much the latter."

I reclaim your hand, winding my fingers through yours, then lean in to kiss you. I feel your distrust as our lips touch, your rekindled wariness, then feel it melt away as your mouth gradually opens to mine. I lay you back on the scratchy blanket and kiss you until I'm dizzy, and some part of me realizes we're careening toward a point from which there will be no going back. It's all I can do to pull away, to remember that you're not mine, that you belong to another world—and another man.

∾

How I wish I could say that's what stopped me that day, that my restraint had to do with some noble twinge of conscience, but it was nothing of the sort. I stopped because I knew you would regret it—regret me—and the thought of being a regret, a reckless lapse in judgment for which you would one day feel remorse, was enough to bring me to my senses. That and the absolute certainty that I wouldn't survive it when you did. Would that I had remembered it later on. Because you did come to regret me, didn't you? Though not nearly as much as I came to regret you, dear Belle. Not nearly as much.

Forever, and Other Lies

(pgs. 29–36)

September 22, 1941
Water Mill, New York

You speak of regret. You of all people. As if you're the only one with cause for such a thing. I assure you, I have causes enough of my own, all of them beginning and ending with you. That you could bring up that day—of all days—astonishes me.

When I think of how you wheedled things out of me. Coaxing me with that smile you have—that very practiced smile—that says you want to know, need to know, all about me, and in every tiny detail. The way you pretended to care. The way you lied. That mouth, so skilled. Words. Kisses. All false. You ask if I remember. Of course I remember. How could I not?

It's just us. That's what you said.

But it wasn't true, was it? She was there with us. Your lady bountiful with her string of newspapers. That day and from the very beginning. Whispering in your ear. Pulling your strings.

Did she teach you, I wonder? How to soften the ground with your charm and your family stories? Or did the lies come naturally? Perhaps you should have gone on the stage. You certainly had me convinced. Why else would I have poured out my heart to you? Given you the ammunition to wound me? To wound us all?

It was only the beginning, that day on the blanket, but yes, I remember. And wonder, even as I write this, how it was possible to not see where it was all headed—where you were headed.

You asked about my mother and I told you some of her story. All my life, she's been a kind of shadow figure, a flicker of softly shifting images, there, then gone, then back again, so that it feels at times as if I've invented her. I haven't, though, however much my father may have wished it were true. She was quite real. And for a time, she was my whole world.

Here are the things I didn't tell you, the lovely things about her that you might have known but never bothered to ask—because you were interested in only the ugly parts. And you made quick work of those bits when you got a hold of them, didn't you? What a banner day it must have been for you. What a laugh you must have had at my expense, fool that I was. But I'll tell you the rest now—not because I imagine you capable of remorse; I know you too well for that—but because I want you to know the woman I knew.

I told you my mother was a beauty. The most beautiful woman in New York, some said. But I didn't tell you that people used to say I looked like her. I have her dark hair and amber eyes, her bone structure, too, I suppose. Perhaps that's why my father never quite looked at me in those days, because I reminded him of the young woman he married, though I could never have held a candle to that girl.

I used to call her Maman, *but only when we were alone. My father didn't like her speaking French in the house. We used to spend afternoons together, just the two of us, tucked away in her room, which smelled of lilies and the creamy French soap she used in the bath. She would pull out the photo album, the one she kept hidden from my father—butter-smooth leather with her initials stamped in gold on the front—and we would flip through the pages. I couldn't read the captions. The letters were funny, not proper English words, but she would read them aloud and tell me stories about them.*

There was a picture of her as a schoolgirl, looking stiff and awkward, her hair swept back in an enormous bow. That was my favorite—because I could see myself in her and I so wanted to be like her when I grew up—but I loved them all. Seaside vacations spent at Les Sables d'Olonne. Family dinners eaten by candlelight. Holiday celebrations that stretched on for days. And everyone smiling. I've always wondered what happened to that album. When I asked Cee-Cee, she claimed she'd never seen it, but not long after we got the call from the hospital, I caught her in our mother's room, going through her things. A few days later, I snuck in again and everything was gone. Her dresser drawers were empty. Her closet was bare. Even the dressing table where she kept her perfumes and creams was stripped clean. It was as if she'd never been there at all, as if she'd been erased.

I vowed then and there never to forget her. Because that's what they wanted—my father and Cee-Cee—for everyone to just forget she was ever a part of our lives. But I remember her. I remember the good and the bad.

She used to laugh a lot when we were together, but even as a child, I sensed that there was something false about her gaiety. I never let on that I noticed, but as time went on, it became harder to pretend. A sudden storm of tears, food trays left untouched, visits from the doctor at all hours of the day and night. It would come on all of a sudden, a kind of curling in on herself, as if someone had drawn a dark cloud over the sun.

To hear the kitchen staff tell it—which I did on one occasion—it started after my sister was born. The baby blues, *the doctor called it. It came on again after my brother came along, but my father was so happy to have a son that he did his best to tolerate her weepy moods. She had given him his young prince, and for a time, it was enough. But after they dragged poor Ernest from the pond, she went into a terrible spiral. A few years later, I came along—a daughter rather than the replacement son my father had hoped for. Once again, my mother struggled with depression. After burying a son, a third bout of the baby blues was more than she could handle. She never recovered and eventually got worse. Much worse.*

I'm not sure how old I was when I realized it. It was gradual at first, little things. She stopped singing. And she slept a lot, sometimes whole afternoons. When I would ask her to retell some of our stories, she would say she was too tired or that she couldn't remember them. But it felt like something else. It felt like she was afraid. I couldn't say of what. I thought grown-ups weren't afraid of anything. But life just seemed to be too much for her. She would lock herself in her room and not come out for days. She wouldn't eat or bathe or let anyone see her. And then out of nowhere, she would reappear as if nothing had happened, and the sun would shine again. Melancholia, *they called it back then.*

My father was no help. He had no patience with her when she got that way, so they fought constantly. My sister would sneak down the hall and listen at her bedroom door: him thundering on about disgracing his good name, her wailing about what she'd given up to be his wife. I crept to the door once and tried to listen, but I couldn't bear it. He hurled such horrible things at her—words I didn't understand then but do now. He was ashamed of her. Ashamed of her frailties—as a woman and as a human being.

But that part you know.

Her bouts grew more frequent with time and lasted longer. One day, she left the house and stayed gone for three days. They found her at a hotel in New Jersey, registered under an assumed name. The papers had a field day. My father dismissed her doctor after that and called in a specialist in female complaints. He was also known for his discretion. He prescribed pills for her nerves. She got better for a time, more manageable. And then one night, my father was holding an important dinner for potential investors in some new venture, and right there at the table, in the middle of a discussion on Henry Ford's newspaper, the Michigan Independent, *and its revived crusade against the international Jew, she had a sort of breakdown.*

I've never forgotten that night—though not for want of trying. The commotion was so loud that Cee-Cee and I scurried from our rooms and crouched at the top of the staircase, watching it all unfold. My father, red-faced and grim, leading my mother from the table. My mother's shrieks ricocheting off the walls as she was forcefully propelled up the stairs. We had to scramble to keep out of sight, but we ducked into one of the guest rooms and watched from the cracked door as my father flung open my mother's bedroom door, shoved her inside, and locked it behind her.

The sight made me sick to my stomach. To see her so broken. To see that he didn't care. There was so much I didn't understand then. But my sister understood. At least she seemed to. I remember her creeping back out into the hall when it was over, listening to my mother's muffled whimpers with a strange expression on her face, not quite a smile but almost. And then my father's voice drifting up the stairs from the dining room, explaining to his guests in the gravest of tones that his wife had been struggling since the death of their son.

"She blames herself, you see. No matter how many times we assure her that it was an accident, she refuses to forgive herself. We hoped things would get better with time, but I'm afraid it's had the reverse effect. It's all been downhill since the arrival of our youngest daughter."

Me. He was talking about me. Blaming me.

This wasn't new. I'd heard him refer to me as a mistake *once, while talking to Cee-Cee, but it was worse somehow, hearing him say it to strangers. I was to blame for my mother's breakdown.*

There were murmurs of pity, female voices mostly, the investors' wives, though I couldn't make out actual words.

"Yes," I heard my father say in answer to someone's question. "It has been difficult. But it's the girls I worry about. The doctor is afraid their mother's behavior may have a lingering impact on them. He's suggested a bit of rest for her, and though I've resisted thus far, I believe he might be right."

Again, the little smile played about Cee-Cee's mouth, like a cat who'd just licked up the last of the cream. "Now we'll see," she whispered, more to herself than to me. "Now we'll just see."

I remember thinking, Now we'll see what? *But I was still crying when she turned and walked away. The doctor arrived a few hours later, after all the guests were gone. The next morning, an ambulance came to take her away to a place called Craig House in Beacon. "For a rest," my father said, patting my seven-year-old head as they wheeled her past me, strapped flat to a gurney, unblinking and pale.*

I wept so hard that day that I made myself sick. Her room—the room where we had shared so many special afternoons—was shut up, the door locked, the key removed, as if my father feared my mother's affliction might be contagious.

The house, never a homey place, became a mausoleum, empty and much too still. And as the days stretched, I began to understand. I was told there would be visits. Sunday drives upstate with flowers and boxes of the chocolate-covered cherries she loved. But there weren't. Not once. And there wouldn't be. A year later, the day before Christmas, the first since she went away, there was a phone call. One of the orderlies had found her that morning—dead. A fall. A knife. A terrible accident. It wasn't an accident, though. It was on purpose. They hushed it up. No one wanted to say the word suicide—*it makes people uncomfortable—but everyone knew.*

These are the things I didn't say that day when you asked about my mother. Because they were painful. And because they were private. Instead, I told you the good things, the things I could bear to say out loud. But it wasn't enough for you. Or her.

You ask if I remember the day of that picnic? As if it were possible to forget a single moment of the whirlwind that was us, those few brief months when you whispered forever—*and I let myself believe. I remember you listening with your hand over mine and that when I finished, you didn't press me for more. Come to that, you never pressed me for anything. But then, you didn't have to. You had other ways of getting what you wanted—as I soon found out.*

SIX

ASHLYN

Like people, it is the books with the most scars that have lived the fullest lies. Faded, creased, dusty, broken. These have the best stories to tell, the wisest counsel to offer.

—*Ashlyn Greer,* The Care & Feeding of Old Books

September 29, 1984
Portsmouth, New Hampshire

Suicide.

The word throbbed like a toothache as Ashlyn closed the book and set it aside, an exposed nerve reawakened. Like Willa Greer, Helene had *chosen* to end her life, *chosen* death over her daughters. Not an accident but a conscious and deliberate choice.

Ashlyn knew firsthand about that kind of loss, the hole left behind when someone you loved left without saying goodbye, without saying they were sorry. She also understood why Belle hadn't revealed those details to Hemi on the day of the picnic. There was a kind of shame in admitting a parent, a mother especially, had simply opted out. That you hadn't been worth hanging around for—worth fighting for. They had that in common now, membership in the club no one liked to talk about: survivors forced to live with the knowledge that they hadn't been enough.

Her own mother's refusal to pursue cancer treatment had been a passive choice, even a noble one, to hear some tell it, a stoic acceptance of God's will, while her father's choice—a shotgun positioned carefully beneath the chin—had been blatant, a lashing out at the God who had taken his wife. Not because he cared for her but because he'd been cheated of something he considered his. Such a thing could not go unpunished. And so he'd climbed up to the attic and, with the twitch of a finger, orphaned his daughter.

That would show God.

He hadn't considered the effect his decision might have on her, the depth of the scars one selfish act could inflict.

But it might have been different for Helene, who'd been forcibly separated from her family and who appeared to have been struggling with mental illness. Perhaps in her state, she hadn't been capable of taking anyone else's feelings into consideration.

Melancholia, Belle had called it—the *baby blues*. It was called *postpartum depression* now, not that terminology mattered. From the sound of things, Helene's symptoms had been severe and seemed to have worsened with each successive birth. Throw in an unsympathetic husband and the death of a son, and you had a recipe for disaster.

But the manner of Helene's death hadn't been the only revelation in this afternoon's reading. She now had a name, or at least a nickname, for the author of *Regretting Belle*. Hemi—short for Hemingway. Yet another artful disguise, but for now at least, she knew what to call him. And his description of that day, of the picnic and their conversation, had been an intriguing one. Part interrogation. Part seduction. And skillful on both sides.

Belle had accused him of wheedling things out of her, of coaxing her with his practiced smile. But he'd as good as admitted to all of that, hinting at ulterior motives, even suggesting they might have to do with the infamous Goldie. Yet he'd sounded conflicted at times, as if he were a reluctant player in someone else's treachery. Had that treachery been what ultimately split them up? And if so, how could Hemi insist the betrayal had been Belle's?

The questions continued to reverberate as Ashlyn pushed to her feet. She was surprised when she glanced up at the old depot clock and saw that it was after six. No wonder her back and neck were stiff. She'd been perched on the same stool since lunch and had lost all track of time.

It happened sometimes. An entire afternoon would pass without a single customer coming in, particularly when the weather was bad, as it was today. A cold rain had been falling all day, driving shoppers to the mall and other indoor venues. Normally, she would have used the downtime to get caught up in the bindery, but after staying late last night to resew the signatures for *The Secret of the Old Clock*, she'd felt justified in parking herself behind the counter with *Forever, and Other Lies* laid open on her lap.

Regretting Belle lay within arm's reach, never far from its mate. It was how she thought of them now, as a pair—a couple. It was a strange thought, even for her, but in her mind, the books were inextricably linked. Like Hemi and Belle. Each a part of the other.

And yet the more she read, the more questions she seemed to have. She was certain Hemi had been deeply and hopelessly in love and that Belle had returned his love. How had they ended up hurting one another so deeply?

But then, given her own disastrous marriage, did she really have to ask? When it came to love, there was always an imbalance, wasn't there? Regardless of the relationship—parents, children, siblings, lovers—one party was always more invested than the other, more willing to hand over their power, to make themselves small, as the price for being loved. She'd always been the more willing one. With her parents *and* her husband.

Daniel.

They'd met at UNH. She was a lit major, he a TA for one of her classes. An aspiring writer working on his PhD, he was always happy to mentor a promising young talent—so long as that talent was female and pretty. He was the complete package, athletically built with a ridiculously sexy smile and eyes the color of a stormy sky, all wrapped up in a glossy academic veneer.

They started meeting for coffee after class, ostensibly to discuss her writing. Coffee progressed to wine, and wine progressed to bed. Six weeks later, she moved out of her grandmother's house and into Daniel's swanky loft apartment. Six weeks after that, they were married and, at Daniel's urging, she quit school and went to work for Frank full-time so he could focus on his writing. He was working on a book, a novel he claimed would take the literary world by storm and finally allow him to give up teaching.

She was fine with putting her own degree on hold while Daniel finished the book, but when he did finally finish and the months began to drag on with no sign of him resuming his full class load, she'd started dropping hints about returning to school herself. Daniel had been firm in his refusal. Until the manuscript sold, he needed her picking up as many hours as she could at the shop so he could focus on querying.

Except the manuscript didn't sell. And every time another rejection letter arrived, he invented a reason to blame *her*. It was never about the book, never about his failure. It was always about her.

And then there were the late nights with the nubile Marybeth, whose work was *entirely fresh but needed direction*. His direction. When she'd asked him point-blank if he was lining up her replacement, he had accused her of being hysterical. But that was part of his pattern too. Deny everything, no matter what the evidence said. Gaslight. Manipulate. Turn the tables. He'd been a master of deflection.

There was talk, of course, whispers about other students. One had supposedly threatened to drown herself when he broke it off. Another had an abortion and left school with a hefty check for her silence. She had written it off at the time, chalking it up to campus gossip. Until she came home early one afternoon and found Marybeth and Daniel in the kitchen, making eggs together. Daniel was in his pajama bottoms. Marybeth was wearing the Brooks Brothers robe Ashlyn had given Daniel for Christmas, her hair still wet from the shower.

True to form, Daniel had blamed her. For not being supportive enough, talented enough, woman enough. And suddenly, horrifyingly, in the middle of all that hurled blame, she realized she'd become her mother. A doormat and a victim. An emotional whipping post for a failed and angry man.

She left that night with nothing but her tote. She just wanted it to be over. But it hadn't been over for Daniel—not *nearly* over. She should have known he'd find a way to punish her, to have the last word. She'd been too late in recognizing who he truly was, a cruel and calculating man willing to destroy them both if he couldn't have what he wanted.

He'd come close too.

In the fading light, the scar on her palm gleamed shiny white, a pale, perfect crescent bisecting the life line of her right hand. Appropriate, since her existence now seemed to be divided into two halves—before Daniel and after Daniel. It had been bothering her of late, small flashes of pain that struck out of nowhere, and she wondered if it had to do with the echoes she'd been picking up from Belle's and Hemi's books. If somehow, like the vibrations of a tuning fork, they had detected and synced up with her own wound.

Perhaps it was time to step back a bit, to focus on work and let her obsession cool before reading any further. Or at all. She needed to work on the holiday newsletter and get it off to the printer, then focus her energy on finishing Gertrude's books in time for Christmas.

She pushed out of the chair, preparing to head up front to lock the door. She tidied as she went, reordering messy signage and straightening shelves, and had just begun to ponder options for supper when she heard the telltale jangle of the shop door bells.

She smothered a groan. *Not one customer all afternoon and now someone walks in at half past six.* "I'm sorry," she called as she approached the front. "I'm afraid we're closed. I was just locking up."

A man in a rain-flecked anorak glanced up from the rack of free handouts near the door. He was thirtysomething, tall and lean, with pale green eyes and close-cropped hair she suspected would have been sandy brown if it weren't wet. He held up a copy of her newsletter. "*The Care & Feeding of Old Books.* Clever title. Your idea?"

Ashlyn frowned, perturbed by what felt like a deliberate brush-off. "Yes. Thank you. But I'm afraid—"

"Good photo of you too."

"Thanks, but as I said, we're closed. We'll be open again at nine tomorrow if you're looking for something special."

The man returned the newsletter to its slot on the rack, pushed his hands into his pockets, and ran his eyes around the shop. He was younger than she'd first thought. A little uncomfortable in his skin but good-looking in a damp, uncombed way.

She forced a smile and tried again. "If you're looking for something specific, a particular title or author, I'd be happy to take your name and number and give you a call tomorrow."

He eyed her blandly. "You already have my number. We spoke a few days ago. I'm Ethan Hillard. I wasn't sure what time you closed, but I took a chance. I was wondering if it would be possible to see the books."

Ashlyn blinked at him, more than a little surprised. When they spoke on the phone, he hadn't seemed the least bit interested. "See them?"

"All right, read them."

His sudden change of heart set off alarm bells. Had he come to demand she return the books? "If you're under the impression that the books are valuable, Mr. Hillard—"

"It's Ethan," he said, cutting her off. "And this isn't about money. After we spoke the other night, the name Belle kept popping into my head and I couldn't think why. And then yesterday I remembered. I have an aunt. She's a great-aunt, actually. The sister of my paternal grandmother. Her real name is Marian, but I'm almost sure I remember the name Belle coming up in conversation between my parents."

Ashlyn felt her pulse tick up. "Marian," she repeated slowly, as if testing the weight of it on her tongue. "You think Belle was your aunt Marian?"

"I have no idea. But the books were in my father's study when he died, and Belle isn't exactly a common name, so I came. I thought if I had a look, I might be able to rule her in or out. There might be names I know—family names—or places I'd recognize."

A surge of adrenaline prickled through Ashlyn's veins at the thought that she might actually be on the verge of confirming her suspicions that Belle and Hemi were real. Maybe she could save him some time. "Do you recognize the name Goldie?"

Ethan thought for a moment, then shook his head. "No."

"A woman?" Ashlyn prodded. "Owned a string of newspapers?"

Another shake of the head. "Doesn't ring any bells. But then, I never knew my aunt, so I'm not likely to recognize the names of her friends."

"I wouldn't say Goldie was a friend of Belle's, but her name appears in both books. Apparently, she was Hemi's boss."

Ethan stared at her blankly. "Who's Hemi?"

Ashlyn's excitement faded. She was hoping he would recognize the name. "He's the author of *Regretting Belle*. That isn't his real name. It's just what Belle calls him. Short for Hemingway, because he's a writer.

Goldie appears to be a nickname as well, though I'm hoping to learn her identity soon. Once I do, I might be able to pin down Hemi's name as well, since he wrote for one of her papers. How about Helene? Does that name jog any memories?"

"None. Who was she?"

"Belle's mother. At least that's the name she used. She'd be your great-grandmother, your father's grandmother. She died when Belle was just a girl . . . by suicide, according to Belle. Apparently, the family did their best to sweep it under the carpet." She paused, registering Ethan's blank face. "None of this rings a bell?"

Ethan shook his head. "No, but it certainly sounds like the Mannings."

Ashlyn blinked at him. "Who?"

"Us," he answered simply. "The Mannings and the Hillards. My father was a Hillard. His mother was a Manning until she married. Do you have a name for Helene's husband?"

Ashlyn shrugged. "She never says. Not even a nickname. At least not in the chapters I've read so far. All I know is he was loaded and something of a tyrant. There are times when Belle sounds almost afraid of him."

Ethan studied her through narrowed green eyes. "You talk about her like you know her."

Ashlyn looked away. How could she possibly explain it? "If you'd read them . . ."

"That's why I'm here. To read them. Or at least have a look."

"Right. Of course." Ashlyn picked up the books from the counter and stepped around Ethan to lock the shop door. "There are a couple of good chairs at the back where we can read."

"Oh, I don't want to keep you. I was just going to take them with me."

Ashlyn experienced a moment of panic at the thought of the books leaving the shop. What if he decided not to return them? "I'd prefer they stay here if you don't mind. But feel free to stay as long as you like."

Ethan seemed surprised, though whether that had to do with her offer to let him stay and read after hours or with her reluctance to let the books out of her possession, she couldn't say. "All right," he said, stripping off his anorak. "If you're sure."

Ashlyn led him to the back of the shop, the books cradled in the crook of her arm. Ethan lagged several steps behind, pausing now and then to survey the exposed brick walls and tin-tiled ceiling. "Quite a place you have here," he said when he finally caught up. "My dad loved old haunts like this. Looks like it's been here awhile. Is it a family business?"

Ashlyn thought of Frank and smiled. "No. Though I did sort of grow up here. The original owner used to let me hang around when I was a kid. He let me do chores in exchange for books. When I got older, I worked here through high school and college. When he died a few years ago, he left me the place."

Ethan's brows shot up. "That was generous."

"He didn't have any family. I was it."

"Still."

Ashlyn nodded. "He was a wonderful man. I still miss him."

An awkward silence descended and for a moment they stood staring at each other, Ashlyn clutching the books, Ethan with his jacket slung over one shoulder. Finally, he pointed to her clasped arms. "I take it those are the books?"

"Oh, sorry. Yes. We can sit here. Take the chair on the left. It's more comfortable."

Ethan glanced at the chair, then back at Ashlyn. "I'm perfectly fine on my own if you have something you need to do."

"It's fine," she replied, taking the chair closest to the window. "I was actually planning to read anyway."

Ethan tossed his jacket over the back of the neighboring chair and sat. "Right. Thanks."

"How do you want to do this?"

"*Do* this?"

"Do you want to jump straight into Belle's book? Or start with Hemi's, since it came first? I've found that if you alternate between them, you get a feel for both sides of the story."

"I don't need a feel for both sides. I just want to know if my aunt wrote the second book."

"And if she did?"

He shrugged. "Then she did."

"No, I mean, what happens to the books? Will you want them back?"

He eyed her with some surprise. "Is that why you think I'm here? To take them back?"

"I just assumed that if they were about your family . . ."

Ethan straightened in his chair, as if he couldn't quite get comfortable. "My parents were my family. That's pretty much where it ends."

"I'm sorry. I didn't mean—"

"Forget it. The family thing just isn't something the Mannings and Hillards do. At least not like other families. We don't get all warm and fuzzy at the holidays or blow out candles and open presents. We share estate planners and probate attorneys—and not much else, unless you count a few threads of DNA."

"Is that why you've never met your aunt?"

He nodded. "Bad blood of some sort. I did meet her kids once when they came to visit, but they didn't stay long. I can't even remember their names."

"You don't happen to know if she's still alive, do you?"

"I don't. I didn't hear from her when my father died, but then I never tried to contact her. Why?"

"I haven't read them all the way through, but what I have read feels awfully personal. If Belle *does* turn out to be your aunt and she's alive, she might not be thrilled about the intimate details of her love life ending up in the hands of a stranger. Come to think of it, how would your father have ended up with them?"

"No idea. He and Marian used to be close—favorite nephew kind of thing—but they eventually lost touch. Maybe they were a gift."

Ashlyn ruled out the possibility immediately. Women didn't generally share those kinds of details with nephews. Even *favorite* ones. "Is there anyone who might have an address for her? Or a phone number?"

"I doubt it. Last I heard, Marian was persona non grata with the family. Even if she is alive, I doubt she'd be in touch with any of them. My father was really the only one she had contact with. She'd call out of the blue once in a while and they'd catch up, or he'd get a card for his birthday, but after a while even that stopped. Never knew why, but then I never asked. Anyway, are we going to do this? There's a good chance this whole conversation has been pointless."

Ashlyn nodded. "Which book do you want first?"

"Let's go with Belle's. With any luck, it won't take long. Doomed romances aren't exactly my thing."

Ashlyn handed him *Forever, and Other Lies*, then realized she'd omitted an important piece of information. "There are inscriptions in both books—one by Belle and one by Hemi—that you really need to read together."

He glanced up from the book, looking faintly annoyed. "Why?"

Ashlyn bit her lip in an effort to hide her annoyance. He had to be the least curious man she'd ever met. "Because they set up the whole story. Listen . . ." She flipped *Regretting Belle* open in her lap, pointing to Hemi's angrily penned line as she read the words aloud. *"How, Belle? After everything . . . how could you do it?"* She glanced up then, meeting Ethan's gaze squarely. "He wrote those words directly to her—an accusation and a question. In the book you're holding, Belle answers him back. Read it and you'll see what I mean."

Ethan opened to the inscription, cradling the book in one hand as he read. *"How??? After everything—you can ask that of me?"* He glanced up, nodding. "Okay, I see what you mean."

"It's all like that. Back and forth, like an argument on paper."

Ethan shot her a tight smile . "I'm just going to read for a bit if that's okay. See if anything feels familiar."

He was telling her to be quiet so he could get on with it. And it was a fair request. She'd been grilling him since he walked in, quizzing him about things he'd already told her he didn't know. If she kept it up, she was going to run him off, and she needed his help.

She returned her attention to Hemi's inscription. Not the words themselves—she'd committed those to memory on day one—but the way the pen strokes pressed deep into the paper, sharp and jagged, like a wound. The question was why.

Regretting Belle

(pgs. 40–47)

4 November 1941
New York, New York

Discovery is a constant threat. More for you than for me, though I'm keenly aware that I risk Goldie's wrath if I'm found out. As it is, she's suspicious about my frequent long lunches and has started keeping tabs on me, like I'm a truant schoolboy. Alibis are harder to come by for us both, rendezvous tricky to arrange. Still, we manage to see one another, living a precarious sort of half-life, detached from reality and all the things we're not meant to have. We pretend it's forever, but as the days grow shorter and winter comes on, things change—as we always knew they would.

It's difficult to pinpoint exactly when things took a turn, but I recall with great clarity the day I suddenly realized they had.

A frigid Tuesday in November. A sky the color of pewter. The threat of snow in the air. You've told your sister you'll be spending the morning at DuBarry, seeing to the fitting of some new dresses you've ordered for the season, but you finish the business in less than an hour and are loitering outside William Barthman, pretending to admire a glitzy window display of bracelets, when I just happen to pull up to the curb.

You've purchased a pair of gloves, to lend weight to your alibi, and the shopping bag dangles from the crook of your arm. We pretend the meeting is pure chance, though we've enacted it many times by now in different locations all over the city. You've become quite adept in the art of subterfuge. But then, you were born to play the femme fatale, a consummate actress, worthy of one of those golden statues they hand out every year.

I wind down the window and wave you over, then offer you a ride. You make a show of demurring but soon open the door and slide onto the seat beside me, smiling politely as I pull away from the curb. We drive out to Long Island for lunch, a car picnic of sandwiches in waxed paper bags and coffee in paper cups, procured from the roadside diner we've patronized a dozen times before.

It's a sunless day, too cold for a real picnic. I park the car near the boat launch so we can look out over the lake and finally lean over to kiss you. My head swims as my mouth closes over yours, hungry after nearly a week of not seeing you.

"We don't have long," you murmur between kisses. "There's a dinner party tonight and I've got to be back in time to dress."

I pull away, annoyed. I've only just shut off the car and you're already talking about getting back. There's always somewhere you're meant to be, somewhere that requires new clothes and an engraved invitation, somewhere I'm not invited. I blow out a breath, disgusted by my own petulance.

"Your father's quite the entertainer," I say, staring at the lake through the windscreen. "Who is it tonight? I'd say Roosevelt, but I know better than to think your old man would invite the president of the United States into his study for cognac and cigars."

You lift your chin, piqued by my tone. "Why would you say that?"

"It's no secret where your father's loyalties lie, Belle. He's a Lindy man, and not quiet about it. And like Lindy and the rest of his America First compatriots, he's dead set against your government getting involved in Europe. And more than fine with Hitler's anti-Semitic policies. Surely you knew."

You shrug. "I told you, I don't bother with politics."

"A luxury members of your class can afford, since their interests will always be protected. Meanwhile, there's a certain faction in this country—men who call themselves patriots—who are quietly working to undermine the very values they claim to stand for. And they're counting on people like you not bothering. They claim to be patriots, ginning up the public with talk about purity and real Americans, but what they really want is to marginalize Jews, remove them from powerful places, deny them a place in society entirely if they have their way. That's how it started in Europe, Belle, with a bunch of patriotic Germans spouting nonsense about purity, and they want to do the same thing here. They're organizing right now, right under your noses. The Bund. Lindbergh and his crowd. Charles Coughlin, a priest with an anti-Semitic radio show. And they're gaining traction. The Bund held a rally in Madison Square Garden. Twenty thousand people doing the Nazi salute on American soil, and no one's paying attention. Some are even cheering them on. The only way to keep those so-called patriots out of power is to pay attention, Belle, to decide where you stand on the issues before you accidentally find yourself on the wrong side."

You wait until I finish, then give me one of your cool looks. "And is there always a wrong side?"

"Maybe not always, but just now—yes, there's a wrong side. Not all the bad guys are in Germany, Belle. People need to realize that. They need to pay attention."

You study me a moment, perplexed and a little annoyed. "Is this why you brought me out here? To lecture me on my patriotic duty as an American? Because it sounds a little odd coming from someone who's over here sleeping in his boss's guest room rather than in his own country joining the fight."

I stiffen. You've brought it up before, in little ways. My lack of means and the fact that I'm a Brit. Sometimes I think you say it as much for your sake as for mine, a reminder that I'm a bad idea. An outsider, not to be trusted. Which happens to be true. I'm not to be trusted. But then, neither are you when it comes to us. I feel it. Have felt it for a long time. Like a dark spot on the horizon, growing steadily larger.

"So," I say, needing to take the edge off the conversation. "No guess as to who tonight's guest of honor might be?"

You shrug, clearly indifferent. "I never know their names. I just show up when I'm told to. But it's guests—plural. Some businessmen from Chicago, a senator from Montana of all places, and a couple men from LA."

Chicago. Montana. Los Angeles. My mind shuffles through a list of possible names. Cobb. Dillon. Regnery. Wheeler. A veritable Who's Who of noninterventionists and Nazi sympathizers.

"Los Angeles is where you keep your movie stars," I say, trying to sound casual.

"In Hollywood, yes."

"Maybe your father has invited a pair of movie moguls. Or film stars. Errol Flynn or that dancing chap Astaire. Perhaps He Who Shall Remain Nameless should be worried one of them will steal you away."

You turn your face to the window, a punishment for breaking the rules. In trying to deflect from my own jealousy, I have blundered onto forbidden ground. After all these weeks—eight glorious, torturous weeks—the subject of your engagement is still avoided. But sooner or later we'll have to discuss it. What it is, what it isn't—and what to do about it.

A better man would have faced it by now, would have tackled it straight on and forced you to choose. But I'm not a better man. I'm a selfish man who wants what he wants, though I'm too craven to press the issue, because deep down I already know what you'll choose—and why. Not for love. You don't love that great clod of a boy. But you'll have him—and all the pretty trimmings that come with his last name.

The money, the standing, the parties. Everything you've been used to. Of course you will. Any woman brought up as you have would. But to say so out loud at this moment would mean the end of what we have, however little it is, and I'm not ready for that. Not yet. And so I swallow my pride—again—and resolve to be happy with what I can have of you.

We finish our sandwiches in silence, washing them down with awful, tepid coffee. I reach into the lunch bag, pull out a packet of molasses cookies, and hand you one. You accept my peace offering and my shoulders relax.

"No doubt you've something smashing to wear this evening. I wish I could see you in whatever it is."

"Blue velvet, off the shoulder, cut rather low in back."

I flash a grin, eyebrow cocked. "I'll have to imagine it."

"No," you say suddenly with a cunning little smile. "No, you won't."

"What?"

"Come to dinner."

"What?"

"Come to dinner. Teddy had to beg off. He's stuck upstate seeing to a problem with his newest stud, so we're a man short. You can get a look at the movie stars."

I blink at you, rerunning what you've just said. Dinner. At your father's table. With his . . . guests, who are almost certainly not movie stars. It's the opportunity I've been angling for. And yet, my conscience chafes. "Do you think that's wise? Parading me around in front of your family?"

You smile, all innocence. "I have no intention of parading you anywhere. And people rarely notice what's right under their noses."

"Your sister won't appreciate a crasher."

"My sister will just have to make the best of it. The kitchen was planning on twelve, and twelve is what they'll get. We're basically talking about rewriting a place card. I'll write it myself if she likes."

There's an alarming whiff of recklessness in your words, a mix of glee and daring that makes me want to give you a shake. "I'm not worried that the foie gras won't stretch, Belle. I'm thinking about the kinds of guests your family is used to having at their table. We both know I'm not up to scratch."

You pin me with one of your dark, steady gazes, the kind meant to make a man squirm, and I find myself wondering where you learned it or if it comes naturally. "Don't you want to meet my father?"

I've wanted nothing more since getting off the boat, *I think to myself. But that isn't the point. "I'm not a suitor, Belle. That's not what we're talking about."*

"What are we talking about?"

I bite my lip, realizing that in my frustration, I've nearly said too much. "Nothing. We're not talking about anything."

"Then what's the problem? You were mooning over not being able to see me in my dress. I'm going to fix it so you will. I thought you'd be . . ."

"Grateful?"

You blink at me. "Glad," you say after a tense beat. "I thought you'd be glad. Instead, you're sniping at me and drumming up excuses not to come."

"I'm not sniping. But part of me does wonder . . ."

"What, Hemi? What do you wonder?"

"What it is we're doing. Or more accurately, what it is you're doing. With me, I mean. When you have—" You warn me with your eyes and I pull up short. "Let's just say, I'm a bit wanting in the pedigree department—not to mention the fortune department—and I can't help thinking you see me as some sort of novelty. A diversion to liven up the social season. Slumming, I think you Yanks call it."

Your eyes cloud, and for a moment, I think you're going to cry. Instead, when your eyes return to mine, they're sharp and hard, like bits of flint. "Slumming?"

"Or maybe it's rebellion. A jab at your father, who'd hardly consider me suitable for his daughter, even if she weren't already . . ."

Sensing where I'm headed, you fling open the car door. Before I know what you're about, you're off at a clip, heading for the lake. I barrel after you, bellowing into the stiff breeze coming off the water. "Where do you think you're going? It's bloody freezing out here."

I've nearly caught up to you when you wheel about, your hair suddenly loose from its pins, tumbling wildly about your face. "Did you ever think I might just want you there? That I'd want to have a . . . friend . . . sitting at that table for a change? Someone who actually cares what I think? Or that I might be tired of only seeing you on the quiet? Of lunches on blankets or in cars, stolen kisses, chance meetings on street corners that aren't chance at all."

Your words stun me. Not the rawness of them, or even the way your eyes pool with tears as you say them, but because you've flung them at me like pebbles, as though the cause of all your unhappiness has to do with me.

"I'm not the impediment here, Belle. If you want things to be different, you have to make them different."

The words are out of my mouth before I can stop them. I haven't said his name, but it's there between us anyway, swirling about us in the spiky November air. Teddy. Revoltingly rich, bloody perfect, not a brain in his head Teddy.

"Please take me back," you say stonily as you step past me. "It's an important dinner and I don't dare be late."

We drive back to the city in silence. I drop you off a block from where I picked you up. You slide out of the car with your package, then hover a moment on the sidewalk. "Will you be there?"

"That depends. Do you still want me there?"

"There will be a place card with your name on it. Come or don't."

Regretting Belle

(pgs. 48–54)

Come or don't, *you said. As if there were ever any question in the matter.*

Still, your head comes around sharply when I'm shown into your father's parlor by a man I assume is the butler. You catch yourself quickly, making your face blank, then murmur some excuse to the woman you're talking to, a matronly type whose too-tight dress puts me in mind of an overripe eggplant. You smile coolly, hand extended as you cross the room to greet me, a vision in midnight-blue velvet. So polite. So gracious.

"It's so good of you to round out our table on such short notice." Your voice is just loud enough to be heard above the hum of conversation. A flawless performance. "Let me get you a drink. What will you have?"

"Gin and tonic, thanks."

Your mouth curls at the corner, the merest hint of a smile. "Of course. The Englishman's drink."

I feel slightly disoriented as you turn and repeat the order to one of the white-coated waiters your father has hired for the occasion, as if time has warped somehow and whisked me back to the night of your engagement party, and then I realize you intended that very thing. You're teasing me, a cat with a mouse.

You take my elbow, seemingly oblivious to the absurdity of the moment, and nod to the opposite side of the room, where your father stands chatting with three men in very expensive-looking suits. "Come, let me introduce you to your host."

Your father looks up as you approach, a ready smile appearing on his squarish face, and for an instant, I see a hint of you in him, the smooth, practiced expression, flipped on like a switch. You have that look in your repertoire too.

He holds out an arm as you come to his side. "Gentlemen, my beautiful daughter and . . ." He pauses, running an eye over me. "I'm sorry, I don't believe I know your friend, my dear."

You give him my name and nothing else. There's a beat of silence, as if he's waiting for me to fill in the blank. When I don't, he thrusts out a hand. He looks me over for another moment, taking my measure, then introduces me to his companions. Wheeler, as I suspected, is one. Cobb is another. Dillon is the third.

"And how do you know my little girl?" he asks in the booming voice of a man who believes he has the world in his pocket.

Somehow, inconceivably, I haven't prepared for this question. To my relief, you jump in. "He's a friend of Teddy's. We met at the St. Regis the night of my engagement party and I happened to run into him today as I was coming out of DuBarry. It was such a raw day that he took pity and offered me a ride. And I thought the least I could do was invite him to dinner as a thank-you. I forgot we were having guests."

What a smooth liar you are, *I think but manage to nod and smile. And then you're whisking me off to introduce me to your sister, where the "old friend of Teddy's" charade is repeated.*

I only glimpsed your sister from a distance that night at the St. Regis, but once again, I'm struck by the differences between you. There are similarities, of course, despite the gap in your ages, a vague resemblance if you look very hard, but she's a bloodless version of you, smaller and paler, as if the years have washed out all her color, and I find myself wondering if she always looked like this or if it's the result of the life she's lived. A husband chosen by her father, a stable of impeccably reared children, years of living up to expectations someone else has set for her. It makes me shudder to think you might look like this after a few years with Teddy.

She offers her hand, eyeing me a little too keenly for comfort. "Well, well. An Englishman. It seems my sister's been hiding you from us. Why do you think that is?"

I shift uncomfortably, expecting you to come to my rescue, but you remain curiously tight-lipped, as if you're enjoying my discomfort. "Well," I say, trying not to sound awkward. "I've been rather busy since coming over. Settling in, getting the lay of the land. I'm afraid I haven't had much time for socializing."

Cee-Cee lifts a sharply penciled brow. Curious and a little skeptical. "It seems an odd time to travel, though, with all the trouble in Europe . . ."

Her words dangle, unfinished. Not quite a question but near enough, and I realize I'll need to tread very carefully. This one does *bother with politics. I nod, acknowledging her point. "It is indeed. But life must go on for the rest of us."*

"Your Mr. Churchill seems determined to drag the entire world into his war," she observes drily, then tsks in mock disapproval. "Is it really wise to leave at a time like this? When your country needs every able-bodied man on the battlefield?"

I reach for my oiliest smile and throw in a wink. "Can you think of a better time to leave?"

Her face lights up, as if she's just recognized a friend. "I take it you're not a fan of war, then?"

"I am of the opinion that war is always to be avoided." It's the most honest thing I've said all evening and it seems to please her.

"I see. Are you political, then?"

"Alas," I say, choosing my next words with special care, "it has been pointed out to me, quite recently in fact, that as a visitor in your country, I

am not entitled to be political. At least not on this side of the pond. Though in certain matters, I admit to holding very particular opinions."

Cee-Cee is clearly intrigued, but before she can ask what those opinions are, I feel your arm wind through mine. "We should keep circulating and give you a chance to meet everyone before we go in to dinner."

But Cee-Cee quickly checks you, claiming my other arm. Her eyes flash in your direction as she pulls me to her side with a saccharine smile. "Don't you dare take him away just when we've found something in common. Why not make yourself useful and go circulate with the wives? They're all green to the gills over that dress. And don't worry about your friend, darling. I'll see that he gets to the dining room when it's time."

You puff up a little, as if you're about to protest, but in the end, you nod coolly and turn away, clearly annoyed that your sister has stolen your mouse.

SEVEN

ASHLYN

Books may be likened to the people who come into our lives. Some will become precious to us; others will be set aside. The key is to discern which is which.

—*Ashlyn Greer,* The Care & Feeding of Old Books

September 29, 1984
Portsmouth, New Hampshire

"It was her," Ethan said, closing *Forever, and Other Lies* and setting it on the table between them. "It was Marian."

Ashlyn looked up from *Regretting Belle*, its cast of guests and white-coated waiters dissolving like a fade shot in a movie. "You're sure?"

"My father used to talk about spending summers in the Hamptons at a farm called Rose Hollow. And the sister—the woman referred to as Cee-Cee—was almost certainly Corinne Manning, my grandmother. I've never laid eyes on the woman, but it all fits."

Ashlyn's stomach did a little somersault. Marian. Corinne. Both real. "Belle mentions Cee-Cee a lot, how she practically raised her after their mother died, but there's not much about her father, except that he was a bit of a tyrant. She doesn't even give him a name."

Ethan grimaced at the mention of his great-grandfather. "His name was Martin Manning. Filthy rich according to my father—and a total bastard. He died not long after I was born. A stroke, I think."

Ashlyn sat a moment with the new information, laying it all out like pieces from a jigsaw puzzle. "I can't believe it," she breathed finally. "We actually found her."

"*You* found her," Ethan corrected. "All I did was confirm her identity."

"And Hemi? Any idea who he might have been?"

"None. And before you ask, I can't help with Teddy either. Neither name is familiar."

"I was hoping you could tell me if she ever married him."

"She never married anyone, as far as I know."

Ashlyn frowned. "I thought you said you met her kids."

"Her *adopted* kids. A boy and a girl. War orphans."

"She adopted two war orphans? From where?"

"I don't remember. Come to think of it, I'm not sure I ever knew. I know she traveled after the war, but I have no idea where. Like I said, the little I do know is from overhearing my parents' conversations."

Ashlyn nodded gloomily. "So what happens now?"

"What do you mean?"

"I mean, where do we go from here?"

Ethan stood and dragged his anorak from the back of the chair. "We don't go anywhere. Belle was my great-aunt Marian. Mystery solved."

Ashlyn looked at him in disbelief. "But that's only a *piece* of the mystery. Aren't you curious about the rest of it?"

"Not in the least."

He was pulling on his jacket now, preparing to leave. Ashlyn pushed to her feet, trailing after him. "Don't you want to know the rest of the story?"

"I know all I care to about the Manning clan."

"You're not curious about who Hemi was and what split them apart?"

"I'm not, actually. But I'm guessing it's in the books if you keep reading." They had reached the front of the store. Ethan plucked a copy of the newsletter from the rack near the door and folded it into quarters before stuffing it into his pocket. "I need to run. I've got an early class tomorrow. History of American Thought."

"You're in school?"

"I'm an adjunct at UNH. Political science."

Like Daniel, Ashlyn thought, curling her fist around the scar on her palm. But Ethan wasn't Daniel. He was the great-nephew of Marian Manning—of Belle—and he was about to leave. "Could I . . . If I run across something . . . would it be all right if I called you? I promise not to be a pest. I'd only call if I needed to verify something."

Ethan shrugged uncomfortably. "I doubt there'd be much I could add, and I'm in the early stages of a new book. I can't really afford distractions."

A soft no, but a no nonetheless. Ashlyn stepped around him, flipping the dead bolt to let him out, then decided to try one more time. "I get why you're not interested in Cee-Cee and Martin, but Hemi— whoever he was—was mad about your aunt, and she was clearly mad about him. Don't you want to know what happened?"

"We know what happened, don't we? Somebody done somebody wrong. Because that's what always happens. Hell, somebody even wrote a song about it."

"B. J. Thomas. 1975."

Ethan frowned, then surprised her by breaking into a grin. "Do I want to know how you happen to have that bit of information on the tip of your tongue?"

"I happen to love that song."

"Okay, never admit that to anyone. Seriously. *Never.*" He ducked his head sheepishly and nodded toward the window. "Looks like it's stopped raining."

"Right." Ashlyn stepped aside, clearing the path to the door. "Thanks for your help. At least I know Belle's name now. It's a place to start."

A gust of chilly air sailed in as he pulled back the door. He lingered a moment, then turned to look at her. "You don't know me, so my advice probably isn't worth much, but I wouldn't hope too hard for a happy ending if I were you. They don't run in the Manning side of the family. Or the Hillard side, for that matter. Unless you count my parents, and they were clearly outliers. Anyway, good luck with your sleuthing."

The bells on the shop door jangled softly as it closed behind him. Ashlyn stepped to the window, watching as Ethan headed down the sidewalk. But his parting words about happy endings not running in his family continued to resonate long after his yellow anorak had disappeared from sight. Perhaps because they rang so true. She looked down at her right hand, at the line of puckered white flesh bisecting her palm. They didn't run in hers either.

EIGHT

ASHLYN

To read a book is to take a journey, to travel into a vast unknown, to hear the voices of angels both living and dead.

—*Ashlyn Greer,* The Care & Feeding of Old Books

September 30, 1984
Portsmouth, New Hampshire

The next afternoon, Ashlyn was in the bindery, still processing what she'd learned during Ethan's unexpected visit to the shop, when the phone rang. She dropped what she was doing and scurried up front to answer it.

"Who's your favorite librarian?" the voice on the other end chirped.

Ashlyn felt the sharp tingle of excitement. She hadn't expected to hear from Ruth so soon, but her triumphant tone certainly seemed to signal good news. "You can't possibly have found her already."

"I have, though it was a bit of a job. Turns out there were more women in the newspaper business in those days than either of us expected. Big names, like Agnes Meyer at *The Washington Post* and Alicia

Patterson at *Newsday*. But neither matched the woman you described. For starters, both were married. So I kept digging. You wouldn't believe how much microfilm I had to comb through, but eventually I hit pay dirt."

"And?"

"Her real name was Geraldine Evelyn Spencer. Born in 1899. Chicago, Illinois. Daughter of Ronald P. Spencer, who made his fortune in coal and owned a string of second-rate dailies as a hobby. Ronald and wife, Edith, were on the SS *Afrique*, bound for Senegal when the ship struck a reef and went down, taking six hundred and three passengers down with it. Geraldine—or Goldie, as her father called her—was twenty-one at the time and inherited the whole kit and caboodle. About six million in 1920, which would equate to more than thirty million today."

Ashlyn was silent as she absorbed the information. A newspaper heiress at the age of twenty-one. The equivalent of more than $30 million. No wonder Goldie didn't care what anyone thought of her.

"Ashlyn? Did I lose you?"

"Oh, no. Sorry. I was just sorting through it all. How on earth did you piece it together?"

"Like I said—microfilm. I also called in a favor from a colleague in Albany. Once I knew who I was looking for, the rest was easy. The press has never been shy about tattling on their own, no matter what they like to pretend. There's more, by the way."

"More?"

"The dirty laundry, you might say. I assumed you'd want that too."

"Whatever you've got, I want."

"Well, she certainly wasn't your typical heiress. Men, booze, a real wild child. No one ever expected her to actually step in and run the publishing arm of Daddy's empire. Caused quite a stir. Ronald Spencer was always fairly moderate in his politics. Didn't like to bother anyone.

Not so for his little girl. She made it clear out of the gate that she wasn't walking on eggshells for anyone. She rolled up her sleeves and took on the social issues of the day. Birth control. Wages for women. Eugenics. Child labor. Had quite a lot to say about the Nazis too. Not the ones in Europe. The ones she claimed lived right here in the US of A. Named names too."

"I'll bet that went over like the proverbial lead balloon."

"She was none too popular with her father's crowd, I can tell you. Labeled a lefty and a commie, but she never backed down. She had a knack for finding dirt on the big boys. Bribery. Corruption. Cronyism. If she got a whiff of something rotten, she dug it up, and then she printed it. Took down more than one bigwig in her day, and by any means necessary. But none of that altered her reputation as a party girl. Actually managed to get herself caught up in a raid at some jazz club in Harlem, complete with photos of her being hauled away in an honest-to-god paddy wagon. Her rivals had a field day, but she didn't care. The woman had no shame. There are quite a lot of photos of her. Always dressed to the nines. And you never saw such jewelry."

"And the rumors about the men she collected?"

"All true. Young. Old. Rich. Poor. She was fond of them all. Never married, as far as I can tell, but she did finally level off when someone named Steven Schwab entered the picture. He appears to have been a longtime protégé and love interest. Looks like he worked for a couple of her newspapers, though I'm not sure which or in what capacity. Maybe he was just, as they say . . . on the payroll. Apparently, they were on and off for years."

Ashlyn felt the hair on her arms prickle. "A love interest?"

"Well, that part's a little murky, but he does appear on her arm in several photos. Definitely younger and handsome as they come. One article mentions his utter devotion to her. Another piece describes him as an aspiring novelist whose aspirations far outweigh his talent. It might be true too. I looked, but I couldn't find a single book attributed to him anywhere. At any rate, he lived with Goldie for the last ten years of her life and she left him a fistful of cash when she died. Clearly, something was going on."

Ashlyn laid the new pieces end to end. Steven Schwab. Young and handsome. Worked for one of Goldie's papers. An aspiring novelist with no books to his credit. Was it possible Hemi and Steven Schwab were one and the same? If her math was right, Hemi was twenty-six when he and Belle met in 1941, which meant he'd be in his sixties now.

The thought raised a host of possibilities. "Ruth, you didn't happen to run across anything that mentioned where Mr. Schwab might be living these days, did you?"

"He doesn't live anywhere. He's dead. Goldie died in '79 and he went a couple years later. I tried to find more on him, but apart from his connection to Goldie, he appears to have been remarkably unremarkable. At any rate, he's dead."

Dead. The word left Ashlyn feeling vaguely deflated. "Right."

"So *now* are you going to tell me what you're working on? I must say, I'm intrigued by the naughty Miss Spencer."

Ashlyn bit her lip. Revealing what she'd stumbled upon, now that she knew Belle and Hemi's story was true, would feel like betraying a confidence.

"I don't blame you for being curious about Goldie. She's certainly a colorful character. But at this point, I don't think I should share much. Partly because I don't know much but also because of privacy issues. For now, I think it best that I keep what I do know to myself and just keep digging."

Ruth blew a sigh into the phone, clearly disappointed. "All right. I get it. I made copies of a few of the articles and photos. I'm guessing you'd like to have those."

"I would. I'm not sure when I can pick them up, though."

"I'm off at two today. I'll run them by the shop if that works."

"Thank you. I owe you huge, Ruth."

"Yes, you do. But honestly, it was fun. I think I may have missed my calling. Maybe I'll pen a series of novels about a crusty New England literary detective and give Agatha Christie and her Miss Marple a run for their money. See you after two."

At ten after two, Ruth Truman dashed into the shop waving a large manila envelope. Ashlyn was in the travel section, helping a customer select a book for her husband's birthday, when she heard the bells on the shop door jangle. She signaled with the wave of a hand, but Ruth kept moving, pausing just long enough to slap the envelope on the counter and explain that she was illegally parked and that her husband had vowed to take away her keys if she came home with one more parking ticket.

It was all Ashlyn could do not to step away from her customer and steal a peek at the envelope. As it was, her customer continued to dither for nearly an hour and ended up leaving empty-handed. Ashlyn didn't care and barely waited until the woman was out the door before making a beeline for the counter.

She held her breath as she unwound the envelope's string closure and slid out the contents. The sight of the pages made her stomach do a little flip. A few had been neatly paper-clipped. Others were single sheets with bold headlines and grainy black-and-white photos. The print quality wasn't good—printed microfilm materials seldom were— but with a magnifying glass, she ought to be able to make out most of it.

She laid out the pieces like a hand of solitaire, arranging them in chronological order. When she was finished, she pulled Frank's enormous magnifying glass from beneath the counter and picked up the first item, a *Chicago Tribune* article dated January 14, 1920.

Chicago Business Mogul Ronald P. Spencer Believed
Dead at Sea

January 15, 1920 (Chicago)—Noted businessman and
Chicago native Ronald Spencer and wife, Edith, are believed to have perished in the sinking of the S.S. *Afrique*
on the early morning of January 13th, when the ship
carrying some 600 passengers and a crew of 135
was driven off course and struck a reef off the French
coast. The ship, owned by French shipping company Compagnie des Chargeurs Réunis, was bound for
Senegal when the accident occurred. Generators in the
engine room are said to have failed during the storm,
leaving the ship unable to maneuver. At 11:58 p.m.,
the ship was thrown against a reef, fatally damaging
the hull. At 3 a.m., all contact with the *Afrique* was lost
and the ship sank soon after. Of the passengers and
crew, only 34 survived. Ronald and Edith Spencer are
survived by one daughter, Miss Geraldine Spencer, 21.

The rest of the article was about Ronald Spencer's net worth and
business holdings. Ashlyn didn't care about any of that. She was much
more interested in the photo of the young woman at the bottom of the
page—GERALDINE "GOLDIE" SPENCER, 21.

She picked up the magnifying glass again, studying Goldie more
closely. Platinum-haired and sloe-eyed, with a perfectly painted bow of
a mouth, staring back at the camera as if someone had dared her to do
it. It wasn't difficult to imagine her as the woman Belle had described,
brazen and flamboyant, with a taste for parties and young men. Hemi's
boss. And lover, too, perhaps.

The second article was also from the *Tribune*, an opinion piece
dated twelve weeks later, lamenting the takeover of Spencer Publishing

by a *"twenty-one-year-old flapper"* who would soon turn her father's redoubtable print holdings into a string of cheap entertainment rags, covering nightclub openings and the latest fashion crazes. The piece ended with a call for the board to take swift steps.

The third piece was much more colorful.

Tattler Owner Goldie Spencer Nabbed in Jazz Club Raid

June 14, 1928 (New York)—In the early-morning hours of June 13, police carried out a secret raid at the basement speakeasy known as the Nitty Gritty Club. Police were acting on a tip that illegally imported liquor was being served at the West 125th Street jazz club. A sizable stockpile of beer and spirits, discovered behind a false wall, was confiscated and is slated to be destroyed. A small amount of marijuana was also found on the premises. Forty-two patrons were taken into custody, including owner Lively Abbot, noted actor and man about town Reginald Bennett, and newspaper heiress Goldie Spencer. Bennett and Spencer were arraigned in county court and ordered to pay a $50 fine. Abbot, who has had repeated brushes with the law, faces up to a year in jail and fines in excess of $700.

Ashlyn scrutinized the grainy photo of a heavily made-up Goldie being muscled into the back of a police wagon. Her platinum hair was cropped short and parted down the middle, her brow adorned with a beaded headpiece—the quintessential flapper. The photographer had caught her with her mouth open, presumably in the act of hurling some epithet at the policeman who had her by the arm. It was hardly a flattering photo, but once again, Goldie's defiance was on full display.

The next two articles—Senator Thuneman Exposed in Bribery Scheme and The Enemy in Our Midst: American Nazis Hiding in Plain Sight—had obviously been included as evidence of Goldie's journalistic bravado. Ashlyn scanned the latter briefly, noting that both Henry Ford and Charles Lindbergh had made it into the piece. The article after that, dated 1971, detailed Goldie's involvement in a rally in defense of a woman named Shirley Wheeler, the first woman to be charged with manslaughter for illegally terminating a pregnancy.

And finally, a tiny tabloid piece dated November 2, 1974. Who's the Hunk on Goldie Spencer's Arm? The photo showed a smiling but noticeably older Goldie at some gala or other. She was wearing a dress trimmed in feathers and a necklace that could have bankrolled a small third-world country. On her arm was an impossibly tall Adonis. A 007 type, with chiseled good looks and a wide white smile, impeccable in black tie. Ashlyn felt a little thrill as she let her magnifying glass hover. Here, at last, was Steven Schwab, considerably younger than Goldie and still quite dashing.

Ashlyn peered more closely at his face, taking in the toothy smile, the sideways cut of his eyes as they sought Goldie's, as if they'd just enjoyed some private joke. Was this the man Marian Manning had loved so desperately, the man who had deceived her and broken her heart? And if so, where did Goldie fit in? Perhaps she'd loved him first and had seen Marian Manning as the interloper. If all was fair in love and war—and Hemi and Steven Schwab *were* in fact the same person— Goldie had clearly been the victor.

According to Ruth, he'd been with her till the end. And the next article—Newspaper Heiress Goldie Spencer Dead at 80—seemed to bear that out, mentioning that Goldie's Park Avenue apartment as well as a sizable portion of her fortune had gone to longtime companion Steven Schwab. In accordance with her will, the remainder of her estate had been divided among various charities championing women's issues, which fit perfectly with the final item from the packet, a multipage spread that had appeared in *The New Yorker* the day of Goldie's memorial service. **Goldie Spencer: A Feminist Legacy.**

Returning to the gala photo and the dashing Steven Schwab, Ashlyn looked for some detail that might confirm that he'd been the love of Marian Manning's life. With the parade of men constantly moving in and out of Goldie's orbit, Hemi could have been anyone. Still, the pieces fit remarkably well. Particularly the part about him being an aspiring novelist. What if Mr. Schwab had done more than just aspire? What if he'd actually written a book—an anonymous book—about a doomed love affair with the daughter of a powerful man?

Hemi . . . is that you?

And even if it was, how could she verify it? He was long past answering questions. As was Goldie. And the deeper she waded into Belle and Hemi's story, the more questions she had. What had become of Marian Manning's poetry? When had she broken her engagement to Teddy, and why, if not to marry Hemi? Might there be photos squirreled away somewhere that included both Steven Schwab and Marian Manning, snapped inadvertently during some party or gala? If so, it would be proof. Or near proof.

None of these things were her business, of course, nor would knowing them change the unhappy outcome. But the *need* to know was like an itch she couldn't reach. At this point, there was only one person who might be able to help, though ability and willingness were two different things. Ethan seemed reluctant to wade any further into his aunt's past, though she suspected he knew more than he realized. Perhaps the names Steven Schwab and Geraldine Spencer would jog his memory.

This time, she thought the call through before dialing. At this time of day, she was likely to get his answering machine, and she wanted to have her ducks in a row. When she was finally clear about what she wanted to say, she rehearsed her pitch once more, then dialed. As expected, Ethan's machine picked up.

"Hey, it's Ashlyn from the bookstore. I know you said you were crazy busy right now, but something's come up. Some names I was hoping to run by you. And a few questions I forgot to ask the other night. Could you maybe call me back?"

By closing time, Ethan still hadn't returned her call and she'd added six new questions to her list. She told herself that didn't necessarily mean he was blowing her off. Maybe he wasn't home yet or he'd forgotten to check his machine. She dialed again, hoping to catch him in person.

"I'm not here. Leave me a message."

Damn.

"Hey, it's me again. I was wondering if you'd gotten my message from this afternoon. A friend of mine did a little digging and came up with a name—Steven Schwab. I was hoping it might ring a bell. I think he might be Hemi. I'm about to close up, but you can reach me at my home number. Anyway . . . thanks."

After a hot shower and a haphazard supper of salad and leftover chicken, Ashlyn spread the contents of the manila envelope out on the kitchen counter and read through them again.

She'd been almost giddy as she combed through it the first time, but her excitement had deflated a little since. Other than the fact that a man named Steven Schwab may or may not have had a romantic relationship with the infamous Goldie, what had she *really* learned? That he *might* have worked for one of the Spencer papers. That he *might* have been a novelist. Nothing that connected Steven Schwab to Marian Manning.

She eyed the phone, keenly aware that it hadn't rung. It was Sunday. Maybe Ethan had gone away for the weekend. Or maybe he had a date. At least she hoped it was something like that and not a deliberate decision to ignore her. She didn't dare call again. Not yet. She'd wait a few days. And in the meantime, she'd keep reading and hope either Belle or Hemi got careless with a detail or two.

Forever, and Other Lies

(pgs. 37–44)

November 4, 1941
New York, New York

I watch as my sister takes you off on her arm and note that you make no move to untangle yourself from her. She has always reminded me of a spider, infinitely patient, waiting for events to shape themselves to her satisfaction. And then she strikes, swiftly and without mercy. The consummate opportunist.

I'm not sure what her plans for you are yet; perhaps her intent is only to annoy me, to remind me, yet again, that she is in charge. As if any of us could forget it. At any rate, you seem quite comfortable being steered about.

How clever you think yourself, a chameleon making your way around the room, chatting and laughing with my father's guests. No one watching would ever guess you weren't one of them or that you had initially balked at my invitation. You play your part flawlessly, so flawlessly that I find myself wondering if your reluctance to come tonight was feigned.

You smile and nod over your gin and tonic, discussing labor disputes and monetary policy like you're a visiting diplomat at a dinner given in your honor. And not so much as a glance in my direction as you mill about. Not even when I nearly burn a hole in your jacket with my eyes, willing you to turn and look at me. It's to spite me, I realize, to pay me back for our argument this afternoon at the lake. I turn away and leave you to Cee-Cee.

Later, when we're called in to dinner, I notice she's had the place cards changed. You're now seated at the far end of the table, as far from me as possible, and I'm forced to watch you fawn over Mrs. Viola Wheeler, smiling that easy smile of yours, charming her Montana-bred ears with your smooth British tongue.

I'm sickened watching her, an old frump in a dress the color of a bruise, giggling like a schoolgirl over whatever you've just said. The husky burr of your laugh drifting down the table. Your unconscious habit of raking your hair off your forehead. So familiar now. Yet you've barely managed a smile for me since you arrived. It's as if we're truly the strangers we're pretending to be. I long for dinner to be over so I can finally peel you away from the rest of them and find some pretext to have you to myself. Instead, after the dessert has been consumed and the coffee drunk, my father suggests the men split off from the ladies and remove to his study for cigars. I'm more than a little surprised when he specifically includes you in the invitation, but as the men push back from the table, I see a look pass between Cee-Cee and my father and realize she approves, and may even have been the one to suggest including you.

The ladies linger at the table with dainty glasses of sherry, clucking about how hard it is to keep a decent cook and their utter disappointment in this year's theatrical season. I nod vacantly, pretending to follow along, but all I can think of is you, sitting in one of the leather club chairs in my father's study, smoking and talking with his oily friends. I feel churlish for thinking it, petulant and resentful, but I didn't ask you here to smoke cigars and rub elbows with a clutch of odious old men.

But as I dispatch a second glass of sherry with one deep swallow, I realize those old men are precisely why you came tonight. For their wealth and connections and whatever they might be able to do for you. I shouldn't be surprised. You introduced yourself as an adventurer the first time I met you. And now here you are under my father's roof, invited into his inner sanctum. How neatly you've managed it. And how quickly. Thanks to me.

I refill my glass, suddenly on the verge of tears. Cee-Cee slants me a silent warning. I pretend not to notice, but I can't help wondering what she sees when she looks at me. Am I as transparent as I fear?

I feel an utter fool.

I wanted you here for your sake. For how I feel when I'm with you— like my heart is too big for my chest. Like I finally belong to someone uncon- nected to this wretched house and my wretched family. But you obviously had different reasons for coming. Reasons that appear to have nothing to do with me. The women are still clucking about hats and hem lengths and suddenly I can't bear another empty word or another sip of sherry. I push to my feet and excuse myself, blurting something about a headache.

My sister shoots me another of her scathing looks as I head for the door. I don't care; I've grown used to her disapproval over the years. And part of me blames her for tonight, for whisking you away and parading you about.

I was always invisible to her, too young to be of any interest. I didn't mind—my mother loved me enough for everyone—but when she died, the loss was like a hole in my chest. And so I latched on to Cee-Cee, following her from room to room, peering in when she was reading or writing letters, asking her to play a game or tell me a story. I needed someone to talk to, someone who remembered Maman and how things were before she got sick. But my sister had no patience for my neediness.

I remember creeping into her bedroom one night and crawling in beside her, desperate for comfort after a horrible dream. Instead of comfort, I received an elbow to the ribs and was sent back to my room. She eventually accepted her role as surrogate mother, though only at my father's request. She never could deny him anything. Including marriage to the stuffy son of one of his business cronies. But then, Cee-Cee was as ambitious as he was, and eager to help the family regain its footing after the Crash. In my father's world, everything comes with a price tag.

A dozen years, one dead husband, and four children later, she has become the matriarch of our family, the arbiter of good taste and good behavior—and a kind of jailer where I'm concerned. She sees it as her duty to keep me properly aligned with my father's wishes, and I generally do what's expected of me. Because it's easier. But not tonight.

I slip out into the hallway and head for the stairs. I have no idea how long my father will be entertaining in his study or what you'll think when you're set free and find I've gone up for the night and left you to fend for yourself. You've made plenty of new friends. Let one of them show you out. Or perhaps Cee-Cee will do the honors. She seems quite taken with you.

I've nearly reached the staircase when I hear muffled footsteps behind me. I turn and find you coming toward me, but you stop abruptly, maintaining an awkward distance.

"I'm going," you say flatly.

"Going? But why?"

"I've had a bellyful of this night. Let's just leave it at that."

You're so cool. So angry. "Has something happened? Has there been a quarrel?"

You smile one of your flinty smiles. "Quite the opposite. I've been welcomed into the fold with open arms. A few weeks more and I'll have been taught the secret handshake."

I frown, trying to make sense of your words, your tone. It's our second argument in the space of a day and it frightens me. "I don't understand. Isn't that why you came?"

"I came for you, Belle. Because you asked me to, remember? You said . . . Did you ever think I might just want you there? *So I came."*

"And the instant you got your foot in the door, I became invisible."

You study me for what feels like a very long time, your mouth drawn down at the corners. Finally, you come a step closer. I expect you to touch me, to kiss me, since there's no one around. Instead, you shake your head. "You parade me in front of your father and sister like some bloody trophy, pretending to barely know me, then get angry because I haven't spent the entire evening pining for you from across the room."

"I didn't expect—"

You hold up a hand, cutting me off. "You seem to think this is some sort of game, Belle. You leave me hanging for days at a time, then tug my chain. And I'm supposed to jump when you call. I was happy to play along—for a while. But things are different now. I can't play anymore."

Your words are like little stones. They sting when they land. "What are you saying?"

"I'm saying that in the future, you should be more careful with your invitations."

You turn then and retreat down the hall. I watch you walk away, your shoulders stiff as you pass through the parlor and slip from sight. Your heels echo against the marble tiles in the foyer, and then I hear the thud of the front door, firm and final.

Much too final.

The next morning, I try to phone you at Goldie's apartment. A man answers—I don't know who—but when I ask to speak to you, he tells me you're no longer in residence, that you moved your things out just this morning. The news catches me off guard and sets off an irrational panic in me. I ask if he knows why you've left so abruptly and then if he knows where you've gone, but he's of no help.

My hands feel shaky as I dial the number for the Review. *We've agreed that I won't call you at work, just as we've agreed that you won't call me here. The woman who answers is brusque and efficient. She tells me over the background thrum of office activity that you haven't shown up for work yet and that no one's heard from you. She suggests I try again after lunch, then, as an afterthought, asks if I want to leave a message.*

For a moment, I'm tempted to dictate some petulant remark about your brusque departure last night, to lash out at you in the only way currently available to me. But once you've read it, what then? I'll only wind up apologizing for my petulance.

"No," I say. "No message." *I'm about to hang up when I blurt out that I'd like to speak with Goldie.*

"I'm afraid Miss Spencer is tied up at the moment. Would you care to leave—"

Her words cut off abruptly, followed by a muffled pause, as if a hand has been placed over the receiver. A moment later, Goldie's voice comes over the line. "What is it you want?"

"I'm calling—"

"I know why you're calling, honey. A little early, though, even for you. I thought yours was more of a lunchtime affair."

Affair. *The word stuns me. The transient nature of it, the impermanence. But then, that's what this is, isn't it? What we're doing? Having an affair? Perhaps not in the completest sense—we've both managed to keep our clothes on—but in every way that matters. Slipping away to meet in secret. Lying about where we've been. Pretending it's different from what other people do. Because we're in* love.

Except we've never actually said the word. Me, because I'm not allowed to say it. Not to you. And you, because . . . Well, I suppose it's part of the bargain we've made, to tiptoe around the truth. To give a thing a name means missing it when you have to let it go. And I'm not sure I can bear the missing. Or the letting go.

Only now, you seem to be the one letting go.

The scratchy silence over the line reminds me that Goldie is still there, waiting for me to respond. I consider denying it, then realize how pointless it would be. There's only one way she could know about our lunchtime rendezvous. You've told her. Everything, it appears.

I hang up, then head down the back stairs and out through the kitchen door. In the garage, I tell Banks, the man who looks after the cars, that I'm

160

going into town to do some shopping and then meeting friends for lunch. As I say it, I realize how smoothly the lie rolls off my tongue and how good I've become at telling them.

I wait nearly two hours across the street from the Review's *offices, watching the entrance, waiting for you to appear. It's a desperate thing to do, I know. A silly, reckless, impetuous thing. But something happened last night, something you seem to believe was my fault, and I think I'm entitled to at least know the nature of my transgression and whether it might have had anything to do with your abrupt change of address. Did you and Goldie quarrel? Over me? And if so, have you lost your job as well as the guest room?*

The possibility that you might already be headed back to England gnaws at me as I watch taxi after taxi pull up to the curb, discharging passengers who aren't you. And then finally, there you are.

I blow the horn, three short taps, until you turn toward the car. Your face goes blank at first, and then you're crossing the street with long, determined strides. You say nothing as you approach, just open the passenger door and slide in.

"What are you doing here, Belle?"

"I called . . . They said you weren't . . . I had to see you."

"I thought we agreed—"

"I don't care what we agreed. They said you moved out this morning."

"Who's they?"

"Whoever answered the phone. What happened?"

You pull off your hat, rake a hand through your hair. For the first time, I notice how tired you look, as if you haven't slept or showered. You study me through narrowed eyes. "How long have you been here? Your lips are blue."

I look away, my throat tight. "I don't know. A couple hours. We need to talk about last night, Hemi. Please."

"We can't sit here. Start the car."

"Where are we going?"

"My place."

Regretting Belle

(pgs. 55–65)

5 November 1941
New York, New York

You say nothing as you maneuver your father's Chrysler through lunch-hour traffic, turning when I tell you to, parking where I tell you to.

I feed the meter, then point to a six-story brick walk-up crouched between its taller neighbors on Thirty-Seventh Street. After a furtive glance in both directions, you follow me into the building, past a bank of metal mailboxes and a scattering of weary chairs and tables. I wonder what you're thinking as you follow me up the narrow flight of stairs, your hand hovering slightly above the banister, so as not to soil your gloves.

I stop in front of apartment 2-B and fumble for the key, still loose in my pocket. The door groans as I push it open and stand aside. You enter tentatively, wary of the dim and vaguely stale interior. There's an uncomfortable moment when I flip on the living room lamp and you take in the handful of sparsely furnished rooms. It isn't bad, but it isn't much either. Certainly a far cry from your father's study with its mahogany-paneled walls and sumptuous leather chairs.

There's a couch covered in some plain, serviceable material; a matching armchair; and a pair of low end tables. The kitchen is at the back, compact, like a ship's galley, with red-and-white curtains and a table built into the wall. Down a short hall, the bedroom is visible, starkly furnished with a bureau, a small desk, and a double bed with a faded chenille spread. My suitcases sit in the doorway, along with my typewriter case and a handful of battered books.

You run your eyes around the place, then turn and blink at me. "This is . . . yours?"

"As of nine thirty this morning, yes. Goldie and I have been experiencing . . . a little friction, so I thought it was time I strike out on my own. It's not a palace, but it's a place to write and sleep, which is all I need."

I watch as your eyes fill with tears. You try to blink them away, but it's too late. They spill down your cheeks. I'm startled when you fall against me with a sob.

"I thought you were going home . . . ," you whisper hoarsely, then tip your head back to look at me. "When I heard you left Goldie's this morning, I thought you were going back to England."

"Why would you assume that?"

"Last night, when you left . . ." You look away, then drop your eyes to the floor. "Why did you leave Goldie's?"

I step away then, needing to put distance between us, and find myself wishing I'd taken up smoking. I could do with a distraction just now, a stall tactic, something to do with my hands. I shove them into my pockets instead. "We had words," I say, clipped, grudging.

"About me?"

"Among other things."

"She knows about us."

There's a hint of accusation in your tone. Deserved, I suppose. "Yes."

Your face goes hard, your tears forgotten. "How could you? Of all the people on earth, how could you tell her? The things she said to me on the phone . . ."

"I'm sorry. We had it out last night when I got back to her place. And then we picked it up again this morning. She means well—"

"Don't make excuses for her."

"She thinks I've crossed the line with you," I reply, a response that's both honest and not quite the truth. "That I've lost my sense of perspective."

"Crossed whose line—hers?"

"No. Mine. But she isn't wrong. And I realized it last night. At dinner."

"What does that mean?"

I pull in a breath, as if bracing for the cauterization of a wound, and then I say it. "It means we have to stop this, Belle. Whatever this is. It has to end. Now."

Your face goes slack. "Because of her?"

"Because of us. Because of you and me and what will happen if this . . ."

"Affair?" you supply in a voice I hardly recognize.

"Yes, all right. Let's call it what it is. What do you suppose will happen if we're found out? You're the daughter of one of the richest men in the country, engaged to one of the most prominent young men in New York. And I'm . . ."

You tilt your chin up. "You're what?"

"A fool," I answer. "Involved with a woman who's about to walk down the aisle with another man. One whose sole redeeming quality—beyond a pair of broad shoulders and a mantel full of polo trophies—is his inclusion in his father's will. And you can stand there, glaring at me, as if I'm on the wrong side. Can you not see the irony?"

"I didn't choose Teddy. I never wanted him."

"You didn't say no, though, did you? You put his ring on your finger and smiled when they toasted the happy couple. I was there, remember?"

"Don't . . ." Your voice falters and your gaze slides to the diamond still glittering on your ring finger. "Please don't talk about that night."

I've struck a nerve and I'm glad. It feels good to have your fiancé out in the open at last, a flesh-and-bone man with a name, rather than a shadow we both pretend not to see. "Why shouldn't I mention it? It was the high point of the season. A posh and unforgettable night, I believe the Times called it."

"I wish I could forget it. Every minute of it." *You break off abruptly and shake your head.* "No, that's not true. Not every minute. Somewhere in the middle, there was you, studying me in your rented suit, smirking and seeing right through me."

"Not quite through you," *I correct.* "If I had, you'd hardly be standing here now. I would have known better—and we would have avoided a great deal of unpleasantness."

"Unpleasantness?" *You stare at me, stricken.* "Of all the words in your writer's repertoire, that's the one you chose at this moment?"

I drop my hands to my sides, shaking my head. I thought I could make the moment easier by wounding you, but there's no satisfaction in it. I soften my voice but make no move to comfort you. I don't dare. "We both knew it would end, Belle. We never talked about it, but we knew."

You swallow hard but manage a nod, acknowledging that much at least. "But why now? When we still have time?"

"When did you think it was going to end? Did you see us carrying on until the eve of your wedding? Perhaps even after?"

You stiffen at the suggestion. "Certainly not."

"No. Certainly not. But you assumed you'd be the one to pull the plug. And until you did, I was supposed to be satisfied with seeing you on the quiet. Playing games like we did last night. Dangerous games for both of us. And once upon a time, I might have been fine with that. But it's messier now. For a lot of reasons."

"It's always been messy, Hemi. Every walk, every picnic, every kiss has been messy. It never mattered—until now."

"It's always mattered. I just forgot."

You stand there, so steely. "I see. And it took Goldie, of all people, to remind you. But why kick you out of the love nest? She's getting what she wants. Me out of the picture."

"She didn't kick me out. I left. That's what set off the row to begin with. Me telling her I'd gotten my own place. She thought it was a bad idea."

"I'll bet she did."

"Not for the reasons you think. She thought I was making a mistake—with you. That this was all a game to you. And last night, I guess I finally saw it too. I'm trying to find my footing here, to do something worthwhile. It's why I came to the States. And for the first time in my life, I'm working on something important. I thought I could keep the two separate, but I can't. And I can't afford to get distracted. Not on this story."

"What's it about?"

"Your father."

You go still. *"My . . . What about my father?"*

"There are . . . stories."

"Stories you heard from Goldie?"

"Some were from Goldie, but not all. You told me yourself, there's been talk for years. Word is your father ran a proper racket back in the twenties. Whisky out of Canada. Rum from Bimini. Had some pretty unsavory friends in those days too. The kind who come in handy when you're involved in rough trade."

You've gone pale now. Not because I've told you anything you didn't already suspect but because I've confirmed it. You're not used to people telling you the truth. But you need to hear it now, because there may come a time when you'll be forced to choose sides, and when that time comes, you should have all the facts.

"Bribes," I continue evenly. *"Shakedowns, even an unsolved disappearance, though they could never prove the connection. He was always careful to stay above the fray. And now he's reinvented himself, converted all that hard-to-explain cash into stocks and bonds and built himself a proper empire. He's collected some powerful allies too—useful in getting him out of the occasional jam—though I suspect he keeps a few of the old ones around too. Just in case. He hides behind the veneer of a buttoned-up businessman, but underneath it all, he's just a thug with a closetful of handmade suits."*

Barbara Davis

"You had no trouble rubbing elbows with his friends last night. If he's so terrible, so dangerous, why drink his cognac and smoke his cigars? Why accept my invitation at all?"

"I accepted your invitation for the same reason you accepted Teddy's ring—because it was to my advantage. Your father appears to have taken a shine to me. He thinks I might be . . . useful."

You eye me warily. "Useful how?"

"He wants me to do a story for the Review.*"*

"What kind of story?"

"A PR piece to help polish up his image."

"And is that what you're planning to write? A piece to . . . polish him up?"

"No."

"But you are going to write something?"

"Yes."

"Something . . . not nice."

"I'm going to write the truth, Belle, wherever that takes me."

"And now that you've gotten your foot in the door, you're through with me."

"Don't put it like that."

"How should I put it?"

"Your father isn't a man to cross. You told me so yourself. What do you think would happen if he found out I've been privately carrying on with his very publicly engaged daughter?"

"I see." You stand rigid, your chin elevated, your arms at your sides. "You're worried about me putting a crimp in your journalistic aspirations."

I'm expecting tears. I'm prepared for tears. But this icy version of you wreaks havoc with my willpower. I summon Goldie's words from this morning—her assertion that I've lost sight of what's important, that I'm in over my head. She wasn't wrong.

168

"I'm being honest, Belle. This is what needs to happen. For both of us. Before someone gets hurt."

Your eyes close briefly, as if to shut out my words. "Why are you doing this?"

I guard my expression as I absorb the question and steel myself for what I know will come next. I won't be made to feel guilty. Not over you. Not over any of it. Not when you're prepared to marry another man. At least you're not looking at me. I'm not sure I could go through with it if you were looking at me.

"Let's not play the whole scene, Belle. We both knew this day would come. You're stung that I've chosen the time and place rather than leaving it to you, but it's time we let each other off the hook, don't you think?"

You blink at me. "Off the hook?"

We're coming to it now, the part I've been dreading. The look of betrayal when you finally understand what I was really after—and why. But it's necessary, this truth-telling, to put the period to us. Because if I don't end it, you will. Maybe not today, but soon, and I prefer to take control of the moment.

"Four months ago, I was an outsider in your world, a bloke with the wrong clothes and a funny accent who'd come here to do a job. But first, I needed an entre, admittance to the kinds of parties your father and his sort throw. Goldie provided that, but only to a point. I needed a more . . . intimate contact." I swallow. Hard. "That's where you came in."

I see the denial creep into your expression, see you not wanting to believe what you've guessed I'm about to tell you. "What are you saying?"

"I'm saying that us meeting wasn't an accident. That there was a reason I turned up the night of your engagement party. I came to the States to write a story and I needed a way in."

"A story for Goldie?"

"She was in London visiting friends last year and we met at a lecture. We ended up going for a drink afterward and got to talking about corruption and politics and war. Your father's name came up at one point. She *already knew quite a lot about his past. What she really wanted to know about were his present-day activities. His plans."*

"So she hired you to help with that."

"Yes."

"And that night at the St. Regis, the flirting with me at dinner the following week, the kiss in the barn—that was about my father too?"

"Yes."

I watch your eyes go dark, like a bitter wind snuffing out a candle. You wanted me to deny it or to at least soften my response, but I promised myself I'd tell it all. Still, now that it's done, I feel as if a part of me has been severed.

Your silence threatens to undo me, and for a moment, I consider taking it all back and telling you the real truth—that it was true once but isn't anymore. That the story I'm working on has taken a turn I never saw coming, one I wish I didn't have to pursue. That I imagine abandoning the whole bloody business and taking you somewhere very far away. And then I remind myself—as Goldie reminded me last night and then again this morning—that you've made your plans and they don't include me.

If I don't speak now, don't finish what I've started, I never will. It'll sting for a while, like a slap you don't see coming—I've taken you for a ride and then tossed you aside—but you'll have Teddy to soften the blow and I'll soon be forgotten.

It helps to remember Teddy. I clear my throat and force myself to meet your gaze. "What we had—what we've been these last few months—has served a purpose for both of us."

Your eyes glitter with unshed tears. "Why are you doing this?"

I thought I could stand whatever you threw at me, but I was wrong. Suddenly, desperately, I need this to be over. "Belle . . ."

"None of it meant anything to you? All these weeks, all the afternoons? It was all for her? For Goldie? When you knew I loved you?"

Love.

The word slices into me like a blade. Neither of us has ever said it before. Me least of all. Instead, I've lived with the knowledge that one day, quite suddenly, it would be our last day. It would have been pointless, not to mention foolhardy, to allow my heart to wander onto such dangerous ground. Now, suddenly, the truth hits me squarely, inescapably. I've loved you from the very first night, the very first look, the very first lie. I let myself believe I was in command of my emotions, that I could conquer them, starve them out of existence. Now I realize that was the biggest lie of all.

I feel unmoored suddenly, adrift now that I've abandoned all my pretenses. "I've been so careful," I say finally, absurdly. "I thought I could keep myself from feeling . . . that I could just beat you to goodbye."

"And now you have." You brush angrily at a fresh spill of tears, as if annoyed that you've allowed them to escape. "What a fool I've been. All this time, I thought . . . I believed you felt what I did."

Your words catch as you make a grab for your handbag. I reach for your arm, staying you. "I did. I do." When your eyes finally meet mine, wet and wide and full of hope, I feel myself falling into them, tumbling end over end. Dizzy. Free. Lost. "I do love you, Belle. I have since that first night, when I crashed your engagement party."

I pull you into my arms then, a man who knows he's irrevocably lost. Goldie was right this morning when she hurled her parting words at my back. I am in over my head. I was prepared to let you go when I left her this morning. As much for my sake as for yours. Now the idea seems unthinkable. You're the answer to a prayer I never thought to pray—and a threat to all my plans—but I'm not strong enough to walk away. I want you. In whatever way it's possible to have you, for however long it's possible to have you. Knowing it's a mistake, knowing it solves nothing. Knowing that one day we will stand here again, on the brink of goodbye.

Forever, and Other Lies

(pgs. 45–49)

November 5, 1941
New York, New York

I barely register the sound of my handbag knocking to the floor as you pull me against you. You wrap me so tightly, I can scarcely tell where I leave off and you begin. And I don't want to. Because it's right. This ache to be near you—to belong to you—has been a part of me since that first night, and now I know it's been a part of you too.

You love me.

There are no words after that from either of us. Your lips on mine, so feverish, so desperate, say everything that needs to be said. And everything that cannot. The promise you can't ask of me because I've already given it to another. The promise that for so many reasons, I'm not free to break. And yet in this feverish, spinning, exquisite moment, I know that I mean to break it—somehow—and to hell with the consequences.

We're both breathless when you pull away, and for a moment I'm afraid you've changed your mind. Then your eyes find mine and I see the question there, silent, needful. The yearning to finish what we've begun, to consummate, at long last, all we've been pretending not to feel.

I press my hand into yours and allow you to lead me down the hall, past your suitcases and your typewriter, and into the bedroom. There's a window looking out onto an alley and an imposing row of brick buildings. The afternoon light slanting in feels cold and stark, a glaring reminder of the world outside.

And then you pull the curtains closed and, without a word, set to work on the buttons of my gloves. It's a startlingly intimate sensation, your fingers, warm and careful, peeling back the fabric. Suddenly I feel vulnerable and exposed, as if my skin is being removed.

I'm trembling and breathless, terrified of I know not what. And yet I never once think to stop you as you slowly undress me and press me back against the spread. We've been inching toward this brink for so long, always careful to pull back at the last second, to preserve some pretense of decency, but there will be no half measures today, no stopping at the water's edge. Decency be damned.

There's an urgency in your touch, a well of pent-up need given free rein at last. I respond instinctively, meeting your hunger with my own, unafraid suddenly, unashamed. The power of it—of us—is like nothing I've imagined. I'm both powerful and powerless, conqueror and conquered. Whole in your arms in a way I never thought possible and, at the same time, utterly shattered as we hurtle headlong over the precipice together. And in that moment, there can be no going back. I'm yours forever. Irrevocably. Indelibly.

I awaken to the sound of your breathing, deep and rhythmic beside me. The light has changed and shadows stretch up the wall and across the carpet. I run my eyes around the room but there's no clock anywhere. I have no idea what time it is or how long we've been asleep.

Your arm is curled about my waist, heavy against my ribs. The weight of it, the fact of it, fills me with a savage rush of joy. This is what it would feel like to be your wife, to wake each morning in a tussle of warm sheets, your breath on the back of my neck, your chest fitted snugly against the curve of my spine. I envision breakfast in bed on the weekends. Eggs and toast on a tray with your paper. And coffee. I'd have to learn to make coffee. Or perhaps you prefer tea. I've never thought to ask.

The realization brings me to earth with a bump. There are so many things I don't know about you, so many things you don't know about me. The little intimacies that develop with time, the things that bind lovers inextricably together, are no part of what we have. In fact, we're still strangers in many ways, two people who stumbled blindly into love, never once imagining a happily ever after.

The thought is still with me when I feel your breathing change. Your arm cinches about my waist and you pull me closer, nuzzling the curve of my shoulder. Suddenly I'm frightened, terrified that this fierce and fledgling joy will wither in the cold glare of reality.

I turn over, cupping your face in both hands, committing your features to memory, as if forgetting them would ever be possible. The subtle cleft at the base of your chin, the crease between your brows that never quite disappears, even when you laugh, the small crescent-shaped scar at the corner of your eye, the result of a childhood fall from a swing. All of it seared on my memory even now, the loss still so raw, it stings.

You cover my hand with yours and the crease between your brows deepens. "What is it? What's wrong?"

"Nothing," I say softly. "I'm just . . . memorizing your face. In case."

"In case . . . what?"

I shrug and reach for the sheet, pulling it up over my shoulders. "I just can't believe I'm here. That we're here—together. It feels like a dream."

"It is a dream," you murmur, your voice still thick from sleep. "One I've had more times than I can count. Only this time, you didn't disappear when I opened my eyes."

You kiss me then, a kiss full of tenderness and wonder. But it turns into something else for me, something fierce and fearful. I cling to you, desperate to prove to myself that it's real, that we're real.

We make love again, more slowly this time, exploring tender topography missed in our first frenzied joining. We cherish each other, every touch and taste and murmur. We whisper promises as the afternoon ebbs into evening. Words like forever *and* tomorrow *and* always. *And we mean them when we say them. Or at least I do. Because I haven't begun to think any of it through. What it will mean. What it will cost. Where it all might lead.*

In the days that follow, we spend every moment we can steal together. I invent outings with girlfriends I haven't seen in months, purchase tickets for concerts I don't attend, invent shopping excursions for clothes I neither need nor want, all to create plausible alibis for my increasingly frequent absences from home. When Cee-Cee assumes I've begun shopping for my trousseau, I don't correct her. I nod and smile, all while trying to work out how to extricate myself from my engagement. Because I will extricate myself. Just as soon as Teddy and his father return from their latest trip to wherever the horses are running this week. For now, though, my time is my own, and it's easy to put those plans off and just enjoy these sweet stolen moments with you.

I try to be at the apartment as often as I can when you come home from work. I use the key I keep secreted in my compact to let myself in, and pretend to ignore the looks I sometimes get from the woman who lives across the hall. The look that says, "I know what you're up to, popping in and out in the middle of the day." *I suppose she does, but it's nothing to me. She's not likely to be part of my father's circle.*

I play at cooking now and then, to surprise you, but I'm not very good at it. That's what comes of having people do for you your whole life. Still, you never complain. We eat together in your tiny kitchen and listen to the news on the radio, keeping careful track of events in Europe and Britain. We do the dishes when we're through, side by side, like proper newlyweds. But we aren't proper newlyweds. We aren't proper anything. And when the dishes are finally put away and the news program ends, I must gather my hat and gloves and kiss you goodbye.

And rehearse a new alibi on the way home.

It's getting harder and harder to leave you, to return to my cold life and my cold family. I'm still wearing Teddy's ring, the symbol of my broken promise. Except that I haven't broken it yet, not officially—not at all, actually—and Cee-Cee has begun to harangue me about setting a date. Teddy, on the other hand, seems in no great hurry to get down the aisle. His telegrams come infrequently and are blessedly brief when they do, perfunctory and almost comically polite.

Perhaps there's a woman like me somewhere, who keeps a key hidden in her compact and slips in and out of his life when she can manage it. I certainly wouldn't begrudge him if there were. Not that he's ever been particularly discreet about such things. Nor, as a man, is discretion demanded.

I keep hoping he'll be the one to break it off, that he'll find someone he prefers or simply acknowledge that we'll never be happy together, but why would he? He loses nothing by marrying me. I, on the other hand, will lose everything. And so I must be the one to end it. And I will.

The how is the thing. And the when.

Forever, and Other Lies

(pgs. 50–56)

November 20, 1941
New York, New York

Teddy has come home.

We've seen each other twice. Both occasions were awkward, since he seemed even less eager to see me than I was to see him. I've realized, to my relief, that he won't put up much of a fight when I tell him I've changed my mind. It's my father's wrath I fear. I need to be with you like I need my next breath, but the thought of defying my father terrifies me.

And so I do nothing.

You're growing impatient, starting to lose faith in me. You haven't said so directly, but I'm aware of a growing friction between us, offhand remarks, sullen silences when Teddy's name unavoidably comes up. You don't understand my reticence. I don't blame you. I barely understand it myself, except to say I'm afraid.

And then one afternoon—you remember it, I'm sure—it all spills out.

We've spent an especially passionate afternoon together, but it's time for me to leave. There's a dinner later—one you'll attend as a guest of my father—and I'll need time to dress. Teddy will be there, too, with me on his arm. It won't be the first time you and I have had to navigate such an evening. We've managed it before. But you've been brooding all afternoon and I sense a storm gathering as I collect my clothes and begin to dress.

You're still in bed, propped up on one elbow, watching me in the mirror with a sulky frown.

"I'm sorry," I say to your reflection. "I know tonight will be awkward."

"Is that what you think? That it will be awkward? Watching the woman I love—the woman I've just made love to—hanging on the arm of another man, fielding questions about her upcoming wedding?"

I turn from the mirror and face you. "I know, Hemi. I do. And I promise—"

"Don't." You throw off the sheets and sit up, reaching for your trousers. "Don't promise me anything, Belle. We both know they're just words. But tonight is the last time. I'm done with whatever game it is you're playing."

Your words pierce me like darts. I've been expecting something, but not this. "You think I enjoy having to pretend you're just some stranger in my father's house? To smile my most charming smile and ask if you need your drink refreshed? I'll remind you that you lied to me to gain access to my father. Now you've gotten exactly what you want and it's my fault."

"Don't make this about me, Belle. You know I'd walk away from all that without batting an eye."

"Then why haven't you?"

"Why should I, when you won't? You've given up exactly nothing for me."

"It isn't that simple, Hemi. You know it isn't."

"But it is, Belle. You tell your father you're not marrying Teddy and you walk away. We'll leave New York. Hell, we'll leave the country if you want. But you have to put it in motion. And you won't. Because when you weigh what you'd be giving up against what you'd be getting, the scales don't balance. I come up short."

"Do you honestly think that's what's holding me back? Money?"

"Not just money, no. But you're used to a way of life I can never give you, and the longer we go on, the more you're starting to realize it."

I blink at you in the mirror, bristling, though I have no right to be angry. "Realize what?"

"That the adventure has run its course. It was exciting in the beginning, the newness of it, the risk of being caught, but the excitement is starting to wear off, and all you're left with is a dingy apartment and a man with limited prospects."

And just like that, my anger is suddenly justified. "You think this has been some kind of experiment? A game?"

"I didn't say that."

"But you did," I fire back. "You said exactly *that."*

I turn away and resume dressing. Moments later, I hear you step into your trousers and leave the room. Tears sting my eyes. I bat them away, too wounded to let you see them. That you could accuse me of such a thing reminds me again how little you know me—and how little I know you.

I never told you how I came to be standing in the ballroom of the St. Regis Hotel the night we met, but I'll tell you now, so you'll understand. Had I been paying better attention, I might have seen what was coming, though what I could have done to prevent it, I still don't know.

It began as so many things in our world did back before my father's fall from grace, with a dinner and a great deal of planning. One night, seemingly out of the blue, I came downstairs to find Teddy and his parents among my father's dinner guests. Teddy lifted his glass as I entered the room, flashing an almost apologetic smile. We grew up in the same circles, largely at a distance, but we'd attended a few dances together and went to the movies once or twice when he was home from school. There were a few kisses of the chaste, good-night variety, but it never went beyond that. He was handsome but too brash for my taste, and not especially bright, as you yourself have pointed out. Nor had he ever expressed any serious interest in me. It was our fathers who were close. Partners in several large business ventures and members of all the same clubs.

My father spotted me as I came down the stairs and waved me over, all smiles as he introduced me to Teddy's mother, who, until that night, had never been invited to our home, as his darling girl. I nodded politely and shook her hand, a hollow sensation in the pit of my stomach, because I suddenly understood what was happening. But I had no intention of marrying Teddy. The moment dinner ended, I pleaded a headache and, to my sister's horror, excused myself for the remainder of the night.

The next morning, I paid for my folly. I was sternly scolded at breakfast for being rude to my guests. My father was not amused when I pointed out that Teddy and his parents were not my guests but his. I also informed him that I had no intention of marrying anyone. I was going to school to study art or education. I folded my napkin, then laid it aside and stood. My father stood, too, and slapped me so hard, I dropped back into my chair.

He'd never struck me before and he took an abrupt step back, as if he'd surprised himself. "You should be careful," he warned, his voice steely soft. "You've always had too much of your mother in you. Too silly and sentimental for your own good. I suggest that in the future, you try to be more malleable. It's spared your sister no end of heartache."

"Is it silly to want to love the man I marry?"

"What you want is of no consequence to me. You have a duty to this family, and you'll do it if you know what's good for you. End of discussion."

Only it wasn't the end. Suddenly I blurted the question I'd always wanted to ask. "Is that the only reason you married Mother? Out of duty?"

I knew I was on dangerous ground, but I couldn't help myself. For a moment, his eyes softened and slipped from mine, refocusing on the far end of the table, where my mother used to sit. But the softness vanished as abruptly as it had come, replaced by something ominous and rigid.

"You are never to speak of your mother to me again, do you understand? Not ever." He brushed the toast crumbs from his vest front and cleared his throat. "As for the other business, it's been decided. Your future in-laws are planning a dinner for the two of you next week. There will be no headaches, no scenes, no theatrics of any kind. You will be attentive and charming and keep his featherbrained mother entertained while her husband and I see

to a bit of business. I don't want to have to persuade you, but I will if you push me. Are we clear?"

I stared at him, stunned. That's what my life was to him, my future. Business. There were a hundred things I longed to throw back at him. Instead, I nodded and looked away.

"I'm head of this house," he continued, his tone milder, almost magnanimous: a man who knew he'd won. "We each have a role to play in this family. Yours is to marry the man I choose for you, and I've chosen Teddy. He's made of the right stuff. Your children will be made of the right stuff."

I was about to protest when Cee-Cee caught my eye, sending a silent warning. I bit my lip and said nothing, fuming as my father turned and walked out of the room.

When we were alone, Cee-Cee reached for the coffeepot, refilled her cup, and dropped in two cubes of sugar. "There now," she said, stirring absently. "That wasn't so difficult, was it?"

I smothered a groan, her superior tone almost more than I could bear. "Do you never get tired of taking his side?"

"It's the only side to take in this house. I'd have thought you'd understand that by now."

"I won't end up like you, a marionette who jumps every time Father pulls your strings."

Cee-Cee sipped her coffee with infuriating nonchalance, then carefully set the cup back in its saucer. "I fear you're in for a rude awakening, sister dear. You'll end up exactly like me. You heard him. What you want doesn't matter. All that matters is what you can do for him. You think you understand what's happening here, that it's about money and real estate—Father's empire—but it's bigger than that. And you need to watch your step."

"Is that supposed to scare me?"

She shrugged off the question as she casually slathered a piece of toast with marmalade. "He was right, you know. You are just like her. And you'll end up just like her if you're not careful. Why keep bringing her up when you know he doesn't want to hear it?"

"It's as if he's trying to pretend she never existed. To erase her. Doesn't that bother you?"

"What do you expect him to do? Keep resurrecting her? Pretend she didn't bring shame on this family with her histrionics?"

"She was sick!"

Cee-Cee rolled her eyes as she tossed the remnants of her toast onto her plate. "How can you be so naive? There's a way things work in the real world. A harsh way, perhaps, but once you accept it, things get . . . easier. That's what Father meant when he used the word malleable. *Accepting the way things work."*

"What things?"

"Everything in life has a pecking order. The strong go to the head of the line, while the weak must give way. Helene was weak."

Her response, so blank and cool, sickened me. "You call her Helene. Like she was some stranger who used to live in our house? She was our mother."

Cee-Cee huffs and rolls her eyes toward the ceiling. "Honestly, you never learn. Families like ours have a duty to future generations, to preserve our way of life, who we are, what we've built. Father has a plan for us. For all of us."

"And if I choose not to be part of his plan?"

"Haven't you been listening? There is no choosing. We're pieces on a chessboard, you and I. Nothing more. He'll move us wherever and however he likes, and he won't stop until he has all the pieces." She pushed back from the table and stood, then hesitated, pinning me with a frosty glare. "You should also know that on occasion, a few pieces have gone missing. Troublesome pieces that didn't matter much to anyone. Don't ever think he won't do it to you."

She walked out then, leaving me to ponder her warning.

A month later, I met you at the St. Regis. You with your slick smile and rented evening clothes. Even then, you were judging me, wondering how in God's name I'd let it happen.

I was wondering too.

NINE

ASHLYN

To lose oneself in the pages of a book is often to find oneself.

—*Ashlyn Greer,* The Care & Feeding of Old Books

October 7, 1984
Rye, New Hampshire

Ashlyn slowed the car and turned onto Harbor Road, a narrow stretch of gravel and crushed oyster shells, curving toward the open harbor. There was a small wooden bridge and beyond, a scattering of rooftops, one of which belonged to Ethan Hillard.

She proceeded over the bridge, past a couple on matching bikes, and began looking for house numbers. The road went farther than she thought, winding along the rock-lined shore for more than a mile. The houses were all on her right and varied in size and style, all sharing an absolutely stunning view of the harbor.

Ashlyn tried to imagine waking up to that glorious vista each morning. Blue sky, silvered sea, the flash of sun on bright white wings. How different the world must look to those who woke to such things. How lovely and clean. How easy.

Suddenly she felt out of place, a trespasser in this idyllic seaside community, and she considered turning around. She'd heard nothing from Ethan since her last phone message a week ago. What did she hope to accomplish by ambushing him at his home? Then again, what did she have to lose?

She had just rounded a deep bend when she spotted a mailbox with the number 58 on the side. She let her foot off the gas, hesitating briefly before pulling into the drive.

The house was large and stately, a classic two-story with a hipped roof, a central widow's walk, and a cupola facing the harbor. Everything looked as if it had just been painted, all clean gray and white, except for the front door, which was a whimsical shade of lemon.

There was a detached three-bay garage to the left of the drive but no sign of a vehicle anywhere. Ashlyn pulled *Forever, and Other Lies* from her tote, eyeing the yellow sticky notes peeking from between its pages. She'd spent several hours this morning writing out each question, then affixing it to the appropriate page. When that was done, she'd composed a polite note asking for his help one more time, then sealed both book and note in a protective plastic sleeve.

Now all she had to do was get the book into his hands, which meant temporarily relinquishing possession of it. Relinquishing the book, even temporarily, wasn't a decision she'd reached lightly, but Ethan had made it abundantly clear that he had no interest in possessing either of them for himself. She'd have to trust him.

Not exactly her strong suit, trust. But she didn't have much choice if she wanted Ethan's help. Before she could change her mind, she headed up the tiered stone terrace and rang the bell. After a second and then a third ring, she had still received no answer and reluctantly resorted to her backup plan, which was to leave the book in the mailbox.

She peered over her shoulder as she walked down the drive, aware that as an outsider in this tiny, well-heeled community, she would almost certainly be thought up to no good if she were spotted poking about in Ethan Hillard's mailbox.

When she was sure the coast was clear, she pulled back the door of the mailbox only to find it stuffed with junk mail and newspaper circulars. Maybe he hadn't been ignoring her after all. Maybe he was just out of town.

She eyed the house again, narrowing her focus to the clear glass storm door. If it was unlocked, she could slip the book between the two doors. It would be safe from any weather in its plastic sleeve, and there'd be no missing it when Ethan returned home, since he'd have to step over it to get in the house.

Tucking the book beneath her arm, she retraced her steps back up the drive. A tentative test of the storm door found it unlocked. She had just thrown another glance over her shoulder and was preparing to pull it back when the actual front door swung open.

"What are you doing?"

Ashlyn was so startled by Ethan's sudden appearance that she fumbled the book, nearly dropping it on the steps. "I was just . . . I didn't think you were home. I rang the bell but no one answered."

"So you thought you'd just let yourself in?"

"No!" She held up the book in her defense. "I was just going to leave this inside the storm door, then call and leave a message when I got back to the shop. I tried the mailbox, but it's full."

Ethan eyed the book, then looked at her, frowning. "It's illegal to go into someone's mailbox."

Ashlyn blinked at him. *Is it really?* "I wasn't going to *take* anything. I was just going to leave the book."

"Why?"

Ashlyn shot him a nervous smile. This wasn't going quite the way she'd hoped. "I have some questions. And I've learned some things since the night you came to the shop. I left you several messages but I never heard back."

"So you came to my house."

It sounded bad when he said it. Intrusive and a little bit creepy. "Not to *see* you. Well, I'd have to see you, but I wasn't planning to bother you. I wrote my questions down on Post-its and stuck them to the pages so you could look them over when you had time. If I had known you were here, I wouldn't have . . ." Ashlyn let the words dangle. He looked tired and annoyed, as if she'd caught him in the middle of something. "I'm sorry. It looks like I picked a bad time."

She was about to head back down the steps when he stopped her. "I never got your messages. That's why I didn't return your calls. I've been holed up with the phone unplugged for the last few days. I'm not sure how many. I've lost track at this point." He paused, scrubbing a hand through his hair. "What's today?"

"Sunday."

He nodded wearily. "A week. Good grief."

She saw it now, the shadow of stubble along his jaw and clothes that looked like they'd been worn for several days. "You've been writing?"

"I promised my editor a look at the first five chapters by next week and it's not going well. I can't seem to get the thing off the ground." He raked back his hair, leaving it standing on end. "Sorry for barking. I'm not good without sleep."

"I'm the one who should be apologizing. I'm sorry about disturbing you while you were working."

Ashlyn was waiting for a response when she realized Ethan's attention had drifted away. She turned, following his gaze, and spotted a plump woman in a lavender tracksuit hovering at the end of the drive with an equally plump springer spaniel. At first glance, it appeared she was having trouble with the dog's leash, but a closer look suggested her attention was actually trained on them.

"That's Mrs. Warren," Ethan said. "Our one-woman neighborhood-watch committee." He smiled tightly, offering the woman an almost comic wave. "I used to steal pickles from her backyard when I was a kid.

Whole jars snatched right off her picnic table. She told my mother I'd end up in prison. She's been keeping an eye on me since I moved back, waiting for me to slip up. You'd better come in before she pegs you as my accomplice. I'm sure she's already memorized your license plate."

Ashlyn was surprised by the invitation but happily followed him inside. At the last minute, she turned in the doorway to throw Mrs. Warren a wave.

Ethan snorted as he closed the door behind them. "That should have tongues wagging by morning."

"Sorry. Busybodies make me crazy. They love to peek through your blinds, but most of them wouldn't lift a finger if your house caught fire."

Ethan's brows shot up. "Is that the voice of experience speaking?"

"Something like that."

They were standing in a large foyer with polished parquet floors and an enormous mirror that caught the light from an overhead fixture of bronze and cut glass. Beyond a curved archway, Ashlyn caught a glimpse of a spacious parlor decorated in soft shades of cream and gray.

"What a beautiful room."

"Care for the full tour?"

She nodded sheepishly. "If you can spare the time."

Ethan said little as he led her from room to room, pointing out a feature here and there but otherwise leaving the rooms to speak for themselves. The house was a study in sophistication and style but with an unfussy cohesion running throughout. Smartly papered walls, fabrics in cool, sedate hues, furnishings chosen for comfort rather than show.

"It's all so beautiful," she said when they arrived back at the kitchen. "Like something out of *House & Garden* but still warm and welcoming."

"Thanks. My mother's doing. When she found out she was sick, she decided to redecorate the place from top to bottom. So everything would be shipshape for my father. And for me when he passed away. That's how she was, always thinking about everybody else. She drove herself crazy to get it right. She was afraid she wouldn't finish in time."

Ashlyn flashed back to the boxes she'd gone through before coming across *Regretting Belle* and the echoes she'd inadvertently picked up. Echoes belonging to someone who was sick and afraid of running out of time. Echoes she now realized had belonged to Ethan's mother.

"I'm so sorry," she said softly. "What was her name?"

"Catherine."

"She sounds lovely."

Ethan smiled, but there was sadness there too. "She was. And a real fighter. They gave her a year when she was diagnosed. She hung in for three."

"And she spent them making sure things would be easier for you and your dad when she was gone."

"That's who she was. She made dozens of lists, phone numbers for all the neighbors, who to call to fix this or that, where she kept the important papers. She even made the housekeeper swear to stay on and look after my father. Now she looks after me. Or tries to."

Ashlyn managed a smile, but she couldn't help comparing the choices her mother had made in the wake of her diagnosis to those of Catherine Hillard, who had done everything in her power to ensure those she loved were looked after. She had chosen to stay. Chosen to fight.

They had wandered back to the kitchen now. Ethan pointed to the stove, where a large pot sat on the back burner. "Can I interest you in a bowl of seafood chowder?"

"You made chowder?"

"Does that seem so impossible?"

"I didn't mean it like that. It's just that Daniel was hopeless in the kitchen. I doubt he could have found a soupspoon, let alone make actual soup."

"Daniel's your ex?"

"Almost ex," she corrected awkwardly. "He died before our divorce was final."

"An accident?"

Ashlyn looked away. She hated the question. Mostly because she never knew quite how to answer. "He was hit by a car. A truck, actually. Four years ago."

"Damn. I'm sorry."

"Thanks."

A silence fell, growing weighty as the seconds ticked by. Ethan stepped to the stove and lifted the lid from the soup pot, peering at the contents. "In the interest of full disclosure, I didn't actually make the chowder. Penny, my inherited housekeeper, brought it by this morning. She's convinced I'll starve to death if she doesn't feed me at least twice a week and I've stopped trying to convince her she's wrong. Her chowder's practically legendary and there's always enough for an army." He paused, lifting his brows. "I'm happy to share."

"No. Really. I didn't come to make a pest of myself." Ashlyn pulled the book from beneath her arm and laid it on the butcher-block counter. "I'll just leave this if that's all right. Maybe you can look at the pages I marked and the questions I jotted down."

Ethan eyed the book with its yellow sticky notes. "What kind of questions?"

"About Goldie Spencer, mostly."

"Who's Goldie again?"

"I mentioned her the night you came to the shop, but I only had a nickname then. Her real name was Geraldine Spencer. She inherited her father's newspaper business when she was just twenty-one and used it to expose corruption. Hemi used to work for her, although it's starting to look like their relationship went deeper than that. And there's a new name I'm hoping might be familiar. Steven Schwab. It's all on the sticky notes, which are attached to the corresponding pages. And there are some photocopies at the back. Pictures I hoped might be familiar."

Ethan removed the book from its protective sleeve and ran a thumb over the protruding yellow Post-its. "That's a lot of notes."

"I know. And I know you don't really care about the books, but I was hoping you could clarify some of the things I've discovered."

"All right," Ethan said grudgingly. "I'll take a look. But chowder first. I'm starving. We can talk while we eat. Can you make a salad? The stuff's in the crisper. You might want to shuck the jacket, though."

Ashlyn nodded as she peeled off her jacket, then stepped to the fridge.

Ethan flipped on the stove and pulled a wooden spoon from a nearby drawer. "You said you have questions about some new things you learned. What kind of things are we talking about?"

Ashlyn ran through her mental list of questions. There were so many she hardly knew where to begin. "Marian mentioned writing poetry when she was a girl. I was wondering if any of her poems might still exist. I was also hoping you'd be able to scare up an old photo or two."

Ethan shrugged. "I don't know anything about poems. Marian wasn't really on my radar growing up, but there might be some photos somewhere. I'm curious about the crusading newspaper heiress, though. Goldie, was it?"

"That's the name she went by. Apparently, she was quite something. Broke all the rules and never apologized for any of it. She may also be the reason Belle and Hemi split. Which brings us to Steven Schwab."

Ethan pulled a pair of bowls from a nearby cabinet and set them beside the stove. "Who's Steven Schwab?"

"He might be the man who broke your aunt's heart. Or he might not be. It's a long story."

"Then we'd better open some wine. Red or white?"

"I don't care. You pick."

What was happening? She'd come to drop off a book. Now Ethan was opening a bottle of Malbec and she was making a salad. And yet it felt strangely good, almost comfortable, despite the unfamiliar surroundings. Maybe he was just glad for the distraction. Whatever the reason, she had his attention and she planned to make the most of it.

TEN

ASHLYN

As with all rare things, regular restorative care is essential. Chronic neglect may result in weakening, warping, or other persistent vulnerabilities.

—*Ashlyn Greer,* The Care & Feeding of Old Books

They ate side by side at the counter, heads bent over the photocopied articles Ruth had dug up, including the piece bearing Steven Schwab's photo. Ashlyn elaborated on her suspicions that Hemi and Goldie had been involved romantically, as well as her reasons for suspecting that Hemi and Steven Schwab were one and the same.

Ethan listened attentively, interrupting now and then to ask a question. His interest was a pleasant surprise, but as she moved on to thornier territory, she reminded herself to tread carefully. Martin Manning was a part of his past, his family. And family was family, no matter what Ethan liked to pretend.

"I hate to ask this, but do you remember your father ever mentioning that Martin may have been involved in anything . . ." She paused, searching for a delicate way to say it. "Less than aboveboard?"

Ethan frowned. "No, but I'd hardly be shocked. Are we talking about white-collar stuff?"

"More like running liquor during Prohibition. Hemi mentioned it to Belle and I got the impression that Marian already knew. I don't think he was ever arrested for it, but it sounds like your great-grandfather had a pretty colorful past. There were other things, too, things about the war."

"Like?"

"Like maybe he was rooting for the wrong side."

Ethan scowled. "I certainly never heard that or anything about illegal liquor. But I wouldn't be surprised. I know there was some big scandal at one point. Essentially ruined him. I have no idea what it was about—my father was pretty tight-lipped about that stuff. My mother was a little freer with her opinions. I once heard her say Martin was so crooked, they'd have to screw him in the ground when he died."

"Sounds like there was no love lost there."

"None. And with good reason. Martin was dead set against my parents getting married. Corinne took his side, of course, and they ganged up on my father. They told him he'd have to choose. My mother or the family. So he chose."

"That's why you know so little about them."

He nodded. "By the time I was old enough to understand any of it, my father and Marian had already fallen out. My mother tried to make peace. She was fond of my aunt, and apparently the feeling was mutual. In fact, Marian told my father to run off and marry her the first time they met." He shook his head, grinning. "Mom swore it was just to get back at Martin and Corinne."

"She might have had a point. Belle was given a similar choice. Though in her case, I'm not sure it was ever really a choice. Martin appears to have been quite the bully."

"That's always been the general consensus."

"There was a son too—Ernest. Did you know?"

"The boy who drowned," Ethan said grimly. "Yeah, I knew. Sad."

"His mother—Marian's mother—never recovered from the loss. She blamed herself and eventually wound up in an asylum. She died there while Marian was still a girl."

"You mentioned that, but I don't think I ever heard it from my parents. All I knew was that she died before my father was born." Ethan paused, scrubbing a hand across his chin. "You know, it's funny. I would have bet my last dollar that I knew almost nothing about the history of either the Hillards or the Mannings, but I'm starting to realize I know a lot more than I thought. Growing up, it was just my parents and me. The rest of them were . . . ghosts. I hate to admit it, but I'm actually curious about what *else* I don't know."

Ashlyn couldn't help grinning. Curious was good. "Then you should read the books. At least Belle's. But I'd love your take on Hemi's side of things too—a man's take."

Ethan stood and began clearing away the bowls. "Is there a man's take versus a woman's take? Or is it just about taking sides based on gender?"

"That's not what I meant." Ashlyn slid off the stool and followed him to the sink with their silverware. "I just meant I'd like an objective opinion, someone to tell me if I'm reading things into the story that aren't actually there. When it comes to romance, I'm not the most objective person on the planet. Trust issues, you might say."

Ethan turned off the kitchen tap and reached for a towel to dry his hands. "Your ex cheated?"

Ashlyn nodded.

"Mine too."

It had never occurred to her that he might once have had a wife. "You were married?"

"Not for long. Just long enough."

"Sorry."

Ethan shrugged, managing something like a grin. "Just 'Another Somebody Done Somebody Wrong' song, right? And here I was thinking we had nothing in common."

Ashlyn smiled awkwardly, seeing the moment as an opportunity to press him again. "Will you read them?"

Ethan sighed. "You're not going to give up, are you? All right." He finished drying his hands and reached for the copy of *Forever, and Other Lies* with its protruding bits of yellow. "I'll read Belle's book. And I'll try to answer your questions. What haven't we covered?"

Ashlyn ran through her list again. They'd already covered quite a lot. But there were still things she was curious about, and she might never catch him in such an obliging mood again. "I'd like to know more about Marian's children. Where they are now. What they're doing."

Ethan sank back down on his stool and reached for his wineglass. "I can't help you there. I only met them once, when I was a kid. Marian had to go to some conference in Boston and they spent the weekend with us. I'm not sure how the subject came up, but the boy—I don't remember his name—was talking about his Bar Mitzvah, going on and on about all the presents he got. I told my mother I wanted a Bar Mitzvah, too, but she explained that Catholics don't have Bar Mitzvahs. I was quite put out."

Ashlyn registered this with some surprise. "I didn't realize Marian was Jewish."

"She wasn't. But her children were, so she converted. I know the papers made a big deal out of it." He went still suddenly. "Come to think of it . . ." He pushed back from the counter abruptly and stood. "Come with me."

"Where are we going?"

"To my father's study."

Ashlyn followed him up a carpeted staircase to the second floor, then down a long open gallery hung with softly hued watercolors. The last door on the left was open. She hesitated when Ethan entered, opting to linger in the doorway. It was a gentleman's room with dark carpeting, heavy furniture, and crowded bookshelves. At the center of the room, facing a large bay window, was an ornately carved desk littered with legal pads and several crumpled pages. An old IBM Selectric had been pushed to one side, a blank sheet of foolscap wilting over the keyboard.

"This is where you write?"

"Where I attempt to write, yes. It's also where my father wrote."

"Your father was a writer too?" *Like Hemi and* his *father.* "How wonderful."

He was rooting around in a closet now, hauling out a series of white office boxes. "He was a professor, actually, but his real gift was words. He had a way of shining a light on the things people didn't want to look at. How our government had sold its soul in the name of profit. How our humanity was slipping away. How prevalent bigotry still is in modern America and the need to guard against it."

"Sounds like he and Goldie Spencer would have been fast friends."

Ethan glanced up from the boxes and smiled. "Maybe."

Ashlyn ventured a little farther into the room. "What are you looking for?"

"Nothing, probably. But my father was an incurable pack rat—to my mother's dismay. I've purged a lot of it, but I haven't had a chance to go through this closet. I've been dreading it, actually. But maybe that's a good thing."

"Why good?"

"Before, when I was telling you about Marian's son, I remembered my parents standing in the kitchen, talking about a newspaper article she'd sent them, and how Corinne had been chapped at learning from a newspaper that her sister had adopted two Jewish kids."

Ashlyn's pulse ticked up. "You think you might have the actual article?"

"Probably not." He lifted the lid off one box, closed it, and set it aside. "My mother probably tossed it during the remodel—she threw out a ton of stuff—but it's worth a look. She obviously let him keep some of his hoard."

Ashlyn eyed the stack of boxes dubiously. "Do you even know what you're looking for?"

"A scrapbook. I only saw the thing a couple of times. My parents weren't terribly nostalgic when it came to my father's side of the family, but I remember it coming out every now and then. It was green leather. Or blue, maybe. Had those metal things on the corners. It would be a miracle if it was still here."

"Can I help?"

"Grab a box and start rooting. We could be here all night, though."

Ashlyn didn't care. She *had* all night. Grabbing a box from the stack, she dropped down onto her knees and lifted the lid. Inside, she found a stack of dog-eared legal pads, a half dozen financial ledgers in red and black, but no scrapbook. The contents of the next box yielded similar results. She was about to reach for a third when Ethan suddenly yelled, "Aha!"

"You found it?"

"I found it." He waved the scrapbook at her, dark green with corner tabs, exactly as he'd described it. "If the article's anywhere, it'll be in here."

Ashlyn held her breath as he laid the book on his knees and began paging through. He was close to the last page when he abruptly stopped.

"There," he said triumphantly, pointing to a small newspaper clipping at the bottom of the page. The clipping was creased down the middle and yellowed with age, affixed with tape that had gone a sticky brown.

Ethan read aloud. "*February 7, 1950. Manning Heiress Returns to US with War Orphans.*" He pointed, then handed Ashlyn the scrapbook. "That's her."

Ashlyn's heart skittered as she came face-to-face with Marian Manning. It was a black-and-white headshot, the kind taken by a professional. Three-quarter profile, head and shoulders. She'd seen similar shots from around the same time. Demure. Fresh-faced. Posed just so. But Marian Manning was none of those things. She met the camera lens as if it were a pair of eyes, challenging, unapologetic, fascinating.

No wonder Hemi had fallen head over heels that first night at the St. Regis.

Ashlyn traced her fingers over the photograph, feeling an instant connection. As if they'd met in another life—which, in a way, they had. "I feel like I know her."

She looked at the photo again. Belle . . . Marian . . . had a face now. A startlingly beautiful face. And an entirely new layer to her story. A mother and a Jewish convert. Choices she had made after losing Hemi. Perhaps to fill the empty place left by his loss. She returned her attention to the article itself, reading aloud.

February 7, 1950 (New York)—Miss Manning surprised all of New York this week, returning unannounced to the States with a pair of newly adopted war orphans in tow: a brother and sister, ages approximately 7 and 5, whose names are not currently known. According to one source who declined to be named, that surprise extended to her own family, who were not made privy to her plans. Miss Manning left the US after the war and has spent the last three years in France, where she became active in the cause of displaced children throughout Europe, many of whom lost entire families in the Nazi death camps. When asked about her decision to adopt despite being unmarried, she replied that she hopes to bring attention to the thousands of

children still awaiting placement around the world and
hopes to set an example for other American families.
She asks for privacy as she resettles her children in the
US and pledges to continue her work on behalf of war
orphans around the world.

"She led by example," Ashlyn said when she finished reading.
"What a wonderful and selfless thing to do."

"It was, though I'm guessing it was the last straw for Martin. He
couldn't have been happy about getting blindsided this way. Which I'm
beginning to suspect delighted Marian no end. I'm also guessing it's why
she ended up being cut out of the will and forbidden to set foot in the
house, though she had to know she was burning her bridges."

"That makes it even more amazing. She defied him, knowing what
the repercussions would be. She was brave."

"I think that's why she and my father hit it off. They were the only
ones to ever buck the system." Ethan took the scrapbook back then,
flipping to the first page. "Let's see what else might be in here."

There were several photos lying loose between the pages, the tape
that once held them in place no longer viable. Ethan studied them one
at a time, turning each photo facedown when he finished with it. "I
don't know any of these people," he said finally. "Aunts and uncles, I
suppose, and cousins. My father was one of four."

"Are any of his siblings still alive?"

Ethan shrugged. "Maybe. I know Robert was killed in Vietnam, shot
down during the Tet Offensive. One of his sisters died a few years ago. He
got a letter from an old college friend, saying he'd seen an announcement
in the paper. And that's all I know. They were never part of our lives."

He tucked the photos back between the pages and moved on, skip-
ping past photos and newspaper clippings that held no meaning for
him. Suddenly he stopped and pointed to a photo of an unsmiling

woman with a fringe of heavy bangs. Beside her stood a tall man with an angular face and small, dark eyes. He, too, was unsmiling.

"I think that's Corinne and her husband. I don't know his name either. He died when my dad was a boy. A lung thing, I think."

"George," Ashlyn supplied. "His name was George."

Ethan cocked an eye at her. "It's weird that you know that and I don't."

"His name is *all* I know. He isn't mentioned much in either book. What about Martin? When did he die?"

"Not too long after I was born. I don't know how. I just know he died and Corinne ascended the throne."

Ashlyn looked at the photo of Corinne—Cee-Cee, as she'd come to know her. She wasn't the beauty her sister was. In fact, there was little resemblance. But it would have been inaccurate to call her unattractive. Her face was square with wide-set eyes and a mouth that was full but ungenerous somehow. A face shaped by unhappiness.

"She doesn't look much like Marian," Ashlyn said.

"She looks exactly the way I imagined she'd look," Ethan said, scowling as he turned to the final page. "Hey. These are the kids. Marian's kids. I had no idea my parents had this. She must have sent it." He ran a thumb beneath the edges of the photo, carefully lifting it from the page, then flipped it over. "Zachary and Ilese on the beach. July 11, 1952."

"That's really them?"

"It is. They're younger here than when I met them, but it's definitely them. I remember him being a kind of prankster. Always giggling. Never sat still. She was the exact opposite. Always had her nose in a book. She barely said a word the entire weekend."

Ashlyn felt a sudden wave of empathy for the girl in the photo. She understood the need to retreat behind a book, to create a physical barrier between you and the world. She'd been doing it for years, seeking refuge in other people's stories.

She studied the children more closely. The girl—Ilese—was pale and small-boned and looked to be eight or nine. Zachary was clearly older, tall and toothy, already hinting at the heartbreaker he would almost certainly become.

"They're very different, aren't they? She's so pale, almost frail-looking. But the boy's a real charmer. It's a shame you lost touch with them."

"I'm not sure you could say we were ever *in* touch. They were both older than me. I barely remember them."

"Do you know where Marian settled when she came back to the States? Did she go back to New York?"

"I have no idea. I doubt it, though. I don't see her wanting to be anywhere near Martin."

"You didn't hear from her when your father passed away?"

"No. For all I know, she's dead too. And if she isn't, there's a good chance she doesn't know he died." He paused, closing the scrapbook and setting it aside. "Why?"

"I was just curious."

His eyes narrowed slightly. "You want to try to find her, don't you?"

Ashlyn didn't bother to hide her excitement. "Do you think it's possible?"

Ethan looked at her, clearly uneasy. "That isn't really the question, is it? The real question is, Would she *want* to be found? A couple of strangers showing up out of the blue, hoping to root through her past? Would *you?*"

"You're not a stranger. You're her nephew."

"I'm actually her nephew's *son*, and I've never laid eyes on the woman. That makes me a stranger."

"All right, maybe you are a stranger. But if she's alive, she hasn't forgotten Hemi. She'd want the books back."

"How do you know?"

Ashlyn looked away, briefly tempted to tell him about the echoes, then realized how strange it would sound. How strange *she* would sound. *Psychometry.* The term had the word *psycho* built in. She couldn't afford to scare him off. Not when she'd come this far.

"A woman doesn't forget the man who shatters her whole world, Ethan. Ever."

"All the more reason to leave it alone. She had her say when she wrote the book. We should let that be it."

Ashlyn watched as Ethan began to gather assorted papers and note-pads and place them back into the carton. She hated to admit it, but he had a point. Reading the books was one thing. She'd stumbled onto those by chance. But tracking down Marian Manning like a blood-hound was something else entirely. Did she really have the right to rummage through someone else's discarded heartbreak? Would she want someone rummaging through hers?

She stood reluctantly, aware that the evening was winding to a close. "I suppose you're right. But thanks for showing me the photographs. I'll at least have some faces to go with names. Can I help you put this stuff back in the closet?"

Ethan glanced around the room, then shook his head. "Nah. Now that I've dragged it all out, I might as well go through it. But not tonight. I'm wiped and I've got class in the morning."

"You're sure?"

"Yeah. It's time I got them sorted out. I'll walk you down."

Downstairs, Ashlyn slipped on her jacket and thanked him for dinner as they walked to the door. "I really didn't mean to horn in on you. Or cause a scandal with your neighbors. At least Mrs. Warren will have gone by now."

Ethan pulled back the door and peered toward the road. "I wouldn't be surprised to find her lurking in the bushes, checking to see if your car's still in the driveway. I'd be careful pulling out if I were you. I'll drop Belle's book off at the shop when I'm through with it."

"Or I can pick it up so you don't have to come all the way to Portsmouth." They were standing in the doorway now, the smell of the sea wafting about them on the damp night air. The moment felt the tiniest bit awkward, like the end of a first date, which it absolutely was not. She fumbled in her pocket for her keys. "I promise not to make a pest of myself and stay all evening."

"I appreciated the distraction, actually. It was nice to have someone to eat with for a change. I was a bit of a jackass that first night. I'm glad I got a chance to redeem myself."

Ashlyn shook her head, laughing. "I can't say I blame you. You didn't know me from Adam, and the whole thing did sound pretty improbable. Anyway, I better go. I've got some reading to do."

"Let me guess, Hemi's book?"

"When I left off, things were starting to get a little bumpy. I'm hoping things smooth out between them."

"Except we know they don't."

"Right," Ashlyn conceded grimly. "We know they don't. Anyway, good luck with your writing." She was halfway down the drive when she turned back. "Is it really illegal to open someone's mailbox?"

"I have no idea. But it sounded good."

"Would you have actually called the police and had me arrested?"

His laugh drifted down the drive. "No. I can't speak for Mrs. Warren, though."

As Ashlyn pulled out of the driveway and headed down Harbor Road, her thoughts were already on Belle and Hemi and the argument they'd had about Belle's reluctance to stand up to her father. Had it been the beginning of the end for them, the first fraying of their doomed romance? Or had they made up only to separate again later? The only way to know was to keep reading. Only this time she'd have a face to go with the words.

Regretting Belle

(pgs. 66–72)

21 November 1941
New York, New York

I've just finished making coffee when I hear your key slide into the lock. I reach for a second cup, set it on the table next to this morning's paper—and wait.

I must say I was surprised when you called to say you were on your way over. I didn't think you'd have the nerve to look me in the eye. But then maybe that was the plan all along, a way to tell me without actually telling me. Perhaps you were afraid I'd make a scene, plead and rail that I'd never let you go. You needn't have worried. I won't chase after you. If you're determined to sell yourself to a man who isn't worthy of you—and it appears you are—then go.

You're nearly perfect when you finally walk into the kitchen, looking like a fashion plate in your smart tweed suit and new hat. It's been snowing on and off all morning and a few flakes still cling to your collar, leaving dark flecks of moisture as they melt. As usual, you're flawless.

For a moment, I regret not putting on a shirt or shoes. What must I look like, standing here in nothing but trousers and an undershirt, my hair still wet from the shower? Then I think—no. It's fitting that this is how you'll remember me, proof that you made the right choice after all.

You stop just inside the doorway and stand very still, as if perplexed by my lack of greeting. I've been rehearsing my first words to you for more than an hour, but somehow I can't make myself say them. I've been dreading this day for so long, since the first time I kissed you, and now that it's come, I'm not prepared.

"Say something," I manage finally.

You frown. "What?"

"Presumably, you've come here to say something to me. Say it."

"I don't . . . What?"

"In fact, you could have just told me over the phone and saved yourself the cost of the meter."

You look me up and down, as if I'm a stranger. "Hemi, what's the matter with you?"

I cross to the table and pick up this morning's paper. Your photo—and Teddy's—looks up at me from the page, along with the headline: WEDDING OF THE SEASON SET FOR JUNE. *I've committed the particulars to memory by now. Church of St. Paul and St. Andrew . . . Waldorf Astoria . . . in a gown designed by English-American couturier Charles James.*

"Congratulations," I say, pushing the paper into your hands. "A June bride. And a reception at the Waldorf. How nice for you."

You stare at it and then at me. "I didn't . . . Hemi, I had nothing to do with this."

Your cheeks have gone a hot, splotchy pink, though I suspect that has more to do with the shame of being caught than with any real outrage. "You're saying the New York Times *ran a story about your upcoming nuptials without your say-so?"*

"Yes!"

"They just made up a date? And a venue?"

Your mouth works silently as you fumble for a response, your face growing more flushed by the minute. "It wasn't me, Hemi. I swear to you." You stare at the headline again, then finally look up at me. "This has Cee-Cee's fingerprints all over it. She's been nagging me for weeks. She obviously thought she could just give them a date and once they printed it, I wouldn't be able to back out. I'll kill her."

I eye you with folded arms, skeptical of your outrage. "What business is it of your sister's when you get married?"

"You still don't understand. None of this is about me. It's about a merger my father's trying to engineer with Teddy's father. But Teddy's parents are getting antsy. Apparently they've made some comments about me dragging my feet."

"And Teddy? Is he getting antsy?"

"Teddy?"

You seem confused by the question, as if you've forgotten him in all of this. "Your fiancé," I remind you coolly.

You close your eyes, sighing wearily. "We've barely seen each other since he and his father got back. His choice as much as mine. He's never said so, but I don't think he's any more eager to say 'I do' than I am. It's our fathers who are hell-bent on getting us down the aisle."

"And apparently they're going to get their way."

You glance at the article once more, then toss the paper on the table. "No, they're not."

"So you've been saying."

"Hemi . . ."

"Do you have any idea what it felt like to open up the paper this morning and see that headline? To realize you've just been stringing me along?"

"Hemi, I promise you—"

"You're always full of promises, Belle."

"Because I mean them."

"Then call the paper. Right now."

"What?"

"Call the Times and tell them they've got it wrong. Demand that they print a retraction. One that quotes you."

You stare at me as if I've just asked you to walk down Fifth Avenue without your clothes. "I can't do that. Not yet. I need more time."

"Time for what?" The words erupt before I can check them, ringing off the kitchen walls. "When will it be time? When you're halfway down the aisle?"

"That isn't fair!"

"Who isn't it fair for? For Teddy? Your father? What about me, Belle? How long am I supposed to wait? I'm tired of playing the fool. I've tried to walk away, to give you an out, but you keep reeling me back in. How many times am I supposed to fall for it?"

Your eyes pool with tears. You look away, your voice suddenly ragged. "What do you want from me?"

And suddenly I see it, the toll all this has been taking on you. You've become the prize in a game of emotional tug-of-war, and I've been too busy nursing my own ego to see just how badly you've begun to fray.

I reach for you, pulling you into my arms. "I want you to marry me, Belle. I want you to walk away from everything—I want us both to walk away—to live in a tent if that's all we can afford and subsist on hamburgers and scrambled eggs. But most of all, I don't want you to be afraid anymore."

You're weeping softly now, all your weight against me. "It isn't that simple."

"But it is," I tell you softly. "We'll just go away. Tomorrow. Now. All you have to do is say yes."

When your eyes lift to mine, I see a glimmer of promise, of hope. "What about the big story you're working on?"

"To hell with the story. Goldie can get someone else to finish it. By the time the thing goes to print, we'll be long gone."

"Where?"

"Who knows? Who cares? Just say yes."

"Yes," you say, and your smile makes my chest feel like it will burst. "Yes, I'll run away with you and live in a tent."

~

A week later, we've begun making plans. We set the date for our departure to coincide with a trip your father has planned to Boston, which will give you a few weeks to prepare. I've already arranged the tickets, a sleeper car on the Broadway Limited. We'll stop in Chicago, find a justice of the peace, then spend a few days in the city, like proper honeymooners, before traveling on to California.

We talk about going to England when the war ends, back to where I grew up, but that's not safe at the moment. There will be time for travel later, time for everything. For now, we'll content ourselves with San Francisco, as far away from your father as I can get you for now.

It's delicious, this secret of ours. We're determined not to give the game away, each of us trying to carry on as if nothing has changed, but inside I'm fit to burst. I feel like a schoolboy, unable to concentrate on anything for more than ten minutes at a stretch, knowing we'll be away soon, just the two of us, beginning a new life together.

I've said nothing to Goldie. She'll be livid when I go. Without a word. Without a thank-you. She's been good to me, giving me this opportunity to prove myself. But lately I've started to worry that she's losing her objectivity, and I'm not sure I have the stomach for what comes next. The piece I've been working on has taken an unexpected turn in recent days. A somewhat disturbing turn, though our sources swear it's true. Still, it could end up being an elaborate ruse, some enemy of your father's looking to settle old business. No doubt he's collected his share of adversaries over the years.

I have a few weeks yet to decide how to tell you—or if I'll tell you at all. You've enough to deal with just now, and it may come to nothing. I almost hope it does.

It's hard to know where my professional loyalties end and my personal loyalties begin. It's precisely what Goldie warned me about the night we argued, and then again the next day, when I moved out. How careful we needed to be about personal entanglements getting in the way of the truth. We must always remember the greater good. Her constant mantra to me. But whose greater good?

Right now, I'm a man with one aim. To get you on that train and out of your father's clutches. I know how hard all this secrecy is. I'm a deceptive man by trade. Artifice, pretense, even outright lying when the need arises. It's part of the work I do. But you're different. All your life, you've had loyalty—to your father, to the family—drilled into your head, and here you are, planning the ultimate betrayal. No note. No phone call. No word of any kind. Just gone—with me.

I'm not foolish enough to think your resolve never wavers. I'm keenly aware of how little I bring to the table, and that from time to time you must question the wisdom of what you're about to do—what you'll be giving up. But you assure me that you will give it up. And so I continue to count the days until we're away from this city with its gritty streets and bankrupt glamour, when it will finally be just the two of us.

I don't see you as often as I'd like. You're busy with your fake wedding plans. Sometimes days go by without a call, and then you appear with a bag of things for the trip. You've been buying up what you'll need, carefully, so as not to draw attention. Drugstore items, cosmetics, shoes, and simple clothes. Things you'll need for the life we'll have in California. That life won't include operas or dinner parties or anything requiring a couture gown.

Will you miss it? I wonder.

The thought comes creeping late at night, when I'm lying alone in the dark, wondering where you are and who you're with. I get up and turn on the lights, to chase away the doubts, and try to settle at my typewriter, reminding myself that you've promised to live in a tent if required.

How silly of me to have pinned all my hopes on a suitcase. You remember the one, don't you? A large leather affair bought especially for the trip? I had your new initials stamped in gold on the top. You teared up when you saw it and traced your fingers over the letters. We talked about all the places we'd go, all the adventures we'd have when the war was over. Paris and Rome and Barcelona. Do you remember it, Belle? The plans and the promises?

Do you remember us?

Regretting Belle

(pgs. 73–86)

5 December 1941
New York, New York

Well, we've got here at last, the end of our story—or very nearly the end. It was always inevitable, I suppose, that the spell we wove during those brief blissful weeks would unravel, that the day would come when you would be forced to choose between loyalty to your family and a life with me, but I never imagined that having made it, you would be able to walk away so cleanly. But time does funny things to the memory, twisting it into something convenient and crooked. And so I'll set the scene, in case the details have slipped your mind.

It's the day before we're set to leave, and I've taken a taxi to the Review *building to do the thing I'm dreading. I've been wrestling with my conscience for some time but made the decision only last night. I was tempted to handle the business by phone, but bad news is always best delivered in person, and the news I have to deliver today will come as very bad news indeed.*

Goldie is seated behind her desk, scanning a page of copy with a pencil caught between her teeth. She glances up, flashing me one of her too-wide smiles. "Well, if it isn't my star reporter. Tell me you're here to say it's finished. *I can't wait to see that bastard twisting in the wind."* Her smile slips suddenly, replaced with a frown as she registers my stony expression. *"Oh god. Please don't tell me there's a problem with the story."*

"The problem is with me, Goldie."

She looks confused but a little relieved too. *"Why? What's happened?"*

"I'm leaving the paper. Leaving New York, actually."

She stares at me, stunned. *"You're . . . what?"*

"This isn't what I want to do. I don't think it ever was. I wish I'd realized it sooner, but I realize it now."

She pushes to her feet, her face like a storm cloud. *"You can't be serious!"*

"But I am. I leave tomorrow. Chicago, then California."

There's a pause, a beat of confused silence as she glares at me. *"If this is a shakedown for more money—"*

"It's not a shakedown, Goldie. I'm just finished."

"You're about to deliver the scoop of the decade. You can't just bail! What about the story? Is it finished?"

"No. And it won't be."

"You said your sources were solid, that everything was checking out. What happened?"

"Nothing's happened. I just decided I can't go ahead with it. Even if I could absolutely prove what I've been told, which I probably can't, it's wrong to print it. Dragging up some poor woman's illness, putting an entire family through the wringer over something that might or might not have happened more than a decade ago. That isn't news. It's ghoulish speculation meant to bring a man to his knees, and as much as I despise the man in question, I've decided I don't want to be part of it."

"This is about her, isn't it? Your precious Belle. She batted those pretty eyes of hers and you've turned to jelly. I knew you had an itch for her, but I never figured you for a guy who'd be led around by his zipper. How could you be so gullible? When you know what's at stake! Her father is a dangerous man, a menace to everything this country's supposed to stand for, and he's

got his eye on a congressional seat. Your story would put an end to those aspirations."

"I don't dispute any of that, and I share your loathing, but you're going to have to find another way to make a case against him, because I can't put my name on the kind of story you're hoping to run. When you approached me about coming to work for you, I told you I wasn't interested in writing tabloid stuff, but that's exactly what this piece is shaping up to be—which is why I've decided to scrap it."

She sneers at me across the desk, hands splayed open on the blotter. "You got plenty interested when you met her, though, didn't you? Moved right in and cozied up to them all. Where were all your scruples then?"

Her words find their target, and for a moment, I'm silent. There's truth in what she says. I did cozy up to you. I convinced myself that it was in the interest of truth, that I was serving some high-minded journalistic purpose, but the lie collapsed the moment I kissed you.

"I'm not proud of any of it," I tell her quietly. "But when this started, I thought you wanted a legitimate piece, an exposé on a shady man with political aspirations. Instead, it's turned into a smear piece full of innuendo and lurid details no one's ever likely to prove."

She rolls her eyes and snorts out a laugh. "Don't tell me you've gone and caught yourself a case of conscience. I hope not, for your sake. It can be fatal in this business." Her eyes narrow suddenly, glittering and feline as they study me. "Or is it something else you've caught? Something with long legs and a trust fund."

I let the remark pass, refusing to take the bait. "That's my business."

"And the Review *is mine. This isn't a courthouse; it's a newspaper office. My job—and yours—is to print the news where we find it. What the public and the police choose to do with it is their business."*

"It's not my job anymore. That's what I came in to tell you. I'm done."

Her face hardens. "Well, I guess I finally know who you were saving yourself for. Not that there was ever much doubt."

"Goldie . . ."

"Get out." *She looks petulant suddenly, a child denied a toy that never really belonged to her.* "Clear out your desk and go. You won't be hard to replace. And when I do replace you, which will take about five minutes, it'll be with someone who understands the job. Go to California and write your damn novel. It had better be good, though, because you can bet your neck you're finished in this business."

I'm headed for my desk when I hear my name over the din. I turn to find her in her office doorway. "Leave your story notes. All of them. Your contacts and your sources. Every last scrap."

"It's my story."

"And it's my newspaper. I paid for the notes. The ink they're written with, the paper they're written on, and yes, the words themselves when you wrote them. I paid for it all."

I stare at her, disgusted that in spite of everything I've just said, she'd still consider pushing ahead with the story. I respected her once, embraced the things I thought she stood for, but she's become so caught up in her need to topple one man that she doesn't care who else she hurts in the process. I'm also aware that if she does manage to piece the story together again, my fingerprints will be all over it. Suddenly I'm very glad that I've kept the grittiest details to myself. I can't stop her from digging it all back up when I'm gone, but I won't help her do it.

"I'm sorry. I've shredded them and thrown them in the bin."

I turn and walk away then, headed for the bullpen and its messy warren of desks. I'm aware of the eyes fastened between my shoulder blades as I paw haphazardly through my desk, tossing some of the contents into a small paper sack, pitching others into the trash with unnecessary force. They'll be settling up on the office pool the minute I'm gone. I beat the last fellow but fell short of the one before him. I know what they thought when I came to work here, and I know what they'll be thinking as I leave. It doesn't make a damn's worth of difference to me.

Tomorrow, I start over. Clean. With you.

~

I'm not expecting to find you at the apartment when I return, but there you are on the sofa, a sheaf of papers clutched in your fist. You say nothing, just sit there with your face hard and white. It takes a moment to realize what's happened. You've found my story notes—the ones I told Goldie I'd thrown away.

"You wrote this . . ." Your hand trembles as you hold out the crumpled pages. "This . . . filth?"

There's nothing to say, no way to explain what you're holding without sounding like a liar. "You weren't supposed to see it. Not like this."

"Of that I'm certain."

Your glare is so full of venom, it's all I can do not to look away. But looking away would be the guilty thing to do. And so I stand there and let you pin me to the spot with those brittle amber eyes. "I was going to tell you tonight," I say evenly. "I was going to explain it all."

You launch up off the sofa, hurling the papers at me. They flutter through the air like a cloud of angry wings before rustling to a stop at my feet. "That's what you think I'm upset about? How I found out? The things I told you . . . All the times we talked about her . . . You were taking it all down, wheedling the details from me so you could twist them into something foul! How could you write these lies? Why would you write them?"

"Nothing's been twisted, Belle. I've learned some things . . . things you didn't know. I never meant for you to learn about them like this, but I swear, every word is true."

"I don't believe you!"

How can I blame you? The words sound clumsy coming out of my mouth, the plea of a man caught in his own lie. All the way home, I rehearsed how I would tell you, the words I would use and how I would begin, but I can't recall any of it now. I'm utterly unprepared for the force of your anger.

"Let me explain," I say feebly. "We'll sit down—"

"It says my mother was Jewish. And that my father . . . that he . . ."

"She was Jewish," I say quietly. "And he did." You've gone still now, your eyes wide and unfocused as you attempt to process what I've said. "I know it's hard to hear, Belle, but it's what happened. Your father had your mother put away. Not because she was sick but because he was ashamed of her. He'd begun making new friends—political friends—and he didn't want them to know he was married to a Jew."

"No." You shake your head repeatedly, as if my words are a swarm of bees you're trying to ward off. "My mother was French."

"Yes. She was French. She was also Jewish. Her maiden name was Treves. Her father, Julien, was the eldest son of a wealthy wine merchant from Bergerac. Her mother, Simone, was the daughter of a rabbi. There was a sister, too, Agnes, who was three years younger than Helene. Did your mother never talk about her family?"

You stand frozen, unblinking.

"Belle?"

"Yes," you say, clearly dazed. "There were pictures. An album full of pictures. But she never said anything. No one knew."

"Your father knew."

Your eyes sharpen suddenly. "How long have you known?"

"The story has been . . . evolving for some time."

"Before or after we met?"

I already see where you're going, but I can't lie "Before. At least some of it."

"I see."

"No, you don't. This isn't what it looks like. I promise you, I had no idea where this would lead when I got involved in this part of it."

"And how did you . . . get involved?"

"It started with a call from a friend of your mother's."

"Who?"

"I can't tell you that."

"Can't or won't?"

"Both."

"I'm just supposed to take your word?"

"There are rules about divulging sources. But I can tell you that the things she told us came from your mother's mouth. About how your father forced her to sever all ties with her family, how she was forbidden to speak a word of Yiddish or even French, ever, and the threats he made if she ever breathed a word about her heritage to you or your sister. But she found a way to tell you anyway. The stories she used to tell, the words that weren't real words. You remember telling me about them, the songs and the prayers. They were Hebrew words, Belle. They were prayers in Hebrew. It was her way of sharing her faith, her heritage, with you without your father knowing."

A pair of tears tracks down your cheeks. You close your eyes, absorbing the pain of it. I search for something to say, something that will comfort you and exonerate me, but there's nothing in the English language for this.

"I'm so sorry, Belle."

But you're not interested in my apology. Your face has gone hard and blank. "The rest of what it says, about the day my mother died and the way she died—her friend couldn't have known that."

"No. She never visited your mother at Craig House, but she had her reasons for being suspicious. Not long before her breakdown, Helene confided that she'd become afraid of your father. Unfortunately, her claims grew more and more outrageous, until one day she made the woman swear that if anything ever happened to her, she'd go to the police and tell them it was your father's doing. The woman began to question everything she'd been told. It sounded like the plot from a Hitchcock film. Then, a few weeks later, Helene suffered her breakdown and was shipped off to Craig House. The woman's first reaction was relief that your mother would finally get the care she needed, but then, not quite a year later, she heard . . ."

"That there'd been an accident."

The way you say it, so flat and empty, makes my gut twist. Your throat convulses as you turn your face away. This isn't how I wanted to tell you, but you were always going to know, and I was always going to be the one to have to tell you. But not like this. Never like this.

"Yes," *I say gently, the way one soothes a child after a nightmare.* "They said it was an accident. But you told me yourself that it wasn't true. The hospital claimed she fell while holding a knife and that by the time she was found, it was too late, but that isn't what happened. There was a knife, but your mother didn't fall. She'd already tried to end her life twice. The first time by throwing herself down the stairs and then by hacking at her wrists with the butter knife from her breakfast tray. They found her and stitched her up, but a few weeks later, she tried again and succeeded. Because your father paid a janitor to drop a utility knife in her room. The kind they use to cut up boxes. He wanted to make sure she made a proper job of it the next time. Because he knew there would be a next time."

You sag back onto the sofa, a sob bubbling up from your throat. I take a step toward you but you hold out a hand, warding me off. The silence spools out, thick, unbearable. Finally, you look up at me. "Why now? If all of this is true, why are you just finding out about it now?"

"Because someone finally started asking questions. The hospital's version of events never smelled right. There was no way a utility knife should have been in a patient's room. And there was talk. Your father made an unscheduled visit just the day before and apparently had a little chat with one of the janitors on your mother's floor. But no one had the guts to say what everyone was thinking—that Helene's so-called accident might actually be a cover for something more sinister. Unfortunately, your father's name carries a lot of weight. Enough to squash the whispers, apparently. And a sanitarium charging thousands of dollars a month wouldn't have wanted the publicity. Better an accident than a suicide. Or worse."

You eye me stonily, giving no sign that what I've just said has registered. "You still haven't answered my question. Why did it take thirteen years for this so-called friend to tell someone? And how did that someone happen to be you?"

"Her husband was an associate of your father's. When she shared her suspicions with him, he forbid her to say anything. A few years ago, he died, leaving her free to come forward, but so much time had passed and your father had become even more powerful. She didn't believe anything would come of it."

"And then a few months ago, out of the blue, she suddenly had a change of heart?"

You're still not convinced, still trying to poke holes in my story. But at least you're asking questions. If I can just keep you talking, keep you listening, I can fix this.

"She did, as a matter of fact. When Lindbergh went to Iowa and said what he said. When she read his comments in the paper, blaming the Jews for Roosevelt's interventionist stance, she remembered something her husband said once. He said your father had praised Hitler as a visionary, predicting that one day this country would come to realize what Germany had—that the only good Jew was a dead Jew. That's when she knew she had to keep her promise to your mother. She felt the public should know what kind of man your father is."

"And this janitor, the one who was supposedly paid to leave the knife in my mother's room—he's admitted this?"

We've reached the part of the story where things start to get murky now, and admitting it isn't going to help me much. But I won't keep anything back. I have to tell you all of it. "He can't admit anything. He's dead. He was quietly fired a week after your mother died, but he did a little bragging on his way out. Two of the staff from that time—an orderly and another janitor—both heard him bragging that he'd cashed in on the French lady."

You glare at me, both horrified and astonished. "So you were writing a story accusing my father of . . . I don't even know what to call it, based on something a dead man is supposed to have said? And you learned all this *because some woman claiming to be a friend of my mother's decided to pick up the phone and call you instead of the police?"*

"She doesn't claim to have been a friend of your mother's—she was a friend of your mother's. I verified it. And she didn't call me—she called Goldie. She didn't think the police would take her seriously. Not after so many years. But she thought the Review *might. Or that we'd at least do a little digging."*

"Or maybe you and Goldie just cooked it all up to sell papers."

In boxing, it's called a sucker punch, the one you don't see coming. Yours lands squarely, low and crippling. "That's what you think of me? That I'm some kind of tabloid hack?"

"This really isn't the day to ask what I think of you."

"Belle . . . please."

"Don't."

"I did all the legwork. Checked out every lead. Because even I thought the story was too incredible to be believed. But it happened, Belle. I'm sure of it."

"This was what you were after. That first night at the St. Regis. It was about this story."

"Partly, yes," I say quietly. "I didn't know all of it then, but Goldie had gotten the call from your mother's friend, and she told me where to look. I had no idea I was walking into anything like this, and then when I did . . ."

"You ran with it."

"I thought it was important. But now . . . I just left Goldie's office. I told her I wasn't finishing the story, that I'd thrown all my notes in the trash."

Your eyes slide to the felled pages on the carpet. "Another lie, since I've just found them on the desk beside your typewriter."

"I was going to tear them up as soon as I got home. And then I was going to tell you. All of it. I didn't realize you'd be here when I got back."

"You still don't understand. It isn't about you killing the story. It's about the fact that you were prepared to use my mother's illness to further your career—when you knew how hard losing her was for me. You claim to love me, but you betrayed my confidence to sell newspapers!"

"You knew I was working on a piece about your father—"

"About his business dealings! Not my mother!"

"I couldn't not pursue the story, Belle. Not when it's about a man as powerful as your father. The public has a right to know—"

"And to hell with me, right?"

"I didn't mean—"

You're on your feet suddenly, hands clenched. "If you were so concerned about the public, why not turn your notes over to the police? I'll tell you why. Because that wouldn't sell nearly as many papers as this . . . horror story. Is this how English newspapers operate? You print whatever you want, things you can't even prove, and then sit back and watch your readers tear the victim to shreds?"

I stare at you, my gut twisting. During all my agonizing about how this conversation might go, I never once prepared for this, for you taking his side, for seeing him as the victim in all this. "I understand that you're angry," I say quietly. "I even understand why. What I can't understand is how—after everything I've told you—you can stand there and defend him to me."

"This isn't about my father. It's about us. About not being able to trust you or believe anything you've ever said to me. You say you were going to tell me. When? After I'd snuck out of my father's house and boarded a train with you to Chicago? Do you know how that would have looked? Like I was part of it! Like I fed you information to take down my own father!"

"That's what's bothering you—what people would have thought? I just walked away from a story I've been working on for months. For you. Went back on my word as a journalist and set fire to any hope of getting another job in the newspaper business. For you. Does none of that matter?"

You regard me with empty eyes. "What do you want me to say? That I don't care about my mother being used as fodder for one of your stories? Or being made a fool of? That in your desperation to prove your journalistic bona fides, you haven't ruined everything? I'm sorry. I can't. Because you have. You've ruined everything."

"You don't mean that. You can't. In less than twenty-four hours, this city and everything in it will be a memory for us. The life we planned, everything we talked about, starts the minute we step on that train. Nothing else matters."

You look at me as if I've said something incomprehensible. "How can I get on that train now? When all I can think about is what else you may have lied about—and what you might lie about next. All I'd be doing is trading a family I can't trust for a man I can't trust."

For the first time, it occurs to me that I could actually lose you over this. "Belle, I swear to you . . ." Your face is so steely, so completely devoid of expression, that the words dry up in my throat. I'd prefer that you rail at me, fly at me, strike me. Instead, you stand there, still and white, icy calm.

"Don't you see?" you say at last. "It doesn't matter what you swear now. It will never matter. Because I'll never believe you. You said you loved me, but you couldn't. Not if you could do something like this. I thought I knew you, but I don't know the man who could do what you meant to. And I don't want to."

"What are you saying?"

"I'm saying I've made a mistake, Hemi. We're just too far apart. How we grew up, the things that matter to us, our sense of right and wrong, apparently. And running away won't change that. I should never have let you into my life. Some part of me knew that. You knew about Teddy and you came at me anyway—because I had something you wanted. And you got it too. Because I let down my guard. Now I see that you're no different from my father. You believe the ends justify the means, that nothing matters so long as you get what you want."

"That isn't fair."

"I agree."

"Belle, please . . ."

"I have to go."

You retrieve your handbag from the arm of the sofa and walk to the door, then look back at me before reaching for the knob. I hold my breath, waiting for you to say something, but you just stand there, staring.

"You can't leave like this, Belle. We need to talk it through."

"I have to go," you say again, as if you haven't heard me.

"Will you be there tomorrow? At the station?"

I hold my breath, waiting. And then you're gone.

ELEVEN

ASHLYN

Protracted neglect is both shameful and sad, and will likely result in reduced value, but there is nothing so unsettling, or so unforgivable, as intentionally inflicted damage.

—*Ashlyn Greer,* The Care & Feeding of Old Books

October 14, 1984
Rye, New Hampshire

Ashlyn rang the bell, then glanced over her shoulder, half expecting to see Mrs. Warren and her plump spaniel lurking at the edge of the drive. The last place she'd expected to find herself on this chilly Sunday afternoon was Ethan's house, but here she was, on his front steps, trying to tamp down her expectations.

She'd been working in the bindery when Ethan called, inviting her over for chili. The invitation had been a pleasant surprise, but it was his hint at some sort of discovery that intrigued her most. He had also asked her to bring *Regretting Belle*—so they could swap. He wanted to read Hemi's versions of events too. Apparently, she wasn't the only one who'd become immersed in Belle and Hemi's story.

Ethan was smiling when he pulled back the door, wearing jeans and a New England Patriots sweatshirt that was badly frayed at the collar. He grinned, noting the direction of her gaze. "No making fun of my lucky sweatshirt. I've had it since college."

Ashlyn eyed him skeptically. "Are you sure it's lucky? The Pats haven't exactly been setting the world on fire the last few years."

The smile morphed into a lopsided grin. "Maybe not, but you watch. One of these days, they're going to get the right guy under center, and when they do, they're going to win so many Super Bowls that the entire country will hate them." He pulled back the door and waved her in. "Come in. It's wicked cold, as my father would say."

In the kitchen, Ashlyn stripped off her jacket and scarf. There was a large pot simmering on the stove and the air was fragrant with the mingled aromas of beef and spices.

"Hungry?"

"Starved actually."

"Me too. I've got the game on in the other room, so I can keep up with the score. Are you a football fan?"

"I know the difference between a screen pass and an out route, if that's what you mean."

Ethan's brows shot up. "I'm impressed. Kirsten certainly wasn't a fan. She found my mild sports addiction enormously aggravating. Your ex was a lucky guy."

Lucky wasn't quite how she thought of Daniel, but she decided to let that part of the remark pass. "Actually, Daniel wasn't a sports fan. I read up on football as a kid because I thought it would get my father's attention."

"Did it?"

"No."

"My dad pulled for the Pats, but he was never a huge football fan. He was crazy for baseball, though. Loved the Sox. He used to take me to Fenway when I was a kid. I loved those afternoons. When he was diagnosed and the doctors told us . . ." He looked away briefly. "I wanted to make sure we got back while he could still enjoy it."

"It's nice that you made those memories."

"Yeah. They were good days. Is your dad still alive?"

Ashlyn shifted uncomfortably. "He died when I was sixteen. Not long after my mother."

Ethan's face softened. "Sorry. That's young to lose both parents. Do you have other family? Siblings? Aunts or uncles?"

"Nope. It's just my books and me."

"Yeah. Me too."

The moment seemed to expand, awkward and unfillable, as they stood looking at each other across the counter. It was Ethan who finally looked away. He moved to the stove and gave the pot a stir. "I'm just reheating this, and then we can dish it up. Can I get you a beer? Wine? Soda?"

"A beer would be great, thanks. Can I do anything?"

"You can keep an eye on the chili. Make sure it doesn't stick."

Ashlyn lifted the lid from the pot, releasing a cloud of fragrant steam, then picked up the wooden spoon. "You really made this? From scratch?"

"Yup. Chopped all the veggies myself. The beans were canned, though. I didn't start it till ten, so I had to take the shortcut."

"It smells delicious. I haven't had chili in—" She broke off, abruptly letting go of the spoon.

Ethan looked around the refrigerator door. "What happened? Did you just burn yourself?"

"No. It's just . . ." She paused, flexing her fingers. "I'm fine."

"Let me see." He was beside her now, reaching for her hand.

"It's okay, really. It's just an old scar. It acts up sometimes. Like pins and needles."

Ethan caught her hand and gently unfurled her fingers. He frowned as he peered at her palm. "That's one hell of a scar. What happened?"

Ashlyn squirmed under his regard. She didn't want to talk about the scar. Or the day she'd gotten it. The memories were still too raw. And always too close to the surface.

After weeks of dodging phone calls, she had agreed to meet Daniel for a drink. He'd pressed for dinner, thinking he could charm her out of going through with the divorce, but her objective for the meeting had been to decide who got the couch and which albums belonged to whom. It hadn't gone well and she'd ended up walking out.

She had just crossed the street to head back to the shop when she heard her name and turned. Daniel stood on the opposite side of the street, wearing his this-isn't-over expression. Time seemed to slow as he stepped off the curb. There was a white panel van and the sickening skid of tires, then a jarring thump as Daniel's body somersaulted up onto the hood, then landed back on the pavement. Suddenly the air was full of shattered glass, shiny shards catching the light as they rained down into the street.

She'd barely noticed the cut, too numb to feel anything as she registered the slick of dark blood already pooling beneath Daniel's head, the impossible angles of his arms and legs. Killed instantly, the coroner's report said. A small mercy, but the sound of shattering glass still woke her now and then, along with Daniel's last words to her. Words she'd never repeated to anyone. Not even her therapist.

"It happened the night Daniel died," she replied finally, uncomfortably aware that Ethan had yet to let go of her hand. "There was a van carrying a huge sheet of glass. When it struck him, glass went everywhere. At some point, I cut myself. I didn't know until one of the medics noticed the blood dripping from my hand."

"I'm sorry."

"It's fine." She withdrew her hand, tucking it out of sight. "Let's eat. You can tell me how far you've gotten with Belle's book and I'll bring you up to speed on Hemi's. There have been some pretty significant developments since we talked. Plus, there are some things about your family—about Martin specifically—that I should warn you about before you start reading. It's . . . not nice."

Ethan nodded somberly. "To be honest, I'd be shocked if it *was* nice, but I think I'd prefer to read it for myself. It's not like I'm emotionally vested in any of it. They're basically strangers."

Ashlyn wondered. It was one thing to grow up knowing your great-grandfather was a bully. It was another to learn he might have been complicit in the death of his wife.

"Are you sure? We're talking about some pretty disturbing stuff."

"Yes, I'm sure. Let's eat. When we're finished, I've got something to show you."

It felt like Christmas morning as Ashlyn followed Ethan upstairs to the study. She'd done her best while they ate not to grill him about what he'd found, though it hadn't been easy. Instead, they had discussed the ins and outs of bookbinding and the curriculum Ethan was developing for a class he hoped to teach next year. Now, finally, her patience was about to be rewarded.

Ethan flipped on the light as they entered. "Sorry about the mess. I thought I'd be through it all in a couple of hours, but I got sidetracked."

Ashlyn stood at the center of the room, surveying the chaos. Eight cartons of assorted files and office paraphernalia scattered in a messy semicircle with several half-full trash bags stationed nearby. "You weren't kidding when you said your father was a pack rat."

Ethan bent down and plucked something off the carpet. It was a paperweight, a clear glass sphere with a deep-blue teardrop at its heart. He stared at it as he rolled it around in his palm. "The man could come up with a reason for hanging on to anything. Didn't matter what it was, he'd find a reason. It drove my mother nuts, but in this case, it was a good thing."

He waved her over to the desk. The old typewriter was still there, with the same blank sheet of paper wilting over the carriage, but the crumpled pages that had littered the floor were gone. Reaching around her, he opened the middle drawer and extracted a small bundle of papers. "I found these in one of the boxes. The last box, as luck would have it, tied with a piece of ribbon."

"What are they?"

"Letters. Cards. Photos. From Marian to my father."

Ashlyn felt a little thrill as she dropped into the chair Ethan had pulled out for her and accepted the stack of correspondence. Unfortunately, the envelopes all seemed to be missing, which meant there were no return addresses. She lifted the first item from the stack, a birthday card with a set of golf clubs on the front. *Happy Birthday, Nephew.* It was dated 1956, signed simply, *Marian.* But there was a brief note jotted in cursive on the opposite side. *Thinking of you and Catherine. Kids are fine. We send our love.*

There were several more cards. Birthday mostly, but there was also a blue-and-silver Hanukkah card with a menorah on the front. *Wishing You Peace and Light.* Each card included a brief note, mentions of the children mostly, but there was nothing earth-shattering about any of them.

Next came a handful of letters, newsy but bland. Talk about the weather, about trips she'd recently taken, the work she continued to do on behalf of displaced children around the world. One included a pair of photos. She peered at the backs of both. *Ilese, age 11. Zachary, 13.*

Once again, Ilese looked broody and serious, while Zachary grinned cheekily for the camera. He was handsome in his dark suit and tie, clutching a violin and bow in his fist, the way one might hold a dead cat—by the tail and slightly away from the body.

Ashlyn folded the photos back into the letter and looked at Ethan. "Are the rest of them like this? Just newsy letters and school photos? I was hoping for something a little more . . . helpful."

"Keep going. You're almost there."

The next piece was a letter dated 1967.

Dearest Dickey,

I hope this finds you well. It's been some time since I dropped you a line. The kids are both great, though I'm not sure I should still be calling them kids at this point. Zachary is wrapping up his graduate studies at Berklee College of Music. Ilese is as brilliant as ever and is looking at master's programs. I'm hoping for either Yale or Princeton but she's leaning toward Bar-Ilan near Tel Aviv, which is an exceptional school but very far away. I suppose all mothers feel like this when it's time for their chicks to fly the nest. And speaking of chicks, I was delighted to receive the photo of my great-nephew in his Easter suit. He's growing up so fast. Cherish him while you have him.

I apologize if I sound morose. I've been a little blue lately, now that the house is so empty. Family is on my mind. Do you by any chance know what happened to the photo album your mother used to keep with her papers? The one with the gold lettering on the front? It belonged to your grandmother Helene and holds especially fond memories for me. Your mother claims to have thrown it away, but I have reason to believe that is not the case. I feel strongly that she not be allowed to keep it, as she held no affection for our mother. If there is any way to discover its whereabouts, I would be grateful.

We've had our differences over the years, you and I. About the decisions I've made and how I've lived my life, but I hope you know how fond of you I've always been and how much I regret the times we allowed sharp words to come between us. I will close for now. I'm off to a luncheon. When the weather warms, perhaps we can get together. You and Catherine are welcome to visit anytime. Though I suggest waiting until the mud season is over. The roads here can be frightful in spring.

Love to all,

Marian

Questions began to bubble as Ashlyn looked up at Ethan. "She mentions tension between the two of them, about decisions she made. I assume that's about Teddy and . . . Wait, you didn't find the album, did you? The one she asked your dad about?"

"I did not."

Ashlyn glowered at him as she slumped back in her chair. "I was hoping for some big revelation, but nothing here gets us any closer to Marian. Or to Hemi, for that matter."

Ethan pointed to the floor, where a folded piece of paper had slid from her lap and onto the carpet. "Maybe you should look at that one."

Ashlyn picked it up, laying it open on her knees. It was a concert schedule, creased into quarters with a circle of red marker ringing a portion of the text.

Boston Symphony Orchestra

August 4, 1969—Featured violinist Zachary Manning
will be performing a selection of chamber pieces this
weekend during his Boston debut. Manning's flawless
technique and delicate approach have already drawn
the attention of some of today's most important con-
ductors and orchestras. A passionate performer, he is
consistently praised for his refreshing interpretations
and artistic sensitivity.

Ashlyn looked up, bewildered. "Am I missing something?"

"Marian's son grew up to be a concert violinist and, from the sound
of it, a fairly prominent one. I figured if we can track him down, we can
at least find out if Marian's still alive."

Ashlyn scanned the page again, dubious. "This is dated 1969. What
are the odds he's still performing? And that we can locate him if he is?"

Ethan's mouth twitched, the beginning of a grin. "I already have."

"What? How?"

"I contacted a buddy at UNH, a music professor I used to play
softball with, and asked him to check it out."

"And?"

"And he called me this morning. Zachary Manning lives in Chicago
and is currently with the Chicago Symphony Orchestra."

Ashlyn stared at Ethan. For a man who'd shown zero interest in his
aunt's story the first time they met, he was certainly proving resourceful.
There was no way to know if Zachary Manning could or would lead
them to Belle, but it was a step in the right direction.

"You actually found him," she said, scanning the flyer again.

"Yup."

"So what now?"

"That's what we need to figure out. I'm not sure picking up the phone and saying, *'Hey, cous, remember me? Is your mom still alive and kicking?'* is a good idea."

Ashlyn shot him a sideways look. "That's definitely *not* a good idea."

"So what *do* I say? We met exactly once, when he was fifteen and I was five. How do I explain tracking him down now, after all this time?"

"Maybe you could use your father's death. You could say you've been going through his things and you found some old letters and photos that you'd like to return to your aunt if he'll tell you how to get in touch with her."

"Hey, that's good. It's also not a lie. If she *is* alive, she probably would want them back. But what do I say to *her*?"

Ethan's intensity surprised her. "I thought you were against trying to find her."

He nodded thoughtfully. "I was. But then I started reading and I think you're right. There's no way she forgets Hemi. I also think she'd want the books back—if only to assure they don't end up in anyone else's hands. The question is how to accomplish it with a modicum of delicacy."

Ashlyn tried to imagine what it would be like to get a call from a stranger who knew the most intimate details of her past. It wasn't a particularly pleasant thought. "I think you cross that bridge when you come to it. The first order of business is to find out if she's alive and then see if you can get a number for her."

While Ashlyn attempted to put the cards and letters back in order, Ethan wandered about the room, presumably mulling over how best to approach Zachary. She was looking for Marian's letter about Helene's photo album when she noticed a hardcover edition of Aldous Huxley's *Brave New World* on the corner of the desk.

It hadn't been there last week—she would have remembered—but it jumped out at her now. By his own admission, Ethan didn't read fiction, which meant it had probably belonged to his father. She ran a finger over the gray dust jacket with its oddly headless man. She felt it instantly, echoes pulling at her like an undertow.

Unable to resist, she picked up the book, breathing in, breathing out, breathing in again. Waiting. But the echoes refused to resolve, like a dissonant chord scraping along her nerves. Self-doubt. Inner turmoil. A man who'd lost his way and desperately wanted to find it again. A man searching for purpose, searching for *himself*.

Ethan's book. Ethan's echoes.

Turning to the title page, she found what she was looking for.

Ethan,
Be brave and do the work. But do it your way.
The world needs your voice.
—Dad

"It was a gift from my father."

Ashlyn started guiltily. She hadn't heard him approach, but he stood just behind her now. She closed the book and returned it to the desk, recalling the inscription she'd found in the battered copy of *The Remains of the Day*. It, too, had mentioned bravery.

"Be brave," she repeated. "It's a lovely inscription."

"It was a thing with my dad—bravery. A guiding principle. I was going through a rough patch when he gave it to me, trying to figure out what I wanted to do with my life, my work."

"You didn't always want to write?"

"No, I did. I just wasn't sure *what* I wanted to write. I had a friend, a guy I went to school with, who'd published a couple of novels. He thought it would be funny to send a manuscript of mine to his editor without telling me. One day, out of the blue, I get a call from a guy I've never heard of, offering me a three-book deal based on the piece my pal had sent him. A political thriller series, of all things."

Ashlyn let the words sink in. A three-book deal. Out of the blue. It was the kind of thing that happened in movies, not real life. "That's amazing. But I thought you didn't do fiction."

"I don't. My friend bet me I couldn't write a four-hundred-page novel in a year, so I did. I was just fooling around, trying to win the bet and shut him up. I never dreamed anyone would ever read it."

"It's the kind of thing every writer dreams of—being discovered."

"Maybe. But I didn't want to be discovered. I know it sounds elitist, but I didn't want to write that stuff. It was, however, what my wife wanted me to write. The advance was six figures and all she could see were dollar signs and movie rights. She was already planning her red-carpet ensemble when I told her I wasn't going to accept."

"I'm guessing she didn't take it well."

"She was furious. When we got married, she tried to get me to reconcile with the family. She thought if I got back in Corinne's good graces, I'd magically be back in the will. She lost her mind when I told her no. So when the book deal happened, she was determined to get her way."

"But she didn't."

"No," Ethan said tightly. "So she found Tony, the personal trainer. But not before she'd dragged me to hell and back over that deal. That's when my father gave me the book. And why he wrote what he did. He knew I had things I wanted to say. He also knew that if I gave in to Kirsten, I'd never say them."

"So you turned down a six-figure, three-book deal, knowing your wife would be furious."

"Yeah."

Ashlyn smiled at him over her shoulder. "You were brave."

"Or stupid."

"It's never stupid to be brave."

"Yeah, the jury's still out on that one. For me, at least."

The Echo of Old Books

Ashlyn studied him, noting, perhaps for the first time, the cloud that seemed to hover about his shoulders. He'd stood his ground with his wife, had made his father proud, and yet there was something that remained unsettled in him, something holding him back.

"I've never done anything brave in my life," she confided quietly. "It was easier to just knuckle under, to be what people expected me to be. You should be proud you didn't."

Ethan responded with a halfhearted shrug, then dropped into a worn leather club chair. "So that's my sad little story. What about you? What happened with Daniel? You said you were in the middle of a divorce when he died."

Ashlyn ran her eyes around the room, in search of a distraction. She didn't want to talk about Daniel, but it felt impolite to refuse when he'd just shared his own story.

Rather than sit beside him, she opted for the edge of the hassock, positioning herself opposite him. She didn't have to tell it all, but she owed him something. "We met at UNH. I was in one of his classes and we started seeing each other on the quiet. The next thing I knew, we were married. It went off the rails pretty quickly after that, but I stayed. I wasn't brave."

"He was the one to leave?"

"No, I left."

"What finally did it?"

"Coming home at three in the afternoon to find a woman named Marybeth in my kitchen—in my husband's bathrobe."

Ethan winced. "Ouch."

"I moved out that night. I felt like such a fool. I'd heard the rumors. The entire faculty knew what he was. But I was too enthralled to hear any of it. He was so brilliant, so talented. I couldn't see how manipulative he was—until I could. And even then, I stayed. Until Marybeth. Even I couldn't unsee that."

239

"He was faculty at UNH?"

She nodded. "He taught my creative writing class."

"Daniel Strayer . . . was your husband?"

Ashlyn wished she weren't sitting directly across from him. "Did you know him?"

Please say no. Please say no. Please say no.

"No, but I've heard the name. He'd been let go the month before I started. Reportedly, after being investigated for some extracurricular activity with a student. Was that your doing?"

"No, it wasn't me. But he *thought* it was. He thought everything was my fault. The night he died, we met for a drink to settle some of the property stuff. It didn't go well. And then when we left . . ." She closed her eyes against the memories, then opened them again when she felt Ethan's touch.

"And then you got this," he said softly, taking her hand and turning it palm-up.

Ashlyn swallowed, suddenly off-balance. "Yes."

"Does it still hurt?"

His voice was unsettlingly soft, the room too warm. "No. Not now."

"I'm glad."

What was happening? Her heart felt like it was tap-dancing on her rib cage and she couldn't seem to make her lungs expand. There hadn't been anyone since Daniel. And not really anyone before him. Certainly no one who made her feel the way she was feeling now.

"You okay?"

She blinked at him, aware that she'd been silent a long time. "Yeah, just . . ."

Ethan abruptly let go of her hand. "Sorry. I didn't mean to make you uncomfortable."

"You didn't. It's just . . . been a while. I guess I'm out of practice. Not that I was ever *in* practice. I just meant . . ."

Oh god, stop talking, Ashlyn. He touched your hand. He didn't invite you to his bedroom.

Ethan's mouth curved softly. "I get it. I haven't been . . . *practicing* much either. The divorce wrecked me. And then my dad got sick. There hasn't been much time for a social life. And to be honest, I've never been very good at this part. The wooing thing, I mean. Picking up on signals, social cues. I'm sorry if I overstepped."

It was Ashlyn's turn to smile. He was nothing like she'd imagined him when he walked into the shop that night. He was charming and funny and kind. "You're doing fine," she told him shyly. "Wooing-wise, I mean."

"We can go slow."

Feathery little wings seemed to take flight in her belly as she met his gaze. "Slow is good."

TWELVE

ASHLYN

Books are rib and spine, blood and ink, the stuff of dreams dreamed and lives lived. One page, one day, one journey at a time.

—*Ashlyn Greer,* The Care & Feeding of Old Books

October 17, 1984
Portsmouth, New Hampshire

Ashlyn ran an eye over the legal pad perched on her knees, pleased with her notes for the shop's annual holiday newsletter. She was working in bed, writing in longhand with Frank Atwater's favorite Conklin fountain pen. She'd type it up later so the typesetter could read it, but there was something deliciously old-fashioned about creating with pen and ink, like a direct line forged from head to hand.

Normally, the entire issue would be written by now and already at the printer's, but between the push to complete Gertrude's Nancy Drew books and the distraction of Hemi's and Belle's books, it had slipped her mind entirely. As it was, she was going to have to scramble to beat the printer's deadline, then get them addressed and mailed.

She had just put down her pen and was considering a cup of tea when the phone rang. She glanced at the clock. Who on earth would be calling at ten o'clock?

"Hello?"

"Is it too late?"

"Ethan?"

The sound of his voice both surprised and pleased her. He'd called on Monday to let her know he'd left a message with Zachary's assistant. Neither of them had mentioned the awkward moment from the night before, though the memory had drifted into her head several times over the course of the day, accompanied each time by an unsettling flush of warmth.

"Yeah, it's me. I didn't wake you, did I?"

"No. I was just working on the holiday newsletter for the store. Are you calling to tell me you just got off the phone with Zachary?"

"Nope. Still haven't heard back."

"Well, it's only been a few days."

"Yeah, I guess."

He sounded distracted, distant. "You sound funny. What's up?"

"I've been reading."

"Ah. How far have you gotten?"

"The stuff about Helene and the asylum. I mean . . . holy hell."

"I know. Are you okay?"

"Yeah. Just, you know . . . processing." There was a pause as he pulled in a breath, then let it out heavily. "My Jewish great-grandmother married a Nazi sympathizer, who locked her up to hide her from his Nazi-loving friends. How did I not know any of that? We're Jewish, or at least partly Jewish, and no one ever said a word. Did my father know? And if so, why keep it a secret? And then Marian, finding out the way she did. My god . . ."

He sounded genuinely rattled. And a little angry. "Are you sure you're all right?"

"Yeah. It's just weird, you know? I never thought of the Mannings as the ideal American family, but this is worse than anything I could have imagined."

Ashlyn thought of her own parents. The mother who couldn't be bothered to save herself. The father who'd climbed up to the attic and put a shotgun under his chin because he wanted to shake his fist at God. "There's no such thing as the ideal American family, Ethan. It's a myth."

"I guess. Have you finished *Forever, and Other Lies* yet?"

"Almost, and it isn't looking good on my end either."

"That's why I stopped. I needed a break." He sighed, weary or disgusted, perhaps both. "I guess we know what happens next, though—and whose fault it ended up being."

Ashlyn considered this a moment. She'd thought so, too, at first. But now she wasn't so sure. She couldn't get past the echoes she'd picked up the first time she touched the books, the eerily similar fusion of bitterness and grief. People lied. Echoes didn't. Belle and Hemi both genuinely believed themselves to be the wronged party, which seemed to suggest that there was more to the story than they currently knew. Perhaps more than they'd *ever* know. But she couldn't say any of that to Ethan.

"Or maybe we just think we know and it was actually something else."

"You think there's something else coming?"

"I'm just saying it feels like that wasn't all of it. He loved Belle, Ethan. Enough to walk away from a story he clearly believed every word of. I could be wrong. Maybe it *was* enough to make Belle walk away—she was certainly furious—but my gut tells me there's something else."

"What makes you think that?"

Ashlyn hesitated, weighing how to answer. "Do you believe in women's intuition?"

"Yeah, I guess."

"Well then, we'll go with that."

"To be honest, I think I know all I want to."

Ashlyn could hear the finality in his tone, and a part of her understood. He hadn't wanted to get involved to begin with, and now he'd learned things about his family that would make anyone reluctant to look deeper.

"I get it. I've been feeling a little like that too. I know there's not going to be a happy ending—both of them make that clear right off the bat—and yet I find myself dragging my feet, dreading the rest of what's coming. I mean, I already know *what's* coming . . . but the actual *how*. Who did what to whom and what happened after. But I will read it. All the way to the end. Because I can't *not* know all of it. Not when we've read this far."

Ethan let out a groan. "I suppose I should at least finish Belle's book."

"Or . . . we could read them together," she suggested on impulse.

"Together? How would that work?"

"Okay, not *together* together. But we could do it over the phone. There aren't that many pages left in either book. We could take turns, with me reading from *Forever, and Other Lies* and you *Regretting Belle*. We could schedule a couple of reading dates. Well, not dates, but you know, set a regular time. Maybe an hour. Or less if you want. Unless you don't have time. And you probably don't with your writing. Never mind, it was a silly idea."

"No," Ethan said when she finally went quiet. "Let's do it."

"Seriously?"

"If it's going to count as a date, then yeah."

A date.

The mere word set off alarm bells in Ashlyn's head. Should she clarify? Tell him that's not what she meant? Did it even matter? They'd be talking on the phone. How dangerous could it be? "All right, then. A reading date. Should I pencil you in for tomorrow night?"

"Actually, I was thinking we could start tonight. Would you mind? I'm not really ready to hang up."

"No, that's fine. It might be a good way to wind down."

"Like a bedtime story," Ethan supplied. "Except those never worked for me. My mom used to read to me when I was a kid, but I'd fight falling asleep in order to keep her reading."

Ashlyn liked that she could hear the smile in his voice. She set her pad and pen aside and settled back against the pillows. "Do you think your mom ever read Belle's and Hemi's books?"

"I don't know for sure, but it's hard to imagine her *not* reading them. My father would certainly have shown them to her. They talked about everything. No secrets."

"No secrets," Ashlyn said wistfully. "What must that be like? To share everything? My parents weren't big on talking. Unless you count screaming at each other. And then with Daniel . . . Let's just say he did most of the talking in our relationship. He was the smart one and I was just expected to do as I was told. The sad part is, for years I did. I was—" She stopped abruptly. "Sorry. Overshare."

"No, it's okay. I like that you feel comfortable telling me those things. And I get what you mean. I'm still trying to figure out how Kirsten and I ever got together. It's like watching a train wreck in slow motion, only one of the trains is you. My parents knew the first time they met her. They saw what I couldn't—or wouldn't."

"I'm sorry."

"Older but wiser, as they say. But it's easy to become gun-shy when you've been burned badly enough, afraid to trust your own judgment. Friends keep trying to fix me up, but . . ." There was a pause, a brief beat of silence. "There really hasn't been anyone since Daniel?"

"No."

"No one in four years?"

"I told you, I don't do brave."

Ethan chuckled. "It requires bravery to let a guy take you to dinner?"

"For me it does."

"But reading on the phone—that's okay, right? That's safe?"

It was Ashlyn's turn to chuckle. Were they flirting? She couldn't tell. It felt a little bit dangerous. But a little bit good too. "I think so, yes."

"Good, then. I'll let you start if that's okay. I think I'd rather just listen tonight."

Once again, Ashlyn heard the weariness in his words. He was rattled, perhaps even a little disillusioned, despite all his feigned ancestral indifference. "Yes. It's okay."

She reached for the copy of *Forever, and Other Lies* on the nightstand, opening to the place she'd marked with a scrap of blue ribbon, then sank back into the pillows and began to read.

Forever, and Other Lies

(pgs. 57–69)

December 5, 1941
New York, New York

I'm seething by the time I get back to the house. To have kept the truth from me, knowing full well you meant to publish every word, has shattered what I thought we had together. But the things you claim to have learned about my father have temporarily eclipsed the pain of your betrayal.

All the way home, I tried to convince myself that you were lying when you wrote those vile things, that you'd invented them out of thin air to please Goldie. But I couldn't make myself believe it. Then I remembered Cee-Cee's warning about my father, how he saw us all as chess pieces and that sometimes the troublesome pieces disappeared, and I realized she meant our mother. Her illness and her Judaism had become troublesome, so he made our mother disappear—not just to Craig House but for good.

I go from room to room, in search of my sister and answers. I find her in my father's study, going through a stack of mail. She looks small behind his desk, diminished by the chair's wide leather shoulders. She glances up as I enter the room, then returns to the stack of envelopes on the blotter.

My father is in Boston, preparing for one of his committee rallies, but his presence is all around us. The smell of his cigars, his lime-scented hair tonic, the pricey vintage cognac he serves his friends, it all hangs in the air, palpable and vaguely unnerving.

My mouth is dry suddenly. I've been rehearsing what to say during the drive back, but now that my sister is looking at me, the words want to stick in my throat. Finally, though, they tumble out. "How long have you known our mother was Jewish?"

Cee-Cee's head comes up, her hands abruptly still. "What?"

"Jewish," I repeat emphatically. "How long have you known our mother was Jewish?"

Her eyes dart toward the open door. "For heaven's sake, lower your voice!"

The panic in her eyes tells me everything I need to know. "Answer the question."

She lifts a letter from the pile with feigned calm and uses a silver letter opener to slit the envelope in one clean stroke. She's in no hurry as she teases out the contents and scans them. Finally, she sets the page aside and looks up. "To whom have you been talking?"

"That's not an answer."

"No. It isn't. But I'm going to ask again. To whom have you been talking?"

"Who I've been talking to doesn't matter."

"Oh, I think it matters a great deal. Shall I guess who it was?" There's the hint of a smile as she says it. The effect is faintly chilling. "It wouldn't be your newspaper friend from the Weekly Review, *would it? The one you've been so cozy with of late?"*

She's trying to divert the conversation, to put me on the defensive. "So you're not even going to try to deny it?"

She tosses her head, as if she's made some point. "Neither are you, apparently."

"Did you know that's why Father sent her away? Because he was ashamed of her . . . Jewishness?" It sounds awkward and ugly coming out of my mouth, but then the things my father has been accused of are ugly.

Cee-Cee folds her hands primly and places them on the blotter. "He was ashamed of her because she embarrassed him in front of his friends."

"She was sick."

"She was weak!"

And there it is. Confirmation, were I still in need of it. "You said once that Father sometimes made the chess pieces disappear. This is what you were talking about. Her. She was the troublesome chess piece."

Cee-Cee pulls in a breath, then squares her shoulders. "You know how she was. You were there that night. You saw and heard the same things I did, the same thing everyone did. Sobbing and ranting like a crazy woman. How much longer was he supposed to endure her tantrums? He had to send her away."

"And the accident," I press. "The way she died."

"What about it?"

"There are people who think it wasn't an accident." I hesitate, not sure I can actually say the rest out loud. Once I do, it's said. There's no taking it back. But I need to say it, to see her face when I say it. "They think someone was paid to drop a knife in her room—that Father paid someone to drop a knife in her room."

She stares at me, aghast. "Don't be ridiculous."

The look of horror on her face fills me with a strange relief. "You didn't know."

"Know what? You're talking nonsense."

"Am I?" I look her up and down, her rattled expression, her rigid posture. "I don't think so. And I think you know it. She didn't die the way they said, Cee-Cee. It wasn't an accident."

I see her needing to deny it, to dismiss it as impossible, and I almost feel sorry for her. The idea that her hero, the father she's worshipped and always striven to please, could be capable of something so horrifyingly cold-blooded has shaken her to her core.

"Of course it wasn't an accident, you little fool. We all know what she did—and why. You said it yourself. She was sick. But no one was going to benefit from the truth coming out, especially if it got out that she'd tried twice before. Suicide *is* an ugly word. Of course they cleaned it up."

I gape at her, incredulous. Not once had the word been mentioned in my presence, but it had clearly been mentioned in hers. "You knew about the other times?"

"Not at first, but after . . . The insurance people were sniffing around, asking questions. Father thought I should know."

"But not me."

"You were a child," *she flings at me before lowering her voice.* "You have no idea how bad it was—how bad she was." *There's a plea in her eyes now, a need to bring me over to her side—to his side.* "The press would have had a field day with her dramatics. It was all so sordid, so . . . messy."

"You make it sound like it was her fault. Like she deserved what happened to her."

"What do you want me to say? It was tragic, horrific. But it was also inevitable. It's why Father sent her there in the first place. He didn't know what else to do with her. She was out of control, spiraling deeper and deeper. It was only a matter of time."

I listen to her, justifying, rationalizing, shifting the blame onto my mother, and I realize she's already absolved him. "You don't care, do you? Whether he did what they say or not. You don't care."

"For the love of god! Will you listen to yourself? What you're suggesting is absurd." *Her eyes harden suddenly, assessing me.* "And in case you've got any wild ideas, it would be a very bad idea to repeat a word of it to anyone."

There's no missing her meaning. How like him she is, *I realize with a wave of revulsion,* trying to back me down with thinly veiled threats.

"Am I next, then? Another chess piece to be disposed of? Who knows? Maybe I'll have an accident too."

She gives me a pained look, as if dealing with an intractable child. "I'd watch my step if I were you." She scoops the stack of mail from the desk then and tucks it under her arm, signaling that our conversation is over. "And don't go getting ideas. The Teddy matter is settled business. You'll walk down the aisle as planned. And until you do, you'll be staying close to home."

"You can't bully me into marrying someone I don't want to marry."

She looks at me as if I've said something amusing. "Of course we can. And you're looking at the proof. Do you think I wanted to marry George and have all these children? That being someone's wife was all I ever aspired to? It wasn't. But here I am, dancing to everyone else's tune—for the good of the family. And soon it'll be your turn."

I lift my chin, willing myself not to blink. "And if I've made other plans?"

She stares at me with an infuriating calm, like a card sharp who knows she's holding the winning hand. "These plans of yours—they wouldn't by any chance include a certain newspaper reporter? One with a seedy little apartment on Thirty-Seventh Street?" She smiles, pleased with herself when she sees my mouth drop open. "Did you really think I wouldn't find out? You're not nearly as clever as you think you are."

I look away, feeling color creep into my cheeks.

Her eyes are riveted to my face as she continues. "I know how often you take the car out, where you go, and how long you stay. I know about the groceries and the wine and what I suspect are very cozy suppers. I know it all."

"You had me followed?"

"I suspected the two of you might be involved the first time he came around. I saw you watching him. And him watching you. Like a pair of hungry cats. I didn't care, so long as you didn't botch the business with Teddy. A friend in the press can be a good thing to have." She pauses, flashing a feral smile. "And something tells me he's very good. A little rough around

the edges, perhaps, but that can be a plus. They say it's fun to go slumming now and then. Is it true?"

The crack of my palm against her cheek echoes off the study walls before I can check myself. Cee-Cee flinches, but her smile never slips. Still, I'm savagely glad to see the hot pink bloom of my handprint along her cheek.

"Right," she says with a cool nod. "That's what I thought."

"I suppose Father knows."

"No. Or not from me, at any rate. I decided as long as you were being discreet, I'd leave it alone. I assumed you'd be through with him by now, though. Instead, here you stand, ready to throw poor Teddy over for the paperboy."

"Hemi is worth ten of Teddy."

"My god . . . You've actually fallen for him. A grubby little reporter paid to invent lurid tales about your own family. And please don't pretend all of this didn't come from him. You sound like a sappy schoolgirl. Well, he chose his mark wisely—I'll give him that."

The remark stings, perhaps because it hits too close to the bone. You did choose wisely. And yet I find myself needing to defend you, too proud to concede that she's right. I feel myself wavering, wanting to justify what you've done—or at least your motives for doing it. But how am I any different from my sister if I'm willing to turn a blind eye to a betrayal simply because I can't bear the truth? And yet, I cannot allow her this petty triumph.

"You're wrong about him," I say evenly. "You've been wrong from the start. He was never going to be on your side. You thought you could buy him, use him to create some hero's narrative, but he was never going to do it. He's not for sale."

"Not for sale?" She actually laughs, a high, mocking trill. "You poor dolt. You never saw him coming. You're a would-be heiress, engaged to one of the most eligible men in the state, but he makes a play for you anyway. He woos you with that pretty face and that stuffy accent. And then, when he's got you on the hook, he begins to pry little bits of information out of

you. He wants to know all about you, how you grew up, and what it was like being the daughter of such an important man. He sets up a little love nest so the two of you can be alone, away from the big bad world, and you play house together. All of this after he's managed to get himself invited to this house and into Father's inner circle. Did it never occur to you to ask yourself what he might hope to gain from all that romancing? Or what would happen once he had what he wanted?"

It sounds so obvious when she lays it all end to end like that, so completely and carefully orchestrated. Because that's exactly how it happened, right down to that first invitation to dinner and the fight we had after. You were in your element that night, smiling and nodding as my sister dragged you around the room, introducing you to people you would have never met otherwise. None of this is news, of course. You admitted as much to me. But knowing that she knows it too—that she sees me for the fool I've been—is a hard pill to swallow.

Tears suddenly threaten. I try to blink them away, but Cee-Cee sees them and huffs impatiently. "You little fool. The man doesn't have two nickels to his name and you were prepared to throw away your entire life for him—to live on love, I suppose. Meanwhile, what have you been giving him?" She rakes her eyes over me, slow and knowing. "Nothing you can get back, I'll wager."

"He hasn't taken a cent from me."

She brushes past me then, without so much as a glance. "I wasn't talking about money."

Hours later, I'm still uncertain what comes next. I've been working on a letter—two letters actually—though I'm not certain I have the strength to finish either. I can't seem to stop weeping. But I have a decision to make. I've been wrestling with the words, with the impossible choice between my heart and my head. But how can I choose? It's as if I've been set adrift and there's no way back to you. No way back to anything. But I must choose. And soon.

I wonder, too, how to deliver the letters once they're written. I could phone instead. Discretion seems pointless now that our secret is no longer secret. But the truth is I'm putting it all on paper because I know I will never be brave enough to say what I almost certainly have to—not once I've heard your voice. And yet, I must say it, mustn't I?

Goodbye.

Cee-Cee was right. I have been naive. About so many things. Living in a fantasy world where the fairy princess and the handsome pauper ride off into the sunset and the wicked king is never heard from again. But life doesn't work like that. The pauper isn't who he seems and the king is all-powerful. There is no sunset, and the princess is a fool.

I'm still at my writing desk when Cee-Cee enters without knocking. I'm startled by her sudden presence and annoyed that she feels entitled to enter without permission. I don't want her to see me like this.

I sit stiffly as she eases her way into the room, peering past me at the sheet of blue notepaper in front of me. "Writing a letter?"

She asks it so casually, as if we haven't just had a cataclysmic argument. I drag my diary across the half-written page and fold my hands over it. "A poem," I lie. "One I've been working on for several weeks."

"I didn't know you were writing again." She tries for a smile, then drops it when she realizes I'm not in the mood for smiles. "May I see it?"

"You've never cared about poetry before. Mine least of all. In fact, I remember you running to Father once with a notebook of mine and getting me in trouble."

She sighs wearily. "Are we going to read through the entire catalog of my sins?"

"If you'd like."

I push to my feet and step away from the desk, prepared to do battle again. Instead, Cee-Cee surprises me by fishing a freshly pressed handkerchief from her pocket and handing it to me. I accept it warily and blot my eyes.

She wanders to the bed and drops down heavily. "We shouldn't fight."

I say nothing. I'm not interested in her olive branch.

"Look, I'm sorry about the things I said earlier. I didn't realize how serious it had gotten with the two of you, and you caught me off guard. You've always been the little sister, and when I see you wandering into trouble, I suppose I still feel a need to protect you."

I can scarcely believe my ears. "When have you ever protected me?"

She drops her gaze. "I know we haven't been close, but that doesn't mean I don't care about you. We're family."

I study her—her wide, soft eyes and turned-down mouth—and wonder who this stranger is sitting on my bed. Certainly no one I've ever met. She looks tired, even a bit shaken. I sit down beside her, stiff, silent.

"You think me harsh," she says quietly. "And I suppose I am. Sometimes out of need, other times out of habit. But I've had so much responsibility since . . . since Mother died. And there's always been such a difference in our ages. I've never quite known how to be with you, how to straddle the line between mother and sister. But you're grown up now. A woman, not a child. We should be friends."

Friends.

I stare at her handkerchief, freshly pressed a moment ago, now wrung into a damp knot. We've barely been sisters. How can we ever be friends? Friends trust one another. And I don't trust anyone anymore.

She brings her face close to mine, offering a tremulous smile. "Can we, do you think? Put the harshness behind us?" She reaches for my hand, tracing her thumb over my knuckles. "Please?"

The moment of softness, so unexpected, so unfamiliar, brings a fresh rush of tears. I try to hold them at bay, but it's useless. I crumple against her, sobbing.

"Poor darling," she croons, patting my back. "It can't be as bad as all that."

I let myself relax against her. Like a child who's suffered a fall, I'm shaken and clingy, desperate for something sure to hold on to. And I'm suddenly so tired.

"We're different people, you and I." Her voice is soft, almost maternal. "We may have different roles to play, but we're family and always will be. Perhaps I've neglected you, even pushed you away, but it was because I didn't know how to take care of you properly. You were so different from me as a child and so much . . . like Helene."

Her voice falters, as if the mention of our mother's name causes her pain. "She and I weren't close the way you two were. You were always her favorite, and I suppose I was jealous. Then she got sick and there was just Father. I was so desperate for his approval. I said and did whatever he wanted me to, but I hurt you in the process. Can you forgive me?"

For as long as I can remember, I have craved my sister's love. When my mother went away and I was left on my own in this cold, enormous house, I longed for the kind of softness she's offering now. But after everything I've learned today, how can I even consider forgiving her? And yet, the pull is there, the temptation to unclench my fists and take what's being offered. But I'm too exhausted to think about it now, too raw, too empty.

She pats my hand as if something's been decided. "You're confused now and hurting. You think you can't live without this man, that he's your night and day, your entire world. But the truth is you barely know him. All you know is what he's told you, what he wants you to believe. But a man who would try to turn you against your family was never going to make you happy. He doesn't understand our way of life. You deserve a man who cares about the things you care about, who can give you the kind of life you're used to. And your children. It's important to think about your children, about the kind of world they'll grow up in."

I nod, barely registering her words. I just want to be alone, to digest all that's happened—all I've been told and all I haven't. My eyes slide to the scrap of blue notepaper just visible beneath my diary—the half-written letter waiting to be finished—and I remember the look on your face when you walked in and realized I'd found your notes. The guilt and the panic, *the scramble to explain yourself. You asked as I was leaving if I would still be there tomorrow. I didn't answer because I didn't know. I still don't.*

"Thank you," I say, pressing Cee-Cee's handkerchief back into her hands. "I'd like to be alone for a while. I have such a terrible headache."

"Of course you do. You should lie down and close your eyes. But first, go and wet a cloth for your eyes. You might make yourself a headache powder while you're at it. Or we can send to the druggist for something stronger, something to help you sleep. You'll see. Everything will look better after a little rest. Go on now. I'll turn back your covers while you get the cloth."

In the bathroom, I prepare a powder and swallow it in two long gulps, retching as the last of it goes down. I stand over the sink, startled by my own reflection. For a moment, my mother looks back at me from the mirror. Raw, red-rimmed eyes. A cloud of messy dark hair. Pale, tearstained cheeks. Exactly how she looked the last time I saw her.

I wash away what's left of my makeup, then carry the washcloth back to bed. I'm startled to find Cee-Cee still hovering. She's turning back the bedspread, rounding up crumpled tissues.

"There now," she says, smiling indulgently. "That's better. But promise me, no more poetry today. Poor thing. You look positively dreadful. Try to rest if you can. I'll send some tea up in a little while. We'll talk again when you're feeling better."

I wait until she's gone and lock the door behind her, then return to my desk and my unfinished letters.

Regretting Belle

(pgs. 87–92)

6 December 1952
London, England

Eleven years on, and it still feels like yesterday, the wound still raw, still fes-
tering. The day you vanished from my life. Shall I tell you how it was? How
it felt? Yes, I think I will. Because I shouldn't be the only one to remember
that day.

 The sun slices through the bedroom blinds right on schedule. I roll off
the bed, still in my clothes. I've waited all night for the phone to ring, lis-
tened for the scrape of your key in the lock. Neither came. But this is a good
sign, I tell myself. If you weren't still planning to be at the station, you would
surely have had the decency to at least pick up the phone. You wouldn't leave
me standing alone on a train platform. And so my things are packed by the
time the sun is fully up, my rented bureau emptied, the medicine cabinet
in the tiny bathroom stripped bare.

 I arrive at Penn Station two hours before our appointed meeting time,
our tickets tucked in the pocket of my coat, a pair of suitcases in one hand
and my father's old typewriter in the other. I enter from Seventh Avenue,

passing through the arcade of posh little shops selling hats and scarves and perfume, and head toward the lunchroom where we've agreed to meet.

I'm immediately swallowed up by the noisy pulse of the concourse. It's a massive space, with an intricate web of wrought-iron arches and gleaming glass panels suspended overhead. The enormous clocks hanging at both ends remind me that I have quite an uncomfortable wait ahead of me.

Eventually, I move to the waiting room, a cavernous chamber with stone columns; a high, vaulted ceiling; and rows of wooden benches that look like church pews. It's less crowded here, quieter. The space reminds me of a cathedral, perhaps because I've been silently praying since I passed through the doors.

I find a place beside a woman with an outlandish feathered hat and enough luggage for an ocean voyage. She eyes me coolly, then nods. I nod back and settle in to pass the next hour. I scan the sea of faces as they blur past. None of them is likely to be yours—it's much too early—but I look anyway, on the off chance that you might be early too.

Every dark-haired woman in a smart hat and heels sends my pulse careening. Several times I push to my feet, sure I've picked you out in the crowd. Then I settle back onto my bench, keenly aware that the woman beside me is growing annoyed. I don't care. I'm exhausted and edgy, checking my watch at three-minute intervals, willing the hands to speed up and put me out of my misery. Eventually, it's time. I wander back to the lunchroom with our cases and station myself near the door to wait.

By 2:45, I know you're not coming.

Still, I head down the stairs to our platform, in case you're running late and decided to go straight to the train. I set down the cases and walk up and down, neck craned, desperate for a glimpse of you in the swarm of travelers.

At precisely 3:04 p.m., the Limited pulls away from the platform. I stand watching, peering through each window as it moves past, hoping there's been some kind of mix-up about where we were supposed to meet. Then I remember both tickets are in my jacket pocket and I realize the Limited will pull into Chicago tomorrow morning with an empty sleeper car.

I should have seen it coming, did see it really. Your excuse-making, your foot-dragging. But I convinced myself we'd gotten past all that. I hated myself for my suspicions, for thinking you were looking for an excuse to run back to your family and your ridiculous fiancé—but in the end, I wound up handing you exactly what you were looking for. Still, you could have spared me the station.

~

I'm numb by the time I return to my apartment. I slide the key into the lock, knowing before I walk through the door that I won't find you on the other side. I drop the suitcases and sag onto the sofa, not bothering to take off my hat and coat. I'm still sitting there when I see something slip beneath the door.

It takes a moment to process what I'm seeing—an envelope with my name scribbled in black ink—and then I'm on my feet, scrambling for the door, stumbling over suitcases and nearly falling out into the hall.

"Belle!"

Your name echoes in the narrow hallway. But instead of you, I see a lanky boy with a tweed cap and a green coat scurrying toward the mouth of the stairs. He turns, wide-eyed, and goes still. His face is familiar. Your sister's boy. The quiet one you call Dickey. His mouth opens, but nothing comes out.

"Where's your aunt?" I say as calmly as I can manage. "Is she with you?" He closes his mouth, shakes his head.

"You're here alone?"

He nods, still silent. I keep one eye on him as I bend down to retrieve the envelope from the floor. "How did you get here?"

"On my bike. I have to go now. I'm not supposed to talk to you."

"She said that?"

"I'm supposed to just push the letter under the door and come straight back."

"Will you tell your aunt something for me?"

His eyes widen and he shakes his head. "I'm not supposed to talk to you."

He turns then and darts down the stairs. I carry the letter to the sofa and slide it out of the envelope, a single sheet of blue stationery. I stare at the page with its loopy, elegant lines. Pretty words meant to absolve you, but you needn't have bothered. It changes nothing.

I've heard people say that at the most terrible moments of their lives, they felt as if the ground had been yanked out from under them. I always thought it a hyperbolic turn of phrase. Now I know better. That moment on the platform, when the train pulled away and I was left standing with the cases, I felt as if I'd been dropped into some bottomless abyss, all my tomorrows black and empty. There's no forgetting a moment like that— no forgiveness. For us, the die was cast the moment that day's 3:00 p.m. Limited left the station without us.

I crumple the note and toss it away, then go to the kitchen and retrieve the bottle of gin I tossed in the bin before I left. I pour myself a glass and swallow half of it in one go, welcoming the trail of fire it leaves on the way to my gut, the brief but woozy kick as it hits bottom.

I've just topped up my glass when the phone rings. I stare at it, heart thumping against my ribs. I can't bear to hear your voice again. Not if you're just going to repeat what's in the note or, worse, say you're sorry. I let it ring. And ring.

But what if you've changed your mind? I lift the receiver, clear my throat. "Hello?"

"I can't believe you didn't call, you bastard!"

Not you. Goldie.

There's a kind of caving in in my chest, the finishing blow. I tell myself to hang up, but I can't make my arm work. Instead, I stand there, clutching my glass of gin, and let her screech.

"I was sure you'd come crawling back when you realized what an idiot you'd been. Throwing away the kind of story every newspaperman dreams of—an honest-to-god bombshell—because you've developed a taste for some expensive bit of skirt? I never took you for a fool, but I guess you are. So it looks like I'm going to have to be the bigger man here. And if I were in your shoes, I'd think very carefully."

Her consonants are thick and slushy, the way they get when she's been drinking. Still, she pushes on. "I'm going to give you one more chance to be a star, you British baboon. Not that you deserve it. And to prove I'm serious, I'm going to let you name your price. Hell, I'll even let you write the headline. But this offer comes with an expiration date. You've got twenty-four hours to make up your mind and get back to your desk or I'll make someone else a star."

I swallow the rest of my gin and thump down the empty glass. "I don't need twenty-four hours."

Forever, and Other Lies

(pgs. 70–76)

December 7, 1941
New York, New York

I slip out of the house before breakfast with nothing but my handbag, duck-ing out through the back door, then make my way along the service alley to the garage. Banks isn't about yet, since my father's away, and the garage is quiet. I lift the keys to the Chrysler from the pegboard on the wall and slide behind the wheel. I feel almost giddy as the motor purrs to life. I imagine you waiting for me across town, pacing and watching the clock, as eager as I am to begin our new life.

Our tickets—the ones you bought for yesterday's Limited—have gone to waste. How I wish I had decided sooner and left in time to make that train. We'd be in Chicago by now, perhaps on our way to the registrar's office. But we'll buy new tickets when we get to the station and at long last wave farewell to New York. A day later than we'd planned, perhaps, but what's one day compared to a lifetime?

It seems a reckless thing to do, to put my trust in you again after what I learned, but after all my weeping and wrestling, I realized I couldn't bear to lose you. But with Cee-Cee watching my every move, I didn't trust the phone. And so I paid Dickey a dollar to deliver my letter on his way to the druggist. When I swore him to secrecy, he eyed me warily, so I wasn't entirely sure he'd see it through. But later, he knocked on my door and told me the deed was done. He could barely look me in the eye, poor thing. He's not cut out for intrigue.

I haven't left Cee-Cee a note; she'll know soon enough where I've gone. And by then I'll have slipped the net for good, never to set foot in my father's house again. I keep my eye on my rearview mirror as I drive, recalling Cee-Cee's gleeful admission that she's been keeping tabs on me. I couldn't bear it if something were to go wrong now.

I have to park a block and a half away from your building, then climb the narrow flight of stairs to the second floor. I'm a little light-headed by the time I reach the top. I half expect to find you hovering in the open doorway, but you're not. I'm even more surprised when I try the knob and find it locked. I dig out my key and let myself in, nearly tripping over my suitcase sitting just inside the door.

I wander through the rooms, casually at first, then more frantically. Looking for you. Looking for your suitcase. In the bedroom, the bureau is bare, the bed still made. The bathroom, too, has been emptied of your things. But that's normal, I tell myself, pushing down a mounting sense of unease. We're going away and you've packed it all. That's why everything feels so empty, so unsettlingly quiet.

I hunt for a note, but there isn't one. There isn't anything—except an empty gin bottle in the sink. Every trace of you is gone. The room wobbles and sways. I close my eyes, waiting for it to stop. When I open them again, I spot the envelope on the floor near the couch, blue, with your name on the front. The flap is open, its contents gone.

I'm still staring at the envelope when a man in a rumpled shirt and a stained cardigan appears in the open doorway. "You can't be in here."

"I'm looking for the man who lives here."

"No one lives here," he says with a trace of annoyance. "Tenant flew the coop last night."

I blink at him as the words sink in. "Flew the coop?"

"Yes, ma'am. Knocked on my door around suppertime to tell me he was clearing out. Said he'd wrapped up his work here and was off to cover the war. I didn't know you could still get over there, but maybe he's got connections. His type usually does."

Suddenly there isn't enough air in the room and I feel as if I'm about to slide to the floor. I grab for the arm of the sofa, dimly aware of the landlord's alarmed expression.

"Hey, are you sick?" His eyes narrow, looking me up and down. "I remember you now. Coming around at odd hours. Never staying long."

The change in his expression makes my cheeks go hot. I consider denying it, assuring him he's mistaken, but it hardly matters now. I straighten and run a hand over my hair. "Did he leave a forwarding address for his mail?"

"No. Nothing like that." He presses his lips together then, as if he's just grasped the situation. "Left you flat, did he?"

I look away. "It would seem so, yes."

"Tough break. But maybe you're better off. Any man who'd leave you to go play in a war needs his head examined."

I stare at him, my throat too tight to reply.

"Well, if you're in need of an apartment, doll, this one's available. I can make you a good deal, too, since your fella paid the month out."

The idea that I would want to live in this apartment is ridiculous, but it suddenly dawns on me that I have no backup plan. It never occurred to me that you wouldn't be here or that I could have miscalculated so completely. Now, the thought of having to return to my father's house, to my sister's gloating smile, is more than I can bear.

"Hey, you okay? You don't look so good."

I shake my head and move toward the door.

He takes a step toward me, as if to block my way, then points to the suitcase parked haphazardly inside the door. "That yours?"

I glance at the suitcase, remembering the weeks I've spent carefully filling it. My trousseau, you teasingly called it. "Yes, it's mine."

"Aren't you going to take it with you?"

"No."

I manage to make it down the stairs and all the way back to the car before falling apart. I lean my head against the icy steering wheel, the thrum of traffic muffled beyond the car windows, and finally, I break. How could you, Hemi? After everything—how could you do it? When you knew I was coming.

I barely remember the drive back to my father's or dropping the car off at the garage. Cee-Cee is in the foyer when I walk in, arranging a bowl of flowers. She peers at me over the blooms as I shrug off my coat, lingering on my face. My eyes feel swollen and gritty, as if I've spent the afternoon in a smoke-filled room.

I expect her to demand to know where I've been, who I've seen. Instead, she inspects me briefly and returns to her gladiolas. I'm so relieved, I could cry. I don't think I could bear another scene with her at this moment. I head for the staircase and manage to make it to the top. I'm so terribly tired all of a sudden, so utterly and completely empty.

Finally, I reach my room and lock myself in. After washing my face and swallowing one of the sleeping powders Dickey brought from the druggist, I fall onto the bed, craving only oblivion. Tomorrow, I'll think about what to do. Tomorrow, I'll make plans.

~

I have no idea what time it is or how long I've been asleep when I hear Cee-Cee outside my door, cursing and banging, rattling the knob.

"Open the door, for heaven's sake! Something's happened!"

I'm still muzzy from sleep, but eventually her words penetrate. Something's happened. *Scenarios tumble through my head as I scramble to sit up. You've changed your mind and come back. My father's gotten wind of our plans and cut his business trip short in order to deal with me. Or perhaps he's already dealt with you. The thought sends a chill through me.* I bolt from the bed and hurry to unlock the door.

Cee-Cee pushes in, grim-faced and out of breath. "The Japanese have bombed the naval base at Pearl Harbor. They just broke in on the radio with a reporter who's there. You could hear the bombs going off in the background, things exploding. It sounds bad."

It takes a moment for my brain to shift gears. *Not you. Not my father. The Japanese.* "How could it happen?"

"A sneak attack, they say. Planes downed. Ships on fire. God knows how many killed. They think Manila's been hit too. Roosevelt will get his war now. They're probably popping the champagne corks as we speak."

I stare at her, horrified. *That's what she's thinking at this moment. No outrage over men dying, no anguish for widowed wives and orphaned children. Just resentment that my father's precious cause—the gift to Hitler of a neutral United States—is almost certainly lost.*

"Has the president spoken?"

"No. But he will. This is exactly what he's been praying for."

"You think the president of the United States has been praying that we'd be attacked and hundreds of people would be killed?"

"You still don't understand, do you, who's pulling the strings and why? This wasn't a random attack. It was orchestrated to drag us into their war. The Jews and the communists want us to use our money and our resources to fight their war for them. Why should we? Let them raise their own army and fend for themselves."

Cee-Cee's words stun me. "The people you're talking about . . . our mother was one of them. Her blood—Jewish blood—runs through your veins the same as mine. They . . . are us."

271

"Never say that again. Not in this house. Not anywhere."

Her eyes glitter coldly as she regards me, reminding me of the night of my mother's breakdown. I flash back to that moment on the stairs, her queer little smile and inexplicable words. Now we'll see. *And afterward, how she slid into my mother's place and systematically removed every trace of her from our lives.*

"He's done this to you," I say, seeing her clearly. Seeing it all clearly. "He poisoned you against her, little by little, and then he rewarded you for it. He taught you to be ashamed of her, ashamed of yourself. Because you're like her. We're both like her."

"I'm not like her!" Cee-Cee shrieks. "I'm an American. A real American. And so are my children. I have a duty to protect our name and our way of life, to keep it unpolluted."

Suddenly my father is staring back at me. The hardness, the hatred, the steely superiority. I see it all in my sister. "Hemi was right about you. About both of you. He had you pegged from the start."

"Ah yes, the paperboy." She flashes a chilly smile. "Come to think of it, why aren't you with him now, having lunch in his squalid little walk-up?" The smile hardens. "Or have you miscalculated again?"

Her words hit me like a dash of cold water. I want to deny it, but how can I when I've been such a fool about everything?

She tips her head to one side and feigns a little pout. "Poor thing. Has he finished with you? If I were you, I'd count myself lucky that I managed to escape relatively unscathed." Her eyebrows lift ever so slightly. "Assuming you have, of course."

"Get out."

She turns, then glances back at me. "I'm not sure when Father will be home, but it won't be long now, and he isn't likely to be in a very good mood when he arrives. I'd think long and hard before mentioning Helene. Or the paperboy. I can promise it won't end well."

Forever, and Other Lies

(pgs. 77–80)

December 10, 1941
New York, New York

I've spent three days in a kind of twilight. Three days believing I've been hurt as deeply as it's possible to be hurt. But I'm wrong. There's more to come.
Shall I tell you how it was? How it felt? It only seems fair.
I'm still avoiding my sister, keeping to my room when I know she's home. I have nothing to say to her, though I suspect at some point she and my father will have a great deal to say to me. About you. About Teddy. About my duty to the family. Because in the end, it always comes back to duty. They have no idea what I've already given up, the scandal they were spared for my sake.
I despise Cee-Cee for being right about you, and myself for being so completely taken in. I find myself reliving every moment you and I spent together, every word, every kiss, every touch, looking for something I should have seen but didn't. Perhaps she's right, though. Perhaps I have dodged a bullet. And perhaps in a few years—a hundred or so—I may even believe it. But it doesn't feel that way just now.

I wait every day for the mail to arrive, hoping there will be something from you. A letter telling me where you are, asking me to come to you. Or at least explaining why you did what you did. There hasn't been, of course. And there won't be. Some part of me knows that.

But there has been a telegram from my father. Cee-Cee made sure it was on this morning's breakfast tray. It seems the Boston rally has been canceled, though my father plans to remain for another week. Since the attack on Pearl Harbor, Lindbergh's beloved America First committee has begun to fray and my father and his friends are hoping to hold it together. The last line is about me: a directive to keep an eye on me until he can come home and deal with me properly.

My sister is toying with me, dangling his return like a threat. I don't care. I refuse to be bullied or remain in this house full of hatred and secrets. He'll cut me off without a cent, but I have some money of my own, from the trust my mother left me when she died. Not a lot by my father's standards, but enough for an easy life by almost anyone else's.

That I will leave here has been decided. It's the where *I haven't quite settled yet. I had pinned all my hopes on California, but that's when it was us. I'm not sure I could bear it now. I should hate you. I do hate you. But I can't help wondering where you are, what you're doing, and if you ever think of me. I shouldn't care. You're not worth my tears. But of course, I care. You knew that when you left.*

The war has begun in earnest. It's just Japan for now, but it's only a matter of time until Roosevelt declares on Germany too. I think of you, of your impassioned speeches about our moral responsibility to join the Europeans in their fight against the Nazis. You were right—about every bit of it—but all I can think of are the horrors of the last war, the blood and death and gore—and you, somewhere in the middle of it, writing it all down for the sake of history.

Your leaving has left me in a kind of strange twilight, a limbo of drowsy days and sleepless nights. I can't seem to get my footing back. But time is running out. I need to make my plans, but I can't think here, with the walls tight around me.

I strip out of my robe and throw on the first thing I find in my closet. I hold my breath as I step out into the hall, expecting to be waylaid and sent back to my room. But there's no sign of Cee-Cee as I make my way downstairs.

Outside, the air is cold and sharp. I welcome the sting of it as I head down Park Avenue. I have no idea where I'm going. Certainly not anywhere I might be recognized. The last thing I want is to run into someone I know, to be forced to smile and make small talk.

I keep my head down and walk briskly for several blocks. Gradually, the scenery changes, stately houses giving way to brownstones and then to squatty brick apartment houses with shops tucked beneath, their windows decorated for the holidays. A pharmacy, a shoe repair shop, a music store with used clarinets and violins in the window. I study the parade of determined faces coming toward me, all too busy to pay me much mind. It feels good to be anonymous, to gaze at face after face without fear of being known. And then I realize what I'm doing. I'm looking for you—your face, your shoulders, your long-legged gait—somewhere in that swift-moving river of humanity.

It's a ridiculous thing to hope. So ridiculous I feel the clutch of tears in my throat. I reverse course abruptly, nearly blundering into a woman with several packages in her arms. Something about her is familiar, the thin mouth and faintly birdlike nose. Lisa. Her name pops into my head. No, Lissa, a seamstress at one of the dress shops I frequent.

I pivot away from her, ducking behind a nearby newsstand. I pretend to browse the racks of magazines, papers, and tabloids. And then I see it—a grainy rendition of my parents' wedding photo staring back at me from the front page of the New York Weekly Review, *along with the garish headline:* GRUESOME ASYLUM DEATH RAISES FRESH EYEBROWS.

My legs go limp and for a moment I think I'm going to be sick right there on the street. I wait until the sensation passes, then pull a copy from the rack. I'm shaking all over and the words shift and blur as I read, but the story is all too familiar.

Multiple suicide attempts, an unexplained knife, the thinly veiled suggestion that what had previously been labeled an accident might not have been an accident at all. There's more on the second page, a laundry list of anti-Semitic and pro-Nazi groups with which my father is said to be affiliated, a longer list than I knew, and finally, the thinly veiled suggestion that he may have gone to nefarious lengths to conceal his wife's Jewish heritage. At the bottom of the second page are two additional photos: one of me and one of Cee-Cee, with our names.

You haven't left anything out. Not even me.

"Buy it or put it back, lady. This ain't a library."

I glance up to find a man with wind-burned cheeks and a day's worth of beard glaring at me. I close the paper and toss it down, too numb to feel relief that he appears not to recognize me. He will by tomorrow.

By tomorrow, everyone will.

Forever, and Other Lies

(pgs. 81–83)

December 18, 1941
New York, New York

There will be no wedding in June.

Teddy's parents have made it official, expressing shock and dismay at the Weekly Review's recent revelations about my father. I suspect they'll waste little time before arranging another matrimonial merger. There are faces to save, after all, and what better way to paper over their son's brief but unfortunate engagement to me than to wed him to some new and unsullied bride—preferably one with pure gentile bloodlines.

My face will not be saved.

I'm the jilted one, unworthy in light of the scandal that has tainted my family, which, in light of my transgressions seems only fair. It's a relief to no longer be thought of as an asset, a thing to be dealt or traded, but it's made me strangely invisible. My father has barely spoken to me since his return from Boston. He's occupied just now, trying to salvage his business interests, which appear to be in free fall. I suspect his newfound visibility has kept him from acting on his first impulse, which was likely to pack me off to some godforsaken place—the way he did my mother.

In that way, at least, your vulgar little exposé has protected me.

It took several days, but eventually, the most lurid details elbowed past the war news. The other papers have picked it up now as well, as you surely knew they would. How proud you must be to have pulled it off.

Father's enemies are ringing bells and drinking champagne. He's threatening a libel suit, but his lawyers warn that a trial would only keep the thing alive and require him to answer uncomfortable questions—publicly and under oath. Wiser, they say, to roundly deny the allegations and let the thing die a natural death.

And so we are all in scandal mode. The phone rings morning and night and the press is camped out on the street in front of the house, waiting to pounce on anyone who happens to enter or exit, rendering us all virtual prisoners. I'm beyond caring about any of it, but Cee-Cee's mood pivots between grief and outrage as, one by one, her friends find reasons to cancel lunches and teas and card games. The usual invitations to holiday parties haven't come and she's been asked to resign from several of her women's clubs. I wish I could feign sympathy, but I can't. There's an old adage about chickens coming home to roost that keeps popping into my head.

I do feel bad for her children, who've been pulled out of school and handed over to a brigade of tutors who come to the house three days a week via the kitchen entrance. It seems I've made rather a mess for everyone, welcoming a viper into our midst.

Poor Dickey seems to be taking it the hardest, avoiding my gaze when we happen to pass in the corridor or on the stairs. I suppose he resents being enlisted to deliver my letter that night, to have, in his mind, unwittingly been part of his family's downfall. I wish I could explain that nothing in that letter had any bearing on what's happening now, that the damage had already been done—and that it was done by you. But Cee-Cee has forbidden me to speak to any of them. It's not so terrible: none of them except Dickey ever paid me much mind. I do regret losing his affection, though. Such a sweet and guileless boy. So unlike the rest of us.

For now, I'll bide my time and get my affairs in order. I must plant myself somewhere, put down roots, and make a life of some kind. I'm not sure what that life will look like. I never planned beyond you. I never imagined I would have to. My mistake.

I wonder now and then if you ever wonder about me. If, when you close your eyes, you still see my face, hear my voice, feel my touch? Or am I already a part of your past? A shadow that briefly crossed your path, nebulous now and unshaped?

I wonder how long it will be until I'm free of you—and what it will feel like when I am. I can't quite imagine it, looking inside myself and not finding you there. Like a piece of me has been carved away, which I suppose it has.

Perhaps I should count myself lucky, feel relief that I found out who you were before things went any further. But no, I don't think I'll let you off quite so easily.

Regretting Belle

(pgs. 93–95)

31 December 1953
London, England

It seems another year is ending, all gone by in another hour or so.

A fitting time to write our epilogue, I suppose, and put an end to this unhappy exercise. I was hoping for a kind of catharsis when I began it, or perhaps exorcism *is a more appropriate word for what I hoped to accomplish. To be released from my sins—and yours.*

A few scribbled pages, I told myself, and it would finally be over. I would let myself bleed until the bleeding was done, until I was emptied of you. How foolish I was to ever think it could be that simple. Still, there are a few things more to say.

I'll begin with the story that appeared in the Review *shortly after I left the States—a story, I might add, I learned about purely by chance, nearly two full years after it was published. That this story happened to contain facts to which I was privy has no doubt led you to conclude that I had some hand in it, but it is a matter of record that the name attached to it was not mine. I gave you my word that day in my apartment—the last time I saw you, as it turns out—and I will not do so again. If you know me so little after all we shared, there's no point in trying to absolve myself.*

And now, in the interest of full disclosure, I will endeavor to flesh out some of the more glaring gaps in my narrative and the semblance of a life I've lived since I lost you.

I was married once. Her name was Laura. A woman with dark hair and amber eyes. She looked like you but she wasn't you, and I couldn't forgive her for it. She deserved better than I could offer, as I told her the night she left. She deserved to be happy and to make someone else happy, but that someone was never going to be me.

You saw to that.

From that very first night at the St. Regis, you have filled my brain, leaving no room for anyone else. Even with an ocean separating us, I could feel you, like the ache of a phantom limb. For a while, I had the war to distract me, and my work. There were stories that needed telling, atrocities that needed to be exposed, whether the world wanted to see them or not. Grinding hunger. Gas chambers. The ovens. Human beings reduced to ash. And then the liberation of the camps. Someone had to cover that, too, so the world would know and never let it happen again. But after the war came an unbearable quiet, an emptiness riddled with wounds that had nothing to do with bullets and battlefields.

And then suddenly there was Laura, sitting across from me at a dinner one night, a ghost promising second chances. We were married four weeks later. I meant to make a go of it, to cauterize the oozing places you left behind, but every time I looked at her, I felt the knife twist, and the bleeding would start all over again. She never knew why it didn't work. She never heard your name—or even knew you existed—but you were always there between us. The other woman.

The only woman.

I almost came looking for you once, in a moment of madness and perhaps more gin than was good for me. I thought if I saw your face one more time, I could walk away clean. I'd shut up the vault with all my memories inside and finally get on with the business of living. By morning I'd come to my senses, of course. Or maybe I just ran out of gin. I can't remember.

Instead, I dragged myself to my typewriter and banged out a pair of books about the war. They were well received and earned several prestigious awards, but they were cool, clinical things, bloodless, academic postmortems. I hated them.

I was weary of war, of its tactics and mechanics and politics. I wanted to write something that felt alive, something with a pulse. But I couldn't get it off the ground. So many false starts and crumpled pages. Wastebaskets full, mocking me for weeks on end. And then one night I woke up in the dark and you were there, the ache of that phantom limb, throbbing with a vengeance. The pulse I'd been searching for.

The words spilled out like poison—the story of us. Alas, dear Belle, it is a story without a happy ending, with no ending at all really, only these few bitter lines. And so, as the old year dies and a new one begins, I will bring this bloody tale of ours to a close. I'll have it bound, I think, and make a present of it to you. A souvenir or a trophy. I shall leave that for you to decide.

By the by, it might surprise you to know that every now and then, I find myself thinking about that suitcase, wondering if anyone ever made use of it or if it's shut up in some attic or basement somewhere, still full of your things. It doesn't matter—how could it after all these years?

Still, I do wonder.

—H

THIRTEEN

ASHLYN

We develop a particular fondness for our favorite books, the way they feel and smell and sound, the memories they invoke, until they begin to exist for us as living, breathing things.

—*Ashlyn Greer,* The Care & Feeding of Old Books

October 21, 1984
Rye, New Hampshire

Ashlyn wrapped her arms tight about her body, warding off the breeze pushing in from the harbor. She couldn't help feeling a pang of disappointment as Ethan closed the copy of *Regretting Belle* and set it on the table between their chairs. It felt like the end of a movie, when the credits start to roll and you realize no one's going to ride off into the sunset. She had known, of course, but it still felt wrong somehow, unfinished.

"I can't believe that's really it."

"For Hemi, at least," Ethan replied. "There's still the last of Belle's book to get through if you want."

Ashlyn shook her head. "No. Not just now. It's not like we don't know how that one ends too."

Ethan frowned. "You sound sad."

"I am, a little. I guess I'm used to books where all the loose ends are tied up in a pretty bow. I knew this one wouldn't end with soaring violins, but it feels unfinished and I'm not sure why. After everything, he never stopped loving her."

"Or hating her, apparently."

"He didn't hate her, Ethan."

"What would *you* call it?"

"Despair," Ashlyn said quietly. "He was heartbroken. Grieving for someone he'd lost. So was Belle. They only pretended to hate one another. Because it felt safer, stronger."

Ethan shrugged. "Maybe. But to just no-show like that was pretty harsh. She could have let him know she wasn't coming. Instead, she bailed. Just left him hanging."

The response should have surprised Ashlyn but didn't. She'd noticed it several times this week, the faint but palpable friction that had started creeping into their conversation, as if they'd each unconsciously stepped into the story and assumed their respective gender roles. Without meaning to, they had chosen sides.

"She didn't leave him hanging, Ethan. She sent him a letter, presumably to tell him she was coming. If anyone bailed, it was Hemi. Can you imagine what it must have felt like to walk into that empty apartment?"

"About the same as finding yourself alone on a train platform, I imagine. And we don't know what the letter said. We only know what Belle implies. What we *do* know is how Hemi reacted after reading it. He went straight for the gin, and it clearly wasn't to pour himself a celebratory shot. I'm not sure I blame him for disappearing. She'd been dragging her feet for weeks. How many times was he supposed to give her the benefit of the doubt? At some point, you have to call it, don't you?"

"Maybe. But something doesn't add up. You said it yourself; we don't know what the letter said. You're assuming from Hemi's reaction that it was a Dear John letter, but why would Belle show up at his apartment if she'd just given him the boot? She expected him to be there, waiting for her."

"That argument goes both ways. If Hemi honestly believed she was coming and all was forgiven, why disappear? The only logical explanation is that the letter was a polite kiss-off."

"And to get even, he went ahead and published the story?"

Ethan blew out a breath. "I'm not saying it was right, but at that point, what did he have to lose?"

"He denies having anything to do with it."

Ethan nodded, though not convincingly. "He does. But both things can't be true, can they? People rewrite history, Ashlyn. They clean up their messes, often by dumping them over someone else's fence. I'm pretty sure that's what we've been reading. Two people trying to tidy up an ugly breakup."

Ashlyn tipped her head back, watching the clouds overhead shred in the wind. Perhaps Ethan was right. Perhaps they were both to blame and hoped to exonerate themselves by rewriting the narrative. Over time, they may even have come to believe their own version of events. A lie, repeated often enough, eventually became the truth. Daniel taught her that. And yet the discrepancies between Belle's and Hemi's versions continued to niggle.

She looked at Ethan squarely, not ready to concede his point. "Does Hemi strike you as the kind of guy who'd go back on his word out of spite?"

Ethan propped his elbows on the railing and looked out over the harbor. "Under normal circumstances, no. But Goldie waved a fistful of cash at precisely the right moment, and Hemi—a.k.a. Steven Schwab—appears to have accepted her offer."

It was true, though Ashlyn hated to admit it. Hemi had both means and motive, and the evidence suggesting he and Steven Schwab were one and the same was hard to deny. "I called Ruth a few days ago and asked her to try to find the actual story. Unfortunately, there isn't much out there from the *Review*. The paper shut down in 1946, but maybe the piece is still floating around on microfilm somewhere."

"And then what? Say we find the story. What have we proven? Come to that, why do we *need* to prove anything? The truth is we're never going to know for sure who did what to whom, and it doesn't matter. Whether we learn the truth or not, nothing changes. I know you don't want to hear this, but I think it's time to admit we're running out of road."

Ashlyn answered with a grudging nod. "I just can't help feeling we've missed something. They loved each other. Enough to throw away everything in order to be together. And then something went wrong. Something that shouldn't have. You don't find it strange that they're both *so* bitter, both convinced that *they* were the *real* victim?"

Ethan rolled his eyes. "Have you ever known a couple who split up where both parties *didn't* think they were the real victim? If you ask me, it's a whitewash job on both their parts."

"I don't believe that," Ashlyn shot back. "I don't believe they were trying to create an alternate version of history. They believed every word they wrote."

"Just wanting something to be true doesn't make it true, Ashlyn."

"I know that."

"Do you?"

"Yes. But this isn't me just wanting it to be true, Ethan. It *is* true. I'm certain of it."

Ethan cocked an eye at her. "You're certain?"

Ashlyn bit her lip, checking an impulse to blurt out that yes, she *was* certain. And *why* she was certain. He didn't understand. But then, how could he? Unless she told him everything.

Ethan was watching her, waiting for a response. "Ashlyn?"

She reached for her beer and took a long pull. Was she actually considering this? Revealing a secret she'd never felt safe enough to share with Daniel, simply to make her point? Risking whatever it was that might be starting between them?

"Can I tell you something?" she said quietly. "Something that's going to sound a little weird? Okay, a *lot* weird."

Ethan straightened, as if sensing the conversation was about to change. "Sure."

"I have this thing. This . . . gift. There's a name for it—psychometry. Most people think it's made-up, but it's real. At least for me." She paused for another sip of beer before continuing. "I can . . . *feel* things. Echoes, I call them."

He was frowning now, clearly perplexed. "Echoes?"

"They're what's left behind when we touch something. You. Me. We all leave echoes. And we leave them on the things we touch, like a residue. The stronger our feelings when we touch an object, the stronger the echoes. And I can read them, with my hands, with all of me, I suppose. At least that's how it feels."

She went quiet then, holding her breath as she attempted to glean his reaction. She could see him trying to work it out in his head, weighing what he'd just heard against the academic side of his nature.

Finally, a furrow appeared between his brows. "You're saying everything you touch gives off these . . . echoes?"

Ashlyn released the breath she'd been holding. A question was good. "Not everything, no. At least not for me. For me, it's just books."

"Books."

"Yes."

He stared at her, blank-faced as he tried to digest what he'd been told. "And you just happen to own a bookstore."

"Go figure, right?"

"How did . . . When . . ." He paused, shaking his head. "I don't even know what to ask. What must that be like? All day. Every day. Surrounded by books that are talking to you. How do you hear yourself think?"

Ashlyn couldn't help smiling at his description. "It isn't like that. It's not words; it's emotion, feelings that come through like tiny vibrations. But it only happens when I touch a book. I can feel what the owner felt when they were reading it—or in this case, when the authors were writing them. That's why I'm certain there was something else going on with Hemi and Belle. Because I feel it when I touch the books. The same betrayal and loss from both of them. The same certainty that they'd been betrayed by the other."

Ethan shook his head, clearly struggling to comprehend. "I'm sorry. I'm still trying to get my head around this. You're saying you can read Belle's emotions—and Hemi's—with your fingers. All these years later. How is that even possible?"

Ashlyn shrugged. "I don't know. It just is. But these books are different from anything I've ever come across. The feelings on both sides are so strong—and so similar. They're just flipped, like mirror images. I know it sounds crazy, and maybe I am obsessing a little, but this isn't some romantic fantasy I'm indulging. I feel it in my bones. There was a reason they both believed they'd been betrayed by the other. I felt it the first time I touched the books, and I *still* feel it."

To her relief, Ethan gave no sign that he found any of this implausible, though he did take several moments to process. "Have you always been able to do it?" he asked finally.

"It started when I was twelve. At first I thought everyone could do it. Then I did some reading about it." She looked down at the beer bottle in her hand, scraping at the soggy label with her thumbnail. "Turns out I'm a bit of a freak."

"Or maybe you're just more tuned in than most people."

She scrunched one eye as she looked at him. "You don't think it's weird?"

"Oh, I think it's *totally* weird. I also think it's amazing."

Ashlyn found her throat suddenly choked with tears. "Thank you."

"For calling you weird?"

"For taking me seriously." She blinked hard and looked away. "I don't talk about it much. Or at all, really. When I told my mother, she made me swear not to breathe a word to anyone, especially not my father, who would say it was the devil's work. The only person I ever told was Frank Atwater, the man who used to own the store . . . and now you."

Ethan came to stand beside her, and for a moment, they stood elbow to elbow, watching a pair of gulls skim over the harbor's silvery surface. The tide was going out. In another few hours, the water would have retreated completely, exposing a stretch of dull gray mud, providing a veritable buffet for hungry gulls and kittiwakes.

"You never told Daniel?" Ethan asked at last.

"I could never have trusted him with something like that, given him that kind of weapon to use against me."

Ethan studied her a moment, his expression thoughtful. "But you trusted me?"

"Yes."

"Don't get me wrong—I'm glad you did. But why?"

Ashlyn ducked her head, shy suddenly. "You told me that first night that you weren't interested in your family history. But you've been so great about letting me pick your brain. So patient with all my questions. I guess I wanted you to understand why it's so personal for me."

Ethan stared at his hands where they gripped the railing, quiet again as the breeze whipped the hair back from his forehead. "Before . . . ," he said finally, awkwardly. "I didn't mean to make light of how you feel. I get now why you're so invested. But it's different for me. I'm not sure how I even got involved. I should be upstairs writing, or at least working on finals.

Instead, I'm up to my ears in some romantic whodunit and I have no idea
how it happened . . . except that it gave me an excuse to keep seeing you."

His final remark caught Ashlyn off guard. "You thought you needed
an excuse?"

"Didn't I?"

The question brought a flush of warmth to her cheeks. "At first.
Maybe."

He reached up to push a lock of hair out of her eyes. "And now?"

It felt like the most natural thing in the world to lean into him,
to melt into the circle of his arms, to yield when his lips touched hers.
Natural and yet terrifying. It had been so long since she'd let herself sur-
render to anything, since she'd felt anything. Now, at a touch, all those
denied sensations flooded through her, like the steps of some long-aban-
doned dance. The winding of his hands through her hair, the rasp of his
breath against her cheek, the dizzying awareness of crumbling barriers.

This is how it starts. Exactly like this.

Ashlyn stiffened as the warning bells began to jangle. Memories of
another first kiss and all that had followed. She'd been so swept up, so
eager to be loved, that she'd forgotten to protect herself. And here she
was, on the verge of doing it again.

Ethan must have registered her sudden misgivings. He eased out of
the kiss and took a step back, looking uncertain and slightly off-balance.
"I seem to remember saying something about going slow. Should I say
I'm sorry?"

Ashlyn felt off-balance, too, registering both regret and relief as she
looked up at him. "*Are* you sorry?"

"No. But I don't want you to be either."

She touched her fingers to her lips, recalling the delicious warmth
of his mouth on hers. She wasn't sorry, but she wasn't sure that what
had just happened was a good idea for either of them.

"Ethan . . ."

He dropped his arms, stepping back. "I know."

She nearly reached for him, then decided she'd only be sending mixed signals. "I'm not sorry about what just happened. In fact, part of me wonders what took us so long, but I'm not sure—"

He held up a hand. "It's okay. I get it."

"No. You don't. I feel what you do. But there's a reason there hasn't been anyone since Daniel. A lot of reasons, actually. I'm better off by myself."

"You don't know that. If there hasn't been anyone, you can't know it."

"But I *do*, Ethan. I have too much baggage to bring to a relationship. And when I say *baggage*, I'm talking whole steamer trunks full. You deserve better than that."

Ethan stared down at the railing, shoulders bunched tightly. "I'm not proposing, Ashlyn. I'm just asking you to keep the door open—and to let me help you carry those bags now and then. No pressure. No strings." He reached for her hand. "You don't even have to give me an answer. Just stick around long enough to give me a chance."

The muffled ring of the house phone suddenly interrupted the quiet. Ethan relinquished her hand with a groan. "I need to get that. One of the professors is on baby watch and I told him I'd cover his classes for a few days if he needed me to. He said he'd call tonight."

"Go," Ashlyn told him, relieved to be spared a response. "I'll be in in a minute."

"You're not going to sneak down the deck stairs and take off while I'm inside, right? You'll be here when I get back?"

Ashlyn shot him a grin. "I'll be in in a minute. Get the phone."

She watched as he disappeared through the french doors, then saw the kitchen light go on. She took her time gathering their empty bottles and straightening the deck chairs. She needed a few minutes before she went in, to digest what had just happened.

Was she *ready* to let Ethan into her life? To risk loving and losing—again? It would be lying to say she hadn't imagined it. She'd been imagining it since that first awkward moment in his study, the first uneasy inkling that something was happening between them. But nothing had come of it. They'd fallen into a kind of partnership after that—collaboration rather than courtship—and she'd convinced herself that it was for the best.

Now, suddenly, things had escalated. She had opened the door and let him in, shared a part of herself that she hadn't even shared with Daniel. Because she trusted him. But trust was a dangerous thing. So was love. And that was where this was headed if she didn't put the brakes on. Was she willing to take that kind of leap again? To give someone the power to shatter the small but careful life she'd managed to rebuild for herself?

And there was something else to consider. The possibility that what they felt was merely a by-product of their involvement with the books. What if they'd simply gotten caught up in Belle and Hemi's story, feeling things that were likely to fade as quickly as they had ignited?

She had no answers, but the sun was nearly down and the temperature was dropping fast, the breeze off the harbor sharp against her cheeks. She had just stepped away from the railing when she heard the patio door open. She turned to find Ethan silhouetted in the doorway. She waited a moment, expecting an announcement, but he just stood there, his face in shadow.

"Well, is it a boy or a girl?"

"Neither. It was Zachary."

Her stomach did a little flip at the mention of the name. "And?"

"And Marian is alive and well and living in Massachusetts, of all places."

FOURTEEN

ASHLYN

In the happiest times of my life, I have reached for my books. In the saddest times of my life, my books have reached back.

—*Ashlyn Greer,* The Care & Feeding of Old Books

October 25, 1984
Rye, New Hampshire

Ethan opened two beers while Ashlyn unpacked the lobster rolls and fries she had picked up on the way over. She'd been more than a little surprised when he called to suggest they get some dinner. They'd spoken twice during the week. Baby watch had finally resulted in an actual baby, which meant he'd been teaching double classes. And when he wasn't teaching, he was chained to his desk, polishing the chapters he'd promised his editor.

Or maybe after their conversation on Sunday, he'd decided to give her a little space. To her relief, the kiss hadn't come up during either phone call. Instead, they'd focused on the fact that it had been days since Zachary had agreed to call Marian and pass along a message from her great-nephew.

Four days.

It wasn't a good sign. Apparently, Marian had little interest in reconnecting. In fairness, Zachary had warned Ethan that a return call was unlikely, as his mother was an extremely private person. Still, she had hoped Marian's affection for Richard Hillard might have tipped the scales in their favor. She'd clearly been too optimistic. They had agreed to wait a full week, then try once more before throwing in the towel. After that—short of stalking the woman—they were out of options.

Ethan handed her a beer, then snuck around her to grab a fry from one of the takeout containers. "How's the newsletter coming?"

Ashlyn raised her beer triumphantly. "Done. And off to the printer as of this morning. I had to beg a little, but I should have it back before Thanksgiving. How about your new classes? Is it weird stepping in midsemester?"

Ethan grabbed another fry, followed by an onion ring. "A little weird, yeah. You'd think college students would be over the whole 'slack when there's a substitute' thing, but they're not." He paused, eyeing the lobster rolls Ashlyn had just pulled from the bag. "Hey, they look good. I've got a fire going if you want to eat in the great room. Or we can just sit at the counter."

"The fire sounds nice."

"Good. You grab the beers and some napkins. I'll bring the food."

He was sliding the Styrofoam containers from the counter when the phone rang. They both went still, looked at the phone, then each other. Ashlyn held her breath as Ethan lifted the receiver, waiting for some sign that the call was what they hoped it was.

"Yes. Thank you. This is Ethan."

He was quiet a moment, listening, then slid his eyes to Ashlyn's, nodding. After another moment, he clicked the speakerphone button and laid the handset on the counter. Ashlyn covered her mouth with both hands, smothering a gasp as a women's voice suddenly filled the kitchen, low and smoky, just the way Hemi had described it.

"My son said you have some letters and cards. Things I sent your father over the years."

"Yes," Ethan replied. "I also came across a few photos while clearing out his study. I thought you might like to have them back."

"Yes," Marian said without hesitation. "I would, yes. I'm sorry I didn't get a chance to see your father before he . . . before he died. I was very fond of him." There was a stretch of silence and then: "Did you happen to find anything else?"

Ethan and Ashlyn exchanged looks.

"The books, you mean?"

"Yes."

The single word, after such a lengthy pause, felt like a confession somehow. Reluctant. Guilty. "Yes," Ethan answered. "They were in my father's study too."

"Both?"

"Yes."

"And you've . . . read them, I take it?"

Ethan hesitated, sliding his eyes back to Ashlyn's. She nodded. It seemed pointless to lie. "We did, yes. We weren't sure what they were."

"Who is *we*?" Marian asked, sounding strangely wary. "Is there a wife?"

"No. There's no wife. It's . . . She's a friend. She's the one who actually found the books. We've been reading them together."

"Well, then. I suppose you'd better come up."

"Up?"

"To Marblehead. You have questions, I'm sure. Can you come on Saturday, you and your . . . friend?"

Ethan looked at Ashlyn, brows raised.

Ashlyn nodded vigorously. It would mean closing for half a day, but there was no way she was passing up an opportunity like this. "In the afternoon," she whispered.

"Yes," Ethan said. "We can come. In the afternoon."

"Come at three and bring the letters. The address is 11 Hathaway Road. It's at the very end of the earth, so be sure you have a good map and give yourself plenty of time."

There was a click, followed by empty silence. Ethan hung up the handset and for a moment they stared at each other. "Holy crap," he said finally. "She actually called. Zachary had me convinced she wouldn't."

"She sounds . . . formidable."

He nodded gravely. "She did. Can you blame her, though? I doubt she ever imagined she'd be dealing with this after forty years."

"No. Probably not. I notice she didn't tell you to bring the books. She said bring the letters, but she didn't include the books."

"Maybe after all this time, she doesn't want them back. I'm not sure I would."

"We'll bring them, though," Ashlyn said. "They're hers."

Ethan nodded as he went to the fridge for another beer. "Can you really make the trip on Saturday? What about the shop?"

"I'll close at one and hang a sign on the door. My customers can do without me for half a day."

"Okay, then. Road trip the day after tomorrow. You know what that means, right?"

"You're going to need a good map?"

"Yeah, that too. But actually, I was talking about the books. If we're bringing them back on Saturday, this is probably the last chance we'll have to read the final pages of Belle's book. What do you say? Are you up for a little after-dinner reading?"

Forever, and Other Lies

(pgs. 84–85)

December 19, 1941
New York, New York

I've made my plans. No one knows what they are yet, though I doubt anyone would try to dissuade me if they did. I'm a pariah now, the architect of my family's downfall and a glaring example of what happens when a woman follows her passions instead of the rules.

I've settled on California after all, a tiny harbor town on the northern coast called Half Moon Bay. No one's ever heard of the place, but during Prohibition, its craggy, fog-drenched coast made it a favorite of Canadian bootleggers. I must admit, I like the irony. It's as far away from my family as it's possible to get just now and as good a place as any to wait out the war. I leave the day after tomorrow. No one will miss me. And I will miss no one. Except you. But then, you were only ever a figment of my imagination.

Still, I owe you one debt. Were it not for you and your precious Goldie, I would never have learned about my mother's heritage—my heritage now. So for that—and only that—I am grateful.

I have made a trip to Craig House in Beacon, to see the place where she died. I didn't go in. I meant to, but I couldn't in the end. Still, I had to see it for myself, to walk its grounds and feel her there. It looked just like the picture in the Review, *a gloomy place for all its antiquated grandeur. I've decided not to remember her there but to instead hold fast to the memories we made in her room, where we spent so many afternoons, singing and telling stories.*

I've tried to find the photo album she kept, the one she used to tell her stories—I would like to at least have something of her to take with me—but Cee-Cee claims to have thrown it away. Perhaps it's best I travel light. There's so little about this part of my life I wish to remember.

I've been back to Rose Hollow too. I don't know why I went. It's closed up now for the season, the horses and trainers all gone to Saratoga. The house and barns all shut up until spring. I unlocked the stable and went inside, stood where we stood the first time you kissed me, and tried to remember what you'd said or done to blind me so completely. Not that I'm likely to ever be so foolish again. You've taught me a great deal.

The follow-up stories have finally slowed to a drip and the press has at long last decamped, gone away to pick the bones of some other family. This will make my defection easier to achieve, as there are no more reporters loitering on the sidewalks, no uncomfortable questions to slow me down. Time is of the essence now.

I must make a future for myself, carve out a life without you. It will not be the life I imagined for myself, but one way or another, it will be the life I'll have chosen.

Forever, and Other Lies

(pgs. 86–99)

June 14, 1955
Marblehead, Massachusetts

At long last, I have settled down to write this final chapter. I admit I had to wrestle myself into the chair. The urge to abandon the thing has been pressing on me. It felt pointless when I began it, turning over such settled ground, rattling the bones of ghosts best left quiet. Yet here I sit with the sun streaming in and nothing left to do but place the headstone as it were.

I've taken no pleasure in it—words are your realm, not mine—but I felt compelled to correct the many inaccuracies in your version of our unfortunate entanglement. You will, I hope, forgive its technical faults. It's been some time since I attempted to put feelings to paper, but I have done my best and will send it along to you the moment I've had it bound to match yours—via our usual messenger, of course. I will also be returning the sadly warped version you sent me. I certainly don't want it.

I do hope this will be the last favor my nephew will be asked to perform concerning us. Poor Dickey. He hardly knew what to make of your mysterious package when it arrived. In fact, he nearly tossed it in the trash.

How I wish he had. Until it arrived, I had forgotten you. Or was at least content to believe I had.

And now, I, too, will finish with a bit of housekeeping. Not that you deserve a word from me, but I will take some small satisfaction in you knowing that I've managed to make a life for myself. A good life, for the most part, once I put myself back together.

It was terrible at first, after you left. Losing you that way, without any real goodbye, seemed unbearable. I thought briefly about tracking you down, of making some hideous scene until you begged my forgiveness. And then the story broke and I realized forgiveness was no longer possible.

It took a few days—Germany and Italy had just declared war on the US and Europe was all anyone could talk about—but eventually, other papers picked it up and the thing caught fire. In the space of two weeks, my father's world came down around his ears. He was hounded almost entirely from business, then lost the rest of his fortune trying to salvage the remains. He was also banned from his club, shunned by the very men he had courted so carefully over the years. If that was your intention, you succeeded beyond your wildest dreams.

I suppose I should have felt some sense of culpability for my role in bringing down the House of Manning, but I felt none. Instead, I got on a train and headed west, desperate for anonymity. I found it, too, using my mother's maiden name. You could do that then, go to some new place and reinvent yourself. No one ever asked for proof of anything in those days. You just gave them a name and that was who you were.

I lived quietly there and made friends. One very special friend, from whom the war had taken everything. She was kind to me when I had stopped believing in kindness and blessed me with a gift I've been trying to repay ever since. But those are private things, memories to which you have no right. And so I will skip ahead.

For the first time in my life, the idea of family—of true family— had become very important to me. When the war ended, I started writing letters, trying to locate my mother's family. The men were all gone, buried or scattered by the war, but I managed to find my mother's sister, Agnes, and several cousins who had fled across the border to Switzerland to escape the occupation. When France was liberated, they returned to their vineyard. My aunt and I wrote letters. They were agonizingly slow in coming and difficult to read when they did. They had lost so much. The land was a ruin, the house stripped bare, but they were determined to resurrect the vineyard and I knew I needed to go.

I needed to belong to them, to belong to their story, and in almost no time at all, I did. Being there, in the home where my mother grew up, surrounded by the people she loved, was like getting a piece of her back. I learned the prayers she wasn't allowed to say, learned the names she was told to forget. Her traditions—the ones she was forced to deny—became my traditions too. Her language, my language. Her faith, my faith. Now, years later, it's how I keep her memory alive, by honoring the woman whose memory you tainted with your story.

While in France, I also learned about the work the OSE—the Œuvre de Secours aux Enfants—was doing to find homes for displaced children. There were so many, all with nothing and no one. It was heartbreaking to see. And a reminder that there were worse things than a lost love. And so began my life's work.

You said something once that I never forgot. You said people like me never accomplish anything meaningful because we don't have to. All anyone expects from us is that we dress well and throw a good party. It stung at the time, because I knew you were only half teasing. Well, I have done something meaningful. Not because I had to but because I chose to. And when my aunt passed away and I returned to the States, I continued that work.

As for marriage, that was never in the cards for me, which is not to say I've been lonely. Far from it. My life has been full and rewarding. I never once thought of trying to find you. At least not seriously. The part of me that believed in such things—in heroes, and sunsets, and happy endings—died the day your story appeared in that rag.

You'll think me bitter, and I was for a time. A very long time. I felt I had paid a higher price for our recklessness than you—as the woman invariably does—and I wanted to punish you. But there's no point, really, in keeping score. We've gone on with our lives, totted up our wins and losses. You've no doubt made mistakes. And I've certainly made mine. You were the first, but there have been others. Some, I've managed to forgive myself for. As for the rest, I continue to atone. But I have learned this. In every wound, there is a gift. Even the self-inflicted ones.

You smashed me to bits when you left, carved my heart into tiny pieces, but chance put me back together again. I learned that I could bear the memory of your face after all. I will never be completely free of you. Your voice, your smile, even that little cleft in your chin will never be far from my thoughts. My cross and my consolation. At least I can say I didn't walk away empty-handed.

As for the suitcase, I have no idea what might have become of it. Perhaps your landlord sold it or gave the contents to his wife. I've never given it much thought. Perhaps because they were never really my things. They belonged to another woman—to Belle, the woman you left behind. But that woman no longer exists. She became someone else that day, and she got on with her life.

M—

FIFTEEN

ASHLYN

The number of lives we are capable of living is limited only by the number of books we choose to read.

—*Ashlyn Greer,* The Care & Feeding of Old Books

October 27, 1984
Marblehead, Massachusetts

It was a glorious day for a drive. Chilly and clear, with the bright autumn sun shining through gold-leafed trees. Ashlyn had closed the shop at one and eaten a sandwich in the car on the way to Ethan's. They had opted to take his Audi and she was perfectly happy to let him drive.

Marian had been right about needing a good map. It had taken them a little over an hour to get to Marblehead, but once there, they found the jumble of narrow roads and even narrower coastal side streets tricky to navigate. It didn't help that many of the street signs were either obscured by foliage, weathered beyond reading, or missing entirely, but eventually they managed to find Hathaway Road, which traced along a rocky, crescent-shaped cove and offered a breathtaking stretch of silver-gray sea.

The house stood on a high granite bluff, an impressive three-story Cape of softly weathered gray and white, with a columned portico, a cluster of red brick chimneys, and a pair of eyebrow dormers that gave the house a vaguely face-like appearance.

Ashlyn hugged her tote to her chest as Ethan pulled up the drive. Inside, the books were tucked safely in their clear plastic sleeves. She'd be giving them up today and the thought made her sad, but they belonged to Marian—if she wanted them. And in a way, it felt right, like they were finally coming home.

Ethan shut off the car and opened his door. The sound of the sea rushed in with the breeze, the distant pull and rush of waves against the rock-strewn shore. "Ready?"

"Ready."

Marian answered the bell almost immediately, as if she'd been hovering nearby. Ashlyn ventured a smile as the door pulled back. It wasn't returned, reminding her that despite Marian's invitation, their intrusion into her life was an unwelcome one.

She was surprisingly tall, almost willowy in a tailored pantsuit of charcoal-gray silk. Her blouse was the color of daffodils and the cleverly knotted scarf at her throat gave her a crisp, tailored air. Minimal makeup, single pearl studs, and a sleek chestnut chignon rounded out her *Town & Country* ensemble. She looked like money. Or at least what Ashlyn always imagined money to look like. Polished and beautiful, untouched somehow by time, despite her sixty-plus years.

Marian stepped back from the doorway, nodding with what felt like resignation. "Come in, then, and take off your coats. I suspect you'll be staying awhile."

The smell of lemon oil and beeswax greeted them as they stepped inside. The entry hall was long and low with a beamed ceiling and gleaming dark-paneled walls. There was a wide staircase with a heavy banister leading to the second floor, and the collection of heavily framed artwork ascending up the wall gave the space a slightly museum-like feel.

Marian hung up their coats, then led them through a parlor furnished with an impressive collection of eighteenth-century antiques, all polished to a high sheen. It was a beautiful room, spacious and surprisingly bright despite the mostly dark furniture, but the real showpiece was a stunning baby grand that took up one full corner of the room.

Ashlyn squinted to read the lettering stenciled in gold above the keys. SAUTER. She wasn't familiar with the name, but it was clearly an expensive instrument. "What a beautiful piano."

"Zachary's," Marian said, her face softening ever so slightly. "I bought it when he was ten. He discovered the violin the following year. It's been gathering dust ever since, but I can't bear to get rid of it. I keep telling myself I'll learn to play one day, but I never do anything about it. It's handy for displaying pictures, though." She pointed to the small collection of framed photos reflected in the piano's glossy black surface. "That's him in the black frame, taken three or four years ago now."

Ashlyn studied the face in the photograph, lean and undeniably handsome. Piercing blue eyes; a thin, straight nose; a heavy wave of dark hair pushed back off his forehead. But it was his mouth, full and faintly sensual, that held her attention. Perhaps it had to do with the smile he seemed to be suppressing. It reminded her of his boyhood photos. Even then, he'd had an infectious smile.

"He's very handsome," Ashlyn said. "Beautiful eyes."

"He was always a charmer. That's Ilese in the red frame. His sister."

The photo was reminiscent of those she had seen of Ilese as a child, the same light eyes and strawberry-blonde mane, the same sober expression. Her head was tipped to one side, but her gaze as she faced the camera was clear and unflinching, almost brash.

"Such a serious girl," Marian said fondly. "But a fierce heart."

"I can see that," Ashlyn said, smiling.

Marian stepped to the doorway, waving them through. "I was about to brew a pot of tea when you arrived. I thought we'd go out to the sunporch to talk."

They passed through a formal dining room with deep-red walls, a long table with seating for ten, and an antique sideboard lined with colorful plates and pitchers. It was like something from a magazine, everything polished and picture-perfect.

The kitchen was large and almost startlingly bright, with a bank of windows looking out over a pebbled beach and a small placid cove. Beyond the cove, a blue-gray sea stretched toward the horizon, flat and shimmery under the autumn sun. A farm table of scrubbed pine sat in front of the windows, adorned with a simple vase of sunflowers. On the opposite wall, a hutch lined with stoneware pitchers gave the room a French country feel, in stark contrast to the more formal living and dining rooms.

"So you're Ethan," Marian said, running her amber eyes over him with a peculiar intensity.

"I am."

"You look like your father. He was always a good-looking boy. You're taller, though. Zachary says you're teaching at the University of New Hampshire and that you've written several books. Dickey must have been so proud of you, following in his footsteps. A teacher *and* a writer."

Ethan frowned. "I don't remember us talking about my work."

"You didn't. Zachary did a little checking after he spoke to you, to make sure you were . . . aboveboard. *A pretty basic guy* was how he described you. Thirty-two. Professor. Writer. Divorced. No children."

"What, no credit report?"

Marian's lips curled faintly. "Don't bristle. Zachary's just protective. And it seems only fair, with you knowing all my secrets, that I know at least a little about you—to level the playing field, as it were." She looked at Ashlyn then, assessing her coolly. "You're the friend. The one who found the books."

"Yes," Ashlyn said awkwardly. "I'm Ashlyn. Ashlyn Greer." She remembered the books suddenly and, after a bit of fumbling, extracted them from her tote.

Marian eyed them almost warily, her hands pinned to her sides, as if she were afraid to even touch them. "Put them over there," she said finally. "On the hutch."

Ashlyn did as she was told, placing the books beside a blue-and-white spatterware bowl, then pulled out the packet of cards and letters and laid them on top. She exchanged an uncomfortable glance with Ethan as Marian proceeded to prepare the tea, equipping a lacquered tray with cups and saucers, and a plate of sugar-dusted cookies. The tension was palpable as the minutes spun out, marked only by the steady ticktock of the clock above the stove.

When the tea was finally ready, Marian lifted the tray and nodded toward a pair of french doors. "Get that, will one of you? It's too cold to go out on the deck, but the view's almost as nice on the porch, and it's much warmer."

The porch was fashioned entirely of glass, like a greenhouse, and ran nearly the full length of the house. Ashlyn went still as she took in the view, a stunning vista of sea and sky. She hadn't realized the back of the house hovered out over the water. The realization left her a little dizzy. "It's like standing at the edge of the world," she said with undisguised awe. "It's breathtaking."

Marian's face softened into a near smile. "It's why I bought the place. I glassed in the porch so I could enjoy it all year round."

They settled at a white wicker table with chairs covered in floral chintz. Marian filled three pretty china cups and handed them around. "Help yourself to cream and sugar, and the cookies are fresh from the bakery downtown."

Another awkward silence fell, this one marked by the clinking of spoons as they quietly doctored their tea. Ashlyn had just reached for a cookie when Marian set down her spoon and turned her gaze on Ethan.

"I'm sorry I wasn't at either of your parents' funerals. Dickey and I had fallen out by the time your mother got sick, but I would have been there for him if I had known. And then *he* got sick. I was out of the country when he died. I didn't find out until I got back and a friend mentioned seeing it in the paper. If I hadn't been so pigheaded . . . I didn't know you at all, but I felt so badly. I should have at least called."

"It was as much my fault as yours," Ethan said. "It honestly never crossed my mind to get in touch with you. Growing up, you were just a name. But I knew you and my father were close for a while."

"We were." She sighed, as if the memory pained her. "We were very close. He was always better than the rest of us. Even as a boy. And dependable. That's why we ended up reconnecting after I came back from France. I needed a favor, so I looked him up."

"What kind of favor?"

"There was a portrait of my mother that used to hang in our dining room. She was wearing a deep blue gown with a spray of lilies pinned to her shoulder and her hair was all done up. It disappeared not long after my father sent her to Craig House. My sister claimed not to know what happened to it, but I didn't believe her. It irked me to think she might have it squirreled away someplace. So I asked him to do a little poking around. He never found it, but he called a few weeks later—to ask *me* for a favor. He was about to graduate from college and he'd met someone he was crazy about. But my sister didn't approve."

"My mother," Ethan said quietly.

"Catherine, yes. He was head over heels, poor boy, but his mother had someone else in mind. Someone more . . . suitable. I was the only person he knew who'd ever stood up to the family and he thought I might have some advice on how to navigate the situation."

"And did you?"

"I told him to walk away—to run if necessary. From them, from the money, from whatever it was they were holding over him. I told him to screw the Mannings—pardon my French—and follow his heart, since he was apparently the only one of us who actually had one. I'm glad he found happiness. Heaven knows not many of us did."

Ashlyn had been quiet, content to hang back and observe, but Marian's last remark struck a slightly false note. Richard hadn't been the only member of the Manning clan with a heart. She could still feel the memory of Belle's echoes in her fingers, the way they had arced through her the first time she touched *Forever, and Other Lies*, the heartbreak so raw it had made the book hard to hold. But it wasn't her place to say so.

Ethan looked awkward holding his teacup and saucer in front of him, uncomfortable and out of place. But his smile was comfortable, genuinely warm. "Thank you. He and my mother both spoke fondly of you, but I've never heard the full story."

Marian took a cookie from the plate and broke off a small piece, then brushed the crumbs from her fingers. "He brought Catherine to meet me a few weeks later. She was so lovely, and she was obviously crazy about him. I told him not to be an idiot, that when it was right it was right and he shouldn't wait for anything. Or let anything come between them."

"She hated that you and my father fell out. But I never knew what happened."

Marian looked away, a shadow briefly darkening her face. "He broke a promise and I lost my temper. I'm sorry about it now. Very sorry. Now, what else would you like to know?"

Ethan put down his cup and saucer and sat back in his chair. "I'd like to know about the books. How they ended up in my father's study. How he wound up in the middle of it all."

"He wound up in the middle of it the way he always did, poor man. He was pressed into service."

"I don't know what that means."

"It means he was minding his business one day when a package arrived from London, a book wrapped in brown paper with a note asking him to pass it along to me, unopened. He nearly threw it away. He didn't trust Hemi, nor should he have after what he'd done to the family. But he sent it in the end."

"Why send it to my father instead of you?"

"Hemi had no idea where I was living. Almost no one did in those days. Scandal has a way of making privacy rather precious. Dickey was easier to find, because of his writing, I suppose. And there was a bit of history there."

"You mean the letter he delivered for you."

A flicker of emotion ruffled Marian's careful composure, a brief ripple of surprise or discomfort. "Yes. The letter."

"It was pretty presumptuous to assume my father would do what he was asking."

"Hemi was nothing if not presumptuous." Her eyes clouded and for a moment she seemed to lose the thread of the conversation. When she looked up again, her eyes were clear but raw with memory. "He believed the ends justified the means—even with me. How else would he have the nerve to send me that book full of lies? You've read all of it by now, I take it? Both of you?"

"Yes," Ethan replied evenly.

"He called me Belle, but there *was* no Belle. Certainly not the one he wrote about. She was a figment of his imagination. An invention."

"And your book was meant to correct the record," Ashlyn said quietly.

Marian's gaze remained fixed on some distant point beyond the glass walls, her eyes wide and empty. "The things he wrote," she said finally. "The distortions and the lies . . . I couldn't let him remember it that way. He blames me, but he knows. We *both* know."

Ashlyn caught Ethan's eye, flashing him an "I told you so" look. It was exactly the point she'd been trying to make about things not adding up. The more she learned, the less she was convinced that either of them actually knew the truth.

Ethan was frowning, pulling thoughtfully at his lower lip. "I'm still not clear about how both books—Hemi's *and* the one you wrote—ended up in my father's study."

"I'm getting to that," Marian replied tightly. She lifted her cup, sipping daintily, then carefully returned it to its saucer. "When I finished *Forever, and Other Lies*, I sent it to one of those places that will print your book for you. I sent Hemi's book with it and asked them to make mine look just like his. It cost a pretty penny too. As soon as it came back, I sent both books to Dickey and asked him to mail them back to Hemi—as a set. I'm not sure why. I suppose I wanted him to know I could give as good as I got."

Ashlyn tried to imagine Hemi's reaction when he opened the package containing both books. "And how did he respond?"

Marian eyed her without expression. "He didn't."

"Not a word?"

She shrugged. "He'd vented his spleen and I'd done the same. What else was there to say?"

Ethan looked confused. "If my father did as you asked and sent them to Hemi, how did they end up back in his study?"

Marian's expression darkened and she shifted in her chair. "A few years later, Hemi phoned Dickey out of the blue and asked if the two of them could meet for a drink. Dickey should have known better, but he agreed. Naturally, I came up in the conversation. He told Dickey that we'd made plans to run away together but that I'd backed out because I was too proud to marry a man with nothing. It wasn't true, of course.

Dickey, of all people, should have known that. He knew better than anyone what losing Hemi had cost me." She paused, shaking her head sadly. "Deep down, he meant well. He always meant well."

"But?"

She shrugged. "But he broke his promise."

Ethan still looked confused. "What was the promise?"

"Your father and I had an agreement. We made it one day after a ferocious argument. He'd been pestering me about the past, about how things had ended with Hemi. He thought I was being too harsh. *Unreasonable*, he called me. And *cruel*. Me . . . cruel." She paused, shaking her head as if baffled. "After everything, he still believed there was a way to go back and fix things. I didn't want his opinion, not about that. I told him that if we were to remain friends, he must promise never to mention Hemi's name to me again. Unfortunately, the promise I extracted said nothing about him speaking *my* name to Hemi.

"When Hemi called, Dickey let it slip that I was scheduled to speak at a conference in Boston the next day, and that afterward, we planned to meet for lunch. At least he *said* it was a slip. At any rate, Hemi wrangled an invitation. Your father agreed, promising to bow out when I arrived. I imagine he thought we'd sip champagne, look into each other's eyes, and live happily ever after, the silly, romantic fool. But when you're happy in love, you think everyone else should be too. Thank heavens for technical difficulties, or who knows what kind of scene there might have been."

"What happened?"

"There was a problem with the hotel's slide projector and we were late getting started. I called the restaurant to let Dickey know I'd been held up. When I asked the hostess if Richard Hillard had already been seated, she said yes, *both* gentlemen had already arrived. When I questioned her, she described Dickey's guest as a tall, good-looking British fellow . . . and I knew.

"I asked her to call your father to the phone. He didn't even bother to deny it. In fact, he tried to convince me to come anyway. I was livid. I never dreamed he would do something so underhanded when he knew . . ." Marian abruptly fell silent, as if she'd said more than intended.

She toyed with a heavy garnet ring on her right hand, spinning it slowly, mindlessly around her finger. "He knew how it was after Hemi left," she said finally, her voice low and filled with pain. "He knew . . . everything. Which is why I was astonished that he could betray me in that way. He was always testing me, trying to soften the ground, but I never dreamed he'd go behind my back that way. At least I was spared the business at the restaurant."

"You didn't go?" Ashlyn asked.

The question seemed to astonish her. "Why on earth would I *go*? I told him I hoped they'd both choke on their soup and I hung up. He called me that night and tried to fix things. I probably would have forgiven him if he hadn't started in again, pushing Hemi at me, insisting I call him. He wouldn't let it go. We fought again. A week later, he called to tell me Hemi had gone back to England but that he'd left both books with him, asking that they be given to me. I told him he could burn them for all I cared, and I hung up. It was the last time we spoke."

Ethan looked stunned. "*That's* why the two of you stopped talking? Because of the books?"

"It wasn't about the books, Ethan. It was about loyalty. Your father set me up to be ambushed."

Ethan folded his napkin carefully and laid it on the table. "It was lunch in a public place, not a dark alley in a shady part of town. I don't think he saw it as an ambush."

"You don't understand." Marian's cup had begun to rattle in its saucer. She set it down carefully and dropped her eyes to her lap. "To look

him in the eye after so many years. After all the lies, all the deception."
Her voice fell to a near whisper. "It wasn't possible."

"You mean the story," Ashlyn said softly.

Marian blinked at Ashlyn once, twice. "Yes. The story. Of course I
mean the story." She closed her eyes, as if remembering caused her physical pain. "He swore he wouldn't print it, but there it was. My mother's
picture. My picture. All of us. And that awful headline splashed across
the front page. I couldn't believe he'd done it."

"He claims he didn't," Ashlyn pointed out gently. "In the book."

Marian's chin came up a notch. "He claims all sorts of things. But
there were things in that article that could only have come from me.
Private things that belonged to *me*." She paused, briefly squeezing her
eyes shut. "He thought he could hide behind an alias, that I wouldn't
know it was him. But I knew. It could only have been him."

Ashlyn blinked at her. "An alias?"

"Steven Schwab," Marian said flatly. "Another convenient
invention."

Ashlyn glanced at Ethan, wondering if he was connecting the dots
too. Marian believed Schwab was an alias . . . Marian didn't know
Steven Schwab . . . Hemi wasn't Steven Schwab.

"He wasn't," Ashlyn blurted. "An invention, I mean. He worked
for Goldie at some point and even appeared with her in several photos.
They were apparently living together when she died. Word is she left
him a tidy portion of her estate."

Marian sat a moment with this new information, presumably
digesting the possibility that for years she'd been wrongly accusing
Hemi. Finally, she met Ashlyn's gaze. "How is it you happen to know
all of this?"

Ashlyn looked down at the teacup balanced on her knee, her cheeks
suddenly warm. "I was convinced that Hemi was Steven Schwab. There
were so many similarities. They both worked for Spencer Publishing.

They were both aspiring novelists. They were both involved with Goldie. It didn't seem like such a leap."

"I have no idea who this Schwab fellow was and I don't care that his name happened to be on that story. Only one person could have written those things because I only shared them with one person, and that person's name was . . . *is* . . . Hugh Garret."

Ashlyn went still as she registered the name, her mind scurrying back over snippets of *Regretting Belle*. Turns of phrase, literary cadence, word choices. *Hugh. Garret.* It couldn't be. And yet, she was absolutely certain it was. Of course it was.

"You're talking about Hugh Garret . . . the *author*?"

"The very same."

Ethan was watching them, clearly at a loss.

"He's a novelist," Ashlyn explained. "An incredibly *successful* novelist with more than twenty books to his name, almost all of them bestsellers." She turned back to Marian. "You were in *love* with Hugh Garret?"

"He wasn't famous then."

"Well, he's certainly famous now. He just released a new novel last month. It went straight to number one, like they all do. Have you read any of his books?"

Marian held her gaze a beat longer than was comfortable. "Just . . . the one."

"Right. Of course. I just wondered . . ."

"I know what you wondered. And the answer is no. I've never been curious. I know all I need to. I have no idea who this Schwab fellow was, and I don't care that his name was on that story. Only one person could have written it."

Coming from anyone else, the response would have felt implausible. But Marian Manning had made her own nephew promise to never speak Hemi's name. It wasn't hard to imagine her walling herself off from anything that might remind her of him.

She was studying Ashlyn now, her eyes narrowed thoughtfully. "I believe it's my turn to ask a question now. Why do you care? What is my love life to you?"

Ethan leaned forward in his chair, apparently feeling the need to step in. "It was Ashlyn who actually found the books. She was combing through some boxes I brought to a secondhand shop when she came across *Regretting Belle*. Your book turned up a week later in a different box."

Marian stared at him. "You . . . gave them away?"

"I didn't know what they were. I needed to clear some shelf space, so I boxed up everything that looked like fiction. The next thing I know, I get a call about a pair of books with no authors. I had no idea what she was talking about."

Marian nodded, appearing to accept his answer, then turned back to Ashlyn. "What is your interest, Miss Greer? Why have you gone to so much trouble?"

Ashlyn felt pinned by those large, wide-set eyes, uncomfortably exposed. How could she answer truthfully without mentioning the echoes? "I thought they were beautiful," she replied earnestly. "And heart-breaking. I kept hoping there would be a different ending. It was like there was a piece of the story missing, like something had been left out."

"What?"

The one-word response erupted from Marian like a hiccup, involuntary and abrupt. Ashlyn took a sip of her tea, then lingered for a second sip. Had she imagined it? The startled blink? The almost imperceptible stiffening of her shoulders? Without meaning to, she had overstepped.

"I only meant we wish things could have turned out differently."

"So do I. But never mind about that." She smiled suddenly, a broad, almost beatific smile that made Ashlyn faintly nervous. "You said *we* just now. I assume you were referring to yourself and Ethan. Are you and my great-nephew an *item*, as we used to say in my day? I can't quite make the two of you out."

All at once, Ashlyn understood the smile. She had turned the tables, deploying a personal question of her own to throw her opponent off guard. Clever. Effective, too, she realized, since she had absolutely no idea how to respond.

"We're still trying to make *each other* out," Ethan said, jumping in to fill the silence. "We only met a few weeks ago."

Marian's smile lost its sharp edges. "Because of the books?"

"Yes."

"I'm glad," she said quietly, her gaze drifting back to the window. "Glad to know something good has come from all the hurt." She rose then and flicked on a pair of lamps at the far end of the porch. "It's getting dark so early now. Will you stay for supper? Nothing fancy. Just some stew I threw together this morning. But I've got a good Burgundy to go with it and some fresh bread from the bakery."

Ethan looked at Ashlyn. "Do you need to get back?"

"Please don't rush off," Marian said with a hopeful smile. "Stay awhile and let me look at you. It's nice to remember Dickey, and there's so much catching up to do. I promise to answer all your questions if you stay. Or most of them, at any rate."

SIXTEEN

ASHLYN

Enemies exist in many forms, all of which may affect both longevity and well-being. One must at all times be vigilant against invaders, both seen and unseen.

—*Ashlyn Greer,* The Care & Feeding of Old Books

Marian hadn't lied about the Burgundy. Apparently, she'd developed quite a palate during her time in France and maintained a nice cellar. Halfway through the stew, Ethan had opened a second bottle. Now they lingered around the table in Marian's large, bright kitchen, sipping from enormous balloon glasses while Marian talked about the nonprofit she'd started almost thirty years ago and the work they continued to do around the world.

Eventually, and perhaps predictably, she moved on to her children, bragging about their many accomplishments. Zachary had become one of the world's most sought-after violinists, performing for heads of state all over the world, and had just rejoined the Chicago Symphony after a five-month European tour. He and his fiancée were planning to marry in the spring. Ilese was currently a professor of women's studies at Yeshiva University in New York and the mother of three beautiful girls.

It made Ashlyn happy to know that after all the heartache, Marian had enjoyed a full and happy life. "To the proud grandma," she said, raising her glass to their hostess. "How old are your granddaughters?"

"Lida is six, Dalia is eight, and Mila, who I call my big girl, is eleven. I wish they lived closer. I miss them since they moved away, but Ilese brings them to see me when she can. And I'll see them next week when I'm in Boston."

"You're going to Boston?"

"There's an awards banquet, a lifetime achievement award. It's to do with the foundation." She paused for a sip of wine, then made a face. "That's how you know you're getting old. They start giving you lifetime achievement awards. It's nice of them, but honestly, I'd rather they just mail me the thing. I'm not much on cities these days, but Ilese and the girls are coming to the banquet, which will be nice. They all got new dresses, so they're very excited."

Ethan reached across the table to refill their glasses before topping off his own. "You haven't mentioned your sister."

Marian's smile evaporated. "Your grandmother?"

"Corinne, yes. Is she still alive?"

"I assume so. I haven't heard otherwise, though I doubt I would have been notified. We haven't spoken since I came home with the children. Almost thirty-five years."

"And the rest of her kids? I know about Robert's plane being shot down and that one of the girls passed away a few years back, but I don't know anything about the others."

"Anne and Christine." She shrugged. "I've no idea where they are now. I burned all those bridges, I'm happy to say. Zachary and Ilese are my family. And my mother's people in France. The children grew very attached to their cousins during our visit. They're still in touch, I'm happy to say."

Visit? The word came as a surprise to Ashlyn. "I just assumed you adopted Ilese and Zachary *while* you were in France. You didn't mention them in the book."

Marian flashed Ashlyn a look of annoyance. "I didn't see the need to mention them. They have nothing to do with what happened back then—nothing to do with *him.*"

"I only meant I wasn't clear on the timing. I thought you adopted them because of your work with the OSE."

Marian's expression softened, as it did anytime she spoke of her children. "It was the other way around, actually. My work with the OSE while I was abroad was *because* of the children. I saw the toll war took on families long before I ever set foot in France. The European refugees—the ones who came over before we stopped accepting them—told terrible stories about what was happening back home. One of them, an Austrian woman who'd fled the Nazis, became my friend when I lived in California. Johanna Meitner was her name. Wait . . . I have a picture of her."

She left the kitchen briefly, returning moments later with a photograph in a simple silver frame. She handed it to Ashlyn. "That's her. Johanna."

Ashlyn studied the face staring back at her from behind the small rectangle of glass. An angular face with sad, pale eyes and a thick fringe of straw-colored hair. She'd been a beauty once, but something—the war, presumably—had dimmed that beauty, leaving her with a vaguely haunted expression. She also appeared to be supporting a gently rounded belly.

"Was she pregnant when this was taken?"

Marian took back the frame, hugging it to her chest. "She was." Her eyes glazed over as she continued to speak, her voice flat and almost robotic, as if she were retrieving the story from some dark place in her memory. "Her husband, Janusz, was a violinist with influential connections. When he learned Johanna was pregnant, he used those connections to arrange for her and their son to leave Austria and come to the States. He was supposed to follow a few weeks later, but he was caught with forged papers and arrested. He died a short time later in one of the camps. She never learned which, but it didn't matter. He was gone and she was alone in a strange country, with a baby on the way."

"And another child to care for," Ashlyn added grimly.

"Yes," Marian said quietly. "Another child."

"How did the two of you become friends?"

"She lived in the house next to mine. She was so lost, broken really, after all that had happened. She was certainly in no shape to be having a baby, but babies come on their own schedule. She needed someone to look after her, to cook and clean and take her mind off things. I was at her house more than I was at mine. We became close, like sisters. She taught me how to prepare for the Sabbath, how to cook the food and say the blessing. The three of us became a family. And then Ilese was born."

Ashlyn's heart caught in her throat. "She was Ilese's mother?"

Marian blinked away tears. "Yes."

"And Zachary . . ."

"Is Ilese's brother." Marian's voice faltered and her eyes slid away. "Johanna died a few days after Ilese was born. She'd lost so much blood, so much . . . everything. The doctor knew she wouldn't make it. She knew it too. She didn't have any fight left. She asked for a pen and paper, then asked me to call her rabbi—to witness what she'd written."

Her eyes were shiny with tears now. "She wanted me to take Ilese . . . to raise her as my own. It never occurred to me to say no. She had no one else. And she knew I would love her—love them—as my own. We were *already* a family. And we would go on being a family. She made the rabbi promise to act as witness, to make sure her wishes were carried out. When he agreed, she closed her eyes and let go."

Marian put down the photo and blotted her eyes with her napkin. "I'm sorry to blubber. All these years later, it's still hard to think of her."

Ashlyn fought the urge to reach for Marian's hand. "I can't imagine taking on two children as a single woman. Was it difficult? Formally adopting them, I mean."

She shook her head. "It wasn't like it is now, with ten families vying for every child. The orphanages were full and the entire world was at war. The men were all gone and women had to go to work. No one was looking for a ready-made family—except me. The biggest hurdle was not being married, but Rabbi Lamm vouched for me and I found a good lawyer to help me navigate all the legal hoops."

"How old was Zachary at the time?"

Marian folded her napkin carefully and laid it aside. "He'd just turned two."

Ashlyn shook her head. "A toddler *and* a newborn. How on earth did you manage?"

"It wasn't as hard as you might think. There was a terrible fuss when we came back to the States, of course. I made the mistake of returning to New York. No one knew who I was in California, but when I came back to the city, it didn't take the press long to sniff me out. When they learned I'd come back from France with a pair of children in tow, they assumed I was married. When they realized I wasn't and that the children were adopted, they created this myth that I'd gone to France specifically to rescue a pair of Jewish war orphans. The stories were ridiculous. To hear them tell it, I crawled through the mud with a bayonet between my teeth and liberated them from Drancy. Of course, I was driven to this selfless act of heroism because of the story in the *Review*—because I'd learned that my mother was a Jew. It was a complete circus. And completely untrue. But it's hard to stop a train once it's gotten momentum."

"Your father must have been thrilled," Ethan observed dryly.

Marian shot him the thinnest of smiles. "Not especially, no. Naturally, Corinne was livid too. The rumors about my mother's death had just started to die down, and there I was, back in the news again with my poor Jewish orphans, resurrecting the scandal. Zachary and Ilese couldn't understand what all the fuss was about." Another smile, this one softer. "The papers made it sound like I saved them, but the truth is *they* saved me. I was so lost after the business with Hemi. Johanna and the children gave me something to care about, something to focus on besides my woes and the war."

"And then after the war, you took the children to France?" Ashlyn said, still trying to fill in the blanks.

Marian fixed her with a pointed stare. "You *are* full of questions, aren't you? Yes, we went to France—to Bergerac. My aunt's health was failing and I wanted to go while there was still time. The children loved it there. They learned French and a little Yiddish and all about growing grapes. It was good for them—good for all of us. And of course, there was my work with the OSE. It was hard but rewarding."

"Do Ilese and Zachary know they were adopted?"

Marian squared her shoulders as if miffed by the question. "Of course they know. I told them when I thought they were old enough to understand. I've told them . . . everything."

Ashlyn picked up Johanna Meitner's photograph again, studying it. "I can see Ilese in her. She has the same coloring and the same angular face."

Marian's eyes narrowed. "I wasn't aware that you knew my daughter?"

"I don't. But Ethan showed me some photos his parents had of the children. They're with the cards and letters we brought back."

Marian seemed to relax. "Yes, of course. I'm just finding all of this a little unnerving. People I've never laid eyes on until today know the most intimate details of my life. It's as if someone's been snooping in my diary, which I suppose you have. When I wrote those things, they were for Hemi's eyes. I never imagined the books falling into anyone else's hands, let alone having to explain any of it."

"I know," Ashlyn replied. "For what it's worth, we never imagined we'd meet you face-to-face. It wasn't until Ethan came across an old concert flyer that we figured out how to find Zachary."

"He told me about that. Boston, I think it was. I wish he was still there, but he's done so well for himself and he's happy. No parent could ask for more."

"And it's wonderful that he takes after his father. Does he remember him at all, do you think?"

Marian blinked at her. "I'm sorry . . . what?"

"You said Janusz was a violinist. I wondered if that's why Zachary decided to learn as well, because he remembered his father playing."

"No. He doesn't remember." She lifted her glass then, draining the last of her wine. "He was too young and Janusz was always away. He remembers Johanna, though—or thinks he does. I used to tell them stories about her, usually at bedtime. I wanted them to know her, to know they had *two* mothers."

"But no father," Ethan pointed out. "Did you *ever* think of marrying?"

Marian dismissed the question with a wave of her hand. "I didn't have time for a husband. I was too busy. And I didn't *need* to be married. Between the children and my work, I had everything I needed." She pushed back from the table then and checked her watch. "Look, we've talked the evening away. It's after ten."

Ashlyn stood and began gathering their empty glasses. "We're sorry to have taken so much of your time. We'll help you clean up and then get out of your hair."

"No, no. Leave it for me. It's not much, and the fog is already settling in. I'll be awfully put out if you end up in a ditch. Go get your coats on. I'll meet you in the foyer."

They were buttoned up and ready to go by the time Marian reappeared carrying a bottle of wine. She handed it to Ethan, then pressed a kiss to his cheek. "*La Famille Treves Sancerre*—for the two of you to share. Lovely with cheese and fruit."

Ethan examined the label. "This is from your family's vineyard."

"Your family too," she reminded him. "Perhaps someday you and Ashlyn will go. Your French cousins would love to meet you, I'm sure."

Ethan shot Ashlyn a lopsided smile. "Guess we'd better start brushing up on our French."

"Don't leave it too long," Marian admonished with a hint of gravity. "Time has a way of getting away from you. Things happen, and before you know it, you've missed your chance."

"All right. We'll do it soon."

She reached up to touch his cheek, letting her hand linger. "They're good people, your cousins. You should know them. And Zachary and Ilese too. And the girls. Please say you'll come back—both of you—and maybe stay a few days. I don't want us to be strangers anymore."

Ethan smiled awkwardly as he shifted the bottle into the crook of his arm. "I'm sorry about the time we missed. I promise to do better."

Marian returned his smile, eyes bright with unshed tears. "We both will. Now go. And please drive safely. I'm looking forward to spending more time with Dickey's boy and his . . . friend."

SEVENTEEN

ASHLYN

Outer condition isn't always indicative of what may lay inside. Perform a thorough assessment, and above all, know when to call in a professional.

—*Ashlyn Greer,* The Care & Feeding of Old Books

Ashlyn settled back against the leather seats as they left the crooked streets of Marblehead behind. A thick fog had rolled in after dark, shrouding the world in a cold, cottony haze, and the wine had made her drowsy.

Beside her, Ethan was unusually quiet, his eyes trained on the road, presumably digesting the day's events. There had been a nice moment in the foyer as they were leaving, when Marian touched his cheek and told him she didn't want them to be strangers. There had also been the slightly awkward moment when he'd committed to the two of them going to France together. Almost certainly a placation on Ethan's part, but he'd seemed genuinely moved at the time. Maybe he would go at some point and meet his French cousins. She hoped so.

She turned to look at him, his profile lit an eerie blue-green by the dashboard lights. He looked pensive and a little subdued. "Are you okay?"

"Yeah. Why wouldn't I be?"

"I don't know. It was a pretty full day and you seem kind of quiet. I thought talking about your parents might have upset you."

"No. It was nice, actually. I liked hearing that Marian could tell my mom was head over heels for my dad. It's nice to think of them like that, like young lovers. We never think of our parents that way, as people with dreams and passions. They're just parents."

Ashlyn preferred not to think of her parents at all, and let the remark pass. "Well, we certainly have a clearer picture of things now. How your father ended up with the books. Why he and Belle lost touch. It's a shame. She seemed genuinely fond of him. And I think she was really glad to meet you."

"Eventually, maybe. But she seemed wary at first. Like she thought we were there to interrogate her. I was surprised when she finally opened up. I was surprised about a lot, actually. She wasn't what I expected."

"What did you expect?"

"I guess I pictured her older. More matronly. I certainly wasn't prepared for the woman who answered the door. I knew she was beautiful. My mother always said she was. But I didn't expect her to still be beautiful."

"She is, though, isn't she? She's also pretty marvelous. Adopting a pair of war orphans, raising them to become very impressive adults, entirely on her own. I don't care how much money you've got—that's a big job. Then starting a nonprofit to help orphaned children all over the world. And to top it off, she makes stew. No wonder she wanted Hemi to know she's lived a full and meaningful life."

"She did say she was too busy for a husband."

"Oh, she was definitely busy, though I'd bet my last dollar that isn't why she never married. I'm guessing it had to do with how things ended with Hemi. You never forget what it feels like to have someone you love hurt you so completely—and to know they did it intentionally."

"Are we still talking about Marian?"

Ashlyn could feel him looking at her and turned her face to the window. "Yes."

"Are you sure?"

"Yes."

Ethan continued to look at her, waiting for her to say more. When she didn't, he let the matter drop. "At least we know his name now—Hugh Garret."

Ashlyn felt herself relax. "I nearly fell out of my chair when she said it. We knew he was a writer—he talked about writing a couple of books about the war—but I never dreamed he'd turn out to be a bestselling author, let alone one so prolific. Marian must have been terrified that their story would show up in a bookshop window one day."

Ethan scrubbed a hand over his chin, frowning. "I wonder why it didn't."

"Maybe it did," Ashlyn blurted, not sure why the thought hadn't occurred to her immediately. "All he'd need to do is change a few names, slap on a new title, and bang, ready-made bestseller. No one but Marian would recognize the story, and she admits she's never read any of his books. I've read a few but not all. He specializes in heartbreak. Real crying-jag stuff. He could have done it and we just don't know."

Ethan pulled to a stop at a traffic light and turned to her. "You're going to go out and buy all his books now, aren't you?"

"Buy them? No. Read all his cover blurbs to see if anything sounds familiar? Absolutely. In fact, if it weren't almost midnight, I'd make you drive to the nearest bookstore right now. Plus, I'm curious to know what he looks like. I'm sure he uses the usual headshot on his jackets, but I can't say I ever paid much attention. Come to think of it, I seem to remember there being a few of his books in the boxes you brought to Kevin's shop."

The light turned green. Ethan flipped on the wipers to clear the windshield, then hit the accelerator. "Those would have belonged to my mother. She loved a good cry."

"Do you think she knew Hemi and Hugh Garret were one and the same?"

"I don't know. My father certainly must have, and I can't imagine him keeping it from her. Like I said, they didn't have secrets."

Ashlyn was quiet a moment, mulling over bits of the day's conversation. So much had finally been made clear, and yet she couldn't help feeling there were things Marian had been unwilling to share. There had been a palpable carefulness to her responses, a thoughtful, almost wary parsing of words. It was a skill she'd perfected herself over the years, knowing what to leave out when answering an uncomfortable question.

"Before," Ethan said, nudging Ashlyn from her thoughts. "When you said I was quiet. You were a little bit right. It *was* weird today. All those years, hearing bits and pieces from my parents about this woman I'd never met, and then there I was this afternoon, sitting on her porch, listening to her talk about them. I think my dad would be glad we met, in spite of their falling-out."

"It's a shame they couldn't have patched things up before he died, but I can see why she was so upset with him. His motives in arranging the lunch might have been pure, but for Marian, it felt like another betrayal, and by the only member of her family she thought she could trust."

"I don't know what happened or why, but I know my father, and he would never have done anything to purposely betray her. He obviously thought she and Hemi had things they needed to talk out."

Ashlyn considered this. She'd never met Richard Hillard, but she'd heard enough to take Ethan's word about his father's motives. Marian had mentioned several times that Hemi had been a repeated point of contention between them, that he kept *pushing him at her*. What she hadn't said was why. Was it possible that Dickey had known the true circumstance surrounding Hemi and Belle's separation? It might explain why he was so determined to reunite them. But why would Marian remain so adamant?

"Did you notice anything odd today while Marian was talking? Anything that felt a little . . . off?"

"Off?"

"I can't put my finger on it, but there were times when she seemed almost defensive. I'd ask her something and she'd change the subject or deflect with a question of her own. It was like there was some line she refused to cross, and any time we got close to it, she shut down."

"I'm not sure I'd call it odd. We're talking about some pretty tough memories. Not to mention being interrogated by two people she didn't know from Adam. I'd probably act weird too. Frankly, I'm surprised she shared what she did."

"Yeah, I guess."

She still wasn't convinced, but it had been a long day and there was a lot to digest. She relaxed against the headrest, sinking into the leather seat. She wished she hadn't left her car at Ethan's. She dreaded having to drive home.

"We've still got an hour," Ethan said, as if reading her thoughts. "Why don't you close your eyes? I'll wake you when we get home."

"The fog's getting worse. I should stay awake. In case you need a second set of eyes."

"I'm good. Get some sleep."

Ashlyn had no idea how long she'd been out when the muffled crunch of tires on gravel woke her. She sat up, blinking at the windshield and the wall of fog shredding in the headlights' twin beams.

"Wow." She turned her neck to the left, then the right, working out a kink. "Sorry I passed out on you."

"No worries. We're almost home."

She squinted at the windshield as he rounded a curve, still trying to get her bearings. She couldn't make out anything through the fog. "I hate driving in stuff like this. I always feel like I'm about to go over a cliff. Please tell me you can see where you're going?"

"We're only a few minutes from the house. I could drive this road blindfolded."

Ashlyn let out a groan. "Why doesn't that make me feel better?"

"You can stay, you know."

Ashlyn's head came around more sharply than she'd intended. "What?"

"You don't have to drive home tonight. You can stay at my place."

"Oh. No. I'll be fine. Thanks."

By the time they pulled into the driveway, Ashlyn had retrieved her tote and was reaching for the door handle, ready to make a hasty exit from the car. "Thanks for driving. It was a good day."

Ethan shut off the car and looked over at her. "Seriously. Stay."

"I'm good. Really. It's twenty minutes, tops."

"I don't think you should drive. It's late and you're tired. To quote Aunt Marian, I'd be very put out if you ended up in a ditch."

Ashlyn smiled in spite of herself. "I promise to steer clear of all ditches." She slid out of the car then and out into the fog, dragging her tote up onto her shoulder. "Oh, I almost forgot the wine."

She was still fumbling to extract the bottle of Sancerre from the tote when Ethan came around the car to stand in front of her. "Stay." His voice was thick, oddly muffled against the fog's insular quiet. "Not *with* me. That's not what I'm asking. I'd just like you to be here when I wake up in the morning, under the same roof. Does that sound strange?"

Ashlyn shook her head. It sounded lovely, actually. "No, it doesn't sound strange. Just . . . faintly terrifying."

There was a smile in his voice when he spoke again. "I can offer you your choice of five bedrooms, two of which overlook the harbor, and all of which have doors that lock. I can't offer you a monogrammed bathrobe, but I'm fairly sure I can scare up an old T-shirt for you to sleep in. There's also a nice continental breakfast, if that influences your decision."

"I'm not worried about door locks, Ethan. It isn't about not *trusting* you."

"Then what *is* it about?"

She closed her eyes, willing the question away. It was the conversation she'd been avoiding, the truth she'd been skirting for weeks. "Trusting *me*, I guess."

"To sleep in my guest room?"

It sounded ridiculous when he put it that way. As if she were worried she might not be able to control herself with him in the next room. But she'd been on this particular precipice before, and to say it had ended badly would be the understatement of the century. She had leapt too soon, fallen too hard, and left herself open to all that came after. She couldn't risk making that mistake again. There'd be no coming back if she did. She'd built a life for herself after Daniel's death. Small. Careful. Safe. It should be enough.

"Ethan . . ."

"Stay," he said again, softer this time but more insistent somehow. "I get that you're scared. I don't know why, but I get it. You don't owe me your story—you don't owe me anything—but I'm a pretty good listener if you're in the mood to share. Or we can just curl up on the couch and watch movies all night and you don't have to tell me anything. Just stay. No strings."

"Won't that just confuse things?"

"Confuse things?" Ethan repeated, as if the question were utterly ridiculous. "Ashlyn, from the moment I met you, I've been confused about everything. This is the first thing I *haven't* been confused about. When Marian asked about us today, you froze. You didn't know how to answer. But I did. I knew exactly what I wanted to say. I wanted to say, *Yes, Marian, we're an item.* And then she reminded me that it was the books that brought us together. Well, the mystery is solved and we no longer have the books, and I'm afraid if I let you leave tonight, that'll be it. You won't have a reason to see me again."

"You think I'm going to just disappear?"

"I don't know what I think. I just know I don't want this to be the end and it feels like it might be. I said it before and I'm saying it again, in case I wasn't clear the last time. I want to see what we're like together. To see if there's an *us*—without Hemi and Belle."

Ashlyn studied him, the sharp lines of his face muted now by the fog. But she didn't need to see his face. His shoulders were bunched, his posture stiff, as if braced for a blow. She wasn't the only one taking a risk. "Okay, then."

"Okay . . . what?"

"Okay, I'll stay."

"We can make scrambled eggs if you want."

Ashlyn frowned at him. "You're hungry?"

"No, but that's what couples always seem to do in the movies late at night. Make scrambled eggs together. Plus it sounded safe, and I want you to feel safe."

"I'll settle for a mug of hot tea and some honey if you have it. It's freezing out here."

Inside, Ethan lit a fire while Ashlyn located a box of Earl Grey and saw to the tea. When she finished, they settled on the sofa with their mugs. They sipped in silence for a time, listening to the crackle and huff of the flames in the grate. Eventually the quiet grew heavy.

"So, what now?" Ashlyn asked, aware that he'd been waiting for her to speak.

"Well, we could tell ghost stories, like we used to do at camp. I think I've got a flashlight around here someplace for effect. Or . . . we can talk.

I pretty much bared my soul to you out there in the driveway—which, by the way, isn't usually my style. Now it's your turn. You've given me scraps here and there—stuff about your dad and your divorce—but I suspect there's more to know."

"Like what?"

"Like why you're so scared. Of me. Of us." He set down his mug and reached for her hand, curling his fingers around her closed fist. "I'm assuming it has to do with Daniel. You told me he cheated on you, but there was something else, wasn't there? Something worse?"

Ashlyn stared at their tightly furled hands, warm and comfortable. But inside her closed fist, she could feel the sting of old memories. Of broken glass and screeching tires.

Yes. There was something else. Something much worse.

She opened her mouth, then closed it again, shaking her head. "I don't know how to talk about this with someone I'm not paying by the hour."

Ethan gave her fingers a squeeze. "Maybe start from the beginning."

The beginning. Yes.

"All right." She closed her eyes, pulled in a breath. "I told you when my mother's cancer came back that she refused treatment, that she chose to die, but I left out the part about my father going up to the attic a few months later and shooting himself while my sixteenth birthday party was happening."

"Oh, Jesus. Ashlyn . . ."

She turned her face away, afraid if she continued to look at him, she wouldn't be able to get through the rest. "I went to live with my grandmother after that. I changed schools and spent every other Thursday on a therapist's couch. A specialist in family trauma. I learned coping skills, healthy grieving, they call it. In time, I adjusted. Or learned to pretend I had. I couldn't bear to talk about it anymore so I pretended I was fine. I finished school and got accepted to UNH. And then I met Daniel."

She extricated her hand from Ethan's and stood, needing to put distance between them. She began to pace, arms clasped tight to her body. "I never saw him coming. He was always careful in his choice of targets, and a consummate actor. I fell for every bit of it. I told him everything, introduced him to all my demons. I gave him the power to hurt me—and he used it."

"The student in your bathrobe?"

"Marybeth," Ashlyn said quietly. "She was hardly the first. But she *was* the catalyst for me leaving. I filed for divorce the next day. He never thought I'd go through with it. When I told him I wasn't coming back, he started hanging around outside the shop, watching me from across the street. He'd call at all hours, begging me to take him back one minute, calling me a bitch the next. His novel still hadn't sold and he was on the verge of being fired from the university. His entire life was spiraling out of control. Naturally, it was all my fault."

"Please tell me you called the police."

The question made Ashlyn cringe. She hadn't, but there hadn't been a day in the last three-plus years that she hadn't wondered if things might have ended differently if she had.

"I didn't. He had enough troubles and I didn't want to add to them. But I couldn't go back, no matter how bad things got for him. I called him one afternoon and asked him to meet me for a drink. He thought I wanted to work things out. Instead, I handed him a list of how I thought our personal property should be divided. It was the last straw."

Ethan was watching her closely now, steeling himself for whatever might be coming. "Last straw . . . meaning?"

Ashlyn moved to the fireplace, her back to him as she stared into the fire. "He started to make a scene, so I got up and left. I had already crossed the street by the time he came out of the bar. I heard my name and turned. He was standing on the curb, looking straight at me with this weird expression. There was a van coming down the street, the kind that carries those big sheets of glass. He watched it come closer . . . and then he stepped off the curb."

She heard Ethan's ragged intake of breath, his long, slow exhale. "My god . . ."

His expression when she turned to face him was one of genuine horror. She squared her shoulders, bracing herself to say the rest. "Just before he stepped into the road, there was a split second . . . He looked up at me and smiled; then he called out, *Say hello to Dr. Sullivan.*"

"Who is Dr.—"

"Dr. Sullivan was my therapist. The one I used to see every other Thursday after my father shot himself."

Ethan's face went slack. "You're saying . . ."

"I'm saying he knew *exactly* what he was doing—and he knew *I* knew it. He knew what it would do to me, that I'd . . . come apart."

"This is what you meant in the car," he said softly. "When you talked about someone you love hurting you intentionally."

"Yes."

"I'm so sorry, Ashlyn. But at least the bastard didn't succeed. I mean, here you are."

"He did, actually. Or nearly did." It was an uncomfortable thing to share, to admit that Daniel's attempt to unravel her had nearly worked. But she needed him to know it all, to understand why they were a bad idea. Why *she* was a bad idea. "Three people," she said thickly. "Three people who were supposed to love me, and they all left—on purpose. With a track record like that, it's hard not to think it's you—that something about you isn't . . . enough. I ended up on another therapist's couch. Tuesdays this time instead of Thursdays. For more than a year."

Ethan was silent for what felt like a long time. Finally, he dragged a hand through his hair. "I get it now," he said quietly. "I get it and I have no idea what to say, except that I'm sorry. For him to do . . . *that*. Knowing what you'd been through. It's inconceivable."

"For a while, I tried to convince myself I'd imagined it."

"You didn't, though."

"No." Ethan's face became a watery blur as she met his gaze, the tears she'd been fighting suddenly spilling free. "It wasn't an accident and it wasn't an act of despair. It was about having the last word."

"Damn it," Ethan whispered, brushing at her tears with the back of his hand. "Damn the bastard. And damn me, too, for pushing you to talk about it."

Ashlyn shook her head, sending another pair of tears sliding down her cheeks. "It's okay." She meant it too. It felt as if a weight had been lifted from her chest, as if trusting herself to say the words aloud, not to a therapist but to someone she cared for, someone who cared for her in return, had robbed them of their power.

The rest came spilling out then, things she'd never told anyone, dark things that brought a fresh round of tears. But these new tears were tears of relief, of liberation and clarity. Suddenly, in that moment, she realized she could forgive Daniel, not only for his final act of brutality but for all of it. The manipulation, the infidelity, the hundreds of tiny cruelties that had made up their marriage. But perhaps even more astonishing, she realized she could forgive herself. For giving him power over her, for seeing too late who he really was—and for staying long after she knew.

Ethan held both her hands as she spoke, remaining silent when she ran out of words. The quiet stretched, leaving only the crackle of flames between them. She looked up at him, managing a shaky smile. "You said you were a good listener and you are. Thank you."

"I'm glad you felt you could trust me."

"You asked me once if there really hadn't been anyone since Daniel. Now you know why. Because I swore I'd never trust anyone again."

"But you *can* trust me, Ashlyn . . . if you want me."

Did she? *Want* him?

She touched her palm to his cheek. On some level, she already knew the answer, had known it for weeks. As always, it was a matter of trust. Not of Ethan but of herself.

"I think I might," she said softly, as much to herself as to him. She waited a beat before pressing her mouth to his. A moment to savor the dizzying thrum of her pulse. A moment to be sure. And she was.

His breath caught as she touched her lips to his, a swift, sharp inhalation that seemed to draw her closer, deeper. She heard his startled groan as his arms tightened around her, his mouth soft and shockingly warm as it opened to hers. She had surprised him, surprised herself, too, and the knowledge sent something primal and delicious spiraling through her.

There was a brief pang of alarm as the kiss began to deepen, a slim window of uncertainty when it might still have been possible to pull away. They were careening toward something irrevocable, a step that would make extrication both messy and painful. But she wanted this—wanted *him*—and whatever came next.

Ethan seemed to sense her decision in that moment. He pulled away and looked down at her, his breathing heavy. "At the risk of blowing the moment, I need to know what this means. I don't want to get it wrong—for either of us."

"It means I want to be here when you wake up tomorrow. And maybe the day after that. If it's what you still want. Me with all my baggage."

His mouth curved, slow, delicious. "I guess that means we're an item."

"I guess it does."

She pulled his mouth down to hers then, both a promise and a plea. She still couldn't say how far she was willing to leap, but she had forced herself to look down and at least judge the distance of the fall. It was a start. And maybe, this time she wouldn't fall alone.

EIGHTEEN

ASHLYN

Maintain a safe distance from known threats.

—*Ashlyn Greer,* The Care & Feeding of Old Books

October 28, 1984
Rye, New Hampshire

Ashlyn opened her eyes to an achingly blue sky and sunlight streaming through unfamiliar blinds. It took a moment to get her bearings, to remember where she was—and why.

Ethan.

The space beside her was empty now, but the sheets were still warm. He hadn't been up long. She lingered beneath the sheets, savoring the moment. It had been years since she'd awakened in a bed that wasn't hers, years since she had allowed herself to be touched, held, loved. Now the memory of Ethan's lovemaking was seared into both her memory and her flesh. Like the echoes of a book, never to be erased.

She waited for the inevitable wave of regret, the realization that it had been a mistake to let him into her life—and into her heart, because he was there too—but none came. Instead, she felt a dreamy and delicious languor, the whole-body tenderness of muscles newly awakened.

When she finally threw back the covers, she was startled to find her clothes scattered across the carpet, hastily shed last night along with Ethan's. She left them, opting for the thick terry-cloth robe draped over the foot of the bed. She slipped it on, inhaling the scent of him as she wandered to the sliding glass doors overlooking a small terrace and the harbor beyond. Was the view always this stunning, or was it the events of last night that made the world look so fresh and bright?

Following the scent of brewing coffee, she padded downstairs to the kitchen. Ethan was at the stove, wielding a spatula. He turned when he heard her enter, flashing a sheepish smile.

"Coffee?"

"Yes please."

He filled a mug and handed it to her, along with a spoon, then pointed to the cream and sugar. She doctored her mug, then sipped. "This is good," she said, not meeting his gaze. She wasn't well versed in morning-after conversation.

"Thanks." He sipped from his own mug, eyeing her over the rim. "Everything okay? With us, I mean. With . . . last night?"

She grinned, charmed by his awkwardness. Apparently, he was no more versed in morning-after conversation than she. "Everything's *very* okay."

"No buyer's remorse?"

"None."

His shoulders relaxed as he turned back to the stove. "You might want to revise your opinion after breakfast. I'm making pancakes—or attempting to—and the jury's still out. Want to grab us some silverware?"

Ashlyn laid out the place settings while Ethan churned out a stack of pancakes and a plate of perfectly browned sausage links. In eight years of marriage, Daniel had never made her so much as a piece of toast. On impulse, she slipped behind Ethan and pressed a kiss to his shoulder.

He turned, surprised but smiling. "What was that for?"

"Pick something."

"What would you like to do today?" he asked as they settled down to breakfast. "Assuming you don't have to work, that is."

The question caught her off guard. She hadn't thought beyond breakfast. "I don't, actually. It's Sunday. But shouldn't you try to get some writing done now that we've wrapped up the Belle and Hemi mystery? Your publisher awaits."

"I probably should, but I'd rather spend the day with you. And I've finally started making some progress, so I've earned a break. We could hit Hillcrest Farm for cider doughnuts and music. Maybe see a movie?"

"Or . . . we could go to a bookstore."

"Ah. I forgot we talked about that last night."

"I just think it's worth checking to see if Hugh Garret ever used Belle and Hemi's story as inspiration for one of his books. And then after, we can hit Hillcrest. I never turn down a cider doughnut."

The phone rang before Ethan could respond. He put down the syrup bottle and held up both hands. "Grab that, would you? I'm all sticky."

Ashlyn did as asked, though she felt awkward answering Ethan's phone. "Hello?"

"Ashlyn, is that you? It's Marian."

"Yes, it's me."

"Whatever are you doing at my nephew's house at this hour?" She laughed then, making it clear that the question had been a rhetorical one. "I'm glad you two finally figured it out."

Ashlyn's cheeks went hot. "Ethan's right here. I'll put him on."

"No, no. That isn't necessary. Listen, I've had a thought. Why don't the two of you come to Boston next Thursday? Ilese will be there with the girls and I'd love for her to meet the two of you. You could stay over and come to the blasted awards dinner on Friday, maybe even make a weekend of it. Take in a show or see some of the museums."

"That's very kind of you, but I'd better give you to Ethan." She covered the mouthpiece as she passed the handset to him. "It's Marian. She wants us to go to Boston on Thursday for dinner, then stay over for the award thing on Friday, but I have the store. You should go, though. Ilese is going to be there. It would be nice for you two to meet."

Ethan wiped his hands and took the phone from her, listening and nodding as Marian repeated her offer. "I wish we could," he said finally. "Unfortunately, I've agreed to pick up some extra classes for a friend and Ashlyn has the store. But we might be able to swing a late dinner on Thursday." He raised his eyes to Ashlyn. "Maybe eight?"

Ashlyn nodded, pleased at the thought of seeing Marian again. They could leave as soon as she closed the shop, then drive back after.

Ethan returned to his breakfast after wrapping up the call. "Eight o'clock, Thursday," he told her over the rim of his coffee mug. "She said she'd call once she booked the reservation." He grinned as he picked up his knife and fork and sliced into a sausage link. "Time to meet the rest of the family."

After breakfast, they headed to Portsmouth and their local Waldenbooks. Ashlyn took a deep breath as they entered the store, inhaling the mingled scents of paper and new ink. It always struck her as a medicinal smell, oily and faintly antiseptic, like iodine. Not unpleasant, but quite different from the woody, smoky, faintly sweet smell she associated with her own shop.

Being in the presence of so many new books felt strange. Shelves and shelves of volumes without pasts—without echoes. They were blank slates now, but one day they would have histories of their own, lives quite separate from the stories captured between their covers.

Something about the promise of stories yet to be written made Ashlyn happy as they made their way to the Fiction & Literature section.

Ethan whistled softly when she pointed to a shelf lined with Hugh Garret titles. "You weren't kidding when you said he was prolific. There are . . ." He paused, trailing a finger over the spines as he counted. "Sixteen books here."

"And that isn't all of them."

She pulled a hardcover from the shelf, presumably his most recent, since there were three copies, all facing out. *A Window to Look Out Of.* On the jacket, a dark-haired woman peered through a rain-spattered window, her pale face slightly out of focus, obscured by water droplets.

"Look." Ashlyn held the book up, pointing to the woman. "It could be her."

Ethan looked skeptical. "It could be *anyone.*"

He was right, of course. But there was something haunting about the cover image, something to do with the deliberate blurring of the woman's face. She turned back the cover, scanning the blurb printed on the inside flap. The synopsis bore no resemblance to Belle and Hemi's story. She picked up a second and read it, then a third. Nothing felt remotely familiar. But on every cover, the same woman—or at least the same *type* of woman. A woman who looked like Belle.

She had just finished with the eighth book and was attempting to reshelve it when it slipped from her hand and thumped to the floor. She bent to retrieve it, then froze as she saw the author's photo staring up at her. Piercing blue eyes and a headful of thick, dark hair, a startlingly sensual mouth. He was distinguished, handsome—and familiar in a way she couldn't explain. As if she'd seen his face somewhere in passing. And then suddenly it hit her. She *had* seen his face.

Yesterday.

"Ethan." She scooped the book from the floor, holding it up. "It's him."

Ethan frowned. "Of course it's him. It says so right there."

"No. Look. It's . . . *him*."

Ethan narrowed his eyes on the photo. Finally, he saw it. "You've got to be kidding me."

"It's Zachary," she breathed. "Hugh Garret is Zachary's father."

"Jesus." Ethan dragged a hand through his hair, eyes still glued to the photo. "Could we be wrong?"

Ashlyn looked at the photo again, recalling something Belle had written near the end of *Forever, and Other Lies*: *I will never be completely free of you. Your voice, your smile, even that little cleft in your chin will never be far from my thoughts. My cross and my consolation.* At the time, she had assumed it had to do with memories, the kind that never left you. Now she realized it was something else entirely.

"No," she said finally. "That's Zachary's face. Look at the eyes, the mouth, the shape of his jaw. It's him to a T. Just forty years older. And it explains Marian's evasiveness, the way she kept deflecting and changing the subject. She must have been pregnant when she left New York, and she made up the story about him being Johanna's to conceal it. It also explains why Zachary and Ilese look nothing alike. They don't share a biological parent."

"I'm guessing Hemi doesn't know he has a son."

"I'd hardly think so. There's no mention of either child in *Forever, and Other Lies*. She wrote about her work, her family in France, but nothing about her children. A woman doesn't forget her children, and certainly not a woman like Marian, who's clearly the proudest mother on the planet. The omission was intentional."

"We can't be sure of any of that."

"I think we can. At the end of the book, she wrote something about Hemi not having the right to know about some parts of her life. This was what she meant. Zachary."

"My god. We're supposed to have dinner with her on Thursday—and with Ilese. This is going to be awkward."

"We can't let it be awkward, Ethan. She can't know we know. She's kept this secret for forty-three years. We should let her keep it if that's what she wants."

NINETEEN

Ashlyn

I love an author the more for having been himself a lover of books.

—Henry Wadsworth Longfellow

November 1, 1984
Boston, Massachusetts

Ashlyn couldn't help feeling awed as she and Ethan stepped into the lobby of the Parker House Hotel. She had visited before. Not as an actual guest but as a sightseer, hoping to soak up some of the rarified air. Strolling through the lobby, with its coffered ceilings and gleaming chandeliers, was like stepping into another time, but it was the history of the place that she truly loved.

Built in 1855, the Parker House had once been home to the Saturday Club, hosting the likes of Nathaniel Hawthorne, Henry Wadsworth Longfellow, and Oliver Wendell Holmes. Other notable guests included Charles Dickens, who had resided at the hotel for five months in 1867, and the villainous John Wilkes Boothe just two years prior.

There were rumors that the hotel was haunted, particularly the tenth floor. The hotel cheerfully embraced this part of its lore and was said to keep a registry of alleged spectral events for interested guests. Ashlyn found the idea charming. If books had echoes, why not buildings? Chairs? Tables? Lamps?

She liked to think that Dickens and Wadsworth might be chatting in some quiet corner, bickering over an obscure bit of literary minutiae. Or lingering over a glass of port in the bar, which had once been a library said to contain more than three thousand books. But tonight, she and Ethan would be dining with the latest recipient of the Children's Welfare Network Lifetime Achievement Award.

The hostess informed them that the rest of their party had already been seated and offered to show them to their table. Ashlyn spotted Marian immediately, seated with a tall blonde and a trio of fidgeting little girls.

"Mila, Dalia, and Lida," Ashlyn whispered to Ethan. "I'm pretty sure Mila is the oldest."

Ethan gave her hand a squeeze. "Got it. Thanks."

Marian's face lit up when she saw them approach. She leaned toward Mila to whisper something, who then whispered something to the other girls, who immediately stopped fidgeting and sat up straight. Ashlyn felt a twinge of nerves when they finally arrived at the table, as if she had just arrived for a job interview.

"Ethan, Ashlyn," Marian said when they had settled themselves in the two empty chairs. "I'm so glad you could come. This is my daughter, Ilese. Girls, this is my nephew's son and your cousin, Ethan, and his girlfriend, Ashlyn."

Ashlyn ducked her head shyly. She hadn't thought about how she might be introduced, but found she rather liked being referred to as Ethan's girlfriend. She nodded at the girls, who were staring at her with wide, curious eyes. "It's especially nice to meet the three of you. Your grandmother has told me a lot about you."

"Only the good bits, though," Marian whispered, sending the girls into a chorus of giggles.

Ilese was sizing them up with pale gray eyes, reminding Ashlyn of a photo Ethan had shown her of a very serious girl with a sharp face and a brash expression. She'd changed surprisingly little since it was taken. Her face was still sharp and triangular, her gaze guarded. And why not? They had appeared out of nowhere, inserting themselves into Marian's cozy and well-brought-up family. A little wariness wasn't unreasonable.

"My mother tells me you own a rare-book shop in Portsmouth," she said to Ashlyn. "And that you and Ethan met because of some old books he found in Dickey's library."

Out of the corner of her eye, Ashlyn saw Marian's shoulders tense. Apparently, Ilese didn't know about the books. "That's right," Ashlyn replied smoothly. "Ethan ran across a few obscure titles while he was clearing space on his father's shelves and they ended up in my hands."

"I'm fascinated by old books. Anything interesting?"

"Not to anyone but the authors," Ashlyn answered and saw Marian's shoulders relax.

"That's too bad. It would have been fun, wouldn't it? To stumble onto some long-lost book by a famous author. Tolstoy or Trollope or someone. You hear about it happening." She turned to Ethan then. "It was sweet of you to track Mom down to return those old letters. Zachary called to tell me he'd heard from you. He wasn't sure you were legit at first. Then he remembered you from that time we stayed with your parents and decided it was okay. She was awfully fond of Dickey. She says you teach at UNH like he did and that you've already written two books. Pretty impressive for someone your age."

Ethan smiled sheepishly. "Not as impressive as it sounds, but thanks."

With the ice broken, the conversation flowed with surprising ease, covering a wide variety of topics, including Ethan's current work in progress, Ilese's ongoing quest for tenure, and the glowing reviews that had come in after Zachary's recent European tour.

By the time their server arrived with coffee and the Parker House's world-famous Boston cream pie, Ilese was bragging about her mother's nonprofit and the work she continued to do on behalf of war-orphaned children.

Marian was clearly embarrassed by her daughter's praise. "I do wish you'd stop, Ilese. You're boring Ashlyn and Ethan to death."

"On the contrary," Ashlyn corrected, and she meant it. The more she learned about Marian, the more impressed she was. "It's easy to see why they're giving you that award tomorrow night. You have so much to be proud of."

"I've been very lucky in my life," Marian said, beaming at her daughter and the girls. "I was born into the kind of privilege most people never know. I walked away from most of it, but not all. There was some money when my mother died. Money my father couldn't touch. It gave me certain . . . freedoms. I was able to pursue the work that was important to me and give my children the kind of life I wanted them to have. But mostly, I've been blessed to have such wonderful children. They're both so bright and so talented. And they were such troupers growing up. I dragged them around quite a lot when they were young. I yanked them away from their friends in California to live on a wreck of a vineyard in Bergerac. They had to learn French so they could attend school. And then, just when they'd fallen in love with farm life and their French cousins, I dragged them back here."

"Yes!" Ilese interjected with a laugh. "You brought us to Marblehead, to that big drafty house. We thought we'd freeze to death that first winter. But then summer came and we learned to swim and sail and dig for clams, and we knew we'd come home. The girls love it too. They can't wait to get back this summer. They're all going to be in Uncle Zachary's wedding, and they're over the moon about it, aren't you, my darlings?"

The girls barely acknowledged their mother's question. That it was well past their bedtime was evident. Lida was heavy-eyed and sullen, and Dalia and Mila were squabbling over the last bite of dessert.

"I wish Zachary could have made it this weekend," Marian said as she signed the dinner check and closed it back up in its little leather folder. "Not for the award dinner but for tonight. It would have been nice for him to meet you in person, but he's just back from tour and doesn't dare take more time away. I wish he lived closer. I so hoped he'd end up here in Boston." She smiled sadly. "I miss his face."

Ashlyn and Ethan exchanged a quick glance.

"You never know," Ilese said, curling an arm around the drowsy Lida and pulling her close. "He may still. The girls would love it if he moved closer. I would, too, I suppose, though I'd never let him know it, the big fathead."

Ashlyn couldn't help smiling. Ilese's fondness for her brother was plain, despite her attempt to pretend otherwise. "Were the two of you close growing up?"

"When we were little, we were inseparable. We moved a lot, so we became each other's best friends, but when we got older, we made new friends and found our own interests. Poor Mom. We fought like cats and dogs during our teens. I was very bookish, very serious about everything, and my brother's never taken *anything* seriously—except his music, of course—so we were always butting heads. But we've always had each other's backs. Nothing has ever changed that—or ever will."

Ashlyn shot Ethan another knowing glance, realizing too late that Marian had witnessed the exchange. Her eyes held Ashlyn's as the seconds stretched, an uneasy acknowledgment and an unspoken plea for silence.

"Well," Ilese said, oblivious to the look that had just passed between Ashlyn and her mother, "I hate to be the one to break up this party, but I need to get the girls up to the room. I promised I'd call Jeffrey before eleven. It's been a wonderful evening. I hope we'll see you both at Mom's this summer. I'll make sure you get an invite to the wedding. And you could come for the holidays. We'll teach you to play dreidel. I warn you, though, we're ruthless." She pushed back her chair, grinning. "And with that word of warning, I'll say good night."

Dalia and Mila slid off their chairs, clearly relieved that the evening was winding to a close, but Lida had already nodded off, her pale head hanging limply to one side. Ilese dragged an enormous tote up onto her shoulder—her mommy bag—then leaned down to pull the sleeping Lida up into her arms. The child whimpered, struggling briefly, before going slack again.

Ilese fought to keep the tote on her shoulder as she made a second attempt to lift her, but the seemingly boneless Lida was in no shape to cooperate. Finally, she turned to Ethan. "At the risk of being presumptuous, I couldn't, by any chance, prevail upon you to assume your new role as cousin and carry this one up to my room while I wrangle these two to the elevator? I used to be able to juggle all three, but Lida's gotten so big. It's hard enough handling them when they're all awake."

Ethan stood and held out his arms. "Hand her over, if you think she won't mind."

"At this point, she's past minding anything. Thank you so much."

Ashlyn couldn't help smiling as she watched Ethan take Lida into his arms. She sagged against him, sighing sleepily as she burrowed her face into the crook of his neck, her legs automatically twining about his hips. Her eyes opened briefly, heavy-lidded and swimming with confusion as she looked for her mother.

Ilese smoothed a hand over her blonde head. "Ethan's going to carry you up so Mommy can get your sisters to the room," Ilese explained softly. "Then I'll call Daddy and you can talk to him if you're still awake. How does that sound?"

Lida tilted her head back just long enough to find Ethan's face before slumping onto his shoulder again. "Sleepy."

"Yes, baby. Sleep. I'll tuck you in as soon as we get upstairs and you can talk to Daddy tomorrow."

Marian mouthed a thank-you to Ethan, then blew Ilese and the girls good-night kisses. "I'll talk to you in the morning, honey. Say hello to Jeffrey and tell him I wish he could have been here."

"I will. It was so good to meet you, Ashlyn. Come on, girls, time to go."

Ashlyn watched as Ilese and Ethan retreated with the girls. He was going to be the kind of cousin the girls would quickly come to adore—more of an uncle, really—and Ilese seemed to have no qualms about welcoming him to the family. It was a shame they didn't live closer.

Marian watched until they were gone, then settled back in her chair and looked squarely at Ashlyn. "How long have you known?"

Ashlyn dropped her gaze, caught off guard by Marian's frankness, but there was no point in pretending she didn't understand the question. "Only a few days."

"How did you figure it out?"

"You showed us Zachary's picture the day we were at your house. The next day, we were at a bookstore and saw Hugh Garret's photo—Hemi's photo. He's the spitting image of his father."

Marian nodded, her smile bittersweet. "He is, isn't he?"

"The story about Johanna . . ."

"Was mostly true. Except the part about Zachary being her son." Marian took a sip of water. Her hands were trembling when she put down the glass. "I suspected I was pregnant when I left New York. By the time I got to California, I was sure. I bought myself a cheap gold band and invented a husband, a pilot who flew for the RAF and was shot down while providing cover for a supply convoy. I got so good at telling the story, I almost believed it myself. When Zachary was born, no one batted an eye. But I hated California. Some places just feel wrong. You don't know why, they just do. Maybe it had to do with Hemi not being there. But I couldn't go back to New York with a child. Corinne would have known the truth in an instant, and I didn't trust my father. I was trying to figure out where to go when Johanna moved in next door. She was alone and so scared. She'd already lost a son, a husband, her parents, and she had a new baby on the way. So I stayed. And then when Ilese was born and she knew she was—" She broke off, her words suddenly choked with emotion. "When she asked me to take her . . ."

"You saw a way to legitimize Zachary," Ashlyn supplied gently.

"No, but *she* did." Her eyes swam with tears. She blinked them away and took another sip of water. "The day I brought Ilese home, I went to Johanna's room. I was still in shock. I couldn't believe she was gone. But I remembered her saying she'd left me something in her bureau. I found it in the top drawer. An envelope with my name on the front. Inside was a birth certificate for a male child named Zachary— the son she lost before coming to the States—and a note."

Ashlyn said nothing, though she was pretty sure she knew what was coming—a brilliant and stunning act of generosity.

"It said, *If you're reading this, my spirit has gone to G-d. Do not grieve for me, but if the child has survived, I leave it to your care, to love and rear as your own. I leave you also my sweet Zachary's name. This is your way home, Marian. Your way to wash all clean. You will have to change his name, of course, but he will have a sister now. May G-d keep you safe and well, and bless you for all your kindnesses,* achot."

Ashlyn frowned. "I don't know that last word. *Achot*, was it?"

"It's Hebrew. It means 'sister.'"

Ashlyn pressed a hand to her mouth, overwhelmed by the thought of a young mother having to write such a letter, the heartbreak of knowing she was unlikely to survive the birth of her child, and the trust it must have taken to give that child over to a woman who, five months earlier, had been a stranger. No wonder Marian had committed every word to memory.

"She was lucky to have you," Ashlyn said quietly. "I can't imagine having to make that kind of decision or write that kind of letter."

"I don't know when she wrote it, but she knew she wasn't coming home before we left for the hospital. I think she was just tired of fighting. It still astonishes me that she could think of me at such a time."

"But you knew what she was suggesting in the letter?"

"Yes. I knew. I used to talk about going home someday. She knew I couldn't, though—and why. And so she made me a gift of her dead son's name—to *wash all clean*. By claiming Zachary was Ilese's older brother and not my natural child, we would both be free of the stigma of illegitimacy. The certificate was dated October 9, 1941, nine months before Thomas was born, but I knew I could make it work. And I did. I never went back to New York. Not to live, anyway. I was still afraid of my father. But I could go where I wanted and start over fresh, and I did. *We* did."

"In Marblehead."

"Yes." She managed a watery smile. "In the house at the end of the earth."

"When Ethan and I figured it out, we agreed not to say anything. We honestly didn't mean for it to come up tonight. Or ever."

"Thank you for that, but I saw you look at Ethan when Ilese was talking about Zachary and I knew you knew. I suppose it doesn't matter now. Zachary is all grown up and long past needing my protection. If anything, he's become *my* protector and I love him for it. He knows, by the way. They both do."

"All of it?"

Marian looked away uncomfortably. "I didn't name names if that's what you're asking. But I sat them down and explained that biologically they weren't *really* brother and sister. Zachary was fourteen. Ilese was twelve. I wanted to wait until they were a little older, but Ilese started asking questions about why she and Zachary looked nothing alike. One of her classmates put the bug in her ear and she wouldn't let it go. So I had the talk."

"How did they take it?"

"Zachary shrugged and asked if he could have a snack. Ilese took a little longer to come around. She didn't care about me having a baby out of wedlock—I actually think she thought that part was brave—but she was terribly upset that I'd lied about Zachary. She's always been that way. Swift to punish if you don't live up to her standards. I was afraid it would come between them. If anything, it made them closer. That's like her too. She has a big heart; she just hides it behind all that ferocity. Later, when Zachary and I were alone, I asked if he wanted to know who his father was. I told him I might be able to arrange for them to meet if he wanted me to."

"And he said no?"

"He said he didn't think it was fair to Ilese that he'd have a father and she wouldn't. He said he'd never had a father before, so why did he need one now? He thought the three of us were doing just fine."

Ashlyn couldn't help being impressed. "What an incredible way to look at it."

Marian smiled. "That's how he is. He rolls with things. And we *were* happy, though I wonder sometimes if he said no because he thought I wanted him to. He always seemed aware of my need for privacy, even if he didn't understand *why* I needed it. Or maybe he just didn't want to upset the balance of things. It would have been a wedge between him and Ilese and he was always very careful about that sort of thing, about maintaining their relationship as siblings, even after they knew the truth. Hemi suddenly entering the picture would have been . . . awkward."

Ashlyn understood. "It's clear from the way Ilese talks about Zachary that they're very close. A father who was his but not hers suddenly turning up might have put a dent in that bond." But what about Hemi? Didn't he have a right to know he had a son? "Did you ever consider telling Hemi?"

"Only every day." Marian's face seemed close to crumpling. She sighed, briefly closing her eyes. "And I would have . . . for Zachary's sake. I had actually resigned myself to it. But when Zachary said no, I was relieved. Telling him would mean opening a door I wasn't ready to reopen. As far as I was concerned, that door closed forever the day he went back on his word and printed that story. There was no way back after that. For either of us."

Ashlyn nodded. "I guess I get it. I just thought if he knew . . ."

Marian's eyes flashed with annoyance. "I know what you thought, that he would have married me for the sake of our son and we would have lived happily ever after. You sound like Dickey."

Ashlyn sat back in her chair, processing Marian's response. "He knew about Zachary?"

"You forget, my nephew actually knew Hemi. It took all of five minutes for him to solve the mystery of my son's paternity—and to start lecturing me about how I was wrong to keep the truth from Hemi. Not just wrong for Zachary's sake, or even for Hemi's, but for my own. All those years later, he still believed we could put it back together. But I didn't want Hemi like that. And he apparently didn't want me at all."

"How can you say that? He wanted to marry you."

"Once, perhaps. But he never came looking for me. Never called or wrote a single letter."

"He wrote you a book," Ashlyn reminded her pointedly.

She nodded wearily. "Yes, he did. I remember the day it came. When I read the inscription, I thought he'd found out about Zachary—that he was asking how I could have kept his son from him. Then I started reading and realized it was just another attempt to paint himself as the injured party. He wasn't interested in the truth. Or in me. It felt like a vindication, proof that he didn't *deserve* to know. I'm sure it looks terrible to an outsider. Heartless and selfish. And perhaps it was. But Zachary was happy growing up and that's what I cared about. I loved him enough for both of us and always will. The rest of it doesn't matter anymore."

"I'm not sure I believe that," Ashlyn replied softly. "I'm not even sure *you* do."

Marian studied her, neatly manicured fingertips drumming on the white tablecloth. "I asked you before and I'll ask you again. What is all this to you?"

"I don't know. I realize it isn't any of my business, but I can't help feeling that you two were truly meant to be together, that what happened was all a terrible mistake."

Marian smiled sadly. "You're so young. Still naive enough to believe love conquers all. I used to think so, too, a million years ago. But I've grown wiser since then." She paused, shaking her head dolefully. "Sometimes it does. More often, it doesn't."

Ashlyn considered her reply carefully. Marian's pain was palpable, despite her efforts to pretend otherwise. "I'm not nearly as naive as you think," she said at last, her voice tinged with sympathy. "I know all about love not working out. I know how badly it hurts when someone you trust betrays you. How all you want to do is hide from the world because you can't believe you could have made such a colossal mistake in trusting someone so unworthy with your heart. I know all this because I've *made* that kind of mistake myself. I gave my heart to someone who never really loved me. But you didn't. Hemi loved you, Marian. And I suspect he never stopped. Just as I suspect you never stopped loving him."

Marian sat stonily, refusing to either confirm or deny Ashlyn's suspicions.

"You could find him, Marian—it wouldn't be hard—and finally tell him the truth. All of it, the way you just told me. Not for Hemi's or Zachary's sake but for yours. Dickey was right about that. Whatever happened all those years ago, whatever happens going forward, you both deserve closure."

Marian's expression remained stony. "You talk as if you think there's some way back for us, that words can fix what happened more than forty years ago, but there was never going to be a happily ever after for us, Ashlyn. Not then and certainly not now."

"This isn't about happily ever after," Ashlyn told her evenly. "It's about choosing to let go of the blame and the anger, to leave it in the past. And it's about forgiveness."

"Forgiveness," Marian repeated, not quite meeting her eyes. "Such an easy word to say but harder to achieve. Forgiving would mean I'd be left with only the memories, stripped of the blame and anger, as you say, and I don't believe I could bear them that way."

Ashlyn understood. She was all too familiar with the need to cloak memories in anger, to insulate herself with bitterness and blame. But she also remembered the almost immediate sense of freedom she had experienced when she finally realized she could forgive Daniel. He'd been dead nearly four years and would never know. But she'd know. In the end, it had been about making a choice to stop punishing herself. Marian could make the same choice.

"None of us can change the past," she told Marian gently. "No matter how badly we wish we could. But we *can* forgive it. We just need to decide to. You can forgive Hemi. And you can forgive yourself for keeping Zachary from him. Accept that at the time, you made a decision you believed was right for your family, even if that isn't the decision you'd make today."

"Let myself off the hook, you mean."

"No, that isn't—"

Before Ashlyn could explain further, Ethan reappeared. "Sorry, that took longer than I expected. Lida came to just as we got to the room and decided I needed to tuck her in; then I needed to read to her, though she conked out after one page of *Goodnight Moon*. What a sweetheart."

To Ashlyn's surprise, Marian pushed to her feet, gesturing to the nearly empty dining room. "I didn't realize it was so late. I think they'd like us to get out of their hair so they can clean up and go home. And you two have a long drive back. I believe it's a school night for Ethan."

Ashlyn picked up her purse and stood, wishing there'd been time to say more. She had learned only recently the power of forgiveness, and had come to understand that the choice to forgive was as much about self-healing as about absolving another of their guilt. Perhaps more. She only wished she had more time to persuade Marian.

She managed a smile. "Thank you so much for dinner, Marian. It was kind of you to include me."

"I'm afraid the night isn't ending on a very bright note. And now that you know all my secrets, the two of you probably wish we'd never connected."

Ethan shot Ashlyn a quizzical look but summoned a smile. "Don't be silly. Six weeks ago, I had no family. Now I have an aunt, and a whole passel of cousins, and an invitation for Hanukkah. Just try getting rid of me."

Marian patted his arm, beaming. "If anything changes and you can make it tomorrow night, you're welcome to come. It'll be deadly dull but the food should be good."

They walked out together, then stopped in the lobby, lingering when it was time to separate. Marian surprised them by wrapping them both in a hug. "Do take care of this girl, Ethan. I suspect she's a treasure."

Ashlyn was surprised by the sharp pang of emotion Marian's words induced. She was afraid she'd overstepped, spoken frankly, perhaps even impertinently, about something that was none of her business, but she suddenly found herself hoping she'd given Marian something to think about.

Ethan shot Ashlyn a crooked grin. "It's a promise."

"I mean it." She took his face between her hands, looking directly into his eyes. "I'll tell you what I told your father all those years ago. Don't let anything come between you." She stepped back then and shot Ashlyn a wink. "And now, I'm off to get my beauty sleep before my big night tomorrow. It seems to take more and more these days."

Ashlyn couldn't help marveling as Ethan's fingers wound through hers and they watched Marian cross the lobby and head toward the elevators. Despite everything, all the heartbreak and loss, Marian Manning hadn't stopped believing in love.

TWENTY

MARIAN

Reading brings us unknown friends.

—*Honoré de Balzac*

November 2, 1984
Boston, Massachusetts

I pat my hair again, finger the single strand of pearls at my throat, wishing I felt steadier. Last night's conversation with Ashlyn kept me tossing and turning until the wee hours. Not what one needs before an ordeal of this sort. It would seem my great-nephew has chosen a woman with a head on her shoulders—and one whom I suspect has endured her share of heartache.

After forty-three years, my secret is out. I have deprived a man I once loved of his son. There was no judgment in her face as I told her my story, only sincere empathy. A rare quality, that, but what she asked of me is impossible. To forgive after so many years, to simply let go. For my sake, she said. But how can it be for my sake? After so many years of clinging to my grief, I'm not sure I know how to live without it. Still, her words linger in a rather inconvenient way as I join Ilese and the girls at our table near the stage.

I feel the beginnings of a headache coming on. The ballroom is uncomfortably warm, thick with a miasma of liquor, hairspray, and designer perfume. Or maybe it's the restless hum of conversation filling all that space that has my nerves strung so tight. It sounds like a hive of angry bees, ready to swarm. My instinct is to flee, but it's too late for that.

Dinner has been cleared away and the dessert served, a sign that the speeches are about to begin. A banner with the words CHILDREN'S WELFARE NETWORK HONORS MARIAN MANNING hangs above the stage. I reach for my wine, then think better of it and sip my water instead. I'm going to need all my wits if I'm going to get up there in front of everyone.

My hands are hot and sticky. I hate these things. Having to truss myself into an evening dress so I can be paraded about as some sort of saint. But it's good exposure for the foundation, so I put up with it when I have to.

I hear my name echo through the mic. There's a startling burst of applause. I push to my feet and mount the steps to the stage. A woman in gold lamé is standing at the podium, Gwendolyn Halliday, president of the CWN. She smiles and presses the award into my hands.

It's surprisingly heavy, a globe fashioned of frosted glass meant to look like the Earth, with my name inscribed on a square of polished blue marble. There are flashbulbs, the sound of shutters clicking, clicking. The press. Always the press.

I look out at the sea of faces, all waiting for me to say something profound. I wish I had written something out on cards, but I never seem to use them when I do, or I get them all out of order, and so I decided not to bother. Oh well.

Ilese and the girls are smiling proudly. They look beautiful in their new dresses with their hair pinned up in little curls. Lida is waving up at the stage excitedly. I wave back and blow her a kiss. "Hello, Lida!"

The audience laughs. I feel myself relax and I open my mouth to speak. I hate the sound of my voice in the high-ceilinged room, but I smile and say the right things. I thank them and they beam. I make a self-deprecating remark about my failings as a public speaker and they titter. I speak earnestly about the importance of finding families for displaced children around the globe and they nod vigorously.

And then a face jumps out at me from the crowd. A man, standing against the back wall. Tall, angular, dark. He isn't nodding. Isn't smiling. But his eyes are locked on me. All these years later, I would know him anywhere.

The room sways and narrows to a pair of dark pinpoints. For a moment, I think my legs will give way and I imagine the headline in tomorrow's social section: Philanthropist Marian Manning Collapses at Dinner Held in Her Honor. I manage to stay on my feet long enough to wrap up my remarks. There's the dull thrum of applause as I leave the stage, but it's strangely muted, as if I've been plunged underwater.

Ilese frowns as I sink down into my chair and dab delicately at the sheen of perspiration along my upper lip. She asks me if I'm all right, remarks that I look shaky. I nod and make myself smile. But all I can think is, *Thank god Zachary couldn't make it tonight.*

Thank god. Thank god.

The girls want to see my award. I hand it to Mila and let them pass it back and forth until Ilese hisses for them to sit back in their chairs and behave. There's a woman talking now, a tall woman in a ruffled yellow dress that reminds me of daffodils. I pretend to listen, but her words are garbled, indistinguishable.

I clap when the others clap, nod when the others nod, and sneak a look now and then to the back of the room. Still there. Still watching

me. The girls are antsy, ready to go now that Mimi—they call me
Mimi—has finished her talk. The women are beginning to gather their
handbags and wraps. The men are folding their napkins and glancing
toward the exits. Things are wrapping up. I'm relieved. And terrified.

There's a final round of applause; then a rush of people are heading in my direction. They surround me, offering congratulations and
shaking my hand. Ilese leans in and kisses me on the cheek, says the
girls have had enough and she needs to put them to bed. She'll see me
for breakfast in the morning. And then she's gone, leaving me to my
crowd of well-wishers.

I manage to smile and say the right things, to be gracious and grateful, but all the time I'm peering over heads and between faces, praying
he'll be gone. Three glimpses later, he's still there, waiting me out as the
crowd steadily thins. Eventually, it's just a handful of hangers-on. The
waiters have begun to clear the tables. There's nothing to do but get it
over with. I tuck my handbag under my arm, pick up my award, and
head for the doorway.

He takes his hands out of his pockets and squares his shoulders as I
approach, still lean but with a new brand of confidence, the kind born
of success rather than hubris. I'm suddenly self-conscious, wondering
if the blue velvet gown I chose for tonight makes me look frumpy.
How is it possible that he hasn't aged since that night in the St. Regis
ballroom? He's wearing a dark suit, impeccably cut with a faint chalk
stripe, the kind he used to make fun of my father's friends for wearing.
In his sixties now, and still breathtakingly handsome.

Zachary will look just like this one day.

The thought nearly knocks the breath out of me.

"Congratulations," he says when I'm standing in front of him.

His voice sends the years spooling backward, to that very first night.
His eyes have lost none of their blue, but there are fine lines fanning out
from the edges now, and his hair is threaded with silver at the temples.

His mouth has changed too. Harder. Less generous. Less prone to smile, I think. He's smiling now, though, if one can call it a smile. The expression doesn't reach his eyes and sharpens his already sharp features.

"Come now. No need for modesty. I've been reading up on you since I saw the announcement about tonight's event in the *Globe*. You're rather impressive."

"Why are you here?" I say, finally finding my tongue.

"How could I pass on the chance to have a drink with an old friend and talk over old times?"

I don't know what to make of him. His words don't match his flinty smile, as if he's got a trick card up his sleeve. "We caught up, remember? You wrote me a book."

"And you wrote one back."

"Which about wraps things up, wouldn't you say?"

"I would have . . . once. But I've had time to think about things since then, to reflect a bit, and it strikes me that you left a few things out of your version of events. Plot holes, we call them."

I stare at him, my heart caught in my throat. How could he know? Did he see Zachary somewhere? On tour perhaps? Surely one look would give the game away. Or maybe he's read something. Zachary is always turning up in this or that paper. Or perhaps he's known all these years. I think of the words inscribed on the title page of *Regretting Belle*. *How, Belle? After everything . . . how could you do it?* Perhaps that's what he's come to ask. But in person this time.

"There's a bar in the lobby," he tells me smoothly. "What do you say we have that drink?"

"I don't want a drink. It's been a long day and I want to go to my room."

"You stood me up the last time we were in Boston."

"I didn't stand you up. I stood Dickey up. We didn't have anything to talk about then and we don't have anything to talk about now." I step to my left then and try to push past him.

He blocks my path. "I think we do. I think it's time we hash it out once and for all. You owe me that, don't you think? Forty years is a long time to keep a man in the dark—no matter what you believe him guilty of."

I can only nod. Forty years *is* a long time. Long enough to actually trick myself into believing my own carefully crafted narrative, to convince myself I could keep such a secret without consequence.

"So . . . the bar," Hemi suggests again.

I nod, because there seems no way out of it. "I'll need a minute to ring my daughter's room so she doesn't worry."

"Here," he says. "Let me free up your hands." Before I can protest, he relieves me of the glass globe, assuring my return. "Shall I order you a drink?"

"I won't be staying that long."

I step past him then, out into the hallway, and head for the alcove where the house phone is located. I don't have to call Ilese. I just need a moment to compose myself and I know the ladies' room is here. I step inside, then sag against the closed door. I've dreaded this moment for so long, and yet I've never once thought how I might handle it, what excuse I might offer for what I've done. Probably because there isn't one. Not for something like this.

It occurs to me, as I stand trembling at one of the black marble sinks, that Ashlyn might be behind Hemi's sudden appearance tonight, that she may have taken it into her head to try to broker a truce between us—like Dickey did. I want it not to be true, but the timing is suspect. Particularly after last night's heartfelt speech about forgiveness. And she knew exactly where I'd be tonight.

Another ambush. Only this time I walked straight into it.

I catch sight of myself in the mirror above the sink. Dressed to the nines and perfectly coiffed for my big night, an elegant updo and flawless makeup. I wonder what he made of me when he walked into the ballroom tonight. Whether he thought the years had been cruel or kind. As if any of that matters now. Still, I fish around in my evening bag for my lipstick and, with shaking hands, touch up my mouth, then dab a bit of powder on my nose. I stand there another moment and study my handiwork.

This is how he will remember me, I think. And then I think, *No . . . this is not what he will remember. He will remember what I did—and what I didn't do.*

I find him at the bar, already sipping a gin and tonic. There's a glass of white wine on the black marble bar top and an empty stool beside him. I slide up onto the gray velvet seat and immediately reach for the glass. I look around the bar, wishing there were more people, wishing there were music. It's so terribly empty, so terribly quiet.

"You look wonderful, Belle." He says it in that low, faintly feline tone that used to make my pulse rush. "Still beautiful."

Don't! I want to scream at him. *Don't sit there and toy with me.*

"Don't call me that," I say instead. "I haven't been Belle for a long time now. And you were never quite as charming as you thought you were."

"I seem to remember you finding me a *little* charming. Not for long, I'll grant, but for a while. Surely you haven't forgotten."

My face flames. I reach for my wine again, my eyes fixed on the rows of liquor bottles lined up shoulder to shoulder, like jewel-colored soldiers behind the bar. "Say what you came to say."

"I didn't come to *say* anything. I came to listen. I thought you might have something you'd like to say to me, something you'd like to explain."

I hide behind my wineglass, watching his face out of the corner of my eye. I have no idea how to make such a confession, which words to use, what order to put them in. Instead, I decide to start with why. "I couldn't trust you. After what you did . . . I could never trust you again. It didn't matter that I was alone. I did what I had to do. I got on with my life."

"Because of the story?"

"Because of everything. But yes, mostly because of the story."

The ice tinkles in his drink as he upends it. He sets down the empty glass and signals the bartender for another. "After all these years, you *still* blame me."

"Who *should* I blame?"

"I went to that bloody station two hours early, dragged both suitcases down there, and waited for you to show. Do you know what it felt like standing on the platform watching that train pull away?"

I stare at him, stunned that he can sit there and talk about hurt—to *me*. Has he forgotten his part in all of it? The promise he made and the breaking of it? His disappearance from my life without a word? "I imagine it felt a lot like walking into your apartment the next day and finding it empty."

"I went to the station as agreed. You didn't come."

"I sent you a note."

"Yes. Your note was quite clear. I'm sorry your wedding plans fell through, by the way. Though I still say you dodged a bullet. Teddy was never good enough for you."

Teddy?

I haven't thought of my ex-fiancé in years and the name catches me off guard. "Why bring up Teddy now?"

He shrugs. "If you must know, it's a question of pride. It still baffles me that you could have chosen that buffoon over me. Even now, I can't quite wrap my head around your words. Or the fact that you thought I could be pacified by such unmitigated tripe."

I put down my glass and look at him squarely. Either I've lost the thread of the conversation or he has. "Which words are we talking about? We wrote so many."

"I'm referring to the letter you had Dickey deliver to my apartment."
The letter. That's what he's talking about. Relief prickles through
me. None of this has been about Zachary. But what he's saying doesn't
make sense. "I never mentioned Teddy in my letter."
The bartender appears with a fresh gin and tonic and takes the
empty glass away. Hemi nods his thanks and turns back to me. "No,
you didn't mention him by name, but I got the gist."
"What gist? What are you talking about?"
He studies me a moment, his blue gaze so intent I'm almost relieved
when he finally speaks. "Why the gaslighting? When we both know
what the letter said? Why does it even matter now?"
"I'm not gaslighting you," I snap, annoyed with whatever game
it is he thinks he's playing. The bartender's eyes slide in our direction.
I throw him an awkward smile and lower my voice. "I know what I
wrote."
Hemi reaches into his jacket pocket. I assume he's reaching for his
billfold, to pay, to leave. Instead, he produces a square of blue paper,
unfolding it with an almost delicate care, and places it in front of me
on the bar. "Perhaps this will refresh your memory."
I stare at the page, sharply creased along its folds, as if it has been
opened and refolded many times. It's been crumpled at some point,
too, but the wrinkles have smoothed over time, and I realize the letter
has been carefully preserved. The ink has faded, but the words *are* mine.

How does one write such a letter? Knowing the pain
it will cause. To end things so bluntly, after so much
planning, seems unthinkable even to me. You'll think
me hard and selfish. Perhaps it's true. Yes, I'm certain
it is. But we would never have been happy, you and
I. Not in the end. I care for you—will always care
for you in my way—but it never would have worked.

We're not matched in the things that really matter, which is why I must now end what should never have begun. If you look at it squarely, as I have, you'll see that it's for the best. In fact, one day I believe you'll be glad I came to my senses. I'm to blame, of course, for letting it go on as long as it did, for letting it happen at all, I suppose. And this is hardly a brave way to end things, a few words scribbled on a scrap of paper. But when your pride has recovered from the sting of this note, you'll realize I've spared us both. The truth is I've promised myself to another and despite my misgivings, I'm not strong enough to break that promise. I'm going away, will already be gone when you read this, too much of a coward to face the mess I've created. Please don't try to contact me. My mind is made up. I beg you to forgive my selfish and fickle heart.

 —Marian

I look up at him, baffled. He's waiting for a response, quite pleased with himself, too, as if he's caught me in a lie of some kind. But the letter's all wrong. Familiar, yes, but *all* wrong. How on earth . . . "Hemi, why do you have this?"

A chilly smile settles at the corners of his mouth. "What can I say? I'm sentimental. Please don't tell me you're going to pretend you didn't write it."

"No. I wrote it—to Teddy. How did *you* get it?"

The smile drops away, and for a moment, his face goes blank. "You sent it. With Dickey."

I blink down at the page, unable to make sense of it. "*This* is the letter he brought you that night?"

"You know damn well it was."

"No," I say, shaking my head emphatically. "I didn't send you this. I wrote two letters. One for Teddy, to explain why I couldn't marry him, and one for you. The one I wrote to you was short. Eight words, to be precise. This is Teddy's letter."

He picks up his drink and lifts it to his lips, then puts it down again without sipping. He's silent for a time, eyes locked straight ahead as he registers what I've just told him. "The one meant for me," he says at last, his face unreadable. "What did it say?"

I look away, recalling the discarded drafts that had ended up in the wastebasket that day, failed attempts to tell him goodbye—all torn to shreds. Because in the end, I realized I couldn't say it. "It said . . . *I'm coming. Wait for me.*"

"That's five words. What else did it say?"

"It doesn't matter now."

"No, but I'd like to know, just the same."

I make the mistake of looking at him then. Our eyes hold a moment, a chilly clash of wills. "I don't remember," I say finally and reach for my wine. "But I do know it didn't say *this*. I can't understand it. I put a stamp on Teddy's letter the minute I sealed it and told Dickey to drop it in the mailbox. He *couldn't* have mixed it up with yours."

"There was no stamp on the envelope he left."

A blade of cold slices through me as the truth dawns, terrible yet inescapable. "They were switched. Somehow Teddy's letter wound up in the envelope meant for you."

He looks skeptical now. "You're saying Dickey opened your letters and read them, then mixed them up when he put them back?"

"I don't know. But something happened. Look." I point to my name—my real name—at the bottom of the page. "It's signed *Marian*." I pause, swallowing past the sudden threat of tears. "I was only ever *Belle* to you. If this was meant for you, why would I sign with my actual name?"

He glances at the signature but shows no sign of being swayed. "What you're suggesting makes no sense. I can't see Dickey risking his hide for a peek at his aunt's letters. The poor kid was scared to death. In fact, when I asked him to relay a message to you, he said he wasn't allowed to talk to me and bolted."

"Was the envelope torn when you got it? Do you remember?"

He eyes me with astonishment. "Do I *remember*?"

I drop my gaze. "I just meant—"

"No. The envelope wasn't torn."

"I don't understand how . . ." I stop midsentence as a thought occurs. "What were you going to ask Dickey to tell me?"

There's a long beat of silence. Finally, I think he's about to answer. Instead, he looks down at his glass, giving the ice at the bottom a shake. "I can't remember."

Fair enough.

I pick up the letter again, scanning the lines I penned so long ago, the vague phrasing and carefully chosen words—words meant for another man—and I imagine Hemi reading them for the first time. My throat aches as I realize how easy it would have been to believe they'd been meant for him and the gut-wrenching pain they must have caused. I try to wrap my head around it. How could it have happened? And then I remember Corinne coming into my room while I was writing the letters and how she was still there, tidying up, when I returned from the bathroom.

"My sister," I say, knowing it's true. "She did this."

I feel his eyes on me as he waits for more, but I'm incapable of speech, the emotions too much to process all at once. I should be stunned, horrified to learn my own flesh and blood would be capable of such deceit, but I'm not. That kind of sabotage is right up Corinne's alley. But I am angry with myself for not having realized it sooner and for not having been more careful with the letters.

The repercussions of her treachery hit like a fist. What's been stolen from me. From *us*. The life we should have shared. The son we would have raised together. The ache of it nearly doubles me over.

Tears blur my vision and I reach for a cocktail napkin to blot my eyes, aware that Hemi is waiting for me to go on. "Corinne came to my room while I was writing the letters. She must have gone snooping while I was in the bathroom and realized I was breaking it off with Teddy. I don't know how she did it, but she must have switched them."

His expression is guarded as he studies me, distant, impervious. I submit to his scrutiny, wondering what he sees and why it should matter after so many years. But it does. Suddenly it matters much too much. Has he grasped the fallout from my sister's actions, or am I the only one lamenting what might have been? "Say something," I say at last.

He looks down at his hands, fisted on the edge of the bar. "What is it you want me to say?"

"I want you to say you believe Corinne switched the letters, and to acknowledge what that means."

"It was a lifetime ago, Marian. At this point, I don't think it matters."

The use of my *real* name—so foreign on his tongue—is like a dash of icy water, but his cavalier response cuts to the bone. I blink at him, stunned. "You came all the way to Boston to crash an awards dinner because you claimed you wanted an explanation. Now it doesn't matter?"

"I didn't *come* all the way to Boston. I live here now. At least part-time."

This is news. Unsettling news. "You *live* here?"

"Two years now. I split time between here and London. More here than there lately."

"You said you read about the awards dinner in the paper. Is that how you knew I'd be here tonight?"

"Yes."

"It wasn't Ashlyn?"

He frowns. "Who's Ashlyn?"

"Never mind. It isn't important."

We fall silent for a time. Hemi nurses his gin and tonic while I stare at my reflection in the bar mirror. I should never have agreed to come. But now that I have, I can't just leave it like this. "You don't believe Corinne switched the letters," I say when I can no longer bear the quiet. "You still believe I meant those words for you."

"Whether you did or didn't isn't the point. Not anymore. Hell, maybe it never was. We were both ready to believe the worst about the other. That doesn't say much for what we had, does it? Maybe we saved ourselves a lot of heartache."

"Saved ourselves a lot of heartache?" I echo, incredulous that he could say such a thing, let alone believe it. "Is that what you've been telling yourself all these years? That you disappearing from my life *saved me a lot of heartache*? That I simply . . . moved on? Never wondering where you were or if I'd ever hear from you again? Tell me you don't actually believe that."

He looks away, his face so steely, I barely recognize him. "Sometimes it's easier to see a thing in the rearview mirror. When there's a bit of distance between it and you."

No. Whatever happened that day, whatever place we've come to now, I won't let him remember us that way—as a pair of reckless young lovers who had narrowly escaped disaster because I got cold feet and ran back to Teddy. "Come with me to talk to Corinne. We'll go together. Tomorrow."

He arches a brow, looking faintly amused. "After more than forty years, you think you're going to just stroll into her parlor and get her to confess?"

"You don't know Corinne. She'd love nothing more than to take credit for coming between us and to gloat about it to my face. I'm sure she sees it as one of her crowning achievements."

"Then why drive all the way to New York to give her the satisfaction?"

"Because I need you to know I'm telling the truth. And because I need her to know I know. If we leave by eight, we can be there by noon."

He empties his glass and sets it down firmly. "No."

I see it clearly then, the flinty layer he's acquired since we parted, an icy detachment he wears like armor. "You'd rather just go on hating me. Is that it?"

He's silent for a time, as if weighing his next words. When he finally does answer, his voice is flat, almost weary. "I've been bitter for a long time, Marian. A very, *very* long time. I'm not sure I could take knowing I've spent the last forty years in purgatory for no damned reason."

"You'd rather remember it wrong?"

"I'd rather not to remember it at all, thank you. But anger is easy. It's also familiar. My default position, you might say."

I blink at him, experiencing an eerie sense of déjà vu. Didn't I say something similar to Ashlyn last night? And yet the cool response stings. "So I'm still the villain—because it's easier. How is that fair?"

"It isn't. I concede that. But tonight was a mistake. I should never have come."

I wait for him to say more, but I can see by the set of his jaw that he's said all he means to. "So that's it? We're finished?"

He nods, eyes fixed straight ahead. "All finished."

I signal the bartender, then open my purse and poke through it for some money. I'm desperate to be away from him, but I refuse to let him pay for my wine. Except there's no cash in my evening bag, only a lipstick, my compact, and my room key.

"Could you please charge the wine to my room?" I ask the bartender when he makes his way over. "Marian Manning. Room 412."

I'm about to slip off the barstool when Hemi touches me, the merest brush of his fingers against the back of my hand. "For what it's worth, I had nothing to do with the story. I never gave Goldie my notes. I threw them away like I said I would. But in my haste to empty out my desk, I left an old notebook behind. Goldie found it and handed it off to Schwab. Schwab admitted it to me when I confronted him. I can't prove it. Both he and Goldie are dead. But it's the truth."

I stare at him, wondering if it's true, wanting so very badly for it to be true. But then I realize he's right. It *won't* change anything. The die was cast more than forty years ago.

"You're right," I say, turning away. "None of it matters now."

I expect him to call after me, to stop me from walking away. It's only when he doesn't that I realize just how badly I want him to.

TWENTY-ONE

MARIAN

Environment must always be considered. Books, like people, absorb what they're around.

—*Ashlyn Greer,* The Care & Feeding of Old Books

November 3, 1984
Boston, Massachusetts

It's nearly eight and my things are packed. My train case, a small suitcase, and a nylon garment bag are on the bed, waiting for the bellman to carry them down. I've called Ilese to let her know that something's come up and I need to get back early. The girls will be disappointed, but I'll see them in a few weeks for Thanksgiving.

I've had little sleep and dread the drive ahead of me. Not home to Marblehead but to New York and Corinne. Strange now that after forty years, this day feels somehow inevitable, as if my sister and I have always been on a collision course. Despite lying awake most of the night, caught between grief and rage, I still haven't decided what to say to her, but I'll have time in the car to choose my words.

I've just swallowed the last of my orange juice when there's a knock at the door. I set the empty glass on the breakfast tray and go to let the bellman in. Instead, I find Hemi standing in the hall, cradling my award in the crook of his arm. "What are you doing here?"

He hands me the glass globe. "Good morning to you too. You left this at the bar last night."

I stand stiffly in the doorway. I'm not prepared to do battle again. At least not with him. "I was just on my way out," I say brusquely. "In fact, I thought you were the bellman."

"The bellman isn't coming. I told him I'd take your bags down."

"What? Why?"

"Because I'm driving you to New York."

I stiffen, caught off guard by his change of heart. "I have my car here."

"I'll bring you back when we're through. If you're actually going to have this conversation, I'm damn sure going to be there to hear it."

In the car, Hemi and I barely speak. Perhaps because I'm preoccupied with what I'm going to say when I finally have Corinne in front of me. I haven't laid eyes on my sister in thirty-five years, nor have I set foot in my father's house in all that time. I have missed neither. Aside from the memories of my mother, there is nothing I remember fondly from that part of my life. And certainly nothing I look forward to revisiting today. Thankfully, what I have to say won't take long.

The silence is numbing, heavy with unsaid things, so that I'm almost relieved when the house finally comes into view, smaller somehow than I remember it, despite its imposing granite facade. My stomach knots as Hemi pulls into the service alley behind the house and cuts the engine. I get out of the car and go around to the front, holding my breath as I ring the bell.

It isn't Corinne who finally answers but a doughy middle-aged woman in nursing whites. She runs an eye over us, already preparing to close the door in our faces. "I'm sorry, there's no soliciting here."

"We're not soliciting," Hemi explains, turning on the special smile he reserves for members of the opposite sex. "This is Mrs. Hillard's sister. We've come all the way from Boston—as a surprise."

He says it with such conviction that I feel a bubble of laughter catch in my throat. I imagine Corinne will be *very* surprised to see me again.

Her posture is still rigid, but some of the wariness has left her eyes. "Mrs. Hillard isn't well. She's waiting for the doctor and can't be disturbed."

I register this news with some surprise. I've never known Corinne to succumb to so much as a cold. Always indomitable. Always in control. "We won't stay long," I assure the nurse. "But there's a rather pressing family matter I feel she'd want resolved immediately. In light of her health, you understand." I feel Hemi's eyes skim my way and sense what feels like admiration. "If you'll just tell her Marian is here, I'm sure she'll want to see me."

The nurse nods grudgingly and ushers us into the foyer. "I'll just go up and check. Please wait here."

I watch as she hurries away in her thick-soled white shoes. When she's out of sight, I wander toward the parlor. Hemi trails slightly behind, maintaining his prickly silence.

The house is a sad echo of itself. Dreary and faded, filled with dated relics from a time when the Mannings boasted one of the finest homes on Park Avenue. Little is familiar, save a few antiques and some of the art on the walls. Even the new furniture—if it can be called new—has seen better days. Tired-looking armchairs and settees with slumping cushions. The carpets are worn to the jute in places, and the once-gleaming floors are dull from lack of care.

It gives me a perverse sense of pleasure to see how far down the Mannings have come in the world, all their careful machinations come to naught, my father's ill-gotten empire smashed. I steal a look at Hemi and see it in his face too.

The rhythmic hiss of thick white stockings alerts us to the return of the nurse. We meet her at the base of the staircase. "She says to go up. She's in her room. It's the last door on the right."

"Yes, thank you. I know where it is."

We push past her, up the staircase, and then along the gallery, and I'm briefly reminded of the night of that fateful dinner party, when Corinne and I hovered at the top of the stairs while my father made excuses for my mother's unseemly behavior. I shove the memory away as we move past my old room and then my mother's. And then I'm standing in front of Corinne's door. It's open. I look around for Hemi and see that he's standing a few steps behind. He nods reassuringly, and for an instant, I glimpse the old Hemi behind his smile.

My stomach churns as I step through the door. The room is overly warm and smells musty, like dirty clothes and unwashed hair. I take a quick inventory of my surroundings. Like the rest of the house, its best days are behind it. The cabbage-rose wallpaper has long since lost its bloom and, despite numerous repairs, is peeling in several places. The draperies are familiar, too, though the once-fine brocade is limp now and rusty with age.

Corinne is seated in a high-backed chair beside the bed. The bed itself is unmade, the covers thrown back as if she's just gotten out of it. She was always lean, but she's reed-thin now and her dressing gown hangs on her, exposing a length of pale collarbone and sallow, crepey skin. Her hair has thinned and lost its color. She wears it in a coil, pinned to the top of her head, like a messy crown. Suddenly I'm reminded of Norma Desmond in *Sunset Boulevard*—the aging maven holding court in her crumbling mansion. The thought fills me with revulsion—and what might become pity if allowed to take root. But I *won't* allow it.

Her eyes settle on me, pale and strangely dull. "Well, well. Look what the wind has blown to my door. Were you homesick, my darling?" Her voice is harsh and phlegmy, her words slightly slurred. She feigns a little pout. "Have you missed me terribly?"

"The nurse said you aren't well," I say, ignoring her sarcasm. "Is it serious?"

The pout falls away, leaving a wan, strained countenance in its wake. "Brain tumors generally are. Whatever you've come to say, I suggest you say it fast. I'm expecting the doctor."

A brain tumor. I absorb the news, wondering briefly where her children are and why they're not here to look after her. Perhaps she's driven them away, too, and has no one but a paid nurse to see to her needs. Perhaps I'll feel sorry for her when I've had time to process it. Perhaps not. For now, I need to focus on why I've come.

"I don't intend to stay long."

Corinne's eyes flash dully. "No, of course not. You're so awfully busy, aren't you? Awards to accept, accolades to receive. It seems that bleeding heart of yours has served you well after all. To hear the papers tell it, you're bucking for sainthood."

I'm startled to learn she's kept track of me and feel a pang of unease about what else she might know. "I see you've managed to keep the house."

"Only just," she says, running slow eyes around the room. "I suspect they'll pull it down the minute I'm gone. Not long now. But not on my watch." Her eyes snap back to mine, suddenly alert. "What do you want? I hope it's not money because that's all gone."

"No. I didn't come for money. I brought you a visitor. An old friend of the family."

Her eyes skitter to the empty doorway, alarmed and then wary. "I don't want to see anyone. And certainly not any friend of yours."

"But this was a friend of yours too," I say, glancing out into the hall. "Let's see if you remember."

As if on command, Hemi steps through the door, wordless, and waits.

Corinne scowls at him, brows knitted over her pale eyes. And then it's there, the recognition I've been waiting for. "You . . . ," she growls, a low, feral rasp. "You!"

"Yes," Hemi says with a languid smile. "It's me."

Her head snaps in my direction. "How dare you bring him to this house. Get out! Both of you!"

I stare at her, unmoved. "We have some things to discuss."

"Out! This instant!"

"The letters, Corinne. What did you do with them?"

Her eyes cloud briefly before sliding away. "I don't know anything about any letters."

"You switched them. How did you do it?"

She stares at me, her face a careful blank. She's as smug and unrepentant as I remember, still convinced she can control everyone and everything. But she's wrong. She was wrong then and she's wrong now.

"We came for answers, Corinne, and we're not leaving until we get them. So unless you're prepared to throw us out bodily, you might as well tell us what we want to know."

She runs her eyes over Hemi, slow, appraising. "So it's *we* now, is it? You and the paperboy, together at last? Have you come for my blessing?"

"There is no *we*," I tell her coldly. "You saw to that. It's the *how* we can't figure out. Tell me how you switched the letters."

Corinne leans forward in her chair, an attempt to look menacing. Instead, she looks sullen and childish—and the tiniest bit shaken. "You've got some nerve waltzing in here and making demands. As if I *owe* you something. I don't owe you anything. Now leave, both of you, or I'll call the police."

"Call them. Call the papers, too, while you're at it. I'm sure they'd love to hear all about this. New Yorkers can't get enough of the Mannings' dirty laundry. I have all afternoon."

Corinne eases back in her chair, arms stretched out beside her, an aging queen on her threadbare throne. She closes her eyes and draws a long breath, her lips blanched of color. "Leave me alone."

Hemi takes a step toward me, shaking his head. "Let it go, Marian. She can't tell you because there's nothing to tell. Though I do applaud your attempts to badger a confession out of a dying woman. Not even your sister could have pulled off what you're alleging."

Corinne sits back in her chair, silent a long moment, as if sizing up her opponents. "And what, *precisely*, is she alleging? What is this thing I couldn't possibly have pulled off?"

"She thinks you got your hands on the letters she wrote before she left New York—one to me and one to Teddy—and that through some clever sleight of hand, you made sure the letter she wrote to Teddy ended up in my hands rather than his. I told her she'd been watching too many movies and that no one was clever enough to pull off what she was talking about."

Corinne sniffs dismissively. "And does she say *why* I might have done such a heinous thing to my own sister?"

"Jealousy," Hemi replies simply.

"Jealousy?" The word seems to astonish Corinne. "Me, jealous of *her*?"

She laughs then, a shrill, grating peal that suddenly brings all her scornful words flooding back. How she never wanted to be a wife or have a houseful of children. How she was tired of dancing to everyone else's tune. How it was my turn to do my duty.

"But you *were* jealous," I remind her, feeling a strange calm flood through me, an understanding that's been far too long in coming. "I used to think it was about what Father wanted, about being obedient to him. But it was more than that. You resented the fact that I wouldn't just roll over and marry Teddy, the way you did with George. You hated me for believing I deserved to make my own choices. You wanted me to be as unhappy as you were. And you knew I would be with Teddy."

Corinne's expression has turned brittle, her careful denial suddenly fallen away, replaced with an almost venomous glee. "And what if I did? Why shouldn't I resent you? When I was never allowed choices and only ever expected to do what other people wanted? You talk about being clever. What do you—*either* of you—know about being clever?" She glares at us now with overbright eyes. "You go sneaking off to some seedy apartment and think no one will know what you're up to. I knew! And you, Mr. Garret, you may have managed to bring us down with your disgusting little story, but that wasn't what you *really* wanted, was it?" She pauses, jabbing a finger at me. "*She* was what you were really after. My pretty little sister. Well, I took care of that, didn't I?" She beams, triumphant at last as she whips her head around to look at Hemi. "Who's clever now, paperboy?"

Hemi catches my eye with the barest of nods. "I do beg your pardon, Corinne. It seems I underestimated you."

"You most certainly did." She aims her sickly-sweet smile at me then. "And you—you silly fool—you certainly helped." She tips her head back, sending a fresh peal of laughter into the air. "You should never have left me alone with your letters, sister dear. It didn't take long to figure out you were planning to run off with the Brit. There was a problem earlier that day, though, wasn't there? A missed appointment of some kind? Hence, your note asking him to wait. What I didn't know was how you planned to get the note to him. I knew you must have a plan, or why write it at all, so I kept an eye out. And who should I catch slipping down the back stairs with his coat under his arm but my little sneak of a son. How lucky for me that you chose such an inept spy."

She smiles then, clearly pleased with herself. "I followed him to the kitchen and saw him take a pair of envelopes from beneath his shirt and slip them into his coat pocket. Poor clumsy boy, I nearly scared him to death when I came up behind him. I scolded him for having his good shoes on. It had rained earlier and everything was muddy. I took his coat and ordered him upstairs to change his shoes, then told him to put on a scarf while he was at it. I needed to make sure I'd have enough time to get the envelopes open."

The last part, delivered so casually—as if she's discussing how to remove a wine stain from a blouse—is faintly shocking. "How do you happen to know how to open sealed envelopes?"

She looks at me, plainly amused. "What a silly question. But then you've never been married, so I suppose you're to be excused. It's easily done when the envelope is freshly sealed, which these were. A few seconds over the teakettle, a carefully applied letter opener—or in this case, a butter knife—and it's done. Initially, I only meant to read them, to learn the extent of your plans, but after reading what you wrote to Teddy, I had a better idea. I knew how it would read to the paperboy. He'd think he'd been given the push. So I swapped them and put the envelopes back into Dickey's coat. Voilà!"

She's so proud of her resourcefulness, like a bank robber bragging about pulling off the perfect heist. Hearing it sickens me, but there are still things I need to know. "What happened to the other letter?"

"You mean the one he was *supposed* to get?" Her gaze flicks to Hemi and she shrugs. "I wrapped it up with the potato peelings from dinner and tossed it into the compost can."

Compost. The thought makes me vaguely queasy. My words—words meant for Hemi—decaying, liquefying, seeping into the dark earth. I slide my eyes to Hemi, vindicated at last, but there's no joy in the moment, no sense of relief or absolution. Only a fresh sense of loss and a terrible reminder of what was stolen from me. From us.

"And Teddy's envelope?" I ask dully. "What happened to *it*?"

"I resealed it, empty, and slipped it back into Dickey's coat. I assume he got it, though I can't say for certain. Lord knows what he thought when he opened the thing. And poor Dickey never had a clue." She's smiling again, a sharp, vicious little smile. "Happy?"

"Am I happy?" I stare at her, incredulous. It's as if some part of her, the warm-blooded part, is missing, and I wonder that we can be related at all. "You've broken my heart all over again, Corinne. Reminded me how close I came to the life I wanted—and how it felt to lose it. But I'm glad it's over, glad to be finished with you and this house, glad to hear they'll pull it down the moment you're gone. I'm going now. I won't be back."

Hemi and I are nearly to the door when she calls my name. I turn, surprised to see her slumped in her chair now, as if all the air has gone out of her. "Go into the closet," she says flatly. "There's a box there with some things in it. Take them with you."

My first reaction is to keep walking, to get as far away from her as possible—as quickly as possible—but something new has crept into her voice, a blend of resignation and defeat. Against my will, I find myself experiencing a pang of sympathy for the sister I know I'll never see again. Grudgingly, I do as she asks.

In the closet, near the back, I find an old hatbox. I open it right there, feeling my breath catch as I lift the lid. Her things. My mother's things. The silver-backed hairbrush that used to sit on her dressing table, a pearl-and-diamond broach, a strand of garnet beads, a packet of old letters postmarked from France—and at the bottom, a brown leather album with my mother's initials embossed in faded gold.

The leather is dry and scarred, the spine completely split, with a pair of large rubber bands employed to secure the pages that have come loose over the years. The sight of it stirs so many memories, beautiful and bittersweet, and for a moment, I'm certain I can hear her, smell her, feel her all around me. *Maman.*

I'm overjoyed, but angry too. I glare at Corinne. "When I asked you about the album, you said you threw it away. You said you threw *everything* away. And all this time . . . you've been keeping these things from me. When you knew she would have wanted me to have them. Why?"

"You've answered your own question," she replies stonily.

"You did it to spite a dead woman?"

"No. To spite you."

Her words knock the breath out of me. I was a child when our mother died. Lonely. Lost. And she purposely withheld the very things that might have offered some comfort. "What have I ever done to you, Corinne? Please help me understand this kind of hatred."

She's silent a moment, frowning as she studies the backs of her hands, as if they belong to someone else. Finally, she drops them to her lap and looks at me. "You weren't born when Ernest died. It was just me. She had a bad time of it. She would shut herself up most days, but when she was having a good day, she would call me to her room. She would brush my hair and sing to me. I was her darling girl. Then you came and I became an afterthought. And then when Father sent her away, I was expected to look after you—the sister I couldn't stand the sight of. I was sixteen, on the verge of having a life of my own. Or so I thought. But I did what was expected of me. I've always done what was expected of me. Including marrying George Hillard, who made my skin crawl. But not *you*. You were too good to marry the man Father chose for you. *You* wanted the paperboy."

"Yes," I say quietly, not daring to look at Hemi. "I did."

"And that was all that mattered, as far as you were concerned. What *you* wanted. You needed to learn your place. To do your duty as *I* was made to. And you *would* have, with him out of the way. Instead, you slipped the hook when the story broke and left me to clean up the mess—again." Her eyes flick to Hemi with open disgust. "You *brought* him to us. Helped him dredge up all that filth and drag Father's name through the mud. He was ruined. We were *all* ruined! And you can stand there and ask what you ever did to me? If I could hurt you in even the tiniest way, I was glad to do it."

She says it all without shame, without batting an eye, and suddenly I understand just how her hatred has warped her. I look down at the contents of the box with fresh eyes. Personal items grudgingly hoarded like trophies from a battlefield. But why keep them at all? And then lie about it?

It strikes me suddenly that Corinne's withholding of our mother's things hasn't been about a grudge against me but about something else entirely, something she refused to admit, even to herself. "You wanted them," I say softly, understanding at last. "You wanted them for yourself. Because they were hers."

She turns her face away. "Do you want them or not?"

"Yes. I want them."

"Take them, then, and get out."

I scoop the box up into my arms; then, before I can change my mind, I lift out the hairbrush and lay it on Corinne's pillow, a gift she doesn't deserve. She doesn't see me do it, but Hemi does. Our eyes touch briefly as he relieves me of the box. I pick up my purse from the bed and head for the door. I don't say goodbye. I don't look back. I've gotten what I came for and now want only to be away from Corinne and out of my father's house.

TWENTY-TWO

MARIAN

Books are the quietest and most constant of friends; they are the most accessible and wisest of counselors, and the most patient of teachers.

—*Charles W. Eliot*

I feel a dull sort of closure as we climb into Hemi's car, a sense of loose ends being tied up. The fall of the Mannings is all but complete. But *our* story—Hemi's and mine—isn't over.

We're silent for much of the drive back. I stare out the window at the passing cars and blurring landscape, trying to process everything that's happened in the last few weeks. Ethan and Ashlyn discovering the books. Hemi showing up out of the blue with a forty-year-old letter in his pocket. Corinne's admission that she'd purposely thwarted my hopes for happiness. And soon, the last piece of the puzzle. The one I've held back.

That four decades of secrets have unwound themselves in so short a time seems impossible but inevitable, too, in some tiny part of my consciousness. Haven't I always been braced for this day? When Hemi's book arrived and I saw what he'd written—*How, Belle?*—wasn't I already preparing for this inevitability? I was. Of course I was.

Ashlyn's words have been festering all day.

Closure.

Is such a thing possible? When anger and loss have been your companions for so long that you can't imagine waking up without them burning in your chest? When the face that has haunted you for so many years is suddenly before you, threatening to reopen wounds you believed scarred over? Ashlyn seems to think so. A belief I can't help feeling comes from personal experience, though she never said so. She claims it's a matter of deciding. And so I've decided. But before closure, there must first be a reckoning.

Mine.

And yet I'm not quite ready to shoulder all the blame.

Beside me, Hemi broods behind the wheel, his expression carefully shuttered as he navigates rush-hour traffic. I feel his eyes stray to my side of the car now and then and sense that he might be about to say something, but when I turn to look at him, he looks away.

"Are we not going to talk about any of it?" I ask when I can no longer bear the quiet. "What she said and what it means?"

He keeps his eyes fixed on the road, his hands wrapped tight around the wheel. "What is there to talk about?"

His response stuns me. "Perhaps we could start with the fact that we've both had it wrong all these years, and that I was telling the truth last night when I told you the letter you showed me was meant for Teddy and not you. I think I deserve at least that."

He says nothing for a time, pretending to be interested in something in the rearview mirror. I wait, watching him. I used to know his face so well, every plane and shadow, but the years have hardened him, making him unreadable.

"And then what?" he says finally. "After forty-three years, we're both sorry. Then what?"

The bitterness in his voice cuts me to the quick. "Then . . . we forgive, Hemi. We stop all the blaming and who hurt who first. It won't change what we've lost. Nothing can change that. But it might pave the way for some kind of closure. For both of us finally being able to let it go."

I hold my breath, waiting for him to respond, to give some sign that he's heard me at all, but he remains mute, unreachable. I turn my face to the window, staring at the highway blurring past. Forgiveness. Closure. Such pretty words. But they felt false as I uttered them. Because I know there's more to come. Much more. And much worse. Perhaps the unforgivable. And yet I must say it. Confession, they say, is good for the soul. But not here, with horns blaring and cars whizzing past. I need to be on my own ground when I tell him.

"Hemi," I say abruptly, before I lose my nerve. "I need you to come back to the house with me. When we get back to the hotel, to my car, I need you to follow me home."

He looks at me finally, his face slightly softened. "Are you not feeling well?"

"I'm fine. But there's something we need to discuss."

"We've been in the car almost three hours and we're still an hour from Boston. Is there some reason we can't discuss whatever it is now?"

"There is," I reply evenly. "There's something I need to show you."

"At your house?"

"Yes."

His expression is suddenly wary. "What?"

"Not here." I turn my face to the window again. "Not yet."

My hands are hot and sticky as I pull up into my driveway. Hemi parks behind me and gets out. I wrestle with my suitcase and the hatbox full of my mother's things from the trunk. The rest will have to wait. And then suddenly Hemi is there, relieving me of the suitcase and box. I murmur an awkward thank-you and head up the drive, leaving him to follow.

In the foyer, I barely look at him as I peel off my coat. He sets down the suitcase and hatbox, then peers over my shoulder into the parlor.

"There's no one here," I tell him and hold out my hand for his coat. "We're alone."

He takes a step back, shaking his head. "I'm fine."

In the parlor, he runs his eyes over the artwork, the furniture, the piano with its collection of framed faces. I hold my breath, waiting for him to see it, but he doesn't.

"Very nice," he says drily. "Not quite what I expected, but nice."

He wanders to the windows. The drapes are open, offering a glimpse of the pebble-strewn beach. The sun is going down and the water is a deep shade of pewter. I leave him to admire the view and go to the kitchen for ice. When I return, he's still at the window, but his coat is off and draped over the arm of the sofa. I pour us both several fingers of gin, then reach for the tonic. He turns when he hears me break the seal on the bottle.

"Your own beach too. I should have known."

There's a whiff of reproach in the words, reminding me of those early days, how he used to set my teeth on edge with his criticism of my privileged childhood and posh lifestyle. I'm briefly tempted to remind him of his Back Bay townhouse but decide to let it pass. "It's shared, actually. But the other family is hardly ever here, so I have it to myself most of the time."

His eyes hold mine for an uncomfortable moment. "We used to talk about living by the sea."

We talked about a lot of things, I want to say. But I can't say it. I can't even think it. Or I won't be able to get through what I *need* to say. I put his drink into his hand. "I know you usually take it with lime, but I'm afraid you'll have to do without. I wasn't expecting company."

He shrugs. "I've learned to do without a lot of things."

"Hemi . . ."

"What should we drink to?"

I look at the floor, at my glass, anywhere but at him. "To your success," I say dully. "How many books now?"

"Twenty-one at last count."

"And most of them bestsellers. Congratulations."

He bunches his shoulders, uncomfortable with my praise. The quiet yawns as we stand staring at each other across the distance of forty-three years. "You're in all of them," he says finally.

The remark catches me off guard. His voice has gone deep and raspy, plucking at nerves I haven't acknowledged in a very long time. "I don't know what that means."

"It means you were every protagonist I ever wrote. No matter what I called them, they were all Belle. All *you*."

"Hemi . . ."

"Have you read any of them?"

"No."

"It started with *Regretting Belle*. It was the first good thing I ever wrote. Maybe the best thing I'll *ever* write." He takes a pull from his drink, grimacing as it goes down. "Whatever happened to it? Do you know?"

"I have it," I say quietly. "I have them both."

This seems to surprise him. And perhaps to please him. "You kept them?"

"No. Dickey did. After he died, his son found them in his study."

"I'm not sure I knew he had a son."

"Ethan," I supply. "Until a week ago, I'd never laid eyes on him, but he looks just like Dickey."

"Am I to assume he read them?"

"Yes," I say, dropping my eyes. "He recognized Rose Hollow and figured out the rest."

"That must have been interesting. Having your love life read by a stranger."

"Your love life too," I remind him coolly. "And yes, it was *very* . . . interesting."

"They know it was me? That I was Hemi? That we . . ."

There's a new scar just below his left eye, at the apex of his cheek. I haven't noticed it until now and I wonder briefly how he got it and when. I fight the urge to touch my fingers to it, to touch *him*. "They know everything," I say instead. "Things even you don't know."

"Belle . . ." He takes a step toward me, then another, his chilly resolve crumbling as he draws near. "I don't know where to start. About last night . . . about this afternoon . . . For forty years, I've been carrying this pain in my gut, blaming you, believing a lie. And all the time . . . I'm so bloody, bloody sorry. For not trusting you. For not *believing* you. And most of all, for the business with the damned story. I should have told you what I was working on. If I had, none of this would have happened. It was a stupid and selfish thing to do and I absolutely own that. But I swear to you, Belle, I didn't have anything to do with it showing up in the *Review*. That was Goldie and Schwab."

"Saboteurs," I say softly.

"What?"

"The life we were supposed to have was derailed by saboteurs. My sister. Goldie. Both had their own agendas and both got what they wanted. What *we* wanted didn't matter."

"Are you happy, Belle? Now, I mean. Are you . . . Is there someone?"

I take a pull from my drink, then set the glass on the bar. "Those are two very different questions. With two very different answers. Yes, I'm happy. I've built a life. I have things I'm passionate about. As I'm sure you do. But no, there's no one."

He puts down his glass and studies me a moment, as if trying to read my thoughts as he weighs his next words. "In my life, I never thought I'd say these words, but god help me, here I am. Here *we* are. There has never been anyone but you, Belle. Before or since. When you didn't come that day and I was left standing on that platform, I was devastated. And then that damned letter. When I read it and thought you'd gone back to Teddy, something in me died and I just stopped caring about anything. I had dreaded it for so long, and there it was in my hands—proof. Only it wasn't. And now we've lost so much time. But I've never forgotten, Belle. I never stopped wishing . . ."

I should resist when he reaches for me, pull back before this goes any further. But I've waited so long to hear those words. The weight of his hand on my arm is achingly familiar, the stony mask he's been hiding behind suddenly fallen away. Here is the Hemi I knew all those years ago, the man I've never stopped loving. The realization makes my throat ache. How can I deny what this moment means, to feel the years spooling backward, to remember how it was with him—how we were together.

When his lips touch mine, it's as if no time at all has passed, like we never lost one another. It feels like coming home, I think, realizing with a shock just how much I've missed the taste of him, the feel of his arms around me. But how is that possible? How could I have forgotten this . . . heaven? An image flickers behind my closed eyes, of tangled limbs and rumpled blue sheets, of bodies fitted close, straining and sheened with sweat. It's been so long. It's been forever. And yet it's been no time at all. Only yesterday.

I melt against him, surrendering to the familiar, aware that it's a mistake, that in a moment it will all come apart. Again. And this time there will be no confusion about who's responsible. The thought hits me like a dash of icy water and I push away from him.

"Hemi . . . wait."

He steps back awkwardly. "I'm sorry."

I shake my head. "Please don't say that. I don't want you to be sorry. And I'm afraid you will be. There's something I need to tell you. Something I should have told you a long time ago."

He says nothing, his expression guarded as he waits for me to continue.

"Before, when you asked if Ethan knew about us, I said he knew everything—even things you *don't*. You didn't ask what things."

I pick up his glass and put it back into his hand, then move to the piano. Zachary looks back at me from his heavy black frame. I wish there had been time to tell him this was happening, but I didn't know myself. I trust he'll forgive me.

Hemi is beside me now, his eyes full of questions as I turn to face him with the photo. I search for words to prepare him for what he's about to hear, but there aren't any words. Not for this. Instead, I put the frame into his hand and wait.

He stares at it, his face blank at first, uncomprehending. "What is this . . . Is this . . ."

"His name is Zachary," I say quietly.

"Zachary." He says the name slowly, rolling it around in his mouth, testing it for familiarity.

"He's ours," I say at last. "Yours and mine."

The truth seems to dawn then, as if he's just been shaken from a long sleep. "You're saying . . ."

"I'm saying we have a son, Hemi. And that I kept him from you. I told everyone he was adopted, but he's mine. And yours."

I brace for the wave of outrage I know is coming. Instead, all expression drains from his face, replaced by the awful blankness of incomprehension. He says nothing, his eyes locked on me as he struggles to process my words. I square my shoulders, forcing myself to hold his gaze as I go on. "I didn't know I was pregnant until I got to California, and by then I had no idea where you were or how to find you."

His expression hardens, gelling into something smooth and impervious. "Did you even try?"

"How? You were off playing war correspondent." The words leave my mouth before I can check them, an excuse I have no right to make. He's not wrong. I could have found him if I wanted to. I chose not to look.

"And later? After the war?" He's bristling now, his words gathering force as he registers the enormity of my transgression. "Dickey knew how to find me. You had him send me a book, remember? One, I'd point out, that omitted any mention of my son."

I nod, blinking back tears, the lump in my throat too large to allow a reply.

"And the day you and Dickey were meant to have lunch. I suppose we know why you bailed the minute you found out I was at the restaurant. And to top it all off, there's the fact that for nearly two decades, my face has been in just about every bookstore window in the country. Please don't tell me you didn't know how to find me, Marian. You've had forty-three years to find me. All you had to do was pick up the phone."

I've prepared myself for his anger, but not for the raw anguish I hear in his voice, the pooling of tears in his eyes. "Hemi . . ."

He turns away from me, stalking to the other side of the room, then wheels around to face me. "You really hated me that much?"

"I never hated you. I wanted to. I tried to, but I couldn't."

"You kept a *child* from me. *Our* son! How could you?"

And there it is. The question he posed to me all those years ago, scribbled on the title page of *Regretting Belle*. Only now it means something different, something unfathomably worse. "You broke my heart," I reply raggedly, knowing it isn't enough, knowing there will never be enough words to fix this. "When you left, and then when the story appeared in the *Review*, I couldn't believe you'd actually done it."

"I hadn't."

"I didn't know that then. How could I?"

"So you felt justified in depriving me of my child." He raked his fingers through his hair, the gesture so familiar it makes my chest hurt. "Christ. He's forty-two years old. A grown man. And I missed it all."

I blink at him through a scrim of tears, searching for something else to say. "I'm sorry, Hemi. So incredibly sorry. From the moment Zachary was born—every moment of every day for the last forty-two years—I've looked at him and seen your face. The man who promised to love me forever, then disappeared without a word. I told myself a man who could do that . . ." My voice breaks and I gulp back a sob. "You would have come back, Hemi, but you would have resented me for it. Enough to eventually leave us both. It's one thing to walk out on a grown woman. It's another to do it to a child. I couldn't risk that happening to Zachary."

"That's who you thought I was? A man who'd turn his back on his own child?"

"I had no idea who *you* were—or *what* you would do. As far as I knew, you had betrayed my confidence and gone back on your word. But I would have forgiven *all* of that. What I couldn't forgive was you walking out of my life without a word, as if I'd been nothing to you. I've seen what happens when a man loses interest in his wife—and what happens to the children when he does." I close my eyes as a fresh round of tears threatens. "I didn't know how to trust you again."

The silence that settles between us is unbearable, as if all our memories together have been swept away, leaving only this terrible new reality. Hemi stands with his shoulders bunched, his face a mix of shadow and sharp angles as he stares at the photo of our son. Finally, he looks up, pinning me with his sharp blue gaze.

"Last night, at the bar, when you said you did what you had to, that you . . . got on with your life. This is what you were talking about. Raising our son. Without me."

I force myself to meet his eyes, eyes so filled with pain they tear at my heart. "I'm so sorry, Hemi."

"Did Dickey know?"

I nod. "Zachary has always been you to a T. We fought about it constantly. He thought you should know. I thought it was none of his business. We had it out once and for all after the business with the lunch. We never spoke again."

"You were so determined to keep him from me that you severed ties with your favorite nephew? Because he thought I deserved to be a part of my son's life?"

How can I make him understand? What I felt. What I feared. Not just for me but for my children and the life I'd carefully built for them. "I couldn't let you back into our lives, Hemi. Not like that. Weekends and holidays and every other summer. Splitting the cost of music camp and bumping into one another at recitals. Polite strangers who happen to share a son. And there was Ilese to consider. What would it have meant for her?"

His face goes blank. "Ilese?"

"My daughter. Zachary was two when I adopted her. They grew up as brother and sister, and I let everyone think that's what they were. Zachary suddenly turning out to have a father would have been awkward."

"As awkward as me finding out I have a forty-two-year-old son?"

I tell myself I have no right to defend myself, that after what I've done I should simply stand here and take whatever he throws at me, but I can't bear the thought that he thinks any of it was easy for me, that there was a single day while Zachary was growing up that I didn't question the choices I made.

"That isn't what I meant, Hemi. By the time I did know how to find you, so much time had passed. It was just the three of us for so long. I was afraid—"

He holds up a hand, cutting me off. "I don't want your excuses. There *are* no excuses for this."

"That isn't what I'm doing. I'm saying I was wrong. No matter what I believed you'd done, I had no right to keep Zachary from you." Tears blur my vision, tears I have no right to. "I don't know how else to say it or what else to do."

He stands with his arms crossed, legs braced wide, unyielding. "What is it you want?"

I stare at him. "What do I *want?*"

"What do you see happening? Surely you had some sort of endgame in mind when you asked me to come here. What was it?"

"I wanted to make things right between us. To tell you I know I was wrong. Terribly and unforgivably wrong—and to ask for forgiveness anyway." I wait for a response, unable to tell if my words have had any impact, but his expression remains blank. "Say something. Please."

A muscle pulses at his jaw. "What would you like me to say?"

"Anything. I don't know. Tell me where we go from here."

"We don't go *anywhere*, Marian. Not now."

I nod, closing my eyes. "Yes. All right. For what it's worth, Zachary is a concert violinist with the Chicago Symphony Orchestra and he's getting married in June."

"Well then, at least I didn't miss *everything.*"

His face, so stony a moment ago, seems to shatter before my eyes, and I feel my heart shatter with it. "I don't know how many times I can say I'm sorry, Hemi, but I'll say it as many times as you ask me to. I'll say it forever."

He shakes his head, his eyes bleak and hollow. "All these years, I've wondered if it could have ended differently. I'd remember how it was between us, all the things we were going to see and do, and think maybe there was a way to get that back. That's why I showed up last night. To see if there was a chance. And then today, for one mad instant, when I kissed you and you kissed me back, I thought there might be. Now I see that we've missed it. Zachary was our chance. After all the what-ifs, all the years apart, *he* was our way back. We might have salvaged something of the life we'd planned. But not now. And the worst part is this time there's no one else to blame. The letter, the story—someone else did those things. *Saboteurs,* you called them. But *you* did this. *You* were the saboteur."

He grabs his coat from the arm of the sofa and heads for the foyer without turning back. I watch him walk away, wishing I knew how to make him stay, but I've used up all the words I know for *I'm sorry.* And he doesn't want to hear them anyway.

Stillness descends as the front door closes behind him, the echo of nothingness threatening to undo me. So complete. So final. I retrieve the photo of Zachary from the bar where Hemi left it and stare down at our son's face. His father's face. I had hoped for closure, but all I feel is the opening of old wounds.

TWENTY-THREE

MARIAN

I have always imagined that closing a book is like pausing a film midframe, the characters frozen in their halted worlds, breath held, waiting for the reader to return and bring it all back to life—like a prince's kiss in a fairy tale.

—*Ashlyn Greer,* The Care & Feeding of Old Books

The sunporch has always been my favorite part of this house, a sanctuary at the sea's edge, even at night. I've been sitting here since Hemi left, with the lights switched off and the sound of the sea all around me. There's not much moon tonight and the dark feels heavy, empty, and yet too full of the past.

I've called Zachary and told him about his father. Told him everything. Or as much as a mother can comfortably tell a grown-up son. I kept to the facts, to names and places. He took it like I thought he would, like he's always taken everything, by asking if *I* was all right. I told him I was. A lie, but sometimes that's easier.

I tried to call Ilese, too, but there was no answer. I'll try again tomorrow, but by then, her brother will have told her everything. They've always had a kind of connection, always able to sense when the other needs a shoulder. But it's done now. The final shoe has fallen. No more secrets festering, waiting to be exposed.

There's a peculiar sense of closure to it all, a sense of things ended, if not truly finished.

On the table in front of me are the books—Hemi's and mine. I don't know why I've brought them out here with me. Certainly not to read. Perhaps it's so I can see them together one last time. Tomorrow, I'll lay a fire in the parlor and do what I told Dickey to do all those years ago—burn them. My past and Hemi's, up in smoke. It seems fitting that a thing that once burned so brightly—too brightly, perhaps—will finally be extinguished. A closure of sorts.

But will it be?

For more than forty years, I pretended it already *was*, shutting myself off from that time, those memories. So very careful. And then in the space of twenty-four hours—less than that, actually—I *forgot* to be careful. I saw his face and let myself remember, felt his arms, his mouth, and let myself hope.

I've clung so voraciously to my anger, steeping myself in blame and bitter memories, as a way to keep from feeling what lay beneath all of it. The unquenchable ache of missing him, feeling him when I'm alone and the house is quiet, gone but a part of me yet. The hollow place the lost years have carved in me. Grief for what might have been, for what nearly was.

Perhaps if I'd told him all of it. How badly losing him had broken me. How much I've ached for him all these years—still ache. But no. He made it clear that any window there might have been closed when I decided to keep Zachary from him. He had it right—I was the saboteur.

I gaze out toward the shore, imagining the horizon stretching beyond it, and wonder if I'll ever be able to put the genie back in the bottle—to forget again. I'm certain the answer is no. This is what I have to look forward to now. Remembering the us that could have been—the family we could have been—had I chosen differently.

I should go in now and get on with whatever comes next. Supper. Bed. Tomorrow. But I don't want to think about tomorrow. Not yet. I stare at the pebble-strewn beach below, the small crescent of sand where land meets sea, and remember Ilese and Zachary there as children, building castles and collecting smooth, shiny stones in a blue plastic pail. I've made good memories here. *They're enough,* I tell myself. They'll have to be.

The tide is out, and in the meager moonlight, the shore seems to give off a pale, almost unearthly light. I close my eyes, listening to the hypnotic rattle of the waves against the stones, the hushed push and pull like breathing. I breathe with it. In, then out. In, then out. Better. Yes, a little better. I can go in now.

I've just opened my eyes when I catch a small flicker of movement along the sand, a blur of dark against bright. It lasts only an instant, but I'm sure I've seen it. I watch, wait, but all is still. *A trick of the moonlight,* I tell myself. Then it happens again.

I peer into the darkness, willing my eyes to adjust. I can't make out anything at first, but eventually I pick out an unfamiliar shape propped against the rocks that separate the beach from the road. Perhaps my neighbors have come back and opened up the house. Unlikely at this time of year, when many of Marblehead's coastal homes have already been shut up for the season. Besides, it's much too cold for an evening on the beach.

Curious, I go to the porch door and push it open. The sound of the sea rushes in on a gust of briny air. The shape, whatever it is, is still there, unmoving but clearer now. I step out onto the deck. My hair catches on the wind, streaming into my eyes. I shove it out of my face, my gaze still fastened on the rocks. I see it then, moonlight caught and reflected back in a brief, bright arc. There, then gone, but familiar somehow.

A flicker of memory. Fingers, long and lean, scraping back a wave of unruly dark hair. A wristwatch catching the candlelight. My heart does a little gallop. It's madness, of course, the figment of a wishful imagination.

And yet I find myself moving to the stairs, taking them carefully in the dark, clinging to the wooden rail until I'm finally standing on the beach. The shadow is still there, an eerie presence silhouetted against the rocks. A man, I realize, with a dizzying jolt of recognition. My heels bite into the sand as I begin to walk, my progress awkward and halting. I feel rather than see him turn to look at me. There's another glint of moonlight, a moment's hesitation, and then he's climbing down from his perch. He stands with his hands at his sides, legs braced wide, watching me approach. Even in the dark, I would know him anywhere.

"Hello," he says when I'm finally standing in front of him. The word gets lost on the wind and sounds strangely disembodied in the darkness. "What are you doing out here?"

"It's my beach. Have you been sitting out here all this time?"

"Not all. I sat in the car for a while."

"Why?"

His shoulders bunch, then fall heavily. "I couldn't make myself leave."

I tell myself it doesn't mean what I think it means, what I *want* it to mean, but the thrum of my pulse and the rush of the sea eclipse all thought. "It's freezing. Where's your coat?"

"The car."

"Hemi, you can't stay out here."

"You want me to go?"

"No. But you can't stay out here. Come inside."

We walk back to the stairs, silent and a careful distance apart. Inside, I flip on a lamp and turn to look at him. His mouth is pinched and bluish, and there's a whiff of cold clinging to him, a briny chill that seems to emanate from his clothes. Without thinking, I touch his face, grazing his cheek with the backs of my knuckles.

"You're freezing."

He stiffens slightly at my touch. "I'm fine."

"Your lips are blue."

"What were you doing on the beach?"

It seems an odd question after I've just found him sitting on the rocks. "I wasn't on the beach. I was sitting up here, looking out, and I saw something move down by the rocks. It turned out to be you."

"You were sitting in the dark?"

I shrug. "So were you."

He's about to respond when he notices the books sitting side by side on the table. He makes no move to touch them, but his eyes flick to mine and I read the question there.

"I pulled them out after you left. I was trying to decide what to do with them."

"And did you?"

"Do you want them?" I ask, sidestepping the question with one of my own.

"No."

The answer comes so quickly, so decisively, that I nearly flinch when he gives it. I nod and step back. "I'll get the tea."

He follows me to the kitchen, watching silently as I put the kettle on and prepare two mugs. For a moment, I'm back in his tiny kitchen in New York, preparing a meal while he reads the paper or pecks away at some story, and it's as if no time has passed. But when I look across the counter at him, I'm reminded just how far we've come from the young lovers we once were.

His face is lined in new ways, though handsome still, God help me. I wish I didn't see the old Hemi when I look at him, but he's there, watching me with those guarded blue eyes, that damn hank of hair hanging over his forehead, not *quite* so dark now but wonderfully and terribly familiar.

I pull out the tea bags and add a splash of milk to Hemi's, the way he used to take it. "This will help," I say, holding the mug out to him.

He takes it and immediately sets it down. Before I can step away, he captures my wrist. "I don't want tea, Belle."

"All right, then. No tea. What do you want?"

His eyes cloud and he drops my wrist. "I want it to be 1941 again. I want it to be the day before I left New York, the day before you found my story notes. I want it to be *before*."

"But it can't be, Hemi."

"No. It can't. It can only be now. But you asked me what I wanted. I've spent the last two and a half hours trying to figure it out."

"And what did you decide?"

"We never said goodbye."

My throat aches as I look up at him. "Is that what you want? To say goodbye?"

"I never wanted to say it."

"Then . . . what?"

"I don't want to be angry anymore, Belle. I have been for so long. Because I thought it was a way to insulate myself from the memories. It never worked, though. It just made me too proud to do what I should have a long time ago."

Belle, not Marian. I drop my gaze, afraid to hope. "Which was?"

"To swallow my bloody pride and come find you. If I had, I would have known Zachary. Been a part of his life—*and yours*. Instead, I wallowed and drank too much and wrote books that turned out the way I wish *we* had." He wanders away then, hands pushed deep into his pockets.

"Hemi . . ."

When he turns back to face me, his eyes are red-rimmed and raw. "We've lost so much time, spent so many years blaming each other for things other people did. I'm still angry that they took so much from us, the time we can't get back. I'll always be angry about that. But I'm through being angry with you. And with myself. But I'm scared blind about what comes next. I don't want to be the only one . . ."

His words trail off and he clears his throat. "Anyway, that's why I showed up last night. Because I had to know if there was a chance. I hoped that there would be. Then I saw you in the ballroom. I knew the exact instant you spotted me. One minute you were all smiles; the next you looked like you were going to throw up. That's when I knew I'd made a mistake."

The anguish in his voice brings tears to my eyes. "I was afraid," I say softly. "Because of Zachary. I wasn't prepared to have that conversation yet. But coming last night wasn't a mistake, Hemi. I'm the one who made the mistake. What I did was unforgivable and I deserved everything you said."

"It wasn't unforgivable. I just . . . when you told me about Zachary, it was like I'd been kicked in the gut. I never thought anything could hurt worse than you not showing up that day, but I was wrong. All I could think about when you told me about Zachary was what I'd lost, not what I'd gained—a son and perhaps a second chance. I never imagined that kind of ending, but here I am, Belle. Here *we* are."

We.

My heart is suddenly thrumming so loudly, I can scarcely hear myself think, and yet I'm afraid to let myself hope. "Is this about Zachary? About being part of his life?"

"It's about everything, Belle. About Zachary, and you, and me. About finally *having* a life. Because up to now, I haven't. Everything— the war stuff, the books, the awards—it was all just killing time. Until I could get back to you. We're different people now. Older. Changed. But some things are the same. At least for me. And I thought . . . *hoped* . . . that maybe there was room for me in your life."

There's no mistaking the plea in his voice, and suddenly I'm afraid. That it's moving too fast. That what we feel in this moment isn't enough. That after everything we've lost, nothing will ever be enough. "We don't know each other anymore, Hemi. You said it yourself—we're different people now. We could be making a huge mistake."

He nods. "You're right. We could. But it's a chance I'm willing to take. However slowly you need to take it. You were Belle then and you'll always be Belle, but you're someone else now too. We both are. And I'd like the chance to know who you turned out to be. I know we've left it a bit late, but I think it's worth finding out if there's a future for us." He reaches for my hand then, searching my eyes. "Is it asking too much?"

I look down at our joined hands, those warm, familiar fingers winding through mine, and recall the advice I gave Dickey all those years ago—the same advice I gave Ethan a few nights ago—to let nothing come between them and love. Can I do this? Risk my heart again? I've made a good life for myself, a full life by almost any standard. I've raised good children and done good work. It should be enough. But I've always known there was a piece missing—and that that missing piece is Hemi.

"No," I say at last. "It isn't asking too much. It's asking just enough."

I open a bottle of wine and put together a makeshift supper of fruit and cheese, then carry it all to the parlor. Hemi builds a fire and we sit on the sofa to begin the business of picking up the loose threads of our lives.

Now and then, his hand wanders to mine, as if to reassure himself that I'm real, just as mine wanders to his cheek for the same reason. The connection we once felt is still there, like a current running between us, and each touch brings with it the temptation to abandon our stories and tumble into bed. How easy it would be to give in to those temptations, to consummate our reunion in the safe and wordless dark. But there are still too many years yawning between us, too many blank spaces that need to be filled. And so we keep talking.

He tells me about the war and the things he saw—some too horrifying to write about—and about his mother's death. How he went home when she got sick and was there when they buried her beside his father, on what would have been their thirty-third anniversary. How, in his grief, he had married a woman who reminded him of me, only to realize on the night of their wedding that he'd made a terrible mistake.

I tell him about California and how it was without him, about how scared I was when I realized I was going to have a baby. I show him Johanna's picture and tell him her story, how we became friends and then sisters, how when she knew she was going to die, she had gifted me with Ilese—and with a new name for the son I had borne out of wedlock.

The hours slip past as our glasses empty and the fire burns low. Over a second bottle of wine, I tell him about Ethan and Ashlyn. How they came into my life because of the books we'd written and already feel like part of my family. How Ethan is the spitting image of Dickey, right down to the size of his heart. And how Ashlyn pushed me to seek closure and finally tell him about Zachary.

And then suddenly, inexplicably, we seem to be out of words. There's more to tell, for both of us. Forty-three years is a lifetime—two lifetimes in this case—but for now, we've said enough. I go to my room, drag the comforter from my bed, then return to Hemi. I say nothing as I extend my hand. He says nothing as he takes it. We head to the sunporch and down the back stairs to the beach below.

We perch on the rocks, silent as we watch the sun rise up out of the sea. The morning air is biting cold, sharp against our cheeks, but beneath the comforter, we're fitted snugly, shoulder to shoulder and limb to limb—each other's shelter. We stay until the sun is well up, the sea a slick of mercury-blue, the sand golden beneath our feet. Eventually, we climb down and stand face-to-face.

I had convinced myself that I was seeking closure, a tidy end to a messy past, but as Hemi pulls me into his arms, it doesn't feel like closure. It feels like a beginning, and I'm suddenly reminded of another kiss, one that happened a lifetime ago, on a rainy day in a stable. That had been a beginning too. Hemi smiles, as if reading my thoughts, then pulls me into the circle of his arms. *This is what it's supposed to be like,* I think as his mouth closes over mine.

This. This. This.

EPILOGUE

ASHLYN

December 7, 1985
Marblehead, Massachusetts

It was well past three, the afternoon sun slanting through the blinds, painting the walls with soft amber light. Ashlyn ran a careful eye over her handiwork, packages wrapped in blue paper and decorated with curlicues of silver and white ribbon spread across the vintage quilt. Hanukkah gifts to be handed out during the first night's festivities.

It was her second Hanukkah with Ethan's new family but her first time participating in the gift-giving, and she was just the tiniest bit nervous. They'd been wonderfully welcoming, treating her like one of their own—and soon she would be. They'd been keeping the secret since just after Thanksgiving, because Ethan wanted to make the announcement when the entire family was together.

It was still hard to believe how much her life had changed in a year and a half. All because a pair of books had found their way into her hands. A seeming coincidence, but was it? Of all the shops in New England, *Regretting Belle* and *Forever, and Other Lies* had ended up in Kevin's shop. And because they had, everything had changed. Not only for herself and Ethan, or even for Hemi and Belle, but for an entire family separated by a decades-old secret.

She thought of the books, now shelved side by side in Marian's office, and recalled the last time she'd run her hands over them. Hemi's first, then Belle's, then both books together. How they had hummed beneath her fingers with the same curious energy. Cool and quiet and gloriously aligned, like notes resonating in perfect harmony.

They had changed their echoes.

That moment had been a kind of revelation for her, a reminder that the echoes a person leaves behind are the by-products of the choices she makes—and perhaps, more critically, that changing those echoes is *always* possible. Now, seated on the edge of the bed, she opened her palm, tracing a fingertip along the puckered line of flesh bisecting her life line. Before and after. It was another reminder—one she vowed never to forget—that people's lives were defined not by the scars they acquired but by what lay on the other side of those scars, by what's done with the life they have left. She'd been given a second chance at love—a second chance at family—and she intended to make the most of both.

She stood when the mantel clock struck four. She should go now and join Ethan and the rest of the family. The sun would be down soon, nearly time to light the menorah. She gathered her armload of gifts from the bed, then added one more to the pile—a special gift meant for Marian.

∼

MARIAN

The sun is nearly down and the menorah gleams brightly, waiting to be lit. I run my eyes around the parlor, my heart near bursting at the sight of our blended family all gathered in one place. It's our second Hanukkah together, but this one feels different, whole at last.

The house is fragrant with the mingled aromas of holiday cooking. Brisket and latkes and sugary, jelly-filled *sufganiyot*. I smile at the girls, flitting anxiously around Ilese and Jeffrey. In their matching blue sweaters, they look like something straight off a Hanukkah card, eagerly awaiting the opening of presents and after-dinner games.

Zachary and Rochelle have come up from Boston to spend a few days. It's good that they've moved closer. The twins are due in March, and while they don't know it yet, they're going to have their hands full. Zachary and Hemi are discussing plans to assemble the cribs and hang the nursery wallpaper. Being a grandfather wasn't something Hemi ever expected, but he's absurdly happy about the idea of being called *Saba*— *Grandfather* in Hebrew.

We were married in August. We waited until after Zachary's wedding was over, then snuck off to the courthouse like a pair of young lovers. Forty-three years later than we planned, but we finally made it. I watch him now, on the other side of the room, so like his son. He rakes the hair back off his forehead, then glances up, as if he suddenly feels my eyes on him. He throws me a wink and sets my heart skittering. After all this time, he can still leave me dizzy.

On the opposite side of the room, Ethan and Ashlyn are in a huddle. Unless I miss my guess, I'll soon be giving them a honeymoon. To France, perhaps, to meet the cousins.

Zachary clears his throat and announces that it's time to light the menorah. Hemi comes to stand beside my chair, his hand warm on my shoulder. We stand and everyone goes quiet, watching as Zachary places a candle on the far-right branch of the menorah, then lights the *shamash*—the helper candle. The girls hold their breaths as the *shamash* is held to the wick of the first candle. There's a faint, collective sigh as it catches.

We sing the blessings then, three on the first night, and I smile at the sound of all our voices blending together. My eyes slide to Ethan, sober and respectful in his borrowed yarmulke. He and Ashlyn know all the words this year, and my heart swells with gratitude that they've become part of our family.

Finally, it's time to eat. Ilese hurries the girls to the powder room to wash up for dinner. The parlor empties but I linger, relishing the rare moment of quiet. I'm tired but happy as I take in my surroundings. The menorah reflected in the darkened window, the stack of gifts wrapped in pretty paper waiting to be opened, the carpet littered with abandoned Barbies and coloring books. How could anyone want for more than this?

Hemi appears suddenly. As if in answer to my question, he holds out a package wrapped in shiny silver paper. "*Hanukkah sameach.*"

I frown as I take the box, wondering why he's giving me my present before supper. There's a curious weight to his gaze as he watches me tear at the silver paper, a sense of expectation that makes me self-conscious. I lift the lid from the box, then peel back several layers of tissue. For a moment, I'm not sure what I'm looking at. It's a book bound in smooth brown leather. I stare at the letters stamped in gold on the front—*H.L.T.*

Helene Louise Treves.

It can't be. But as I lift the book out onto my lap, I see that it is—my mother's album beautifully and painstakingly restored. I run my hands over it, astonished. The leather is supple and buttery soft, the once-broken spine seamlessly mended, the pages intact with no sign of the ghastly rubber bands. It's Ashlyn's work, of course, and the transformation is nothing short of miraculous.

I hold my breath as I turn back the cover, my throat tight with threatening tears. And then suddenly she's looking up at me, the woman I remember from those special afternoons. Young and fresh and beautiful. The *Maman* of my memories. My hands tremble a little as I turn the pages, slowly, wonderingly.

From the dining room, I can hear them gathering around the table, the clink of plates and silverware, the trill of girlish laughter and the hum of conversation—the sounds of family. They'll be calling us soon, wondering where we've gotten to. I close the album reluctantly and return it to its box. There'll be time later to savor my gift. Right now, supper is waiting.

I push to my feet, smiling at Hemi through a shimmer of tears, grateful for the memories he's given back to me—and for the new memories we'll make together.

ACKNOWLEDGMENTS

And now, it's time to say thank you to everyone who made this book possible while building a house and orchestrating a cross-country move. Every book takes a village (this one took an *especially* large village), a group of dedicated individuals willing to stand in the creative fire with you and make sure you come out whole on the other side, people who believe in your project and in you—even when you don't—and somehow help you keep your head on straight. There's absolutely no way to thank them all, but I'm about to try.

First, to my amazing agent, Nalini Akolekar: it's been a wonderful journey. Thank you for every step of it. I can't wait to see what's next! And of course, a huge shout-out goes to the entire Spencerhill team, who are always working behind the scenes to make sure the trains are running on time.

To my original editor, Jodi Warshaw, who believed in this book from the start and has always been an enormous pleasure to work with: thank you a million times for all your faith in me. To the lovely Chris Werner, who stepped in midproject and was nothing short of amazing in his support and dedication down the homestretch. And to Danielle Marshall, with whom it has been my absolute delight to work. I couldn't ask to be in better hands! Also, a huge shout-out to Gabe Dumpit,

Alex Levenberg, Hannah Hughes, and every single member of the Lake Union / Amazon Publishing team. From marketing to design, you guys are without a doubt the best in the biz.

To my developmental editor, Charlotte Herscher, without whom I would be completely lost. (It's true, I would!) Thank you for the gentle nudges and all your wonderful insights—and for managing it all with such grace. As Hemi would say, you help me find the pulse in each and every book.

To the book bloggers, whose generosity and love of the written word keep readers engaged and reading. Special thanks to Susan "Queenie" Peterson, Kathy Murphy (a.k.a. the Pulpwood Queen), Kate Rock, Annie McDowell, Denise Birt, Linda Gagnon, and Susan Leopold. You all are nothing short of amazing.

To my fabulous colleagues at Blue Sky Book Chat, Patricia Sands, Alison Ragsdale, Marilyn Simon Rothstein, Bette Lee Crosby, Soraya Lane, Lainey Cameron, Aimie K. Runyan, and Christine Nolfi: thanks for the fun and the friendship and for your unending support during this very hairy year!

To the lovely and talented Kerry Schafer, colleague, admin, and most of all, friend. Thank you for all of it. The brainstorming, the hand-holding, the creative input, the positivity, and the gentle nudge when I needed it. You should have a cape made. (Seriously.)

To the ladies of the Glitter Girls Book Club, who I was forced to leave when I moved to Florida. Thanks for the fun. You will be missed (but not forgotten)!

To my mom, Patricia Crawford, who continues to be my biggest and loudest cheerleader. Thank you for the shoulder and our 6:00 p.m. chats. Love you to the moon and back!

And finally to Tom, my newly retired husband (though all he's done since leaving work is pack boxes and unpack boxes). Thank you for carrying the load and giving me space to write while our lives were temporarily turned upside down. There are not enough ways to say thank you, but I hope I show you every day.

DISCUSSION QUESTIONS

1. Psychometry is defined as the ability to discover facts about an event or person by touching objects associated with them. Would you view that kind of ability as a gift or a burden? If you could have that ability, but limited to only one type of object, what object would you choose and why?

2. Ashlyn has come to see her work in the bindery as a vocation, a sacred calling. How are rebinding and book repair used throughout the story as metaphors for healing emotional wounds?

3. On the surface, Ashlyn and Marian are vastly different women, but on an emotional level, they share some similarities. In what ways do Ashlyn's and Marian's characters mirror one another?

4. How does Ashlyn's personal history with love and romantic relationships influence her need to immerse herself in Belle and Hemi's relationship? How did her experiences help connect her to Belle on a visceral and emotional level?

5. It's often said that forgiveness is more about our own healing than about letting someone who caused us pain or harm off the hook. Do you subscribe to this theory? If

so, do you believe there are circumstances in which forgiveness is simply not possible, or should we always strive to forgive, no matter how severe the transgression?

6. Throughout the book, Ashlyn is plagued by a troublesome scar on the palm of her right hand. What does the scar symbolize for her at the beginning of the novel? By the end of the novel, how has the scar's significance changed for her?

7. Both Hemi and Belle admit that they chose to cling to their anger rather than allow themselves to experience the deep grief they felt at losing one another. Have there been times in your own life when you held on to anger in order to mask deeper emotional wounds? If so, do you regret the choice?

8. How does the issue of trust—or the lack of it—play into the relationships between Ashlyn and Ethan and Belle and Hemi? Discuss the events in both women's lives that might have contributed to their inability to trust.

9. Marian and Corinne have a deeply conflicted relationship. Marian still harbors feelings of rejection and betrayal. Corinne is an extension of her father, cold and controlling. But by the end of the book, the power dynamic has shifted, giving Marian the upper hand. And yet, despite Corinne's admissions, Marian offers an olive branch of sorts. Why do you think she made this choice rather than clinging to her outrage, and under the circumstances, would you have been able to do the same?

10. Early on, Ashlyn tells Ethan she's never done anything brave, but by the end of the book, she seems to have a new idea about what the word means. Discuss how and why you feel her opinion of her own bravery has changed.

ABOUT THE AUTHOR

Photo © 2015 Lisa Aube

Barbara Davis is the Amazon Charts bestselling author of eight novels, including *The Keeper of Happy Endings* and *The Last of the Moon Girls*. She spent more than a decade as an executive in the jewelry business before leaving the corporate world to pursue her lifelong passion for writing. Originally a Jersey girl, Barbara has lived in Florida, North and South Carolina, and New Hampshire. She has recently returned to Florida with her newly retired bubby, Tom, where she is currently working on her next book. For more information, visit www.barbaradavis-author.com.